'A work of great brilliance and depth . . . Munro's power of analysis, of sensation, and thoughts, is almost Proustian in its sureness.'

New Statesman

'With their surface serenity and long echoes, these stories shift their ground, exploring the ambiguities of love. At first glance Alice Munro is simple. At second reading she has a touch of genius.'

Mail on Sunday

'Beautifully precise writing . . . Minor events are rendered strangely fascinating; sudden melodrama, as in *Fits*, is as thrilling as a fire-alarm.' *Sunday Telegraph*

'These short stories take long views but never blur; vivid detail distinguishes them; at the heart of many is some incident sharply displaying an individual's – often enigmatic – uniqueness.'

Independent

'Particularly interesting to men who want to know what women think of them and know about them.' *London Review of Books*

Also by Alice Munro

Dance of the Happy Shades
Lives of Girls and Women
Something I've Been Meaning to Tell You
The Beggar Maid
The Moons of Jupiter

THE PROGRESS OF LOVE

Alice Munro was born in Canada in 1931. She has published one novel and four collections of stories, most recently *Something I've Been Meaning To Tell You*. Her book, *The Beggar Maid*, was shortlisted for the 1980 Booker Prize, and she has also won both the Governor General's Award and the Canada/Australia Prize. Her work appears regularly in *The New Yorker*, and she lives in Ontario.

'One of the best short story writers alive.'

PHILIP HOWARD/*The Times*

'In range and depth her short stories are almost novels . . . complete, complex and brilliantly structured . . . one of the finest living short-story writers.'

Daily Telegraph

'Alice Munro has earned glowing testimonials for her previous collections of short stories and *The Progress of Love* will bring her many more of them. She deserves them all. Her prose is of a quality that makes most of her peers look like clumsy apprentices.'

Standard

'Alice Munro is already well known here as a Canadian writer of great sensitivity and delicacy. Her new collection of stories show no falling off in her gift for putting the ordinary into a sharp, clear perspective: her characters, like flowers in a glass paperweight, seem very near and also very far away.'

Guardian

'Alice Munro's beat is small town rural Ontario where she moves among ordinary men and women, farmers, truckers, high-school kids, storekeepers like an alley cat gliding over trash cans, quiet and effortless. She touches but does not disturb their lives, and she has ways of making the unremarkable seem remarkable.'

Glasgow Herald

'Only a few writers continue to create those full-bodied miniature universes of the old school. Some of her short stories are so ample and fulfilling that they feel like novels. They present whole landscapes and cultures, whole families of characters.

ANNE TYLER/*The New Republic*

'She brings to each story a freshness of vision, a breadth of sympathy and a wide-ranging imagination that make her work both unpredictable and scrupulously true ... One senses Munro's conviction that human nature is mysterious and wonderful. Her stories are magically captivating; they will stand the test of time.'

Publishers Weekly

'Alice Munro is a born teller of tales who can transform the anecdotal or apparently digressive into a rich parable of life in our fickle times,' *Washington Post Book World*

'Draws her readers irresistibly into the undergrowth of other people's private lives.' *Cosmopolitan*

'Each of the eleven pieces in *The Progress of Love* seems to contain enough material for a fair-sized novel; Munro's art of compression emphasises amplitudes rather than economies.' *Time*

'Like a scrapbook ... where each image unleashes a string of memories ... hindsight, however, rarely intrudes on the simplicity and ingenuousness of the descriptions, giving the whole a freshness and lighthearted sensitivity reminiscent of Laurie Lee and Mark Twain.' *Time Out*

'At the end of one of the stories she writes, 'This is a message; I really believe it; but I don't know how to deliver it.' Oh, but she does ... 'Honest' and 'lovely' indeed. Ironic, too, precise and witty.'

NINA BAWDEN

'An exceptionally polished and engaging book.'

Times Literary Supplement

Alice Munro

THE PROGRESS OF LOVE

Published by Fontana Paperbacks

First published in Great Britain
by Chatto & Windus Ltd 1987

This Flamingo edition
first published in 1988
by Fontana Paperbacks
8 Grafton Street, London W1X 3LA

Flamingo is an imprint of
Fontana Paperbacks, part of
The Collins Publishing Group.

Made and printed in Great Britain by
William Collins Sons & Co. Ltd, Glasgow

The following stories have been previously published, some of them in slightly different forms: "Eskimo" in *Gentlemen's Quarterly*; "Monsieur les Deux Chapeaux" and "Fits" in *Grand Street*; "A Queer Streak" in *Granta*; "Jesse and Meribeth" (originally titled "Secrets Between Friends") in *Mademoiselle*; "The Progress of Love", "Lichen", "Miles City, Montana", "The Moon in the Orange Street Skating Rink" and "White Dump" in *The New Yorker*; and "Circle of Prayer" in *The Paris Review*.

Grateful acknowledgement is made to Diplomat Music Corporation for permission to reprint an excerpt from "Today" by Lenny Stack and Janelle Cohen from the film *C. C. & Co.* Reprinted by Permission.

For my sister, Sheila

CONTENTS

THE PROGRESS OF LOVE

I got a call at work, and it was my father. This was not long after I was divorced and started in the real-estate office. Both of my boys were in school. It was a hot enough day in September.

My father was so polite, even in the family. He took time to ask me how I was. Country manners. Even if somebody phones up to tell you your house is burning down, they ask first how you are.

"I'm fine," I said. "How are you?"

"Not so good, I guess," said my father, in his old way—apologetic but self-respecting. "I think your mother's gone."

I knew that "gone" meant "dead." I knew that. But for a second or so I saw my mother in her black straw hat setting off down the lane. The word "gone" seemed full of nothing but a deep relief and even an excitement—the excitement you feel when a door closes and your house sinks back to normal and you let yourself loose into all the free space around you. That was in my father's voice, too—behind the apology, a queer sound like a gulped breath. But my mother hadn't been a burden—she hadn't been sick a day—and far from feeling relieved at her death, my father took it hard. He never got used to living alone, he said. He went into the Netterfield County Home quite willingly.

He told me how he found my mother on the couch in the kitchen when he came in at noon. She had picked a few tomatoes, and was setting them on the windowsill to ripen; then she must have felt weak, and lain down. Now, telling this, his voice went wobbly—meandering, as you would expect—in his amazement. I saw in my mind the couch, the old quilt that protected it, right under the phone.

"So I thought I better call you," my father said, and he waited for me to say what he should do now.

My mother prayed on her knees at midday, at night, and first thing in the morning. Every day opened up to her to have God's will done in it. Every night she totted up what she'd done and said and thought, to see how it squared with Him. That kind of life is dreary, people think, but they're missing the point. For one thing, such a life can never be boring. And nothing can happen to you that you can't make use of. Even if you're racked by troubles, and sick and poor and ugly, you've got your soul to carry through life like a treasure on a platter. Going upstairs to pray after the noon meal, my mother would be full of energy and expectation, seriously smiling.

She was saved at a camp meeting when she was fourteen. That was the same summer that her own mother—my grandmother—died. For a few years, my mother went to meetings with a lot of other people who'd been saved, some who'd been saved over and over again, enthusiastic old sinners. She could tell stories about what went on at those meetings, the singing and hollering and wildness. She told about one old man getting up and shouting, "Come down, O Lord, come down among us now! Come down through the roof and I'll pay for the shingles!"

She was back to being just an Anglican, a serious one, by the time she got married. She was twenty-five then, and my father was thirty-eight. A tall good-looking couple, good dancers, good card-players, sociable. But serious people—that's how I would try to describe them. Serious the way hardly anybody is anymore. My father was not religious in the way my mother was. He was an Anglican, an Orangeman, a Conservative, because that's what he had been brought up to be. He was the son who got left on the farm with his parents and took care of them till they died. He met my mother, he waited for her, they married; he thought himself lucky then to have a family to work for. (I have two brothers, and I had a baby sister who died.) I have a feeling that my father never slept with any woman before my mother, and never with her until he married her. And he had to wait, because my mother wouldn't get married until she had paid back to her own father every cent he had spent on her since her mother died. She had kept track of everything—board, books, clothes—so that she could pay it back. When she married, she had no nest egg, as teachers usually did, no hope chest, sheets, or dishes. My father used to say, with a somber, joking face, that he had hoped to get a woman with money in the bank. "But you take the money in the bank, you have to take the face that goes with it," he said, "and sometimes that's no bargain."

The house we lived in had big, high rooms, with dark-green blinds on the windows. When the blinds were pulled down against the sun, I used to like to move my head and catch the light flashing through the holes and cracks. Another thing I liked looking at was chimney stains, old or fresh, which I could turn into animals, people's faces, even distant cities. I told my own two boys about that, and their father, Dan Casey, said, "See, your mom's folks were so poor, they couldn't afford TV, so they got these stains on the ceiling—your mom had to watch the stains on the ceiling!" He always liked to kid me about thinking poor was anything great.

When my father was very old, I figured out that he didn't mind people doing new sorts of things—for instance, my getting divorced—as much as he minded them having new sorts of reasons for doing them.

Thank God he never had to know about the commune.

"The Lord never intended," he used to say. Sitting around with the other old men in the Home, in the long, dim porch behind the spirea bushes, he talked about how the Lord never intended for people to tear around the country on motorbikes and snowmobiles.

And how the Lord never intended for nurses' uniforms to be pants. The nurses didn't mind at all. They called him "Handsome," and told me he was a real old sweetheart, a real old religious gentleman. They marvelled at his thick black hair, which he kept until he died. They washed and combed it beautifully, wet-waved it with their fingers.

Sometimes, with all their care, he was a little unhappy. He wanted to go home. He worried about the cows, the fences, about who was getting up to light the fire. A few flashes of meanness—very few. Once, he gave me a sneaky, unfriendly look when I went in; he said, "I'm surprised you haven't worn all the skin off your knees by now."

I laughed. I said, "What doing? Scrubbing floors?"

"Praying!" he said, in a voice like spitting.

He didn't know who he was talking to.

I don't remember my mother's hair being anything but white. My mother went white in her twenties, and never saved any of her young hair, which had been brown. I used to try to get her to tell what color brown.

"Dark."

"Like Brent, or like Dolly?" Those were two workhorses we had, a team.

"I don't know. It wasn't horsehair."

"Was it like chocolate?"

"Something like."

"Weren't you sad when it went white?"

"No. I was glad."

"Why?"

"I was glad that I wouldn't have hair anymore that was the same color as my father's."

Hatred is always a sin, my mother told me. Remember that. One drop of hatred in your soul will spread and discolor everything like a drop of black ink in white milk. I was struck by that and meant to try it, but knew I shouldn't waste the milk.

. . .

All these things I remember. All the things I know, or have been told, about people I never even saw. I was named Euphemia, after my mother's mother. A terrible name, such as nobody has nowadays. At home they called me Phemie, but when I started to work, I called myself Fame. My husband, Dan Casey, called me Fame. Then in the bar of the Shamrock Hotel, years later, after my divorce, when I was going out, a man said to me, "Fame, I've been meaning to ask you, just what is it you are famous for?"

"I don't know," I told him. "I don't know, unless it's for wasting my time talking to jerks like you."

After that I thought of changing it altogether, to something like Joan, but unless I moved away from here, how could I do that?

In the summer of 1947, when I was twelve, I helped my mother paper the downstairs bedroom, the spare room. My mother's sister, Beryl, was coming to visit us. These two sisters hadn't seen each other for years. Very soon after their mother died, their father married again. He went to live in Minneapolis, then in Seattle, with his new wife and his younger daughter, Beryl. My mother wouldn't go with them. She stayed on in the town of Ramsay, where they had been living. She was boarded with a childless couple who had been neighbors. She and Beryl had met only once or twice since they were grown up. Beryl lived in California.

The paper had a design of cornflowers on a white ground. My mother had got it at a reduced price, because it was the end of a lot. This meant we had trouble matching the pattern, and behind the door we had to do some tricky fitting with scraps and strips. This was before the days of pre-pasted wallpaper. We had a trestle table set up in the front room, and we mixed the paste and swept it onto the back of the paper with wide brushes, watching for lumps. We worked with the windows up, screens fitted under them, the front door open, the screen door closed. The country we could see through the mesh of screens and the wavery old window glass was all hot and flowering—milkweed and wild carrot in the pastures, mustard rampaging in the clover, some fields creamy with the buckwheat people grew then. My mother sang. She sang a song she said her own mother used to sing when she and Beryl were little girls.

> *"I once had a sweetheart, but now I have none.*
> *He's gone and he's left me to weep and to moan.*
> *He's gone and he's left me, but contented I'll be,*
> *For I'll get another one, better than he!"*

I was excited because Beryl was coming, a visitor, all the way from California. Also, because I had gone to town in late June to write the Entrance Examinations, and was hoping to hear soon that I had passed with honors. Everybody who had finished Grade 8 in the country schools had to go into town to write those examinations. I loved that—the rustling sheets of foolscap, the important silence, the big stone high-school building, all the old initials carved in the desks, darkened with varnish. The first burst of summer outside, the green and yellow light, the townlike chestnut trees, and honeysuckle. And all it was was this same town, where I have lived now more than half my life. I wondered at it. And at myself, drawing maps with ease and solving problems, knowing quantities of answers. I thought I was so clever. But I wasn't clever enough to understand the simplest thing. I didn't even understand that examinations made no difference in my case. I wouldn't be going to high school. How could I? That was before there were school buses; you had to board in town. My parents didn't have the money. They operated on very little cash, as many farmers did then. The payments from the cheese factory were about all that came in regularly. And they didn't think of my life going in that direction, the high-school direction. They thought that I would stay at home and help my mother, maybe hire out to help women in the neighborhood who were sick or having a baby. Until such time as I got married. That was what they were waiting to tell me when I got the results of the examinations.

You would think my mother might have a different idea, since she had been a schoolteacher herself. But she said God didn't care. God isn't interested in what kind of job or what kind of education anybody has, she told me. He doesn't care two hoots about that, and it's what He cares about that matters.

This was the first time I understood how God could become a real opponent, not just some kind of nuisance or large decoration.

My mother's name as a child was Marietta. That continued to be her name, of course, but until Beryl came I never heard her called by it. My father always said Mother. I had a childish notion—I knew it was childish—that Mother suited my mother better than it did other mothers. Mother, not Mama. When I was away from her, I could not think what my mother's face was like, and this frightened me. Sitting in school, just over a hill from home, I would try to picture my mother's face. Sometimes I thought that if I couldn't do it, that might mean my mother was dead. But I had a sense of her all the time, and would be reminded of her by the most unlikely things—an upright piano, or a tall white loaf of bread. That's ridiculous, but true.

Marietta, in my mind, was separate, not swallowed up in my mother's grownup body. Marietta was still running around loose up in her town of Ramsay, on the Ottawa River. In that town, the streets were full of horses and puddles, and darkened by men who came in from the bush on weekends. Loggers. There were eleven hotels on the main street, where the loggers stayed, and drank.

The house Marietta lived in was halfway up a steep street climbing from the river. It was a double house, with two bay windows in front, and a wooden trellis that separated the two front porches. In the other half of the house lived the Sutcliffes, the people Marietta was to board with after her mother died and her father left town. Mr. Sutcliffe was an Englishman, a telegraph operator. His wife was German. She always made coffee instead of tea. She made strudel. The dough for the strudel hung down over the edges of the table like a fine cloth. It sometimes looked to Marietta like a skin.

Mrs. Sutcliffe was the one who talked Marietta's mother out of hanging herself.

Marietta was home from school that day, because it was Saturday. She woke up late and heard the silence in the house. She was always scared of that—a silent house—and as soon as she opened the door after school she would call, "Mama! Mama!" Often her mother wouldn't answer. But she would be there. Marietta would hear with relief the rattle of the stove grate or the steady slap of the iron.

That morning, she didn't hear anything. She came downstairs, and got herself a slice of bread and butter and molasses, folded over. She opened the cellar door and called. She went into the front room and peered out the window, through the bridal fern. She saw her little sister, Beryl, and some other neighborhood children rolling down the bit of grassy terrace to the sidewalk, picking themselves up and scrambling to the top and rolling down again.

"Mama?" called Marietta. She walked through the house to the back yard. It was late spring, the day was cloudy and mild. In the sprouting vegetable gardens, the earth was damp, and the leaves on the trees seemed suddenly full-sized, letting down drops of water left over from the rain of the night before.

"Mama?" calls Marietta under the trees, under the clothesline.

At the end of the yard is a small barn, where they keep firewood, and some tools and old furniture. A chair, a straight-backed wooden chair, can be seen through the open doorway. On the chair, Marietta sees her mother's feet, her mother's black laced shoes. Then the long, printed cotton summer work dress, the apron, the rolled-up sleeves. Her mother's shiny-looking white arms, and neck, and face.

Her mother stood on the chair and didn't answer. She didn't look at Marietta, but smiled and tapped her foot, as if to say, "Here I am, then. What are you going to do about it?" Something looked wrong about her, beyond the fact that she was standing on a chair and smiling in this queer, tight way. Standing on an old chair with back rungs missing, which she had pulled out to the middle of the barn floor, where it teetered on the bumpy earth. There was a shadow on her neck.

The shadow was a rope, a noose on the end of a rope that hung down from a beam overhead.

"Mama?" says Marietta, in a fainter voice. "Mama. Come down, please." Her voice is faint because she fears that any yell or cry might jolt her mother into movement, cause her to step off the chair and throw her weight on the rope. But even if Marietta wanted to yell she couldn't. Nothing but this pitiful thread of a voice is left to her—just as in a dream when a beast or a machine is bearing down on you.

"Go and get your father."

That was what her mother told her to do, and Marietta obeyed. With terror in her legs, she ran. In her nightgown, in the middle of a Saturday morning, she ran. She ran past Beryl and the other children, still tumbling down the slope. She ran along the sidewalk, which was at that time a boardwalk, then on the unpaved street, full of last night's puddles. The street crossed the railway tracks. At the foot of the hill, it intersected the main street of the town. Between the main street and the river were some warehouses and the buildings of small manufacturers. That was where Marietta's father had his carriage works. Wagons, buggies, sleds were made there. In fact, Marietta's father had invented a new sort of sled to carry logs in the bush. It had been patented. He was just getting started in Ramsay. (Later on, in the States, he made money. A man fond of hotel bars, barbershops, harness races, women, but not afraid of work—give him credit.)

Marietta did not find him at work that day. The office was empty. She ran out into the yard where the men were working. She stumbled in the fresh sawdust. The men laughed and shook their heads at her. No. Not here. Not a-here right now. No. Why don't you try upstreet? Wait. Wait a minute. Hadn't you better get some clothes on first?

They didn't mean any harm. They didn't have the sense to see that something must be wrong. But Marietta never could stand men laughing. There were always places she hated to go past, let alone into, and that was the reason. Men laughing. Because of that, she hated barbershops, hated their smell. (When she started going to dances later on with my father, she asked him not to put any dressing on his hair, because the smell reminded her.) A bunch of men standing out on the street, outside a hotel, seemed to Marietta like a clot of poison. You tried not to hear what they were saying, but you could be sure it was vile. If they didn't say anything, they laughed and vileness spread out from them—poison—just the same. It was only after Marietta was saved that she could walk right past them. Armed by God, she walked through their midst and nothing stuck to her, nothing scorched her; she was safe as Daniel.

Now she turned and ran, straight back the way she had come. Up the hill, running to get home. She thought she had made a mistake leaving her mother. Why did her mother tell her to go? Why did she want her father? Quite possibly so that she could greet him with the sight of her own warm body swinging on the end of a rope. Marietta should have stayed—she should have stayed and talked her mother out of it. She should have run to Mrs. Sutcliffe, or any neighbor, not wasted time this way. She hadn't thought who could help, who could even believe what she was talking about. She had the idea that all families except her own lived in peace, that threats and miseries didn't exist in other people's houses, and couldn't be explained there.

A train was coming into town. Marietta had to wait. Passengers looked out at her from its windows. She broke out wailing in the faces of those strangers. When the train passed, she continued up the hill—a spectacle, with her hair uncombed, her feet bare and muddy, in her nightgown, with a wild, wet face. By the time she ran into her own yard, in sight of the barn, she was howling. "Mama!" she was howling. "Mama!"

Nobody was there. The chair was standing just where it had been before. The rope was dangling over the back of it. Marietta was sure that her mother had gone ahead and done it. Her mother was already dead—she had been cut down and taken away.

But warm, fat hands settled down on her shoulders, and Mrs. Sutcliffe said, "Marietta. Stop the noise. Marietta. Child. Stop the crying. Come inside. She is well, Marietta. Come inside and you will see."

Mrs. Sutcliffe's foreign voice said, "Mari-et-cha," giving the name a rich, important sound. She was as kind as could be. When Marietta lived with the Sutcliffes later, she was treated as the daughter of the household, and it was a household just as peaceful and comfortable as she had imagined other households to be. But she never felt like a daughter there.

In Mrs. Sutcliffe's kitchen, Beryl sat on the floor eating a raisin cookie and playing with the black-and-white cat, whose name was Dickie. Marietta's mother sat at the table, with a cup of coffee in front of her.

"She was silly," Mrs. Sutcliffe said. Did she mean Marietta's mother or Marietta herself? She didn't have many English words to describe things.

Marietta's mother laughed, and Marietta blacked out. She fainted, after running all that way uphill, howling, in the warm, damp morning. Next thing she knew, she was taking black, sweet coffee from a spoon held by Mrs. Sutcliffe. Beryl picked Dickie up by the front legs and offered him as a cheering present. Marietta's mother was still sitting at the table.

Her heart was broken. That was what I always heard my mother say. That was the end of it. Those words lifted up the story and sealed it shut. I never asked, Who broke it? I never asked, What was the men's poison talk? What was the meaning of the word "vile"?

Marietta's mother laughed after not hanging herself. She sat at Mrs. Sutcliffe's kitchen table long ago and laughed. Her heart was broken.

I always had a feeling, with my mother's talk and stories, of something swelling out behind. Like a cloud you couldn't see through, or get to the end of. There was a cloud, a poison, that had touched my mother's life. And when I grieved my mother, I became part of it. Then I would beat my head against my mother's stomach and breasts, against her tall, firm front, demanding to be forgiven. My mother would tell me to ask God. But it wasn't God, it was my mother I had to get straight with. It seemed as if she knew something about me that was worse, far worse, than ordinary lies and tricks and meanness; it was a really sickening shame. I beat against my mother's front to make her forget that.

My brothers weren't bothered by any of this. I don't think so. They seemed to me like cheerful savages, running around free, not having to learn much. And when I just had the two boys myself, no daughters, I felt as if something could stop now—the stories, and griefs, the old puzzles you can't resist or solve.

Aunt Beryl said not to call her Aunt. "I'm not used to being anybody's aunt, honey. I'm not even anybody's momma. I'm just me. Call me Beryl."

Beryl had started out as a stenographer, and now she had her own typing and bookkeeping business, which employed many girls. She had arrived with a man friend, whose name was Mr. Florence. Her letter had said that she would be getting a ride with a friend, but she hadn't said whether the friend would be staying or going on. She hadn't even said if it was a man or a woman.

Mr. Florence was staying. He was a tall, thin man with a long, tanned face, very light-colored eyes, and a way of twitching the corner of his mouth that might have been a smile.

He was the one who got to sleep in the room that my mother and I had papered, because he was the stranger, and a man. Beryl had to sleep with me. At first we thought that Mr. Florence was quite rude, because he wasn't used to our way of talking and we weren't used to his. The first morning, my father said to Mr. Florence, "Well, I hope you got some kind of a sleep on that old bed in there?" (The spare-room bed was heavenly, with a feather tick.) This was Mr. Florence's cue to say that he had never slept better.

Mr. Florence twitched. He said, "I slept on worse."

His favorite place to be was in his car. His car was a royal-blue Chrysler, from the first batch turned out after the war. Inside it, the upholstery and floor covering and roof and door padding were all pearl gray. Mr. Florence kept the names of those colors in mind and corrected you if you said just "blue" or "gray."

"Mouse skin is what it looks like to me," said Beryl rambunctiously. "I tell him it's just mouse skin!"

The car was parked at the side of the house, under the locust trees. Mr. Florence sat inside with the windows rolled up, smoking, in the rich new-car smell.

"I'm afraid we're not doing much to entertain your friend," my mother said.

"I wouldn't worry about him," said Beryl. She always spoke about Mr. Florence as if there was a joke about him that only she appreciated. I wondered long afterward if he had a bottle in the glove compartment and took a nip from time to time to keep his spirits up. He kept his hat on.

Beryl herself was being entertained enough for two. Instead of staying in the house and talking to my mother, as a lady visitor usually did, she demanded to be shown everything there was to see on a farm. She said that I was to take her around and explain things, and see that she didn't fall into any manure piles.

I didn't know what to show. I took Beryl to the icehouse, where chunks of ice the size of dresser drawers, or bigger, lay buried in sawdust. Every few days, my father would chop off a piece of ice and carry it to the kitchen, where it melted in a tin-lined box and cooled the milk and butter.

Beryl said she had never had any idea ice came in pieces that big. She seemed intent on finding things strange, or horrible, or funny.

"Where in the world do you get ice that big?"

I couldn't tell if that was a joke.

"Off of the lake," I said.

"Off of the lake! Do you have lakes up here that have ice on them all summer?"

I told her how my father cut the ice on the lake every winter and hauled it home, and buried it in sawdust, and that kept it from melting.

Beryl said, "That's amazing!"

"Well, it melts a little," I said. I was deeply disappointed in Beryl.

"That's really amazing."

Beryl went along when I went to get the cows. A scarecrow in white slacks (this was what my father called her afterward), with a white sun hat tied under her chin by a flaunting red ribbon. Her fingernails and toenails—she wore sandals—were painted to match the ribbon. She wore the small, dark sunglasses people wore at that time. (Not the people I knew—they didn't own sunglasses.) She had a big red mouth, a loud laugh, hair of an unnatural color and a high gloss, like cherry wood. She was so noisy and shiny, so glamorously got up, that it was hard to tell whether she was good-looking, or happy, or anything.

We didn't have any conversation along the cowpath, because Beryl kept her distance from the cows and was busy watching where she stepped. Once I had them all tied in their stalls, she came closer. She lit a cigarette. Nobody smoked in the barn. My father and other farmers chewed tobacco there instead. I didn't see how I could ask Beryl to chew tobacco.

"Can you get the milk out of them or does your father have to?" Beryl said. "Is it hard to do?"

I pulled some milk down through the cow's teat. One of the barn cats came over and waited. I shot a thin stream into its mouth. The cat and I were both showing off.

"Doesn't that hurt?" said Beryl. "Think if it was you."

I had never thought of a cow's teat as corresponding to any part of myself, and was shaken by this indecency. In fact, I could never grasp a warm, warty teat in such a firm and casual way again.

Beryl slept in a peach-colored rayon nightgown trimmed with écru lace. She had a robe to match. She was just as careful about the word "écru" as Mr. Florence was about his royal blue and pearl gray.

I managed to get undressed and put on my nightgown without any part of me being exposed at any time. An awkward business. I left my underpants on, and hoped that Beryl had done the same. The idea of sharing my bed with a grownup was a torment to me. But I did get to see the contents of what Beryl called her beauty kit. Hand-painted glass jars contained puffs of cotton wool, talcum powder, milky lotion, ice-blue astringent. Little pots of red and mauve rouge—rather greasy-looking. Blue and black pencils. Emery boards, a pumice stone, nail polish with an overpowering smell of bananas, face powder in a celluloid box shaped like a shell, with the name of a dessert—Apricot Delight.

I had heated some water on the coal-oil stove we used in summertime. Beryl scrubbed her face clean, and there was such a change that I almost expected to see makeup lying in strips in the washbowl, like the old wallpaper we had soaked and peeled. Beryl's skin was pale now, covered with fine cracks, rather like the shiny mud at the bottom of puddles drying up in early summer.

"Look what happened to my skin," she said. "Dieting. I weighed a hundred and sixty-nine pounds once, and I took it off too fast and my face fell in on me. Now I've got this cream, though. It's made from a secret formula and you can't even buy it commercially. Smell it. See, it doesn't smell all perfumy. It smells serious."

She was patting the cream on her face with puffs of cotton wool, patting away until there was nothing to be seen on the surface.

"It smells like lard," I said.

"Christ Almighty, I hope I haven't been paying that kind of money to rub lard on my face. Don't tell your mother I swear."

She poured clean water into the drinking glass and wet her comb, then combed her hair wet and twisted each strand round her finger, clamping the twisted strand to her head with two crossed pins. I would be doing the same myself, a couple of years later.

"Always do your hair wet, else it's no good doing it up at all," Beryl said. "And always roll it under even if you want it to flip up. See?"

When I was doing my hair up—as I did for years—I sometimes thought of this, and thought that of all the pieces of advice people had given me, this was the one I had followed most carefully.

We put the lamp out and got into bed, and Beryl said, "I never knew it could get so dark. I've never known a dark that was as dark as this." She was whispering. I was slow to understand that she was comparing country nights to city nights, and I wondered if the darkness in Netterfield County could really be greater than that in California.

"Honey?" whispered Beryl. "Are there any animals outside?"

"Cows," I said.

"Yes, but wild animals? Are there bears?"

"Yes," I said. My father had once found bear tracks and droppings in the bush, and the apples had all been torn off a wild apple tree. That was years ago, when he was a young man.

Beryl moaned and giggled. "Think if Mr. Florence had to go out in the night and he ran into a bear!"

Next day was Sunday. Beryl and Mr. Florence drove my brothers and me to Sunday school in the Chrysler. That was at ten o'clock in the morning. They came back at eleven to bring my parents to church.

"Hop in," Beryl said to me. "You, too," she said to the boys. "We're going for a drive."

Beryl was dressed up in a satiny ivory dress with red dots, and a red-lined frill over the hips, and red high-heeled shoes. Mr. Florence wore a pale-blue summer suit.

"Aren't you going to church?" I said. That was what people dressed up for, in my experience.

Beryl laughed. "Honey, this isn't Mr. Florence's kind of religion."

I was used to going straight from Sunday school into church, and sitting for another hour and a half. In summer, the open windows let in the cedary smell of the graveyard and the occasional, almost sacrilegious sound of a car swooshing by on the road. Today we spent this time driving through country I had never seen before. I had never seen it, though it was less than twenty miles from home. Our truck went to the cheese factory, to church, and to town on Saturday nights. The nearest thing to a drive was when it went to the dump. I had seen the near end of Bell's Lake, because that was where my father cut the ice in winter. You couldn't get close to it in summer; the shoreline was all choked up with bulrushes. I had thought that the other end of the lake would look pretty much the same, but when we drove there today, I saw cottages, docks and boats, dark water reflecting the trees. All this and I hadn't known about it. This, too, was Bell's Lake. I was glad to have seen it at last, but in some way not altogether glad of the surprise.

Finally, a white frame building appeared, with verandas and potted flowers, and some twinkling poplar trees in front. The Wildwood Inn. Today the same building is covered with stucco and done up with Tudor beams and called the Hideaway. The poplar trees have been cut down for a parking lot.

On the way back to the church to pick up my parents, Mr. Florence turned in to the farm next to ours, which belonged to the McAllisters. The McAllisters were Catholics. Our two families were neighborly but not close.

"Come on, boys, out you get," said Beryl to my brothers. "Not you," she said to me. "You stay put." She herded the little boys up to the porch, where some McAllisters were watching. They were in their raggedy home clothes, because their church, or Mass, or whatever it was, got out early. Mrs. McAllister came out and stood listening, rather dumbfounded, to Beryl's laughing talk.

Beryl came back to the car by herself. "There," she said. "They're going to play with the neighbor children."

Play with McAllisters? Besides being Catholics, all but the baby were girls.

"They've still got their good clothes on," I said.

"So what? Can't they have a good time with their good clothes on? I do!"

My parents were taken by surprise as well. Beryl got out and told my father he was to ride in the front seat, for the legroom. She got into the back, with my mother and me. Mr. Florence turned again onto the Bell's Lake road, and Beryl announced that we were all going to the Wildwood Inn for dinner.

"You're all dressed up, why not take advantage?" she said. "We dropped the boys off with your neighbors. I thought they might be too young to appreciate it. The neighbors were happy to have them." She said with a further emphasis that it was to be their treat. Hers and Mr. Florence's.

"Well, now," said my father. He probably didn't have five dollars in his pocket. "Well, now. I wonder do they let the farmers in?"

He made various jokes along this line. In the hotel dining room, which was all in white—white tablecloths, white painted chairs—with sweating glass water pitchers and high, whirring fans, he picked up a table napkin the size of a diaper and spoke to me in a loud whisper, "Can you tell me what to do with this thing? Can I put it on my head to keep the draft off?"

Of course he had eaten in hotel dining rooms before. He knew about table napkins and pie forks. And my mother knew—she wasn't even a country woman, to begin with. Nevertheless this was a huge event. Not exactly a pleasure—as Beryl must have meant it to be—but a huge, unsettling event. Eating a meal in public, only a few miles from home, eating in a big room full of people you didn't know, the food served by a stranger, a snippy-looking girl who was probably a college student working at a summer job.

"I'd like the rooster," my father said. "How long has he been in the pot?" It was only good manners, as he knew it, to joke with people who waited on him.

"Beg your pardon?" the girl said.

"Roast chicken," said Beryl. "Is that okay for everybody?"

Mr. Florence was looking gloomy. Perhaps he didn't care for jokes when it was his money that was being spent. Perhaps he had counted on something better than ice water to fill up the glasses.

The waitress put down a dish of celery and olives, and my mother said, "Just a minute while I give thanks." She bowed her head and said quietly but audibly, "Lord, bless this food to our use, and us to Thy service, for Christ's sake. Amen." Refreshed, she sat up straight and passed the dish to me, saying, "Mind the olives. There's stones in them."

Beryl was smiling around at the room.

The waitress came back with a basket of rolls.

"Parker House!" Beryl leaned over and breathed in their smell. "Eat them while they're hot enough to melt the butter!"

Mr. Florence twitched, and peered into the butter dish. "Is that what this is—butter? I thought it was Shirley Temple's curls."

His face was hardly less gloomy than before, but it was a joke, and his making it seemed to convey to us something of the very thing that had just been publicly asked for—a blessing.

"When he says something funny," said Beryl—who often referred to Mr. Florence as "he" even when he was right there—"you notice how he always keeps a straight face? That reminds me of Mama. I mean of our mama, Marietta's and mine. Daddy, when he made a joke you could see it coming a mile away—he couldn't keep it off his face—but Mama was another story. She could look so sour. But she could joke on her deathbed. In fact, she did that very thing. Marietta, remember when she was in bed in the front room the spring before she died?"

"I remember she was in bed in that room," my mother said. "Yes."

"Well, Daddy came in and she was lying there in her clean nightgown, with the covers off, because the German lady from next door had just been helping her take a wash, and she was still there tidying up the bed. So Daddy wanted to be cheerful, and he said, 'Spring must be coming. I saw a crow today.' This must have been in March. And Mama said quick as a shot, 'Well, you better cover me up then, before it looks in that window and gets any ideas!' The German lady—Daddy said she just about dropped the basin. Because it was true, Mama was skin and bones; she was dying. But she could joke."

Mr. Florence said, "Might as well when there's no use to cry."

"But she could carry a joke too far, Mama could. One time, one time, she wanted to give Daddy a scare. He was supposed to be interested in some girl that kept coming around to the works. Well, he was a big good-looking man. So Mama said, 'Well, I'll just do away with myself, and you can get on with her and see how you like it when I come back and haunt you.' He told her not to be so stupid, and he went off downtown. And Mama went out to the barn and climbed on a chair and put a rope around her neck. Didn't she, Marietta? Marietta went looking for her and she found her like that!"

My mother bent her head and put her hands in her lap, almost as if she was getting ready to say another grace.

"Daddy told me all about it, but I can remember anyway. I remember Marietta tearing off down the hill in her nightie, and I guess the German lady saw her go, and she came out and was looking for Mama, and somehow we all ended up in the barn—me, too, and some kids I was playing with—and there was Mama up on a chair preparing to give Daddy the fright of his life. She'd sent Marietta after him. And the German lady starts wailing, 'Oh, Missus, come down Missus, think of your little *kindren*'—'*kindren*' is the German for 'children'—'think of your *kindren*,' and so on. Until it was me standing there—I was just a little squirt, but I was the one noticed that rope. My eyes followed that rope up and up and I saw it was just hanging over the beam, just flung there—it wasn't tied at all! Marietta hadn't noticed that, the German lady hadn't noticed it. But I just spoke up and said, 'Mama, how are you going to manage to hang yourself without that rope tied around the beam?' "

Mr. Florence said, "That'd be a tough one."

"I spoiled her game. The German lady made coffee and we went over there and had a few treats, and, Marietta, you couldn't find Daddy after all, could you? You could hear Marietta howling, coming up the hill, a block away."

"Natural for her to be upset," my father said.

"Sure it was. Mama went too far."

"She meant it," my mother said. "She meant it more than you give her credit for."

"She meant to get a rise out of Daddy. That was their whole life together. He always said she was a hard woman to live with, but she had a lot of character. I believe he missed that, with Gladys."

"I wouldn't know," my mother said, in that particularly steady voice with which she always spoke of her father. "What he did say or didn't say."

"People are dead now," said my father. "It isn't up to us to judge."

"I know," said Beryl. "I know Marietta's always had a different view."

My mother looked at Mr. Florence and smiled quite easily and radiantly. "I'm sure you don't know what to make of all these family matters."

The one time that I visited Beryl, when Beryl was an old woman, all knobby and twisted up with arthritis, Beryl said, "Marietta got all Daddy's looks. And she never did a thing with herself.

Remember her wearing that old navy-blue crêpe dress when we went to the hotel that time? Of course, I know it was probably all she had, but did it have to be all she had? You know, I was scared of her somehow. I couldn't stay in a room alone with her. But she had outstanding looks." Trying to remember an occasion when I had noticed my mother's looks, I thought of the time in the hotel, my mother's pale-olive skin against the heavy white, coiled hair, her open, handsome face smiling at Mr. Florence—as if he was the one to be forgiven.

I didn't have a problem right away with Beryl's story. For one thing, I was hungry and greedy, and a lot of my attention went to the roast chicken and gravy and mashed potatoes laid on the plate with an ice-cream scoop and the bright diced vegetables out of a can, which I thought much superior to those fresh from the garden. For dessert, I had a butterscotch sundae, an agonizing choice over chocolate. The others had plain vanilla ice cream.

Why shouldn't Beryl's version of the same event be different from my mother's? Beryl was strange in every way—everything about her was slanted, seen from a new angle. It was my mother's version that held, for a time. It absorbed Beryl's story, closed over it. But Beryl's story didn't vanish; it stayed sealed off for years, but it wasn't gone. It was like the knowledge of that hotel and dining room. I knew about it now, though I didn't think of it as a place to go back to. And indeed, without Beryl's or Mr. Florence's money, I couldn't. But I knew it was there.

The next time I was in the Wildwood Inn, in fact, was after I was married. The Lions Club had a banquet and dance there. The man I had married, Dan Casey, was a Lion. You could get a drink there by that time. Dan Casey wouldn't have gone anywhere you couldn't. Then the place was remodelled into the Hideaway, and now they have strippers every night but Sunday. On Thursday nights, they have a male stripper. I go there with people from the real-estate office to celebrate birthdays or other big events.

The farm was sold for five thousand dollars in 1965. A man from Toronto bought it, for a hobby farm or just an investment. After a couple of years, he rented it to a commune. They stayed there, different people drifting on and off, for a dozen years or so. They raised goats and sold the milk to the health-food store that had opened up in town. They painted a rainbow across the side of the barn that faced the road. They hung tie-dyed sheets over the windows, and let the long grass and flowering weeds reclaim the yard. My parents had finally got electricity in, but these people didn't use it. They preferred oil lamps and the wood stove, and taking their dirty clothes to town. People said they wouldn't know how to handle lamps or wood fires, and they would burn the place down. But they didn't. In fact, they didn't manage badly. They kept the house and barn in some sort of repair and they worked a big garden. They even dusted their potatoes against blight—though I heard that there was some sort of row about this and some of the stricter members left. The place actually looked a lot better than many of the farms round about that were still in the hands of the original families. The McAllister son had started a wrecking business on their place. My own brothers were long gone.

I knew I was not being reasonable, but I had the feeling that I'd rather see the farm suffer outright neglect—I'd sooner see it in the hands of hoodlums and scroungers—than see that rainbow on the barn, and some letters that looked Egyptian painted on the wall of the house. That seemed a mockery. I even disliked the sight of those people when they came to town—the men with their hair in ponytails, and with holes in their overalls that I believed were cut on purpose, and the women with long hair and no makeup and their meek, superior expressions. What do you know about life, I felt like asking them. What makes you think you can come here and mock my father and mother and their life and their poverty? But when I thought of the rainbow and those letters, I knew they weren't trying to mock or imitate my parents' life. They had displaced that life, hardly knowing it existed. They had set up in its place these beliefs and customs of their own, which I hoped would fail them.

That happened, more or less. The commune disintegrated. The goats disappeared. Some of the women moved to town, cut their hair, put on makeup, and got jobs as waitresses or cashiers to support their children. The Toronto man put the place up for sale, and after about a year it was sold for more than ten times what he had paid for it. A young couple from Ottawa bought it. They have painted the outside a pale gray with oyster trim, and have put in skylights and a handsome front door with carriage lamps on either side. Inside, they've changed it around so much that I've been told I'd never recognize it.

I did get in once, before this happened, during the year that the house was empty and for sale. The company I work for was handling it, and I had a key, though the house was being shown by another agent. I let myself in on a Sunday afternoon. I had a man with me, not a client but a friend—Bob Marks, whom I was seeing a lot at the time.

"This is that hippie place," Bob Marks said when I stopped the car. "I've been by here before."

He was a lawyer, a Catholic, separated from his wife. He thought he wanted to settle down and start up a practice here in town. But there already was one Catholic lawyer. Business was slow. A couple of times a week, Bob Marks would be fairly drunk before supper.

"It's more than that," I said. "It's where I was born. Where I grew up." We walked through the weeds, and I unlocked the door.

He said that he had thought, from the way I talked, that it would be farther out.

"It seemed farther then."

All the rooms were bare, and the floors swept clean. The woodwork was freshly painted—I was surprised to see no smudges on the glass. Some new panes, some old wavy ones. Some of the walls had been stripped of their paper and painted. A wall in the kitchen was painted a deep blue, with an enormous dove on it. On a wall in the front room, giant sunflowers appeared, and a butterfly of almost the same size.

Bob Marks whistled. "Somebody was an artist."

"If that's what you want to call it," I said, and turned back to the kitchen. The same wood stove was there. "My mother once burned up three thousand dollars," I said. "She burned three thousand dollars in that stove."

He whistled again, differently. "What do you mean? She threw in a check?"

"No, no. It was in bills. She did it deliberately. She went into town to the bank and she had them give it all to her, in a shoebox. She brought it home and put it in the stove. She put it in just a few bills at a time, so it wouldn't make too big a blaze. My father stood and watched her."

"What are you talking about?" said Bob Marks. "I thought you were so poor."

"We were. We were very poor."

"So how come she had three thousand dollars? That would be like thirty thousand today. Easily. More than thirty thousand today."

"It was her legacy," I said. "It was what she got from her father. Her father died in Seattle and left her three thousand dollars, and she burned it up because she hated him. She didn't want his money. She hated him."

"That's a lot of hate," Bob Marks said.

"That isn't the point. Her hating him, or whether he was bad enough for her to have a right to hate him. Not likely he was. That isn't the point."

"Money," he said. "Money's always the point."

"No. My father letting her do it is the point. To me it is. My father stood and watched and he never protested. If anybody had tried to stop her, he would have protected her. I consider that love."

"Some people would consider it lunacy."

I remember that that had been Beryl's opinion, exactly.

I went into the front room and stared at the butterfly, with its pink-and-orange wings. Then I went into the front bedroom and found two human figures painted on the wall. A man and a woman holding hands and facing straight ahead. They were naked, and larger than life size.

"It reminds me of that John Lennon and Yoko Ono picture,"

I said to Bob Marks, who had come in behind me. "That record cover, wasn't it?" I didn't want him to think that anything he had said in the kitchen had upset me.

Bob Marks said, "Different color hair."

That was true. Both figures had yellow hair painted in a solid mass, the way they do it in the comic strips. Horsetails of yellow hair curling over their shoulders and little pigs' tails of yellow hair decorating their not so private parts. Their skin was a flat beige pink and their eyes a staring blue, the same blue that was on the kitchen wall.

I noticed that they hadn't quite finished peeling the wallpaper away before making this painting. In the corner, there was some paper left that matched the paper on the other walls—a modernistic design of intersecting pink and gray and mauve bubbles. The man from Toronto must have put that on. The paper underneath hadn't been stripped off when this new paper went on. I could see an edge of it, the cornflowers on a white ground.

"I guess this was where they carried on their sexual shenanigans," Bob Marks said, in a tone familiar to me. That thickened, sad, uneasy, but determined tone. The not particularly friendly lust of middle-aged respectable men.

I didn't say anything. I worked away some of the bubble paper to see more of the cornflowers. Suddenly I hit a loose spot, and ripped away a big swatch of it. But the cornflower paper came, too, and a little shower of dried plaster.

"Why is it?" I said. "Just tell me, why is it that no man can mention a place like this without getting around to the subject of sex in about two seconds flat? Just say the words 'hippie' or 'commune' and all you guys can think about is screwing! As if there wasn't anything at all behind it but orgies and fancy combinations and non-stop screwing! I get so sick of that—it's all so stupid it just makes me sick!"

In the car, on the way home from the hotel, we sat as before—the men in the front seat, the women in the back. I was in the middle, Beryl and my mother on either side of me. Their heated bodies pressed against me, through cloth; their smells crowded out the smells of the cedar bush we passed through, and the pockets of bog, where Beryl exclaimed at the water lilies. Beryl smelled of all those things in pots and bottles. My mother smelled of flour and hard soap and the warm crêpe of her good dress and the kerosene she had used to take the spots off.

"A lovely meal," my mother said. "Thank you, Beryl. Thank you, Mr. Florence."

"I don't know who is going to be fit to do the milking," my father said. "Now that we've all ate in such style."

"Speaking of money," said Beryl—though nobody actually had been—"do you mind my asking what you did with yours? I put mine in real estate. Real estate in California—you can't lose. I was thinking you could get an electric stove, so you wouldn't have to bother with a fire in summer or fool with that coal-oil thing, either one."

All the other people in the car laughed, even Mr. Florence.

"That's a good idea, Beryl," said my father. "We could use it to set things on till we get the electricity."

"Oh, Lord," said Beryl. "How stupid can I get?"

"And we don't actually have the money, either," my mother said cheerfully, as if she was continuing the joke.

But Beryl spoke sharply. "You wrote me you got it. You got the same as me."

My father half turned in his seat. "What money are you talking about?" he said. "What's this money?"

"From Daddy's will," Beryl said. "That you got last year. Look, maybe I shouldn't have asked. If you had to pay something off, that's still a good use, isn't it? It doesn't matter. We're all family here. Practically."

"We didn't have to use it to pay anything off," my mother said. "I burned it."

Then she told how she went into town in the truck, one day almost a year ago, and got them to give her the money in a box she had brought along for the purpose. She took it home, and put it in the stove and burned it.

My father turned around and faced the road ahead.

I could feel Beryl twisting beside me while my mother talked. She was twisting, and moaning a little, as if she had a pain she couldn't suppress. At the end of the story, she let out a sound of astonishment and suffering, an angry groan.

"So you burned up money!" she said. "You burned up money in the stove."

My mother was still cheerful. "You sound as if I'd burned up one of my children."

"You burned their chances. You burned up everything the money could have got for them."

"The last thing my children need is money. None of us need his money."

"That's criminal," Beryl said harshly. She pitched her voice into the front seat: "Why did you let her?"

"He wasn't there," my mother said. "Nobody was there."

My father said, "It was her money, Beryl."

"Never mind," Beryl said. "That's criminal."

"Criminal is for when you call in the police," Mr. Florence said. Like other things he had said that day, this created a little island of surprise and a peculiar gratitude.

Gratitude not felt by all.

"Don't you pretend this isn't the craziest thing you ever heard of," Beryl shouted into the front seat. "Don't you pretend you don't think so! Because it is, and you do. You think just the same as me!"

My father did not stand in the kitchen watching my mother feed the money into the flames. It wouldn't appear so. He did not know about it—it seems fairly clear, if I remember everything, that he did not know about it until that Sunday afternoon in Mr. Florence's Chrysler, when my mother told them all together. Why, then, can I see the scene so clearly, just as I described it to Bob Marks (and to others—he was not the first)? I see my father standing by the table in the middle of the room—the table with the drawer in it for knives and forks, and the scrubbed oilcloth on top—and there is the box of money on the table. My mother is carefully dropping the bills into the fire. She holds the stove lid by the blackened lifter in one hand. And my father, standing by, seems not just to be permitting her to do this but to be protecting her. A solemn scene, but not crazy. People doing something that seems to them natural and necessary. At least, one of them is doing what seems natural and necessary, and the other believes that the important thing is for that person to be free, to go ahead. They understand that other people might not think so. They do not care.

How hard it is for me to believe that I made that up. It seems so much the truth it is the truth; it's what I believe about them. I haven't stopped believing it. But I have stopped telling that story. I never told it to anyone again after telling it to Bob Marks. I don't think so. I didn't stop just because it wasn't, strictly speaking, true. I stopped because I saw that I had to give up expecting people to see it the way I did. I had to give up expecting them to approve of any part of what was done. How could I even say that I approved of it myself? If I had been the sort of person who approved of that, who could do it, I wouldn't have done all I have done—run away from home to work in a restaurant in town when I was fifteen, gone to night school to learn typing and bookkeeping, got into the real-estate office, and finally become a licensed agent. I wouldn't be divorced. My father wouldn't have died in the county home. My hair would be white, as it has been naturally for years, instead of a color called Copper Sunrise. And not one of these things would I change, not really, if I could.

Bob Marks was a decent man—good-hearted, sometimes with imagination. After I had lashed out at him like that, he said, "You don't need to be so tough on us." In a moment, he said, "Was this your room when you were a little girl?" He thought that was why the mention of the sexual shenanigans had upset me.

And I thought it would be just as well to let him think that. I said yes, yes, it was my room when I was a little girl. It was just as well to make up right away. Moments of kindness and reconciliation are worth having, even if the parting has to come sooner or later. I wonder if those moments aren't more valued, and deliberately gone after, in the setups some people like myself have now, than they were in those old marriages, where love and grudges could be growing underground, so confused and stubborn, it must have seemed they had forever.

LICHEN

Stella's father built the place as a summer house, on the clay bluffs overlooking Lake Huron. Her family always called it "the summer cottage." David was surprised when he first saw it, because it had none of the knotty-pine charm, the battened-down coziness, that those words suggested. A city boy, from what Stella's family called "a different background," he had no experience of summer places. It was and is a high, bare wooden house, painted gray—a copy of the old farmhouses nearby, though perhaps less substantial. In front of it are the steep bluffs—they are not so substantial, either, but have held so far—and a long flight of steps down to the beach. Behind it is a small fenced garden, where Stella grows vegetables with considerable skill and coaxing, a short sandy lane, and a jungle of wild blackberry bushes.

As David turns the car into the lane, Stella steps out of these bushes, holding a colander full of berries. She is a short, fat, white-haired woman, wearing jeans and a dirty T-shirt. There is nothing underneath these clothes, as far as he can see, to support or restrain any part of her.

"Look what's happened to Stella," says David, fuming. "She's turned into a troll."

Catherine, who has never met Stella before, says decently, "Well. She's older."

"Older than what, Catherine? Older than the house? Older than Lake Huron? Older than the cat?"

There is a cat asleep on the path beside the vegetable garden. A large ginger tom with ears mutilated in battle, and one grayed-over eye. His name is Hercules and he dates from David's time.

"She's an older woman," says Catherine in a flutter of defiance. Even defiant, she's meek. "You know what I mean."

David thinks that Stella has done this on purpose. It isn't just an acceptance of natural deterioration—oh, no, it's much more. Stella would always dramatize. But it isn't just Stella. There's the sort of woman who has to come bursting out of the female envelope at this age, flaunting fat or an indecent scrawniness, sprouting warts and facial hair, refusing to cover pasty veined legs, almost gleeful about it, as if this was what she'd wanted to do all along. Man-haters, from the start. You can't say a thing like that out loud nowadays.

He has parked too close to the berry bushes—too close for Catherine, who slides out of the car on the passenger side and is immediately in trouble. Catherine is slim enough, but her dress has a full skirt and long, billowy sleeves. It's a dress of cobwebby cotton, shading from pink to rose, with scores of tiny, irregular pleats that look like wrinkles. A pretty dress but hardly a good choice for Stella's domain. The blackberry bushes catch it everywhere, and Catherine has to keep picking herself loose.

"David, really, you could have left her some room," says Stella.

Catherine laughs at her predicament. "I'm all right, I'm okay, really."

"Stella, Catherine," says David, introducing.

"Have some berries, Catherine," says Stella sympathetically. "David?"

David shakes his head, but Catherine takes a couple. "Lovely," she says. "Warm from the sun."

"I'm sick of the sight of them," says Stella.

Close up, Stella looks a bit better—with her smooth, tanned skin, childishly cropped hair, wide brown eyes. Catherine, drooping over her, is a tall, frail, bony woman with fair hair and sensitive skin. Her skin is so sensitive it won't stand any makeup at all, and is easily inflamed by colds, foods, emotions. Lately she has taken to wearing blue eye shadow and black mascara, which David thinks is a mistake. Blackening those sparse wisps of lashes emphasizes the watery blue of her eyes, which look as if they couldn't stand daylight, and the dryness of the skin underneath. When David first met Catherine, about eighteen months ago, he thought she was a little over thirty. He saw many remnants of girlishness; he loved her fairness and tall fragility. She has aged since then. And she was older than he thought to start with—she is nearing forty.

"But what will you do with them?" Catherine says to Stella. "Make jam?"

"I've made about five million jars of jam already," Stella says. "I put them in little jars with those artsy-fartsy gingham tops on them and I give them away to all my neighbors who are too lazy or too smart to pick their own. Sometimes I don't know why I don't just let Nature's bounty rot on the vine."

"It isn't on the vine," says David. "It's on those god-awful thornbushes, which ought to be cleaned out and burned. Then there'd be room to park a car."

Stella says to Catherine, "Listen to him, still sounding like a husband."

Stella and David were married for twenty-one years. They have been separated for eight.

"It's true, David," says Stella contritely. "I should clean them out. There's a long list of things I never get around to doing. Come on in and I'll get changed."

"We'll have to stop at the liquor store," says David. "I didn't get a chance."

Once every summer, he makes this visit, timing it as nearly as he can to Stella's father's birthday. He always brings the same present—a bottle of Scotch whiskey. This birthday is his father-in-law's ninety-third. He is in a nursing home a few miles away, where Stella can visit him two or three times a week.

"I just have to wash," Stella says. "And put on something bright. Not for Daddy, he's completely blind now. But I think the others like it, the sight of me dressed in pink or blue or something cheers them up the way a balloon would. You two have time for a quick drink. Actually, you can make me one, too."

She leads them, single file, up the path to the house. Hercules doesn't move.

"Lazy beast," says Stella. "He's getting about as bad as Daddy. You think the house needs painting, David?"

"Yes."

"Daddy always said every seven years. I don't know—I'm considering putting on siding. I'd get more protection from the wind. Even since I winterized, it sometimes feels as if I'm living in an open crate."

Stella lives here all year round. In the beginning, one or the other of the children would often be with her. But now Paul is studying forestry in Oregon and Deirdre is teaching at an English-language school in Brazil.

"But could you get anything like that color in siding," says Catherine. "It's so nice, that lovely weather-beaten color."

"I was thinking of cream," says Stella.

Alone in this house, in this community, Stella leads a busy and sometimes chaotic life. Evidence of this is all around them as they progress through the back porch and the kitchen to the living room. Here are some plants she has been potting, and the jam she mentioned—not all given away but waiting, she explains, for bake sales and the fall fair. Here is her winemaking apparatus; then, in the long living room, overlooking the lake, her typewriter, surrounded by stacks of books and papers.

"I'm writing my memoirs," says Stella. She rolls her eyes at Catherine. "I'll stop for a cash payment. No, it's okay, David, I'm writing an article on the old lighthouse." She points the lighthouse out to Catherine. "You can see it from this window if you squeeze right down to the end. I'm doing a piece for the historical society and the local paper. Quite the budding authoress."

Besides the historical society, she says, she belongs to a play-reading group, a church choir, the winemakers' club, and an informal group in which the members entertain one another weekly at dinner parties that have a fixed (low) cost.

"To test our ingenuity," she says. "Always testing something."

And that is only the more or less organized part of it. Her friends are a mixed bag. People who have retired here, who live in remodelled farmhouses or winterized summer cottages; younger people of diverse background who have settled on the land, taking over rocky old farms that born-and-bred farmers won't bother about anymore. And a local dentist and his friend, who are gay.

"We're marvellously tolerant around here now," shouts Stella, who has gone into the bathroom and is conveying her information over the sound of running water. "We don't insist on matching up the sexes. It's nice for us pensioned-off wives. There are about half a dozen of us. One's a weaver."

"I can't find the tonic," yells David from the kitchen.

"It's in cans. The box on the floor by the fridge. This woman has her own sheep. The weaver woman. She has her own spinning wheel. She spins the wool and then she weaves it into cloth."

"Holy shit," says David thoughtfully.

Stella has turned the tap off, and is splashing.

"I thought you'd like that. See, I'm not so far gone. I just make jam."

In a moment, she comes out with a towel wrapped around her, saying, "Where's my drink?" The top corners of the towel are tucked together under one arm, the bottom corners are flapping dangerously free. She accepts a gin-and-tonic.

"I'll drink it while I dress. I have two new summer outfits. One is flamingo and one is turquoise. I can mix and match. Either way, I look stupendous."

Catherine comes from the living room to get her drink, and takes the first two gulps as if it were a glass of water.

"I love this house," she says with a soft vehemence. "I really do. It's so primitive and unpretentious. It's full of light. I've been trying to think what it reminds me of, and now I know. Did you ever see that old Ingmar Bergman movie where there is a family living in a summer house on an island? A lovely shabby house. The girl was going crazy. I remember thinking at the time, That's what summer houses should be like, and they never are."

"That was the one where God was a helicopter," David says. "And the girl fooled around with her brother in the bottom of a boat."

"We never had anything quite so interesting going on around here, I'm afraid," says Stella over the bedroom wall. "I can't say I ever really appreciated Bergman movies. I always thought they were sort of bleak and neurotic."

"Conversations tend to be widespread around here," says David to Catherine. "Notice how none of the partitions go up to the ceiling? Except the bathroom, thank God. It makes for a lot of family life."

"Whenever David and I wanted to say something private, we had to put our heads under the covers," Stella says. She comes out of the bedroom wearing a pair of turquoise stretch pants and a sleeveless top. The top has turquoise flowers and fronds on a white background. At least, she seems to have put on a brassière. A light-colored strap is visible, biting the flesh of her shoulder.

"Remember one night we were in bed," she says, "and we were talking about getting a new car, saying we wondered what kind of mileage you got with a such-and-such, I forget what. Well, Daddy was always mad about cars, he knew everything, and all of a sudden we heard him say, 'Twenty-eight miles to the gallon,' or whatever, just as if he were right there on the other side of the bed. Of course, he wasn't—he was lying in bed in his own room. David was quite blasé about it; he just said, 'Oh, thank you, sir,' as if we'd been including Daddy all along!"

When David comes out of the liquor store, in the village, Stella has rolled down the car window and is talking to a couple she introduces as Ron and Mary. They are in their mid-sixties probably, but very tanned and trim. They wear matching plaid pants and white sweatshirts and plaid caps.

"Glad to meet you," says Ron. "So you're up here seeing how the smart folks live!" He has the sort of jolly voice that suggests boxing feints, playful punches. "When are you going to retire and come up here and join us?"

That makes David wonder what Stella has been telling them about the separation.

"It's not my turn to retire yet."

"Retire early! That's what a lot of us up here did! We got ourselves out of the whole routine. Toiling and moiling and earning and spending."

"Well, I'm not in that," says David. "I'm just a civil servant. We take the taxpayers' money and try not to do any work at all."

"That's not true," says Stella, scolding—wifely. "He works in the Department of Education and he works hard. He just will never admit it."

"A simple serpent!" says Mary, with a crow of pleasure. "I used to work in Ottawa—that was eons ago—and we used to call ourselves simple serpents! Civil serpents. Servants."

Mary is not in the least fat, but something has happened to her chin that usually happens to the chins of fat women. It has collapsed into a series of terraces flowing into her neck.

"Kidding aside," says Ron. "This is a wonderful life. You wouldn't believe how much we find to do. The day is never long enough."

"You have a lot of interests?" says David. He is perfectly serious now, respectful and attentive.

This a tone that warns Stella, and she tries to deflect Mary. "What are you going to do with the material you brought back from Morocco?"

"I can't decide. It would make a gorgeous dress but it's hardly me. I might just end up putting it on a bed."

"There's so many activities, you can just keep up forever," Ron says. "For instance skiing. Cross-country. We were out nineteen days in the month of February. Beautiful weather this year. We don't have to drive anywhere. We just go down the back lane—"

"I try to keep up my interests, too," says David. "I think it keeps you young."

"There is no doubt it does!"

David has one hand in the inner pocket of his jacket. He brings out something he keeps cupped in his palm, shows it to Ron with a deprecating smile.

"One of my interests," he says.

"Want to see what I showed Ron?" David says later. They are driving along the bluffs to the nursing home.

"No, thank you."

"I hope Ron liked it," David says pleasantly.

He starts to sing. He and Stella met while singing madrigals at university. Or that's what Stella tells people. They sang other things, too, not just madrigals. "David was a skinny innocent bit of a lad with a pure sweet tenor and I was a stocky little brute of a girl with a big deep alto," Stella likes to say. "There was nothing he could do about it. Destiny."

"O, Mistress mine, where are you roaming?" sings David, who has a fine tenor voice to this day:

> *"O, Mistress mine, where are you roaming?*
> *O, Mistress mine, where are you roaming?*
> *O, stay and hear, your true love's coming,*
> *O, stay and hear, your true love's coming,*
> *Who can sing, both High and Low."*

Down on the beach, at either end of Stella's property, there are long, low walls of rocks that have been stacked in baskets of wire, stretching out into the water. They are there to protect the beach from erosion. On one of these walls, Catherine is sitting, looking out at the water, with the lake breeze blowing her filmy dress and her long hair. She could be posed for a picture. She might be advertising something, Stella thinks—either something very intimate, and potentially disgusting, or something truly respectable and rather splendid, like life insurance.

"I've been meaning to ask you," says Stella. "Is there anything the matter with her eyes?"

"Eyes?" says David.

"Her eyesight. It's just that she doesn't seem to be quite focussing, close up. I don't know how to describe it."

Stella and David are standing at the living-room window. Returned from the nursing home, they each hold a fresh, restorative drink. They have hardly spoken on the way home, but the silence has not been hostile. They are feeling chastened and reasonably companionable.

"There isn't anything wrong with her eyesight that I know of."

Stella goes into the kitchen, gets out the roasting pan, rubs the roast of pork with cloves of garlic and fresh sage leaves.

"You know, there's a smell women get," says David, standing in the living-room doorway. "It's when they know you don't want them anymore. Stale."

Stella slaps the meat over.

"Those groins are going to have to be rewired entirely," she says. "The wire is just worn to cobwebs in some places. You should see. The power of water. It can wear out tough wire. I'll have to have a work party this fall. Just make a lot of food and ask some people over and make sure enough of them are able-bodied. That's what we all do."

She puts the roast in the oven and rinses her hands.

"It was Catherine you were telling me about last summer, wasn't it? She was the one you said was inclined to be fey."

David groans. "I said what?"

"Inclined to be fey." Stella bangs around, getting out apples, potatoes, onions.

"All right, tell me," says David, coming into the kitchen to stand close to her. "Tell me what I said?"

"That's all, really. I don't remember anything else."

"Stella. Tell me all I said about her."

"I don't, really. I don't remember."

Of course she remembers. She remembers the exact tone in which he said "inclined to be fey." The pride and irony in his voice. In the throes of love, he can be counted on to speak of the woman with tender disparagement—with amazement, even. He likes to say that it's crazy, he does not understand it, he can plainly see that this person isn't his kind of person at all. And yet, and yet, and yet. And yet it's beyond him, irresistible. He told Stella that Catherine believed in horoscopes, was a vegetarian, and painted weird pictures in which tiny figures were enclosed in plastic bubbles.

"The roast," says Stella, suddenly alarmed. "Will she eat meat?"

"What?"

"Will Catherine eat meat?"

"She may not eat anything. She may be too spaced out."

"I'm making an apple-and-onion casserole. It'll be quite substantial. Maybe she'll eat that."

Last summer, he said, "She's a hippie survivor, really. She doesn't even know those times are gone. I don't think she's ever read a newspaper. She hasn't the remotest idea of what's going on in the world. Unless she's heard it from a fortune-teller. That's her idea of reality. I don't think she can read a map. She's all instinct. Do you know what she did? She went to Ireland to see the Book of Kells. She'd heard the Book of Kells was in Ireland. So she just got off the plane at Shannon Airport, and asked somebody the way to the Book of Kells. And you know what, she found it!"

Stella asked how this fey creature earned the money for trips to Ireland.

"Oh, she has a job," David said. "Sort of a job. She teaches art, part time. God knows what she teaches them. To paint by their horoscopes, I think."

Now he says, "There's somebody else. I haven't told Catherine. Do you think she senses it? I think she does. I think she senses it."

He is leaning against the counter, watching Stella peel apples. He reaches quickly into his inside pocket, and before Stella can turn her head away he is holding a Polaroid snapshot in front of her eyes.

"That's my new girl," he says.

"It looks like lichen," says Stella, her paring knife halting. "Except it's rather dark. It looks to me like moss on a rock."

"Don't be dumb, Stella. Don't be cute. You can see her. See her legs?"

Stella puts the paring knife down and squints obediently. There is a flattened-out breast far away on the horizon. And the legs spreading into the foreground. The legs are spread wide—smooth, golden, monumental: fallen columns. Between them is the dark blot she called moss, or lichen. But it's really more like the dark pelt of an animal, with the head and tail and feet chopped off. Dark silky pelt of some unlucky rodent.

"Well, I can see now," she says, in a sensible voice.

"Her name is Dina. Dina without an 'h.' She's twenty-two years old."

Stella won't ask him to put the picture away, or even to stop holding it in front of her face.

"She's a bad girl," says David. "Oh, she's a bad girl! She went to school to the nuns. There are no bad girls like those convent-school girls, once they decide to go wild! She was a student at the art college where Catherine teaches. She quit. Now she's a cocktail waitress."

"That doesn't sound so terribly depraved to me. Deirdre was a cocktail waitress for a while when she was at college."

"Dina's not like Deirdre."

At last, the hand holding the picture drops, and Stella picks up her knife and resumes peeling the apples. But David doesn't put the picture away. He starts to, then changes his mind.

"The little witch," he says. "She torments my soul."

His voice when he talks about this girl seems to Stella peculiarly artificial. But who is she to say, with David, what is artificial and what is not? This special voice of his is rather high-pitched, monotonous, insistent, with a deliberate, cruel sweetness. Whom does he want to be cruel to—Stella, Catherine, the girl, himself? Stella gives a sigh that is noisier and more exasperated than she meant it to be and puts down an apple half-peeled. She goes into the living room and looks out the window.

Catherine is climbing off the wall. Or she's trying to. Her dress is caught in the wire.

"That pretty li'l old dress is giving her all sorts of trouble today," Stella says, surprising herself with the bad accent and a certain viciousness of tone.

"Stella. I wish you'd keep this picture for me."

"Me keep it?"

"I'm afraid I'll show it to Catherine. I keep wanting to. I'm afraid I will."

Catherine has disengaged herself, and has spotted them at the window. She waves, and Stella waves back.

"I'm sure you have others," says Stella. "Pictures."

"Not with me. It's not that I want to hurt her."

"Then don't."

"She makes me want to hurt her. She hangs on me with her weepy looks. She takes pills. Mood elevators. She drinks. Sometimes I think the best thing to do would be to give her the big chop. Coup de grâce. Coup de grâce, Catherine. Here you are. Big chop. But I worry about what she'll do."

"Mood elevator," says Stella. "Mood elevator, going up!"

"I'm serious, Stella. Those pills are deadly."

"That's your affair."

"Very funny."

"I didn't even mean it to be. Whenever something slips out like that, I always pretend I meant it, though. I'll take all the credit I can get!"

These three people feel better at dinnertime than any of them might have expected. David feels better because he has remembered that there is a telephone booth across from the liquor store. Stella always feels better when she has cooked a meal and it has turned out so well. Catherine's reasons for feeling better are chemical.

Conversation is not difficult. Stella tells stories that she has come across in doing research for her article, about wrecks on the Great Lakes. Catherine knows something about wrecks. She has a boyfriend—a former boyfriend—who is a diver. David is gallant enough to assert that he is jealous of this fellow, does not care to hear about his deep-water prowess. Perhaps this is the truth.

After dinner, David says he needs to go for a walk. Catherine tells him to go ahead. "Go on," she says merrily. "We don't need you here. Stella and I will get along fine without you!"

Stella wonders where this new voice of Catherine's comes from, this pert and rather foolish and flirtatious voice. Drink wouldn't do it. Whatever Catherine has taken has made her sharper, not blunter. Several layers of wispy apology, tentative flattery, fearfulness, or hopefulness have simply blown away in this brisk chemical breeze.

But when Catherine gets up and tries to clear the table it becomes apparent that the sharpening is not physical. Catherine bumps into a corner of the counter. She makes Stella think of an amputee. Not much cut off, just the tips of her fingers and maybe her toes. Stella has to keep an eye on her, relieving her of the dishes before they slide away.

"Did you notice the hair?" says Catherine. Her voice goes up and down like a Ferris wheel; it dips and sparkles. "He's dyeing it!"

"David is?" says Stella, in genuine surprise.

"Every time he'd think of it, he'd tilt his head back, so you couldn't get too close a look. I think he was afraid you'd say something. He's slightly afraid of you. Actually, it looks very natural."

"I really didn't notice."

"He started a couple of months ago. I said, 'David, what does it matter—your hair was getting gray when I fell in love with you, do you think it's going to bother me now?' Love is strange, it does strange things. David is actually a sensitive person—he's a vulnerable person." Stella rescues a wineglass that is drooping from Catherine's fingers. "It can make you mean. Love can make you mean. If you feel dependent on somebody, then you can be mean to them. I understand that in David."

They drink mead at dinner. This is the first time Stella has tried this batch of homemade mead and she thinks now how good it was, dry and sparkling. It looked like champagne. She checks to see if there is any left in the bottle. About half a glass. She pours it out for herself, sets her glass behind the blender, rinses the bottle.

"You have a good life here," Catherine says.

"I have a fine life. Yes."

"I feel a change coming in my life. I love David, but I've been submerged in this love for so long. Too long. Do you know what I mean? I was down looking at the waves and I started saying, 'He loves me, he loves me not.' I do that often. Then I thought, Well, there isn't any end to the waves, not like there is to a daisy. Or even like there is to my footsteps, if I start counting them to the end of the block. I thought, The waves never, ever come to an end. So then I knew, this is a message for me."

"Just leave the pots, Catherine. I'll deal with them later."

Why doesn't Stella say, "Sit down, I can manage better by myself"? It's a thing she has said often to helpers less inept than Catherine. She doesn't say it because she's wary of something. Catherine's state seems so brittle and delicate. Tripping her up could have consequences.

"He loves me, he loves me not," says Catherine. "That's the way it goes. It goes forever. That's what the waves were trying to tell me."

"Just out of curiosity," says Stella, "do you believe in horoscopes?"

"You mean have I had mine done? No, not really. I know people who have. I've thought about it. I guess I don't quite believe in it enough to spend the money. I look at those things in the newspapers sometimes."

"You read the newspapers?"

"I read parts. I get one delivered. I don't read it all."

"And you eat meat? You ate pork for dinner."

Catherine doesn't seem to mind being interrogated, or even to notice that this is an interrogation.

"Well, I can live on salads, particularly at this time of year. But I do eat meat from time to time. I'm a sort of very lackadaisical vegetarian. It was fantastic, that roast. Did you put garlic on it?"

"Garlic and sage and rosemary."

"It was delicious."

"I'm glad."

Catherine sits down suddenly, and spreads out her long legs in a tomboyish way, letting her dress droop between them. Hercules, who has slept all through dinner on the fourth chair, at the other side of the table, takes a determined leap and lands on what there is of her lap.

Catherine laughs. "Crazy cat."

"If he bothers you, just bat him off."

Freed now of the need to watch Catherine, Stella gets busy scraping and stacking the plates, rinsing glasses, cleaning off the table, shaking the cloth, wiping the counters. She feels well satisfied and full of energy. She takes a sip of the mead. Lines of a song are going through her head, and she doesn't realize until a few words of this song reach the surface that it's the same one David was singing, earlier in the day. "What's to come is still unsure!"

Catherine gives a light snore, and jerks her head up. Hercules doesn't take fright, but tries to settle himself more permanently, getting his claws into her dress.

"Was that me?" says Catherine.

"You need some coffee," Stella says. "Hang on. You probably shouldn't go to sleep right now."

"I'm tired," says Catherine stubbornly.

"I know. But you shouldn't go to sleep right now. Hang on, and we'll get some coffee into you."

Stella takes a hand towel from the drawer, soaks it in cold water, holds it to Catherine's face.

"There, now," says Stella. "You hold it, I'll start the coffee. We're not going to have you passing out here, are we? David would carry on about it. He'd say it was my mead or my cooking or my company, or something. Hang on, Catherine."

David, in the phone booth, begins to dial Dina's number. Then he remembers that it's long distance. He must dial the operator. He dials the operator, asks how much the call will cost, empties his pockets of change. He picks out a dollar and thirty-five cents in quarters and dimes, stacks it ready on the shelf. He starts dialling again. His fingers are shaky, his palms sweaty. His legs, gut, and chest are filled with a rising commotion. The first ring of the phone, in Dina's cramped apartment, sets his innards bubbling. This is craziness. He starts to feed in quarters.

"I will tell you when to deposit your money," says the operator. "Sir? I will tell you when to deposit it." His quarters clank down into the change return and he has trouble scooping them out. The phone rings again, on Dina's dresser, in the jumble of makeup, panty hose, beads and chains, long feathered earrings, a silly cigarette holder, an assortment of windup toys. He can see them: the green frog, the yellow duck, the brown bear—all the same size. Frogs and bears are equal. Also some space monsters, based on characters in a movie. When set going, these toys will lurch and clatter across Dina's floor or table, spitting sparks out of their mouths. She likes to set up races, or put a couple of them on a collision course. Then she squeals, and even screams with excitement, as they go their unpredictable ways.

"There doesn't seem to be any answer, sir."

"Let it ring a few more times."

Dina's bathroom is across the hall. She shares it with another girl. If she is in the bathroom, even in the bathtub, how long will it take her to decide whether to answer it at all? He decides to count ten rings more, starting now.

"Still no answer, sir."

Ten more.

"Sir, would you like to try again later?"

He hangs up, having thought of something. Immediately, energetically, he dials information.

"For what place, sir?"

"Toronto."

"Go ahead, sir."

He asks for the phone number of a Michael Read. No, he does not have a street address. All he has is the name—the name of her last, and perhaps not quite finished with, boyfriend.

"I have no listing for a Michael Read."

"All right. Try Reade, R-E-A-D-E."

There is indeed an M. Reade, on Davenport Road. Not a Michael but at least an M. Check back and see, then. Is there an M. Read? Read? Yes. Yes, there is an M. Read, living on Simcoe Street. And another M. Read, R-E-A-D, living on Harbord. Why didn't she say that sooner?

He picks Harbord on a hunch. That's not too far from Dina's apartment. The operator tells him the number. He tries to memorize it. He has nothing to write with. He feels it's important not to ask the operator to repeat the number more than once. He should not reveal that he is here in a phone booth without a pen or pencil. It seems to him that the desperate, furtive nature of his quest is apparent, and that at any moment he may be shut off, not permitted to acquire any further information about M. Read or M. Reade, on Harbord or Simcoe or Davenport, or wherever.

Now he must start all over again. The Toronto area code. No, the operator. The memorized number. Quick, before he loses his nerve, or loses the number. If she should answer, what is he going to say? But it isn't likely that she will answer, even if she is there. M. Read will answer. Then David must ask for Dina. But perhaps not in his own voice. Perhaps not in a man's voice at all. He used to be able to do different voices on the phone. He could even fool Stella at one time.

Perhaps he could do a woman's voice, squeaky. Or a child's voice, a little-sister voice. *Is Dina there?*

"I beg your pardon, sir?"

"Nothing. Sorry."

"It's ringing now. I will let you know when to deposit your money."

What if M. Read is a woman? Not Michael Read at all. Mary Read. Old-age pensioner. Career girl. What are you phoning me for? Sexual harassment. Back to information, then. Try M. Read on Simcoe. Try M. Reade on Davenport. Keep trying.

"I'm sorry. I can't seem to get an answer."

The phone rings again and again in M. Read's apartment, or house, or room. David leans against the metal shelf, where his change is waiting. A car has parked in the liquor-store lot. The couple in it are watching him. Obviously waiting to use the phone. With any luck, Ron and Mary will drive up next.

Dina lives above an Indian-import shop. Her clothes and hair always have a smell of curry powder, nutmeg, incense, added to what David thinks of as her natural smell, of cigarettes and dope and sex. Her hair is dyed dead black. Her cheeks bear a slash of crude color and her eyelids are sometimes brick red. She tried out once for a part in a movie some people she knew about were making. She failed to get the part because of some squeamishness about holding a tame rat between her legs. This failure humiliated her.

David sweats now, trying not to catch her out but to catch her any way at all, to hear her harsh young voice, with its involuntary tremor and insistent obscenities. Even if hearing it, at this moment, means that she has betrayed him. Of course she has betrayed him. She betrays him all the time. If only she would answer (he has almost forgotten it's M. Read who is supposed to answer), he could howl at her, berate her, and if he felt low enough—he *would* feel low enough—he could plead with her. He would welcome the chance. Any chance. At dinner, talking in a lively way to Stella and Catherine, he kept writing the name Dina with his finger on the underside of the wooden table.

People don't have any patience with this sort of suffering, and why should they? The sufferer must forgo sympathy, give up on dignity, cope with the ravages. And on top of that, people will take time out to tell you that this isn't real love. These bouts of desire and dependence and worship and perversity, willed but terrible transformations—they aren't real love.

Stella used to tell him he wasn't interested in love. "Or sex, even. I don't think you're even interested in sex, David. I think all you're interested in is being a big bad boy."

Real love—that would be going on living with Stella, or taking on Catherine. A person presumed to know all about Real Love might be Ron, of Ron-and-Mary.

David knows what he's doing. This is the interesting part of it, he thinks, and has said. He knows that Dina is not really so wild, or so avid, or doomed, as he pretends she is, or as she sometimes pretends she is. In ten years' time, she won't be wrecked by her crazy life, she won't be a glamorous whore. She'll be a woman tagged by little children in the laundromat. The delicious, old-fashioned word "trollop," which he uses to describe her, doesn't apply to her, really—has no more to do with her than "hippie" had to do with Catherine, a person he cannot now bear to think about. He knows that sooner or later, if Dina allows her disguise to crack, as Catherine did, he will have to move on. He will have to do that anyway—move on.

He knows all this and observes himself, and such knowledge and observation has no effect at all on his quaking gut, zealous sweat glands, fierce prayers.

"Sir? Do you want to keep on trying?"

The nursing home that they visited, earlier in the day, is called the Balm of Gilead Home. It is named after the balm-of-Gilead trees, a kind of poplar, that grow plentifully near the lake. A large stone mansion built by a nineteenth-century millionaire, it is now disfigured by ramps and fire escapes.

Voices summoned Stella, from the clusters of wheelchairs on the front lawn. She called out various names in answer, detoured to press hands and drop kisses. Vibrating here and there like a fat hummingbird.

She sang when she rejoined David:

"I'm your little sunbeam, short and stout,
Turn me over, pour me out!"

Out of breath, she said, "Actually it's teapot. I don't think you'll see much change in Daddy. Except the blindness is total now."

She led him through the green painted corridors, with their low false ceilings (cutting the heating costs), their paint-by-number pictures, their disinfectant—and other—smells. Out on a back porch, alone, her father sat wrapped in blankets, strapped into his wheelchair so that he wouldn't fall out.

Her father said, "David?"

The sound seemed to come from a wet cave deep inside him, to be unshaped by lips or jaws or tongue. These could not be seen to move. Nor did he move his head.

Stella went behind the chair and put her arms around his neck. She touched him very lightly.

"Yes, it's David, Daddy," she said. "You knew his step!"

Her father didn't answer. David bent to touch the old man's

hands, which were not cold, as he expected, but warm and very dry. He laid the whiskey bottle in them.

"Careful. He can't hold it," said Stella softly. David kept his own hands on the bottle while Stella pushed up a chair, so that he could sit down opposite her father.

"Same old present," David said.

His father-in-law made an acknowledging sound.

"I'm going to get some glasses," Stella said. "It's against the rules to drink outside, but I can generally get them to bend the rules a bit. I'll tell them it's a celebration."

To get used to looking at his father-in-law, David tried to think of him as a post-human development, something new in the species. Survival hadn't just preserved, it had transformed him. Bluish-gray skin, with dark-blue spots, whitened eyes, a ribbed neck with delicate deep hollows, like a smoked-glass vase. Up through this neck came further sounds, a conversational offering. It was the core of each syllable that was presented, a damp vowel barely held in shape by surrounding consonants.

"Traffic—bad?"

David described conditions on the freeway and on the secondary highways. He told his father-in-law that he had recently bought a car, a Japanese car. He told how he had not, at first, been able to get anything close to the advertised mileage. But he had complained, he had persisted, had taken the car back to the dealer. Various adjustments had been tried, and now the situation had improved and the figure was satisfactory, if not quite what had been promised.

This conversation seemed welcome. His father-in-law appeared to follow it. He nodded, and on his narrow, elongated, bluish, post-human face there were traces of old expressions. An expression of shrewd and dignified concern, suspicion of advertising and of foreign cars and car dealers. There was even a suggestion of doubt—as in the old days—that David could be trusted to handle such things well. And relief that he had done so. In his father-in-law's eyes David would always be somebody learning how to be a man, somebody who might never learn, might never achieve the steadfastness and control, the decent narrowness of range. David, who preferred gin to whiskey, read novels, didn't understand the stock market, talked to women, and had started out as a teacher. David, who had always driven small cars, foreign cars. But that was all right now. Small cars were not a sign of any of the things they used to be a sign of. Even here on the bluffs above Lake Huron at the very end of life, certain shifts had registered, certain changes had been understood, by a man who couldn't grasp or see.

"Hear anything about—Lada?"

It happens luckily that David has a colleague who drives a Lada, and many boring lunch and coffee breaks have been taken up with the discussion of this car's strengths and failings and the difficulty of getting parts. David recounted these, and his father-in-law seemed satisfied.

"Gray. Dort. Gray-Dort. First car—ever drove. Yonge Street. Sixty miles. Sixty miles. Uh. Uh. Hour"

"He certainly never drove a Gray-Dort down Yonge Street at sixty miles an hour,"said Stella when they had got her father and his bottle back to his room, had said goodbye, and were walking back through the green corridors. "Never. Whose Gray-Dort? They were out of production long before he had the money to buy a car. And he'd never have taken the risk with anybody else's. It's his fantasy. He's reached the stage where that's his big recreation—fixing up the past so anything he wishes had happened did happen. Wonder if we'll get to that stage? What would your fantasy be, David? No. Don't tell me!"

"What would yours be?" said David.

"That you didn't leave? That you didn't want to leave? I bet that's what you think mine would be, but I'm not so sure! Daddy was so pleased to see you, David. A man just means more, for Daddy. I suppose if he thought about you and me he'd have to be on my side, but that's all right, he doesn't have to think about it."

Stella, at the nursing home, seemed to have regained some sleekness and suppleness of former times. Her attentions to her father, and even to the wheelchair contingent, brought back a trace of deferential grace to her movements, a wistfulness to her voice. David had a picture of her as she had been twelve or fifteen years before. He saw her coming across the lawn at a suburban party, carrying a casserole. She was wearing a sundress. She always claimed in those days that she was too fat for pants, though she was not half so fat as now. Why did this picture please him so much? Stella coming across the lawn, with her sunlit hair—the gray in it then merely made it ash blond—and her bare toasted shoulders, crying out greetings to her neighbors, laughing, protesting about some cooking misadventure. Of course the food she brought would be wonderful, and she brought not only food but the whole longed-for spirit of the neighborhood party. With her overwhelming sociability, she gathered everybody in. And David felt quite free of irritation, though there were times, certainly, when these gifts of Stella's had irritated him. Her vivacious exasperation, her exaggeration, her wide-eyed humorous appeals for sympathy had irritated him. For others' entertainment he had heard her shaping stories out of their life—the children's daily mishaps and provocations, the cat's visit to the vet, her son's first hangover, the perversity of the power lawnmower, the papering of the upstairs hall. A charming wife, a wonderful person at a party, she has such a funny way of looking at things. Sometimes she was a riot. *Your wife's a riot.*

Well, he forgave her—he loved her—as she walked across the lawn. At that moment, with his bare foot, he was stroking the cold, brown, shaved, and prickly calf of another neighborhood wife, who had just come out of the pool and had thrown on a long, concealing scarlet robe. A dark-haired, childless, chain-smoking woman, given—at least at that stage in their relationship—to tantalizing silences. (His first, that one, the first while married to Stella. Rosemary. A sweet dark name, though finally a shrill trite woman.)

It wasn't just that. The unexpected delight in Stella just as she was, the unusual feeling of being at peace with her, didn't come from just that—the illicit activity of his big toe. This seemed profound, this revelation about himself and Stella—how they were bound together after all, and how as long as he could feel such benevolence toward her, what he did secretly and separately was somehow done with her blessing.

That did not turn out to be a notion Stella shared at all. And they weren't so bound, or if they were it was a bond he had to break. We've been together so long, couldn't we just tough it out, said Stella at the time, trying to make it a joke. She didn't understand, probably didn't understand yet, how that was one of the things that made it impossible. This white-haired woman walking beside him through the nursing home dragged so much weight with her—a weight not just of his sexual secrets but of his middle-of-the-night speculations about God, his psychosomatic chest pains, his digestive sensitivity, his escape plans, which once included her and involved Africa or Indonesia. All his ordinary and extraordinary life—even some things it was unlikely she knew about—seemed stored up in her. He could never feel any lightness, any secret and victorious expansion, with a woman who knew so much. She was bloated with all she knew. Nevertheless he put his arms around Stella. They embraced, both willingly.

A young girl, a Chinese or Vietnamese girl, slight as a child in her pale-green uniform, but with painted lips and cheeks, was coming along the corridor, pushing a cart. On the cart were paper cups and plastic containers of orange and grape juice.

"Juice time," the girl was calling, in her pleasant and indifferent singsong. "Juice time. Orange. Grape. Juice." She took no notice of David and Stella, but they let go of each other and resumed walking. David did feel a slight, very slight, discomfort at being seen by such a young and pretty girl in the embrace of Stella. It was not an important feeling—it simply brushed him and passed—but Stella, as he held the door open for her, said, "Never mind, David. I could be your sister. You could be comforting your sister. *Older* sister."

"Madam Stella, the celebrated mind reader."

It was strange, the way they said these things. They used to say bitter and wounding things, and pretend, when they said them, to be mildly amused, dispassionate, even kindly. Now this tone that was once a pretense had soaked down, deep down, through all their sharp feelings, and the bitterness, though not transformed, seemed stale, useless and formal.

. . .

A week or so later, when she is tidying up the living room, getting ready for a meeting of the historical society that is to take place at her house, Stella finds the picture, a Polaroid snapshot. David has left it with her after all—hiding it, but not hiding it very well, behind the curtains at one end of the long living-room window, at the spot where you stand to get a view of the lighthouse.

Lying in the sun had faded it, of course. Stella stands looking at it, with a dust cloth in her hand. The day is perfect. The windows are open, her house is pleasantly in order, and a good fish soup is simmering on the stove. She sees that the black pelt in the picture has changed to gray. It's a bluish or greenish gray now. She remembers what she said when she first saw it. She said it was lichen. No, she said it looked like lichen. But she knew what it was at once. It seems to her now that she knew what it was even when David put his hand to his pocket. She felt the old cavity opening up in her. But she held on. She said, "Lichen." And now, look, her words have come true. The outline of the breast has disappeared. You would never know that the legs were legs. The black has turned to gray, to the soft, dry color of a plant mysteriously nourished on the rocks.

This is David's doing. He left it there, in the sun.

Stella's words have come true. This thought will keep coming back to her—a pause, a lost heartbeat, a harsh little break in the flow of the days and nights as she keeps them going.

Monsieur les Deux Chapeaux

"Is that your brother out there?" Davidson said. "What's he up to?"

Colin went over to the window to see what Ross was up to. Not much. Ross was using the long-handled clippers to clip the grass along the sidewalk to the front door of the school. He was working at a normal rate and seemed to be paying attention to what he was doing.

"What's he up to?" Davidson said.

Ross was wearing two hats. One was the green-and-white peaked cap he had got last summer at the feed store, and the other one, on top, was the old floppy hat of pinkish straw that their mother wore in the garden.

"Search me," said Colin. Davidson was going to think that was smart-arse.

"You mean why has he got the two hats on? I don't know. I honestly don't know. Maybe he forgot."

This was in the front office, during school hours on Friday afternoon, the secretaries bent over their desks but keeping their ears open. Colin had a gym class going on at the moment—he had just come into the office to find out what had happened about a boy who had begged off sick half an hour before—and he hadn't expected to find Davidson prowling around here. He hadn't come prepared to provide explanations about Ross.

"Is he a forgetful kind of person?" the principal said.

"No more than average."

"Maybe it's supposed to be funny."

Colin was silent.

"I've got a sense of humor myself but you can't start being funny around kids. You know the way they are. They'll see enough to laugh at anyway, without giving them extra. They'll make any little thing an excuse for distraction and then you know what you've got."

"You want me to go out and talk to him?" Colin said.

"Leave it for now. There's probably a couple of classrooms already have their eye on him and that'd just get them more interested. Mr. Box can speak to him if somebody has to. Actually, Mr. Box was mentioning him."

Coonie Box was the school janitor, who had hired Ross for the spring cleanup of the grounds.

"Oh? What?" said Colin.

"He says your brother keeps his own hours a bit."

"Does he do the work all right?"

"He didn't say he didn't." Davidson gave Colin one of his tight-lipped, dismissive, much-imitated smiles. "Just that he's inclined to be independent."

Colin and Ross looked rather alike, being tall, as their father had been, and fair-skinned and fair-haired, like their mother. Colin was athletic, with a shy, severe expression. Ross, though younger, was soft around the middle; he had a looser look. And he had an expression that seemed both leering and innocent.

Ross was not retarded. He had kept up with his age group in school. His mother said he was a genius of the mechanical kind. Nobody else would go that far.

"So? Is Ross getting used to getting up in the morning? Has he got an alarm?" Colin said to his mother.

"They're lucky to have him," Sylvia said.

Colin hadn't known whether he'd find her at home. She worked shifts as a nurse's aide at the hospital, and when she wasn't working she was often out. She had a lot of friends and commitments.

"And you're lucky I'm in," she said. "I'm on the early shift this week and next, but usually I go over to Eddy's after work and do a bit of housecleaning for him."

Eddy was Sylvia's boyfriend, a dapper seventy-year-old, twice a widower, with no children and plenty of money, a retired garage owner and car dealer who could certainly have afforded to hire somebody to clean his house. What did Sylvia know about housecleaning, anyway? All last summer, she had kept the winter plastic tacked up over her front windows to save the trouble of putting it up again. Colin's wife, Glenna, said that it gave her the same feeling as bleary glasses—she couldn't stand it. And the house—the same Insul-brick-covered cottage Sylvia and Ross and Colin had always lived in—was so full of furniture and junk some rooms had turned into passageways. Most surfaces were piled high with magazines, newspapers, plastic and paper bags, catalogues, circulars, and fliers for sales that had come and gone, in some cases for businesses that had folded and products that had disappeared from the market. In any ashtray or ornamental dish you might find a button or two, keys, cutout coupons promising ten cents off, an earring, a cold capsule still in its plastic wrap, a vitamin pill turning to powder, a mascara brush, a broken clothespin. And Sylvia's cupboards were full of all kinds of cleaning fluids and polishes—not the regular kind bought in stores, but products supposedly of unique and dazzling effectiveness, signed for at parties. She was kept broke paying for all the things she had signed for at parties—cosmetics, pots and pans, baking utensils, plastic bowls. She loved giving and going to those parties, also bridal showers and baby showers, and goodbye showers for her co-workers leaving the hospital. Here in these deeply cluttered rooms, she had dispensed, on her own, a great deal of careless, hopeful hospitality.

She poured water from the kettle onto the powdered coffee in their cups, which she had rinsed lightly at the sink.

"Was it boiling?" said Colin.

"Near enough."

She shook some pink-and-white marshmallow cookies out of their plastic package.

"I told Eddy I needed the afternoon off. He's getting to think like he owns me."

"Can't have that," said Colin.

About her boyfriends, he usually took a lightly critical tone.

Sylvia was a short woman with a large head—made larger by her fluffy, graying hair—and broad hips and shoulders. One of her boyfriends used to tell her she looked like a baby elephant, and she took that—at first—as an endearment. Colin thought there was something clumsy and appealing about her figure and her wide-open face with its pink, soft skin, clear blue eyes under almost nonexistent eyebrows, her eager all-purpose smile. Something maddening as well.

The subject of Ross was one of the few things that could make her face tighten up. That, and the demands and peculiarities of boyfriends, once they were on the wane.

Was Eddy on the verge of waning?

Sylvia said, "I've been telling him he's just too darn possessive." Then she told Colin a joke that was going round at the hospital, about a black man and a white man at the urinal.

"If you're working the early shift," said Colin, "how do you know what time Ross gets up?"

"Somebody complaining about Ross, is that it?"

"Well. They're just saying he likes to keep his own hours."

"They'll find out. If they have any mechanical thing or electrical thing that goes wrong, they'll be glad they got Ross. Ross has just as many brains as you do but they have gone in a different direction."

"I won't argue that," said Colin. "But his job is on the grounds."

Glenna said that the reason Sylvia proclaimed Ross to be a genius—aside from the fact that he really was clever about engines—was that he had the other side of a genius. He was absentminded and not very clean. He called attention to himself. He was weird, and that was the way a genius was supposed to be. But taken by itself, said Glenna, that wasn't enough proof.

Then she always said, "I like Ross, though. You can't help

liking him. I like him *and* your mother. I like her, too." Colin believed she did like Ross. He wasn't so sure she liked his mother.

"I only go over to your place when I'm invited, Colin," was what his mother said. "It's your home, but it's Glenna's home, too. Nevertheless I'm glad Ross feels so welcome."

"I went in the office today," Colin said, "and there was Davidson looking out the window." He hadn't known whether or not he was going to tell his mother about the hats. As usual, he wanted to get her a little upset about Ross, but not too upset. The sight of Ross working away there, with the electric clippers, all alone on the school grounds, a floppy pink straw hat perched on his seed-corn cap, had seemed to Colin something new, newly disturbing. He had seen Ross in odd getups before—once in the supermarket wearing Sylvia's blond wig. That seemed more calculated than today's appearance, more definitely a joke, with an audience in mind. Today, too, Ross could be thinking about all the kids behind the windows. And teachers and typists and Davidson and anybody driving by. But not them particularly. Something about Ross today suggested the audience had grown and faded—it included the whole town, the whole world, and Ross was almost indifferent to it. A sign, Colin thought. He didn't know what of—just a sign that Ross was farther along the way that Ross was going.

Sylvia didn't seem concerned with that part of it. She was upset, but for another reason.

"My hat. He's bound to lose it. I'll give him Hail Columbia. I'll give him proper *hell*. It may not look like much, but I really value that hat."

The first words Ross ever spoke directly to Glenna were "Do you know the only thing that's the matter with you?"

"What?" said Glenna, looking alarmed. She was a tall, frail girl with dark curly hair, a white skin, very light blue eyes, and a habit of holding on to her bottom lip with her teeth, which gave her a wistful, worried air. She was the sort of girl who often wears pale blue (she had a fuzzy sweater on, of that color), and a delicate chain around her neck, with a cross or heart on it, or a name.

(Glenna wore her name, because people had trouble spelling it.)

"The only thing the matter with you," said Ross, chewing and nodding, "is that I didn't find you first!"

A relief. They all laughed. This was during Glenna's first dinner at Sylvia's house. Sylvia and Colin and Glenna were eating take-out Chinese food—Sylvia had set a pile of plates and forks and even paper napkins beside the cardboard cartons—and Ross was eating a pizza, which Sylvia had ordered especially for him because he didn't like Chinese food.

Glenna suggested that Ross might like to come to the drive-in with them that night, and he did. The three of them sat on top of Colin's car, with Glenna in the middle, drinking beer.

It became a family joke. What would have happened if Glenna had met Ross first?

Colin wouldn't have had a chance.

Finally, Colin had to ask her, "What if you *had* met him first? Would you have gone out with him?"

"Ross is sweet," Glenna said.

"But would you have gone out with him?"

She looked embarrassed, which was really all the answer Colin needed.

"Ross isn't the type you go out with."

Sylvia said, "Ross, someday you are going to find a wonderful girl."

But Ross seemed to have given up looking. He stopped calling up girls and crowing like a rooster into the phone; he no longer drove slowly along the street, trailing them, sounding the horn as if in Morse code. One Saturday night, at Colin's and Glenna's house, he said he had given up on women, it was so hard to find a decent one, and anyway he had never gotten over Wilma Barry.

"Wilma Barry, who was that?" said Glenna. "Were you in love, Ross? When?"

"Grade Nine."

"Wilma Barry! Was she pretty? Did she know how you felt about her?"

"Yeah. Yeah. Yeah, I guess."

Colin said, "Jesus, the whole school knew!"

"Where is she now, Ross?" said Glenna.

"Gone. Married."

"Did she like you, too?"

"Couldn't stand me," said Ross complacently.

Colin was remembering the persecution of Wilma Barry—how Ross would go into empty classrooms and write her name on the blackboard, in little dots of colored chalk, or little hearts; how he went to watch the girls' basketball games, in which she played, and carried on like a madman every time she got near the ball or the basket. She dropped off the team. She took to hiding in the girls' washroom and sending out scouts to tell her if the coast was clear. Ross knew this, and hid in broom closets so he could pop out and whistle mournfully at her. She dropped out of school altogether and married at seventeen. Ross was too much for her.

"What a shame," said Glenna.

"I did love that Wilma," Ross said, and shook his head. "Colin, tell Glenna about me and the piece of pie!"

So Colin told that story, a favorite with everybody who had gone to high school around their time. Colin and Ross always brought their lunch to school because their mother worked and the cafeteria was too expensive. They always had bologna-and-ketchup sandwiches and store pie. One day, they were all being kept in at noon for some reason, Grades 9 and 10 together, so Ross and Colin were in the same room. Ross had his lunch in his desk and right in the middle of whatever lecture they were getting, he took out a big piece of apple pie and started to eat it. "What in the devil do you think you're doing?" the teacher yelled, and Ross without a moment's hesitation thrust the pie under his bum and sat on it, bringing his sticky hands together in a clap of innocence.

"I didn't do it to be funny!" Ross told Glenna. "I just couldn't think what to do with that pie but stick it underneath me!"

"I can just see you!" said Glenna, laughing. "Oh, Ross, I can just see you! Like some character on television!"

"Didn't we ever tell you that before?" said Ross. "How come we never?"

"I kind of think we did," said Colin.

Glenna said, "You did, but it's funny to hear it again."

"All right, Colin, tell her about the time you shot me dead!"

"You told me that, too, and I don't want to ever have to hear it again," said Glenna.

"Why not?" said Ross, disappointed.

"Because it's horrible."

Colin knew that when he got home from Sylvia's Ross would be there ahead of him, working on the car. He was right. It was nearly the end of May now, and Ross had started his car-wrecking and combo-building in Colin's yard as soon as the snow was gone. There wasn't enough room for this activity at Sylvia's.

Plenty of room for it here. Colin and Glenna had bought a run-down cottage set far back from the street, in the remains of an orchard. They were fixing it up. They used to live over the laundromat, and when Glenna had to quit work—she was a teacher, too, a primary specialist—because of being pregnant with Lynnette, she took on the job of managing the laundromat so that they could live rent free and save money. They talked then about moving—right away, to someplace remote and adventurous-sounding like Labrador or Moosonee or Yellowknife. They talked about going to Europe and teaching the children of Canadian servicemen. Meanwhile this house came up for sale, and it happened to be a house Glenna had always looked at and wondered about when she took Lynnette for a walk in the carriage or stroller. She had grown up in Air Force bases all over the country, and she loved to look at old houses.

Now, Glenna said, with all the work there was to do on this place, it looked as if they knew where they'd be and what they'd be doing forevermore.

Ross had two cars to wreck and one to build. The Chevy was a 1958 model that had been in an accident. The windshield was smashed, and the radiator and fan shoved back on the engine. The wiring was burned. Ross hadn't been able to tell how the engine ran until he got the fan and the radiator and the banged-up sheet metal out of the way. Then he hot-wired it and filled the block with water. It ran. Ross said he knew it would. That was what he had bought the car for, the body being so damaged it was no use to him. The body he was using belonged to a 1971 Camaro. The top coat of paint had fallen off in sheets when he used the stripper, but now he was having to work with the hose and scouring pads on what was underneath. He was going to have to take out the dents in the roof with a body hammer and cut out the rusted sections of the floorboards to put in an aluminum panel. That and a lot more. It looked as if the job might take all summer.

Right now Ross was working on the wheels, with Glenna helping him. Glenna was polishing the trim rings and center caps, which had been taken off, while Ross scoured the wheels themselves and went over them with a wire brush. Lynnette was in her playpen by the front door.

Colin sniffed the air for stripper. Ross didn't use a respirator; he said you didn't need to in the fresh air. Colin knew he should trust Glenna not to expose herself and Lynnette to that. But he sniffed, and it was all right; they hadn't been using any stripper. To cover up, he said, "Smells like spring."

"You don't need to tell me," said Glenna, who was subject to hay fever. "I can feel the clouds of pollen just getting ready to move in."

"Did you get your shots?" said Colin.

"Not today."

"That was dumb."

"I know," said Glenna, polishing like mad. "I was going to walk over to the hospital. Then I got fooling around with these and I got sort of hypnotized."

Lynnette walked cautiously around the sides of her playpen, holding on, then lifted her arms and said, "Up, Dad." Colin was delighted with the firm, businesslike way she said "Dad"—not "Da" as other babies did.

"What I've decided I'm going to do," said Ross. "I'm going to put on a rust remover that's a conditioner and then a conversion coating and then a primer. But I got to get every last bit of the old filler out, because the stripper could've got into it and it'd look like a mess through the new paint. I'm going to use acrylic lacquer. What do you think?"

"What color?" said Colin. He was talking to two rear ends, both in jeans. Glenna's jeans were cutoffs, baring her long, powdery-white legs. No sign of either hat on Ross now. He sobered up remarkably whenever he got near his car.

"I was thinking yellow. Then I thought red always looks good on a Camaro."

"We'll get the paint chart and hold it up in front of Lynnette and let her choose," said Glenna. "Okay, Ross? Whatever she points to? Will we do that?"

"Okay," said Ross.

"She'll point to red. She loves red."

"Take it easy," said Colin to Lynnette as he went past her into the house. She started to complain, not too seriously. He got three bottles of beer out of the refrigerator. During the winter, they had worked inside the house, pulling off wallpaper and tearing up linoleum, and they had got the place now to a stage where all the innards were showing. There were batts of pink insulating material held in place under sheets of plastic. Piles of lumber to be used in the new partitions sat around drying. You walked on springy wide boards in the kitchen. Ross had shown up regularly to help, but had not offered since he started on the car.

Glenna had said, "I think he started thinking about the car when he realized he wasn't going to live with us in the house."

Colin said, "Ross always fooled around with cars."

But Ross had never cared so much before about what a car looked like. He had cared about the getaway speed and top speed and whatever menacing or ridiculous-sounding noise he could force out of it. He had had two accidents. Once, he rolled his car into a ditch and walked away without a scratch. Another time, he had taken a shortcut, as he said, through a vacant lot in town and run into a heap of junk that included an old bathtub. When Colin came home from college on the weekend, there was Ross with purple bruises along the side of his face, a cut over one ear, and his ribs taped.

"I had a collision with a bathtub."

Had he been drunk, or high?

"I don't think so," said Ross.

This time he seemed to have something else in mind than gunning the engine and fishtailing down the street, leaving a trail of burn marks on the pavement. He wanted a real car, what the magazine he read called a "street car." Could that be to get girls? Or just to show himself off in, driving in a respectable style with an occasional flash of speed or powerful growl when he took off at the lights? Maybe this time he could even do without a trick horn.

"This is one car isn't going to be run up and down the main street like a maniac or hittin' a hundred on the gravel," he said.

"That's right, Ross," said Glenna. "Time you graduated."

"Beer," said Colin, and put it down where Ross could reach.

"Ross?" said Glenna. ("Thank you," she said to Colin.) "Ross, you're going to have to rip the carpet off the doors. You are. It looks okay but really it stinks. I can smell it. Over here."

Colin sat on the step with Lynnette on one knee, knowing he wasn't going to bring up the matter of being on time, let alone the hats. He wasn't going to remind Ross that this was the first job he'd had in over a year. He was too tired, and now he felt too peaceful. Some of this peacefulness was Glenna's doing. Glenna didn't ally herself with anybody who was completely weird, or with any futile undertaking. And there she was, looking at her face in the caps, sniffing the carpet panels, taking Ross and his car seriously—so seriously that when Colin first got out of the car and saw her squatted down, polishing, he had felt like asking if this was the way things were going to go all summer, with her so involved with Ross's car she wouldn't have time to work on the house. He'd be kicking himself now if he'd said that. What would he do if she didn't like Ross, if she hadn't liked him from the start and agreed to have him around? When Ross said what the one thing wrong was, at their first meeting, and Glenna smiled, not politely or condescendingly but with true surprise and pleasure, Colin had felt more than relief. He had felt as if from now on Ross could stop being a secret weight on him; he would have someone to share Ross with. He had never counted Sylvia.

The other thought that had crossed Colin's mind was dirty in every sense of the word. Ross never would. Ross was a prude. He glowered and stuck his big lip out and looked as if he half felt like crying when there was a sexy scene at the movies.

On Saturday morning, there was a large package of chicken pieces thawing on the counter, reminding Colin that Glenna had asked Sylvia and Eddy and her friend—their friend—Nancy to come over for supper.

Glenna had gone to the hospital, walking, with Lynnette in the stroller, to get her hay-fever shots. Ross was already working. He had come into the house and put a tape on, leaving the door open so that he could hear it. *Chariots of Fire*. That was Glenna's. Ross usually listened to country and Western.

Colin was just home from the builders'-supply store, where they didn't have his ceiling panels in yet, in spite of promises. He went out to look at the grass he had planted last Saturday, a patch of lawn to the side of the house, fenced off with string. He gave it some water, then watched Ross sanding the wheels. Before long and without quite intending to, he was sanding as well. It was hypnotizing, as Glenna had said; you just kept on at it. After they were sufficiently sanded down, the wheels had to be painted with primer (the tires protected from that with masking tape and paper), and when the primer was dry, they had to be scuffed off with a copper pad and cleaned again with a wax-and-grease remover. Ross had all this planned out.

They worked all morning and then all afternoon. Glenna made hamburgers for lunch. When Colin told her he couldn't do the kitchen ceiling because the panels hadn't come, she said he couldn't have worked on the kitchen anyway, because she had to make a dessert.

Ross went uptown and bought a touch-up gun and some metallic charcoal paint, as well as Armor-All for the tires. This was a good idea—the touch-up gun made it a lot easier to get into the recesses of the wheels.

Nancy arrived about the middle of the afternoon, driving her dinky little Chevette and wearing a strange new outfit—rather long, loose shorts and a top that was like a bag with holes cut for the head and arms, the whole thing dirt-colored and held at the waist with a long raggedy purple sash. Nancy had been brought in that year to teach French from kindergarten to Grade 8, that being the new requirement. She was a rangy, pale, flat-chested girl with frizzy, corn-yellow hair and an intelligent, mournful face. Colin found her likable and disturbing. She came around like an old friend, bringing her own beer and her own music. She chattered to Lynnette, and had a made-up name for her—Winnie-Winnie. But whose old friend was she? Before last September, none of them had ever set eyes on her. She was in her early thirties, had lived with three different men, and did not think she would ever marry. The first time she met Sylvia and Eddy, she told them about the three men and about the drugs she had taken. Sylvia egged her on, of course. Eddy didn't know what she was talking about, and when she mentioned acid, he may have thought she was referring to battery acid. She told you how she felt every time you saw her. Not that she had a headache or a cold or swollen glands or sore feet, but whether she was depressed or elated or whatever. And she had an odd way of talking about this town. She talked about it as if it were a substance, a lump, as if the people in it were all glued together, and as if the lump had—for her—peculiar and usually discouraging characteristics.

"I saw you yesterday, Ross," said Nancy. She sat on the step, having opened a beer and put on Joan Armatrading, "Show Some Emotion." She got up and lifted Lynnette out of the playpen. "I saw you at the school. You were beautiful."

Colin said, "There's stuff lying all around here she could put in her mouth. Little nuts and stuff. You have to watch her."

"I'll watch her," said Nancy. "Winnie-Winnie." She was tickling Lynnette with the fringe of her sash.

"Monsieur les Deux Chapeaux," she said. "I had Grade Three all looking out the window and admiring you. That's what we decided to call you. Monsieur les Deux Chapeaux. Monsieur of the Two Hats."

"We do know some French. Strange as it may seem," said Colin.

"I don't," said Ross. "I don't know what she's talking about."

"Oh, Ross," said Nancy, tickling Lynnette. "Aren't you my little honey bear, my little Winnie-Winnie? Ross, you were beautiful. What an inspiration on a dull dragged-out old Friday afternoon."

Nancy had a way of making Ross turn sullen. To her face behind her back, he often said that she was crazy.

"You're crazy, Nancy. You never saw me. You're seeing things. You got double vision."

"Sure," said Nancy. "Absolutely, Monsieur les Deux Chapeaux. So what are you doing? Tell me. You taking up car-wrecking?"

"We're painting these wheels, at the moment," said Colin. Ross wouldn't say anything.

"I once took a course," said Nancy. "I took a course in elementary mechanics so I would know what was going on with my car and I wouldn't have to go into the garage squeaking like a little woman." She squeaked like a little woman, "Oh, there's this funny noise and tell me what's under the hood, please? Good heavens, it's an engine! Well, so I wouldn't do that I took this course and I got so interested I took another course and I was actually thinking about becoming a mechanic. I was going to get down in the grease pit. But really I'm too conventional. I couldn't face the hassle. I'd rather teach French."

She put Lynnette on her hip and walked over to look at the engine.

"Ross? You going to steam-clean this?"

"Yeah," said Ross. "I'll have to see about renting one."

"Also, I lived with a guy who was involved with cars and you know what he did? When he had to rent a steamer, he used to ask around to see if anybody else wanted it done, and then he'd charge them ten dollars. So he made money on the rent."

"Yeah," Ross said.

"Just suggesting. You'll need a different radiator brace, won't you? V-8s mount the radiator behind the brace."

After that Ross came out of his sulk—he saw he might as well—and started showing her things.

. . .

"Come on, Colin," Nancy said. "Glenna says we need more whipping cream. We can go in my car. You hold Lynnette."

"I haven't got a shirt on," said Colin.

"Lynnette doesn't care. I'll go into the store. Come on. Glenna wants it now."

In the car she said, "I wanted to talk to you."

"I figured that."

"It's about Ross. About what he's doing."

"You mean him going around in those hats? What? What did Davidson say?"

"I don't mean anything about that. I mean that car."

Colin was relieved. "What about the car?"

"That engine. Colin, that engine is too big. He can't put that engine in that body."

Her voice was dramatically deep and calm.

"Ross knows quite a bit about cars," Colin said.

"I believe you. I never said Ross was dumb. He does know. But that engine, if he puts it in, I'm afraid it will simply break the drive shaft—not immediately but sooner or later. And sooner rather than later. Kids do that a lot. They put in a big powerful engine for the pickup and speed they want, and one day, you know, really, it can take the whole car over. It literally flips it over. Breaks the shaft. The thing is, with kids, something else often goes wrong first or they wreck it up. So he could have done this before and gotten away with it. Thought he was getting away with it. I'm not just doing the big expert, Colin. I swear to God I'm not."

"Okay," said Colin. "You're not."

"You know I'm not? Colin?"

"I know you're not."

"I just could not bring myself to say anything to Ross. He is so steamed up about it. That's what they say here, isn't it? Steamed up? I couldn't come out with a major criticism like that. Anyway, he might not believe me."

"I don't know if he'd believe me," said Colin. "Look. You are dead sure?"

"Don't say dead!" Nancy begged him, in that phony-sounding voice he had to believe was sincere. "I am absolutely and undeniably sure and if I wasn't I would not have opened my big mouth."

"He knows he's putting in a bigger engine. He knows that. He must figure it's all right."

"He figures wrong. Colin, I love Ross. I don't want to upset his project."

"You better not let Sylvia hear you say that."

"Say what? She doesn't want him killed, either."

"That you love Ross."

"I love you all, Colin," said Nancy, pulling into the Mac's Milk lot. "I really do."

"This is what I did, I'll tell you," said Sylvia, speaking mostly to Nancy, after a fourth glass of rosé. "I gave myself a twenty-fifth wedding anniversary party. What do you think of that?"

"Marvellous!" said Nancy. Sylvia had just told her the joke about the black man and white man at the urinal, and Colin could see that it had given her some difficulty.

"I mean, without a husband. I mean, he wasn't still living with me. I wasn't still living with him. He was still living. In Peterborough. He isn't still living now. But I said, 'I have been married twenty-five years, and I still am married. So don't I deserve to have a party?' "

Nancy said, "Certainly."

They were sitting at the picnic table out in the back yard, just a few steps from the kitchen door, under the blossoming black-cherry tree. Glenna had spread a white cloth and used her wedding china.

"This will be a patio by next year," Glenna said.

"See," said Sylvia. "If you had've used plastic, you could scoop all this up now and put it in the garbage."

Eddy lit Sylvia's cigarette. He himself had not stopped smoking throughout the meal.

Nancy picked a soggy strawberry out of the ruined crown of meringue. "It's lovely here now," she said.

"At least no bugs yet," said Glenna.

Sylvia said, "True. Strawberries would have been a lot cheaper by next week, but you couldn't've ate out here because of the bugs."

That seemed funny to Nancy. She started laughing, and Eddy joined in. For some unstated reason—with him it would have to be unstated— he admired Nancy and all she did. Sylvia, bewildered but good-humored, with her face as pink as a tissue-paper rose starting to look pretty crumpled round the edges, said, "I don't see what's funny. What did I say?"

"Go on," said Ross.

"Go on what?"

"Go on and tell about the anniversary party."

"Oh, Ross," said Glenna. She got up and turned on the lights in the colored plastic lanterns that were strung along the wall of the house. "I should have made Colin get up and put some in the cherry tree," she said.

"Well, Colin was thirteen at the time and Ross was twelve," Sylvia said. "Oh, everybody knows this backwards and forwards except you, Nancy. So, twenty-five years married and my oldest kid is thirteen? You could say that was the problem. Such a long time without kids, we were just counting on never having any. First counting on having them and then being disappointed and then getting used to it, and being used to it so long, over ten years married, and I'm pregnant! That was Colin. And not even twelve months later, eleven months and three days later, another one! That was Ross!"

"Whoopee!" said Ross.

"The poor man, I guess he got scared from then on I would just be dropping babies every time he turned around, so he took off."

"He was transferred," Colin said. "He worked for the railway, and when they took off the passenger train through here they transferred him to Peterborough."

He had not many memories of his father. Once, walking down the street, his father had offered him a stick of gum. There was a kindly, official air about this gesture—his father was wearing his uniform at the time—rather than a paternal intimacy. Colin had the impression that Sylvia couldn't manage sons and a husband, somehow—that she had mislaid her marriage without exactly meaning to.

"He didn't just work for the railway," said Sylvia. "He was a conductor on it. After he first was transferred, he used to come back sometimes on the bus, but he hated travelling on the bus and he couldn't drive a car. He just gradually quit visiting and he died just before he would've retired. So maybe he would've come back then, who knows?"

(It was Glenna's idea, relayed to Colin, that all this easygoing talk about throwing her own anniversary party was just Sylvia's bluff—that she had asked or told her husband to come, and he hadn't.)

"Well, never mind him, it was a party," Sylvia said. "I asked a lot of people. I would've asked Eddy but I didn't know him then so well as I do now. I thought he was too high class." She jabbed Eddy's arm with her elbow. Everybody knew it was his second wife who had been too high class. "It was August, the weather was good, we were able to be outside, like we are here. I had trestle tables set up and I had a washtub full of potato salad. I had spareribs and fried chicken and desserts and pies and an anniversary cake I got iced by the bakery. And two fruit punches, one with and one without. The one with got a lot more with as the evening wore on and people kept pouring in vodka and brandy and whatever they had and I didn't know it!"

Ross said, "Everybody thought Colin got into the punch!"

"Well, he didn't," said Sylvia. "That was a lie."

Earlier, Colin and Nancy had cleared the table together, and when they were alone in the kitchen Nancy said, "Did you say anything to Ross?"

"Not yet."

"You will, though? Colin? It's serious."

Glenna coming in with a platter of chicken bones heard that, though she didn't say anything.

Colin said, "Nancy thinks Ross is making a mistake with his car."

"A fatal mistake," said Nancy. Colin went back outside, leaving her talking in a lowered, urgent voice to Glenna.

"And we had music," Sylvia said. "We were dancing on the sidewalk round the front, as well as partying at the back. We had records playing in my front room and the windows open. The night constable came down and he was dancing along with us! It was just after they put the pink streetlights up on that street, so I said, 'Look at the lights they put up for my party!' Where are you going?" she said to Colin, who had stood up.

"I want to show Eddy something."

Eddy stood up, looking pleased, and padded around the table. He was wearing brown-and-yellow checked pants, not too bold a check, a yellow sports shirt and dark-red neckerchief. "Doesn't he look nice?" said Sylvia, not for the first time. "Eddy, you're such a dresser! Colin just don't want to hear me tell the rest."

"The rest is the best," Ross said. "Coming up!"

"I want to show Eddy something and ask him something," Colin said. "In private."

"This part of it is like something you would read in the newspaper," said Sylvia.

Glenna said, "It's horrible."

"He's going to show Eddy his precious grass," said Sylvia. "Plus, he really does want to get away from me telling it. Why? Wasn't his fault. Well, partly. But it's the kind of thing has happened over and over again with others, only the outcome has been worse. Tragic."

"It sure could've been tragic," Ross said, laughing.

Colin, guiding Eddy around to the front of the house, could hear Ross laughing. He got Eddy past the string fence and the new grass. In the front yard there was some light from the streetlight, not really enough. He turned on the light by the front door.

"Now. How good can you see Ross's car?" Colin said.

Eddy said, "I seen it all before."

"Wait."

Colin's car was parked so that the lights would shine where he wanted them to, and he had the keys in his pocket. He got in and started the motor and turned on the lights.

"There," he said. "Take a look at the engine now while I got the lights on."

Eddy said, "Okay," and walked over into the car light and stood contemplating the engine.

"Now look at the body."

"Yeah," said Eddy, doing a quarter-turn but not stooping to look. In those clothes, he wouldn't want to get too close to anything.

Colin turned off the lights and the motor and got out of the car. In the dark he heard Ross laughing again.

"Somebody was saying to me that the engine was too big to be put in there," Colin said. "This person said it would break the universal and the drive shaft would go and the car would somersault. Now, I don't know enough about cars. Is that true?"

He wasn't going to say that the person was Nancy, not because Nancy was a woman but because Eddy was apt to regard anything Nancy said or did with such mesmerized delight that you would never be able to get an opinion out of him. It was not easy to get opinions out of him in any case.

"It's a big engine," Eddy said. "It's a V-8 350. It's a Chevy engine."

Colin didn't say he knew this already. "Is it too big?" he said. "Is it a danger?"

"It is a bit big."

"Have you seen them put this kind of an engine in this kind of body before?

"Oh, yeah. I seen them do everything."

"Would it cause an accident, like this person said?"

"Hard to say."

After most people say that, they go on and tell you what it is that is hard to say. Not Eddy.

"Would it be sure to break the universal?"

"Oh, not sure," said Eddy agreeably. "I wouldn't say that."

"It might?"

"Well."

"Should I say anything to Ross?"

Eddy chuckled nervously. "Sylvia don't take it too well when you say anything to Ross."

Colin had not been into the spiked punch. He and Ross and the half-dozen other boys did not go that close to the heart of the party. They ignored the party, staying on the fringes of it, drinking only out of cans—cans of Coca Cola and Orange that somebody had brought and left beside the back steps. They ate potato chips that were provided, but did not bother with the food set out on tables that required plates or forks. They did not pay attention to what the adults were doing. A few years ago, they would have been hanging around watching everything, with the idea, mostly, of making fun of and disrupting it. Now they would not give that world—the world of adults, at the party or anywhere else—credit for existing.

Things that belonged to adults were another story. Those were still interesting, and in the cars parked along the black lane they found plenty. Tools, shovels, last winter's chains, boots, some traps. Torn raincoats, a blanket, magazines with dirty pictures. A gun.

The gun was lying along the back seat of an unlocked car. It was a hunting rifle. There was no question that they would have to lift it out, look at it and comment on it in a knowledgeable way, aim it at imaginary birds.

Some said to be careful.

"It isn't loaded."

"How do you know?"

Colin never heard how that boy knew. He was thinking how Ross must not get his hands on this gun, or, loaded or not, it would explode. To prevent such a thing happening. Colin grabbed it himself, and what happened then he absolutely did not know, or remember, ever. He didn't remember pointing the gun. He couldn't have pointed it. He didn't remember pulling the trigger, because that was what he couldn't have done. He couldn't have pulled the trigger. He couldn't remember the sound of a shot but only the knowledge that something had happened—the knowledge you have when a loud noise wakes you out of sleep and just for a moment seems too distant and inevitable to need your attention.

Screams and yells broke on his ears at this same time. One of the screams came from Ross, which should have told Colin something. (Do people shot dead usually scream?) Colin didn't see Ross fall. What he did see—and always remembered—was Ross lying on the ground, on his back, with his arms flung out, a dark stain spilled out from the top of his head.

That could not actually have been there—was there a puddle?

Not despising the world or help of adults anymore, one or two boys raced down the lane to Sylvia's house, yelling, "Ross is shot! Colin shot him! Ross! He's shot! Colin shot him! Ross! Colin! Ross!"

By the time they made the people sitting around the table in the back yard understand this—some had heard the shot but thought of firecrackers—and by the time the first men, running down the lane, came to the scene of the tragedy, Ross was sitting up, stretching his arms, with a sly, abashed look on his face. The boys who hadn't run to get help had seen him stir, and thought he must be alive but wounded. He wasn't wounded at all. The bullet hadn't come near him. It had hit the shed a little way down the lane, a shed where an old man sharpened skates in the wintertime. Nobody was hurt.

Ross claimed he had been knocked out, or knocked over, by the sound of the shot. But everybody, knowing Ross, believed or suspected that he had put on an act on purpose, on the spur of the moment. The gun was lying in the grass by the side of the lane, where Colin had thrown it. None of the boys had picked it up; nobody wanted to touch it or be associated with it, though it was clear to them now that everything must come out—how they took it from the car when they had no business to, how they were all to blame.

But Colin chiefly. Colin was to blame. And he had run.

That was the cry, after the first commotion about Ross.

"What happened? Ross, are you all right? Are you hit? Where is the gun? Are you really all right? Where did you get the gun? Why did you act like you were shot? Are you sure you're not shot? Who shot the gun? *Who*? Colin!"

"Where is Colin?"

Nobody even remembered the direction he had gone in. Nobody remembered seeing him go. They called, but there was no answer. They looked along the lane to see if he might be hiding. The constable got into the police car, and other people got into their cars, and they drove up and down the strets, even drove a few miles out onto the highway to see if they could catch him running away. No sign of him. Sylvia went into the house and looked in the closets and under the beds. People were wandering around, bumping into each other, shining flashlights into bushes, calling for Colin.

Then Ross said he knew the place to look.

"Down at the Tiplady Bridge."

This was an iron bridge of the old-fashioned kind spanning the Tiplady River. It had been left in place though a new, concrete bridge had been built upriver, so that the widened highway now bypassed that bit of town. The road leading down to the old bridge was closed off to cars and the bridge itself declared unsafe, but people swam or fished off it, and at night cars bumped around the ROAD CLOSED sign to park. The pavement there was broken up, and the streetlight had burned out and not been replaced. There were rumors and jokes about this light, implying that members of the council were among those who parked, and preferred darkness.

The bridge was only a couple of blocks from Sylvia's house. The boys ran ahead, not led but followed by Ross, who took a thoughtful pace. Sylvia stuck close to him and told him to get a move on. She was wearing high heels and a teal-blue sheath dress, too tight across the hips, which hampered her.

"You better be right," she said, confused now about which son she was most angry at. She hadn't had time to recover from Ross's not being shot when she had to wonder if she would ever see Colin again. Some party guests were drunk or tactless enough to wonder out loud if he could have jumped into the Tiplady River.

The constable stuck his head out of the car and told them to remove the roadblock. Then he drove through and shone his headlights on the bridge.

The top of the bridge did not show up very well in this light, but they could see somebody sitting there.

"Colin!"

Colin had climbed up and settled on the iron girders. He was there.

"Colin! I can't believe you did that!" Sylvia yelled up at him. "Come on down off that bridge!"

Colin didn't move. He seemed dazed. He was, in fact, so blinded by the lights of the police car that he couldn't have climbed down if he had wanted to.

Now the constable ordered him, and others ordered him. He wouldn't budge. In the midst of the orders and reproaches, it struck Sylvia that of course he didn't know that Ross wasn't dead.

"Colin, your brother isn't shot!" she called to him. "Colin! Your brother is alive here beside me! Ross is alive!"

Colin didn't answer but she thought she saw his head move, as if he was peering down.

"Get those stupid lights off him," she said to the constable, who was a sort of boyfriend. "Turn the lights on Ross if you want to turn them on something."

"Why don't we stand Ross out in the lights?" the constable said. "Then we can turn them off and let the boy climb down.

"Okay, Colin," the constable called out. "We're going to show you Ross standing here—he isn't hurt or anything!"

Sylvia pushed Ross into the light.

"Open your mouth, for crying out loud," she said. "Tell your brother you're alive."

Colin was helping Glenna clean up. He thought about what his mother had said, about plastic dishes and tablecloths that you could just scoop up and throw in the garbage. There was not a chance in a million that Glenna would ever do that. His mother understood nothing about Glenna, nothing at all.

Now Glenna was exhausted, having created a dinner party

more elaborate than necessary that nobody but herself could appreciate.

No, that was wrong. He appreciated, even if he didn't understand the necessity. Every step she took him away from his mother's confusion, he appreciated.

"I don't know what to say to Ross," he said.

"What about?" said Glenna.

She was so tired, he thought, that she had forgotten what Nancy told her. He found himself thinking of the night before their wedding. Glenna had five bridesmaids, chosen for their size and coloring rather than particular friendship, and she had made all their dresses to a design of her own. She made her wedding dress as well, and all the gloves and headdresses. The gloves had sixteen little covered buttons each. She finished them at nine-thirty the night before the wedding. Then she went upstairs, looking very white. Colin, who was staying in the house, went up to see how she was and found her weeping, still holding some scraps of colored cloth. He couldn't get her to stop, and called her mother, who said, "That's just the way she is, Colin. She overdoes things."

Glenna sobbed and said, among other things, that she saw no use in being alive. The next day, she was angelically pretty, showing no ravages, drinking in praise and wishes for her happiness.

This dinner wasn't likely to have worn her out as much as the bridesmaids' outfits, but she had reached the stage where she had a forbidding look, a harsh pallor, as if there were a lot of things that she might call in question.

"He is not going to want to go hunting for another engine," Colin said. "How can he afford one? He owes Sylvia for that one. Anyway, he wants a big engine. He wants the power."

Glenna said, "Does it make that much difference?"

"It makes a difference. In the pickups and the power. Sure. An engine like that makes a difference."

Then he saw that she might not have meant that. She might not have meant "Does the engine make a difference?" She might have meant "If it's not this, it'll be something else."

(She sat on the grass; she polished the caps. She sniffed at the door panels. She said, "Let Lynnette choose the color.")

She might have meant "Why don't we just let it go?"

Colin shook the garbage down in the plastic bag and tied it at the neck. "I don't want you and Lynnette riding around with him, if there's anything like that."

"Colin, I wouldn't," said Glenna, in a gentle, amazed voice. "Do you think I ever would ride with him in that car or let Lynnette ride with him? I never would."

He took the garbage out and she began to sweep the floor. When he came back, she said, "I just thought of something. I thought, Soon I'll be sweeping the black and white tiles and I won't even be able to picture what these old boards look like. We won't be able to remember. We should take some pictures so we can remember what we've done."

Then she said, "I think Nancy sort of dramatizes sometimes. I mean it about me and Lynnette. But I think she overdramatizes."

Glenna had surprised him, in fact, with the way she could picture things. The house, each of its rooms, in its finished state. She had placed the furniture they hadn't yet bought; she had chosen the colors in accordance with a northern or southern exposure, morning or evening light. Glenna could hold in her mind an orderly succession of rooms, an arrangement that was ordained, harmonious, and, by her, completely understood.

A problem wouldn't just thrust itself on Glenna, and throw her into doubts and agonies. Solutions were waiting like a succession of rooms. There was a way she would see of dealing with things without talking or thinking about them. And all her daily patience and sweetness wouldn't alter that way, or touch it.

At first, with the lights and the hollering, his only idea was that they had come to blame him. That didn't interest him. He knew what he had done. He hadn't run away and cut down here and climbed the bridge in the dark so that they couldn't punish him. He was not afraid; he wasn't shivering with the shock. He sat on the narrow girders and felt how cold the iron was, even on a summer night, and he himself was cold, but still calm, with all the jumble of his life, and other people's lives in this town, rolled back, just like a photograph split and rolled back, so it shows what was underneath all along. Nothing. Ross lying on the ground with a pool around his head. Ross silenced, himself a murderer. Still nothing. He wasn't glad or sorry. Such feelings were too puny and personal; they did not apply. Later on, he found out that most people, and apparently his mother, believed he had climbed up here because he was in a frenzy of remorse and was contemplating throwing himself into the Tiplady River. That never occurred to him. In a way, he had forgotten the river was there. He had forgotten that a bridge was a structure over a river and that his mother was a person who could order him to do things.

No, he hadn't forgotten those things so much as grasped how silly they were. How silly it was that he should have a name and it should be Colin, and that people should be shouting it. It was silly, in a way, even to think that he had shot Ross, though he knew he had. What was silly was to think in these chunks of words. Colin. Shot. Ross. To see it as an action, something sharp and separate, an event, a *difference*.

He wasn't thinking of throwing himself into the river or of anything else he might do next, or of how his life would progress from this moment. Such progress seemed not only unnecessary but impossible. His life had split open, and nothing had to be figured out anymore.

They were telling him Ross wasn't dead.

He isn't dead, Colin.

You never shot him.

It was a hoax.

It was Ross playing a joke.

Ross's joke.

You never shot anybody, Colin. Gun went off but nobody was hurt.

See, Colin. Here he is.

Here's Ross. He ain't dead.

"I ain't dead, Colin!"

"Did you hear that? Did you hear what he said? He said he ain't dead!"

So now you can come on down.

Now you can come down.

Colin. Come on down.

That was when everything started to go back to being itself again. He saw Ross unwounded, unmistakably himself, lit up by car lights. Ross risen up, looking cheerful and slightly apprehensive, but not really apologetic. Ross, who seemed to caper even when he was standing still, and to laugh out loud even when he was working hard at keeping his mouth shut.

The same.

Colin felt dizzy, and sick with the force of things coming back to life, the chaos and emotion. It was as painful as fiery blood pushing into frozen parts of your body. Doing as he was told, he started to climb down. Some people clapped and cheered. He had to concentrate to keep from slipping. He was weak and cramped from sitting up there. And he had to keep himself from thinking, too suddenly, about what had just missed happening.

He knew that to watch out for something like that happening—to Ross, and to himself—was going to be his job in life from then on.

Miles City, Montana

My father came across the field carrying the body of the boy who had been drowned. There were several men together, returning from the search, but he was the one carrying the body. The men were muddy and exhausted, and walked with their heads down, as if they were ashamed. Even the dogs were dispirited, dripping from the cold river. When they all set out, hours before, the dogs were nervy and yelping, the men tense and determined, and there was a constrained, unspeakable excitement about the whole scene. It was understood that they might find something horrible.

The boy's name was Steve Gauley. He was eight years old. His hair and clothes were mud-colored now and carried some bits of dead leaves, twigs, and grass. He was like a heap of refuse that had been left out all winter. His face was turned in to my father's chest, but I could see a nostril, an ear, plugged up with greenish mud.

I don't think so. I don't think I really saw all this. Perhaps I saw my father carrying him, and the other men following along, and the dogs, but I would not have been allowed to get close enough to see something like mud in his nostril. I must have heard someone talking about that and imagined that I saw it. I see his face unaltered except for the mud—Steve Gauley's familiar, sharp-honed, sneaky-looking face—and it wouldn't have been like that; it would have been bloated and changed and perhaps muddied all over after so many hours in the water.

To have to bring back such news, such evidence, to a waiting family, particularly a mother, would have made searchers move heavily, but what was happening here was worse. It seemed a worse shame (to hear people talk) that there was no mother, no woman at all—no grandmother or aunt, or even a sister—to receive Steve Gauley and give him his due of grief. His father was a hired man, a drinker but not a drunk, an erratic man without being entertaining, not friendly but not exactly a troublemaker. His fatherhood seemed accidental, and the fact that the child had been left with him when the mother went away, and that they continued living together, seemed accidental. They lived in a steep-roofed, gray-shingled hillbilly sort of house that was just a bit better than a shack—the father fixed the roof and put supports under the porch, just enough and just in time—and their life was held together in a similar manner; that is, just well enough to keep the Children's Aid at bay. They didn't eat meals together or cook for each other, but there was food. Sometimes the father would give Steve money to buy food at the store, and Steve was seen to buy quite sensible things, such as pancake mix and macaroni dinner.

I had known Steve Gauley fairly well. I had not liked him more often than I had liked him. He was two years older than I was. He would hang around our place on Saturdays, scornful of whatever I was doing but unable to leave me alone. I couldn't be on the swing without him wanting to try it, and if I wouldn't give it up he came and pushed me so that I went crooked. He teased the dog. He got me into trouble—deliberately and maliciously, it seemed to me afterward—by daring me to do things I wouldn't have thought of on my own: digging up the potatoes to see how big they were when they were still only the size of marbles, and pushing over the stacked firewood to make a pile we could jump off. At school, we never spoke to each other. He was solitary, though not tormented. But on Saturday mornings, when I saw his thin, self-possessed figure sliding through the cedar hedge, I knew I was in for something and he would decide what. Sometimes it was all right. We pretended we were cowboys who had to tame wild horses. We played in the pasture by the river, not far from the place where Steve drowned. We were horses and riders both, screaming and neighing and bucking and waving whips of tree branches beside a little nameless river that flows into the Saugeen in southern Ontario.

The funeral was held in our house. There was not enough room at Steve's father's place for the large crowd that was expected because of the circumstances. I have a memory of the crowded room but no picture of Steve in his coffin, or of the minister, or of wreaths of flowers. I remember that I was holding one flower, a white narcissus, which must have come from a pot somebody forced indoors, because it was too early for even the forsythia bush or the trilliums and marsh marigolds in the woods. I stood in a row of children, each of us holding a narcissus. We sang a children's hymn, which somebody played on our piano: "When He Cometh, When He Cometh, to Make Up His Jewels." I was wearing white ribbed stockings, which were disgustingly itchy, and wrinkled at the knees and ankles. The feeling of these stockings on my legs is mixed up with another feeling in my memory. It is hard to describe. It had to do with my parents. Adults in general but my parents in particular. My father, who had carried Steve's body from the river, and my mother, who must have done most of the arranging of this funeral. My father in his dark-blue suit and my mother in her brown velvet dress with the creamy satin collar. They stood side by side opening and closing their mouths for the hymn, and I stood removed from them, in the row of children, watching. I felt a furious and sickening disgust. Children sometimes have an access of disgust concerning adults. The size, the lumpy shapes, the bloated power. The breath, the coarseness, the hairiness, the horrid secretions. But this was more. And the accompanying anger had nothing sharp and self-respecting about it. There was no release, as when I would finally bend and pick up a stone and throw it at Steve Gauley. It could not be understood or expressed, though it died down after a while into a heaviness, then just a taste, an occasional taste—a thin, familiar misgiving.

. . .

Twenty years or so later, in 1961, my husband, Andrew, and I got a brand-new car, our first—that is, our first brand-new. It was a Morris Oxford, oyster-colored (the dealer had some fancier name for the color)—a big small car, with plenty of room for us and our two children. Cynthia was six and Meg three and a half.

Andrew took a picture of me standing beside the car. I was wearing white pants, a black turtleneck, and sunglasses. I lounged against the car door, canting my hips to make myself look slim.

"Wonderful," Andrew said. "Great. You look like Jackie Kennedy." All over this continent probably, dark-haired, reasonably slender young women were told, when they were stylishly dressed or getting their pictures taken, that they looked like Jackie Kennedy.

Andrew took a lot of pictures of me, and of the children, our house, our garden, our excursions and possessions. He got copies made, labelled them carefully, and sent them back to his mother and his aunt and uncle in Ontario. He got copies for me to send to my father, who also lived in Ontario, and I did so, but less regularly than he sent his. When he saw pictures he thought I had already sent lying around the house, Andrew was perplexed and annoyed. He liked to have this record go forth.

That summer, we were presenting ourselves, not pictures. We were driving back from Vancouver, where we lived, to Ontario, which we still called "home," in our new car. Five days to get there, ten days there, five days back. For the first time, Andrew had three weeks' holiday. He worked in the legal department at B. C. Hydro.

On a Satuday morning, we loaded suitcases, two thermos bottles—one filled with coffee and one with lemonade—some fruit and sandwiches, picture books and coloring books, crayons, drawing pads, insect repellent, sweaters (in case it got cold in the mountains), and our two children into the car. Andrew locked the house, and Cynthia said ceremoniously, "Goodbye, house."

Meg said, "Goodbye, house." Then she said, "Where will we live now?"

"It's not goodbye forever," said Cynthia. "We're coming back. Mother! Meg thought we weren't ever coming back!"

"I did not," said Meg, kicking the back of my seat.

Andrew and I put on our sunglasses, and we drove away, over the Lions Gate Bridge and through the main part of Vancouver. We shed our house, the neighborhod, the city, and—at the crossing point between Washington and British Columbia—our country. We were driving east across the United States, taking the most northerly route, and would cross into Canada again at Sarnia, Ontario. I don't know if we chose this route because the Trans-Canada Highway was not completely finished at the time or if we just wanted the feeling of driving through a foreign, a very slightly foreign, country—that extra bit of interest and adventure.

We were both in high spirits. Andrew congratulated the car several times. He said he felt so much better driving it than our old car, a 1951 Austin that slowed down dismally on the hills and had a fussy-old-lady image. So Andrew said now.

"What kind of image does this one have?" said Cynthia. She listened to us carefully and liked to try out new words such as "image." Usually she got them right.

"Lively," I said. "Slightly sporty. It's not show-off."

"It's sensible, but it has class," Andrew said. "Like my image."

Cynthia thought that over and said with a cautious pride, "That means like you think you want to be, Daddy?"

As for me, I was happy because of the shedding. I loved taking off. In my own house, I seemed to be often looking for a place to hide—sometimes from the children but more often from the jobs to be done and the phone ringing and the sociability of the neighborhood. I wanted to hide so that I could get busy at my real work, which was a sort of wooing of distant parts of myself. I lived in a state of siege, always losing just what I wanted to hold on to. But on trips there was no difficulty. I could be talking to Andrew, talking to the children and looking at whatever they wanted me to look at—a pig on a sign, a pony in a field, a Volkswagen on a revolving stand—and pouring lemonade into plastic cups, and all the time those bits and pieces would be flying together inside me. The essential composition would be achieved. This made me hopeful and lighthearted. It was being a watcher that did it. A watcher, not a keeper.

We turned east at Everett and climbed into the Cascades. I showed Cynthia our route on the map. First I showed her the map of the whole United States, which showed also the bottom part of Canada. Then I turned to the separate maps of each of the states we were going to pass through. Washington, Idaho, Montana, North Dakota, Minnesota, Wisconsin. I showed her the dotted line across Lake Michigan, which was the route of the ferry we would take. Then we would drive across Michigan to the bridge that linked the United States and Canada at Sarnia, Ontario. Home.

Meg wanted to see, too.

"You won't understand," said Cynthia. But she took the road atlas into the back seat.

"Sit back," she said to Meg. "Sit still. I'll show you."

I could hear her tracing the route for Meg, very accurately, just as I had done it for her. She looked up all the states' maps, knowing how to find them in alphabetical order.

"You know what that line is?" she said. "It's the road. That line is the road we're driving on. We're going right along this line."

Meg did not say anything.

"Mother, show me where we are right this minute," said Cynthia.

I took the atlas and pointed out the road through the mountains, and she took it back and showed it to Meg. "See where the road is all wiggly?" she said. "It's wiggly because there are so many turns in it. The wiggles are the turns." She flipped some pages and waited a moment. "Now," she said, "show me where we are." Then she called to me, "Mother, she understands! She pointed to it! Meg understands maps!"

It seems to me now that we invented characters for our children. We had them firmly set to play their parts. Cynthia was bright and diligent, sensitive, courteous, watchful. Sometimes we teased her for being too conscientious, too eager to be what we in fact depended on her to be. Any reproach or failure, any rebuff, went terribly deep with her. She was fair-haired, fair-skinned, easily showing the effects of the sun, raw winds, pride, or humiliation. Meg was more solidly built, more reticent—not rebellious but stubborn sometimes, mysterious. Her silences seemed to us to show her strength of character, and her negatives were taken as signs of an imperturbable independence. Her hair was brown, and we cut it in straight bangs. Her eyes were a light hazel, clear and dazzling.

We were entirely pleased with these characters, enjoying the contradictions as well as the confirmations of them. We disliked the heavy, the uninventive, approach to being parents. I had a dread of turning into a certain kind of mother—the kind whose body sagged, who moved in a woolly-smelling, milky-smelling fog, solemn with trivial burdens. I believed that all the attention these mothers paid, their need to be burdened, was the cause of colic, bed-wetting, asthma. I favored another approach—the mock desperation, the inflated irony of the professional mothers who wrote for magazines. In those magazine pieces, the children were splendidly self-willed, hard-edged, perverse, indomitable. So were the mothers, through their wit, indomitable. The real-life mothers I warmed to were the sort who would phone up and say, "Is my embryo Hitler by any chance over at your house?" They cackled clear above the milky fog.

We saw a dead deer strapped across the front of a pickup truck.

"Somebody shot it," Cynthia said. "Hunters shoot the deer."

"It's not hunting season yet," Andrew said. "They may have hit it on the road. See the sign for deer crossing?"

"I would cry if we hit one," Cynthia said sternly.

I had made peanut-butter-and-marmalade sandwiches for the children and salmon-and-mayonnaise for us. But I had not put any lettuce in, and Andrew was disappointed.

"I didn't have any," I said.

"Couldn't you have got some?"

"I'd have had to buy a whole head of lettuce just to get enough for sandwiches, and I decided it wasn't worth it."

This was a lie. I had forgotten.

"They're a lot better with lettuce."

"I didn't think it made that much difference." After a silence, I said, "Don't be mad."

"I'm not mad. I like lettuce on sandwiches."

"I just didn't think it mattered that much."

"How would it be if I didn't bother to fill up the gas tank?"

"That's not the same thing."

"Sing a song," said Cynthia. She started to sing:

> *"Five little ducks went out one day,*
> *Over the hills and far away.*
> *One little duck went*
> *'Quack-quack-quack.'*
> *Four little ducks came swimming*
> *back."*

Andrew squeezed my hand and said, "Let's not fight."

"You're right. I should have got lettuce."

"It doesn't matter that much."

I wished that I could get my feelings about Andrew to come together into a serviceable and dependable feeling. I had even tried writing two lists, one of things I liked about him, one of things I disliked—in the cauldron of intimate life, things I loved and things I hated—as if I hoped by this to prove something, to come to a conclusion one way or the other. But I gave it up when I saw that all it proved was what I already knew—that I had violent contradictions. Sometimes the very sound of his footsteps seemed to me tyrannical, the set of his mouth smug and mean, his hard, straight body a barrier interposed—quite consciously, even dutifully, and with a nasty pleasure in its masculine authority—between me and whatever joy or lightness I could get in life. Then, with not much warning, he became my good friend and most essential companion. I felt the sweetness of his light bones and serious ideas, the vulnerability of his love, which I imagined to be much purer and more straightforward than my own. I could be greatly moved by an inflexibility, a harsh propriety, that at other times I scorned. I would think how humble he was, really, taking on such a ready-made role of husband, father, breadwinner, and how I myself in comparison was really a secret monster of egotism. Not so secret, either—not from him.

At the bottom of our fights, we served up what we thought

were the ugliest truths. "I know there is something basically selfish and basically untrustworthy about you," Andrew once said. "I've always known it. I also know that that is why I fell in love with you."

"Yes," I said, feeling sorrowful but complacent.

"I know that I'd be better off without you."

"Yes. You would."

"You'd be happier without me."

"Yes."

And finally—finally—racked and purged, we clasped hands and laughed, laughed at those two benighted people, ourselves. Their grudges, their grievances, their self-justification. We leapfrogged over them. We declared them liars. We would have wine with dinner, or decide to give a party.

I haven't seen Andrew for years, don't know if he is still thin, has gone completely gray, insists on lettuce, tells the truth, or is hearty and disappointed.

We stayed the night in Wenatchee, Washington, where it hadn't rained for weeks. We ate dinner in a restaurant built about a tree—not a sapling in a tub but a tall, sturdy cottonwood. In the early-morning light, we climbed out of the irrigated valley, up dry, rocky, very steep hillsides that would seem to lead to more hills, and there on the top was a wide plateau, cut by the great Spokane and Columbia rivers. Grainland and grassland, mile after mile. There were straight roads here, and little farming towns with grain elevators. In fact, there was a sign announcing that this county we were going through, Douglas County, had the second-highest wheat yield of any county in the United States. The towns had planted shade trees. At least, I thought they had been planted, because there were no such big trees in the countryside.

All this was marvellously welcome to me. "Why do I love it so much?" I said to Andrew. "Is it because it isn't scenery?"

"It reminds you of home," said Andrew. "A bout of severe nostalgia." But he said this kindly.

When we said "home" and meant Ontario, we had very different places in mind. My home was a turkey farm, where my father lived as a widower, and though it was the same house my mother had lived in, had papered, painted, cleaned, furnished, it showed the effects now of neglect and of some wild sociability. A life went on in it that my mother could not have predicted or condoned. There were parties for the turkey crew, the gutters and pluckers, and sometimes one or two of the young men would be living there temporarily, inviting their own friends and having their own impromptu parties. This life, I thought, was better for my father than being lonely, and I did not disapprove, had certainly no right to disapprove. Andrew did not like to go there, naturally enough, because he was not the sort who could sit around the kitchen table with the turkey crew, telling jokes. They were intimidated by him and contemptuous of him, and it seemed to me that my father, when they were around, had to be on their side. And it wasn't only Andrew who had trouble. I could manage those jokes, but it was an effort.

I wished for the days when I was little, before we had the turkeys. We had cows, and sold the milk to the cheese factory. A turkey farm is nothing like as pretty as a dairy farm or a sheep farm. You can see that the turkeys are on a straight path to becoming frozen carcasses and table meat. They don't have the pretense of a life of their own, a browsing idyll, that cattle have, or pigs in the dappled orchard. Turkey barns are long, efficient buildings—tin sheds. No beams or hay or warm stables. Even the smell of guano seems thinner and more offensive than the usual smell of stable manure. No hints there of hay coils and rail fences and songbirds and the flowering hawthorn. The turkeys were all let out into one long field, which they picked clean. They didn't look like great birds there but like fluttering laundry.

Once, shortly after my mother died, and after I was married—in fact, I was packing to join Andrew in Vancouver—I was at home alone for a couple of days with my father. There was a freakishly heavy rain all night. In the early light, we saw that the turkey field was flooded. At least, the low-lying parts of it were flooded—it was like a lake with many islands. The turkeys were huddled on these islands. Turkeys are very stupid. (My father would say, "You know a chicken? You know how stupid a chicken is? Well, a chicken is an Einstein compared with a turkey.") But they had managed to crowd to higher ground and avoid drowning. Now they might push each other off, suffocate each other, get cold and die. We couldn't wait for the water to go down. We went out in an old rowboat we had. I rowed and my father pulled the heavy, wet turkeys into the boat and we took them to the barn. It was still raining a little. The job was difficult and absurd and very uncomfortable. We were laughing. I was happy to be working with my father. I felt close to all hard, repetitive, appalling work, in which the body is finally worn out, the mind sunk (though sometimes the spirit can stay marvellously light), and I was homesick in advance for this life and this place. I thought that if Andrew could see me there in the rain, red-handed, muddy, trying to hold on to turkey legs and row the boat at the same time, he would only want to get me out of there and make me forget about it. This raw life angered him. My attachment to it angered him. I thought that I shouldn't have married him. But who else? One of the turkey crew?

And I didn't want to stay there. I might feel bad about leaving, but I would feel worse if somebody made me stay.

Andrew's mother lived in Toronto, in an apartment building looking out on Muir Park. When Andrew and his sister were both at home, his mother slept in the living room. Her husband, a doctor, had died when the children were still too young to go to school. She took a secretarial course and sold her house at Depression prices, moved to this apartment, managed to raise her children, with some help from relatives—her sister Caroline, her brother-in-law Roger. Andrew and his sister went to private schools and to camp in the summer.

"I suppose that was courtesy of the Fresh Air fund?" I said once, scornful of his claim that he had been poor. To my mind, Andrew's urban life had been sheltered and fussy. His mother came home with a headache from working all day in the noise, the harsh light of a department-store office, but it did not occur to me that hers was a hard or admirable life. I don't think she herself believed that she was admirable—only unlucky. She worried about her work in the office, her clothes, her cooking, her children. She worried most of all about what Roger and Caroline would think.

Caroline and Roger lived on the east side of the park, in a handsome stone house. Roger was a tall man with a bald, freckled head, a fat, firm stomach. Some operation on his throat had deprived him of his voice—he spoke in a rough whisper. But everybody paid attention. At dinner once in the stone house—where all the dining-room furniture was enormous, darkly glowing, palatial—I asked him a question. I think it had to do with Whittaker Chambers, whose story was then appearing in the *Saturday Evening Post*. The question was mild in tone, but he guessed its subversive intent and took to calling me Mrs. Gromyko, referring to what he alleged to be my "sympathies." Perhaps he really craved an adversary, and could not find one. At that dinner, I saw Andrew's hand tremble as he lit his mother's cigarette. His Uncle Roger had paid for Andrew's education, and was on the board of directors of several companies.

"He is just an opinionated old man," Andrew said to me later. "What is the point of arguing with him?"

Before we left Vancouver, Andrew's mother had written, "Roger seems quite intrigued by the idea of your buying a small car!" Her exclamation mark showed apprehension. At that time, particularly in Ontario, the choice of a small European car over a large American car could be seen as some sort of declaration—a declaration of tendencies Roger had been sniffing after all long.

"It isn't that small a car," said Andrew huffily.

"That's not the point," I said. "The point is, it isn't any of his business!"

We spent the second night in Missoula. We had been told in Spokane, at a gas station, that there was a lot of repair work going on along Highway 2, and that we were in for a very hot, dusty drive, with long waits, so we turned onto the interstate and drove through Coeur d'Alene and Kellogg into Montana. After Missoula, we turned south toward Butte, but detoured to see Helena, the state capital. In the car, we played Who Am I?

Cynthia was somebody dead, and an American, and a girl.

Possibly a lady. She was not in a story. She had not been seen on television. Cynthia had not read about her in a book. She was not anybody who had come to the kindergarten, or a relative of any of Cynthia's friends.

"Is she human?" said Andrew, with a sudden shrewdness.

"No! That's what you forgot to ask!"

"An animal," I said reflectively.

"Is that a question? Sixteen questions!"

"No, it is not a question. I'm thinking. A dead animal."

"It's the deer," said Meg, who hadn't been playing.

"That's not fair!" said Cynthia. "She's not playing!"

"What deer?" said Andrew.

I said, "Yesterday."

"The day before," said Cynthia. "Meg wasn't playing. Nobody got it."

"The deer on the truck," said Andrew.

"It was a lady deer, because it didn't have antlers, and it was an American and it was dead," Cynthia said.

Andrew said, "I think it's kind of morbid, being a dead deer."

"I got it," said Meg.

Cynthia said, "I think I know what morbid is. It's depressing."

Helena, an old silver-mining town, looked forlorn to us even in the morning sunlight. Then Bozeman and Billings, not forlorn in the slightest—energetic, strung-out towns, with miles of blinding tinsel fluttering over used-car lots. We got too tired and hot even to play Who Am I? These busy, prosaic cities reminded me of similar places in Ontario, and I thought about what was really waiting there—the great tombstone furniture of Roger and Caroline's dining room, the dinners for which I must iron the children's dresses and warn them about forks, and then the other table a hundred miles away, the jokes of my father's crew. The pleasures I had been thinking of—looking at the countryside or drinking a Coke in an old-fashioned drugstore with fans and a high, pressed-tin ceiling—would have to be snatched in between.

"Meg's asleep," Cynthia said. "She's so hot. She makes me hot in the same seat with her."

"I hope she isn't feverish," I said, not turning around.

What are we doing this for, I thought, and the answer came—to show off. To give Andrew's mother and my father the pleasure of seeing their grandchildren. That was our duty. But beyond that we wanted to show them something. What strenuous children we were, Andrew and I, what relentless seekers of approbation. It was as if at some point we had received an unforgettable, indigestible message—that we were far from satisfactory, and that the most commonplace success in life was probably beyond us. Roger dealt out such messages, of course—that was his style—but Andrew's mother, my own mother and father couldn't have meant to do so. All they meant to tell us was "Watch out. Get along." My father, when I was in high school, teased me that I was getting to think I was so smart I would never find a boyfriend. He would have forgotten that in a week. I never forgot it. Andrew and I didn't forget things. We took umbrage.

"I wish there was a beach," said Cynthia.

"There probably is one," Andrew said. "Right around the next curve."

"There isn't any curve," she said, sounding insulted.

"That's what I mean."

"I wish there was some more lemonade."

"I will just wave my magic wand and produce some," I said. "Okay, Cynthia? Would you rather have grape juice? Will I do a beach while I'm at it?"

She was silent, and soon I felt repentant. "Maybe in the next town there might be a pool," I said. I looked at the map. "In Miles City. Anyway, there'll be something cool to drink."

"How far is it?" Andrew said.

"Not so far," I said. "Thirty miles, about."

"In Miles City," said Cynthia, in the tones of an incantation, "there is a beautiful blue swimming pool for children, and a park with lovely trees."

Andrew said to me, "You could have started something."

But there was a pool. There was a park, too, though not quite the oasis of Cynthia's fantasy. Prairie trees with thin leaves—cottonwoods and poplars—worn grass, and a high wire fence around the pool. Within this fence, a wall, not yet completed, of cement blocks. There were no shouts or splashes; over the entrance I saw a sign that said the pool was closed every day from noon until two o'clock. It was then twenty-five after twelve.

Nevertheless I called out, "Is anybody there?" I thought somebody must be around, because there was a small truck parked near the entrance. On the side of the truck were these words: "We have Brains, to fix your Drains. (We have Roto-Rooter too.)"

A girl came out, wearing a red lifeguard's shirt over her bathing suit. "Sorry, we're closed."

"We were just driving through," I said.

"We close every day from twelve until two. It's on the sign." She was eating a sandwich.

"I saw the sign," I said. "But this is the first water we've seen for so long, and the children are awfully hot, and I wondered if they could just dip in and out—just five minutes. We'd watch them."

A boy came into sight behind her. He was wearing jeans and a T-shirt with the words "Roto-Rooter" on it.

I was going to say that we were driving from British Columbia to Ontario, but I remembered that Canadian place names usually meant nothing to Americans. "We're driving right across the country," I said. "We haven't time to wait for the pool to open. We were just hoping the children could get cooled off."

Cynthia came running up barefoot behind me. "Mother. Mother, where is my bathing suit?" Then she stopped, sensing the serious adult negotiations. Meg was climbing out of the car—just wakened, with her top pulled up and her shorts pulled down, showing her pink stomach.

"Is it just those two?" the girl said.

"Just the two. We'll watch them."

"I can't let any adults in. If it's just the two, I guess I could watch them. I'm having my lunch." She said to Cynthia, "Do you want to come in the pool?"

"Yes, please," said Cynthia firmly.

Meg looked at the ground.

"Just a short time, because the pool is really closed," I said. "We appreciate this very much," I said to the girl.

"Well, I can eat my lunch out there, if it's just the two of them." She looked toward the car as if she thought I might try to spring some more children on her.

When I found Cynthia's bathing suit, she took it into the changing room. She would not permit anybody, even Meg, to see her naked. I changed Meg, who stood on the front seat of the car. She had a pink cotton bathing suit with straps that crossed and buttoned. There were ruffles across the bottom.

"She *is* hot," I said. "But I don't think she's feverish."

I loved helping Meg to dress or undress, because her body still had the solid unself-consciousness, the sweet indifference, something of the milky smell, of a baby's body. Cynthia's body had long ago been pared down, shaped and altered, into Cynthia. We all liked to hug Meg, press and nuzzle her. Sometimes she would scowl and beat us off, and this forthright independence, this ferocious bashfulness, simply made her more appealing, more apt to be tormented and tickled in the way of family love.

Andrew and I sat in the car with the windows open. I could hear a radio playing, and thought it must belong to the girl or her boyfriend. I was thirsty, and got out of the car to look for a concession stand, or perhaps a soft-drink machine, somewhere in the park. I was wearing shorts, and the backs of my legs were slick with sweat. I saw a drinking fountain at the other side of the park and was walking toward it in a roundabout way, keeping to the shade of the trees. No place became real till you got out of the car. Dazed with the heat, with the sun on the blistered houses, the pavement, the burned grass, I walked slowly. I paid attention to a squashed leaf, ground a Popsicle stick under the heel of my sandal, squinted at a trash can strapped to a tree. This is the way you look at the poorest details of the world resurfaced, after you've been driving for a long time—you feel their singleness and precise location and the forlorn coincidence of your being there to see them.

Where are the children?

I turned around and moved quickly, not quite running, to a

part of the fence beyond which the cement wall was not completed. I could see some of the pool. I saw Cynthia, standing about waist-deep in the water, fluttering her hands on the surface and discreetly watching something at the end of the pool, which I could not see. I thought by her pose, her discretion, the look on her face, that she must be watching some byplay between the lifeguard and her boyfriend. I couldn't see Meg. But I thought she must be playing in the shallow water—both the shallow and deep ends of the pool were out of my sight.

"Cynthia!" I had to call twice before she knew where my voice was coming from. "Cynthia! Where's Meg?"

It always seems to me, when I recall this scene, that Cynthia turns very gracefully toward me, then turns all around in the water—making me think of a ballerina on point—and spreads her arms in a gesture of the stage. "Dis-ap-peared!"

Cynthia was naturally graceful, and she did take dancing lessons, so these movements may have been as I have described. She did say "Disappeared" after looking all around the pool, but the strangely artificial style of speech and gesture, the lack of urgency, is more likely my invention. The fear I felt instantly when I couldn't see Meg—even while I was telling myself she must be in the shallower water—must have made Cynthia's movements seem unbearably slow and inappropriate to me, and the tone in which she could say "Disappeared" before the implications struck her (or was she covering, at once, some ever-ready guilt?) was heard by me as quite exquisitely, monstrously self-possessed.

I cried out for Andrew, and the lifeguard came into view. She was pointing toward the deep end of the pool, saying, "What's that?"

There, just within my view, a cluster of pink ruffles appeared, a bouquet, beneath the surface of the water. Why would a lifeguard stop and point, why would she ask what that was, why didn't she just dive into the water and swim to it? She didn't swim; she ran all the way around the edge of the pool. But by that time Andrew was over the fence. So many things seemed not quite plausible—Cynthia's behavior, then the lifeguard's—and now I had the impression that Andrew jumped with one bound over this fence, which seemed about seven feet high. He must have climbed it very quickly, getting a grip on the wire.

I could not jump or climb it, so I ran to the entrance, where there was a sort of lattice gate, locked. It was not very high, and I did pull myself over it. I ran through the cement corridors, through the disinfectant pool for your feet, and came out on the edge of the pool.

The drama was over.

Andrew had got to Meg first, and had pulled her out of the water. He just had to reach over and grab her, because she was swimming somehow, with her head underwater—she was moving toward the edge of the pool. He was carrying her now, and the lifeguard was trotting along behind. Cynthia had climbed out of the water and was running to meet them. The only person aloof from the situation was the boyfriend, who had stayed on the bench at the shallow end, drinking a milkshake. He smiled at me, and I thought that unfeeling of him, even though the danger was past. He may have meant it kindly. I noticed that he had not turned the radio off, just down.

Meg had not swallowed any water. She hadn't even scared herself. Her hair was plastered to her head and her eyes were wide open, golden with amazement.

"I was getting the comb," she said. "I didn't know it was deep."

Andrew said, "She was swimming! She was swimming by herself. I saw her bathing suit in the water and then I saw her swimming."

"She nearly drowned," Cynthia said. "Didn't she? Meg nearly drowned."

"I don't know how it could have happened," said the lifeguard. "One moment she was there, and the next she wasn't."

What had happened was that Meg had climbed out of the water at the shallow end and run along the edge of the pool toward the deep end. She saw a comb that somebody had dropped lying on the bottom. She crouched down and reached in to pick it up, quite deceived about the depth of the water. She went over the edge and slipped into the pool, making such a light splash that nobody heard—not the lifeguard, who was kissing her boyfriend, or Cynthia, who was watching them. That must have been the moment under the trees when I thought, Where are the children? It must have been the same moment. At that moment, Meg was slipping, surprised, into the treacherously clear blue water.

"It's okay," I said to the lifeguard, who was nearly crying. "She can move pretty fast." (Though that wasn't what we usually said about Meg at all. We said she thought everything over and took her time.)

"You swam, Meg," said Cynthia, in a congratulatory way. (She told us about the kissing later.)

"I didn't know it was deep," Meg said. "I didn't drown."

We had lunch at a take-out place, eating hamburgers and fries at a picnic table not far from the highway. In my excitement, I forgot to get Meg a plain hamburger, and had to scrape off the relish and mustard with plastic spoons, then wipe the meat with a paper napkin, before she would eat it. I took advantage of the trash can there to clean out the car. Then we resumed driving east, with the car windows open in front. Cynthia and Meg fell asleep in the back seat.

Andrew and I talked quietly about what had happened. Suppose I hadn't had the impulse just at that moment to check on the children? Suppose we had gone uptown to get drinks, as we had thought of doing? How had Andrew got over the fence? Did he jump or climb? (He couldn't remember.) How had he reached Meg so quickly? And think of the lifeguard not watching. And Cynthia, taken up with the kissing. Not seeing anything else. Not seeing Meg drop over the edge.

Disappeared.

But she swam. She held her breath and came up swimming.

What a chain of lucky links.

That was all we spoke about—luck. But I was compelled to picture the opposite. At this moment, we could have been filling out forms. Meg removed from us, Meg's body being prepared for shipment. To Vancouver—where we had never noticed such a thing as a graveyard—or to Ontario? The scribbled drawings she had made this morning would still be in the back seat of the car. How could this be borne all at once, how did people bear it? The plump, sweet shoulders and hands and feet, the fine brown hair, the rather satisfied, secretive expression—all exactly the same as when she had been alive. The most ordinary tragedy. A child drowned in a swimming pool at noon on a sunny day. Things tidied up quickly. The pool opens as usual at two o'clock. The lifeguard is a bit shaken up and gets the afternoon off. She drives away with her boyfriend in the Roto-Rooter truck. The body sealed away in some kind of shipping coffin. Sedatives, phone calls, arrangements. Such a sudden vacancy, a blind sinking and shifting. Waking up groggy from the pills, thinking for a moment it wasn't true. Thinking if only we hadn't stopped, if only we hadn't taken this route, if only they hadn't let us use the pool. Probably no one would ever have known about the comb.

There's something trashy about this kind of imagining, isn't there? Something shameful. Laying your finger on the wire to get the safe shock, feeling a bit of what it's like, then pulling back. I believed that Andrew was more scrupulous than I about such things, and that at this moment he was really trying to think about something else.

When I stood apart from my parents at Steve Gauley's funeral and watched them, and had this new, unpleasant feeling about them, I thought that I was understanding something about them for the first time. It was a deadly serious thing. I was understanding that they were implicated. Their big, stiff, dressed-up bodies did not stand between me and sudden death, or any kind of death. They gave consent. So it seemed. They gave consent to the death of children and to my death not by anything they said or thought but by the very fact that they had made children—they had made me. They had made me, and for that reason my death—however grieved they were, however they carried on—would seem to them anything but impossible or unnatural. This was a fact, and even then I knew they were not to blame.

But I did blame them. I charged them with effrontery, hypocrisy. On Steve Gauley's behalf, and on behalf of all children, who knew that by rights they should have sprung up free, to live a new, superior kind of life, not to be caught in the snares of vanquished grownups, with their sex and funerals.

Steve Gauley drowned, people said, because he was next thing to an orphan and was let run free. If he had been warned enough and given chores to do and kept in check, he wouldn't have fallen from an untrustworthy tree branch into a spring pond, a full gravel pit near the river—he wouldn't have drowned. He was neglected, he was free, so he drowned. And his father took it as an accident, such as might happen to a dog. He didn't have a good suit for the funeral, and he didn't bow his head for the prayers. But he was the only grownup that I let off the hook. He was the only one I didn't see giving consent. He couldn't prevent anything, but he wasn't implicated in anything, either—not like the others, saying the Lord's Prayer in their unnaturally weighted voices, oozing religion and dishonor.

At Glendive, not far from the North Dakota border, we had a choice—either to continue on the interstate or head northeast, toward Williston, taking Route 16, then some secondary roads that would get us back to Highway 2.

We agreed that the interstate would be faster, and that it was important for us not to spend too much time—that is, money—on the road. Nevertheless we decided to cut back to Highway 2.

"I just like the idea of it better," I said.

Andrew said, "That's because it's what we planned to do in the beginning."

"We missed seeing Kalispell and Havre. And Wolf Point. I like the name."

"We'll see them on the way back."

Andrew's saying "on the way back" was a surprising pleasure to me. Of course, I had believed that we would be coming back, with our car and our lives and our family intact, having covered all that distance, having dealt somehow with those loyalties and problems, held ourselves up for inspection in such a foolhardy way. But it was a relief to hear him say it.

"What I can't get over," said Andrew, "is how you got the signal. It's got to be some kind of extra sense that mothers have."

Partly I wanted to believe that, to bask in my extra sense. Partly I wanted to warn him—to warn everybody—never to count on it.

"What I can't understand," I said, "is how you got over the fence."

"Neither can I."

So we went on, with the two in the back seat trusting us, because of no choice, and we ourselves trusting to be forgiven, in time, for everything that had first to be seen and condemned by those children: whatever was flippant, arbitrary, careless, callous—all our natural, and particular, mistakes.

FITS

The two people who died were in their early sixties. They were both tall and well built, and carried a few pounds of extra weight. He was gray-haired, with a square, rather flat face. A broad nose kept him from looking perfectly dignified and handsome. Her hair was blond, a silvery blond that does not strike you as artificial anymore—though you know it is not natural—because so many women of that age have acquired it. On Boxing Day, when they dropped over to have a drink with Peg and Robert, she wore a pale-gray dress with a fine, shiny stripe in it, gray stockings, and gray shoes. She drank gin-and-tonic. He wore brown slacks and a cream-colored sweater, and drank rye-and-water. They had recently come back from a trip to Mexico. He had tried parachute-riding. She hadn't wanted to. They had gone to see a place in Yucatán—it looked like a well—where virgins were supposed to have been flung down, in the hope of good harvests.

"Actually, though, that's just a nineteenth-century notion," she said. "That's just the nineteenth-century notion of being so preoccupied with virginity. The truth probably is that they threw people down sort of indiscriminately. Girls or men or old people or whoever they could get their hands on. So not being a virgin would be no guarantee of safety!"

Across the room, Peg's two sons—the older one, Clayton, who was a virgin, and the younger one, Kevin, who was not—watched this breezy-talking silvery-blond woman with stern, bored expressions. She had said that she used to be a high-school English teacher. Clayton remarked afterward that he knew the type.

Robert and Peg have been married for nearly five years. Robert was never married before, but Peg married for the first time when she was eighteen. Her two boys were born while she and her husband lived with his parents on a farm. Her husband had a job driving trucks of livestock to the Canada Packers Abattoir in Toronto. Other truck-driving jobs followed, taking him farther and farther away. Peg and the boys moved to Gilmore, and she got a job working in Kuiper's store, which was called the Gilmore Arcade. Her husband ended up in the Arctic, driving trucks to oil rigs across the frozen Beaufort Sea. She got a divorce.

Robert's family owned the Gilmore Arcade but had never lived in Gilmore. His mother and sisters would not have believed you could survive a week in such a place. Robert's father had bought the store, and two other stores in nearby towns, shortly after the Second World War. He hired local managers, and drove up from Toronto a few times during the year to see how things were getting on.

For a long time, Robert did not take much interest in his father's various businesses. He took a degree in civil engineering, and had some idea of doing work in underdeveloped countries. He got a job in Peru, travelled through South America, gave up engineering for a while to work on a ranch in British Columbia. When his father became ill, it was necessary for him to come back to Toronto. He worked for the Provincial Department of Highways, in an engineering job that was not a very good one for a man of his age. He was thinking of getting a teaching degree and maybe going up North to teach Indians, changing his life completely, once his father died. He was getting close to forty then, and having his third major affair with a married woman.

Now and then, he drove up to Gilmore and the other towns to keep an eye on the stores. Once, he brought Lee with him, his third—and, as it turned out, his last—married woman. She brought a picnic lunch, drank Pimm's Number 1 in the car, and treated the whole trip as a merry excursion, a foray into hillbilly country. She had counted on making love in the open fields, and was incensed to find they were all full of cattle or uncomfortable cornstalks.

Robert's father died, and Robert did change his life, but instead of becoming a teacher and heading for the wilderness, he came to live in Gilmore to manage the stores himself. He married Peg.

It was entirely by accident that Peg was the one who found them.

On Sunday evening, the farm woman who sold the Kuipers their eggs knocked on the door.

"I hope you don't mind me bringing these tonight instead of tomorrow morning," she said. "I have to take my daughter-in-law to Kitchener to have her ultrasound. I brought the Weebles theirs, too, but I guess they're not home. I wonder if you'd mind if I left them here with you? I have to leave early in the morning. She was going to drive herself but I didn't think that was such a good idea. She's nearly five months but still vomiting. Tell them they can just pay me next time."

"No problem," said Robert. "No trouble at all. We can just run over with them in the morning. No problem at all!" Robert is a stocky, athletic-looking man, with curly, graying hair and bright brown eyes. His friendliness and obligingness are often emphatic, so that people might get the feeling of being buffeted from all sides. This is a manner that serves him well in Gilmore, where assurances are supposed to be repeated, and in fact much of conversation is repetition, a sort of dance of good intentions, without surprises. Just occasionally, talking to people, he feels something else, an obstruction, and isn't sure what it is (malice, stubbornness?) but it's like a rock at the bottom of a river when you're swimming—the clear water lifts you over it.

For a Gilmore person, Peg is reserved. She came up to the woman and relieved her of the eggs she was holding, while Robert went on assuring her it was no trouble and asking about the daughter-in-law's pregnancy. Peg smiled as she would smile in the store when she gave you your change—a quick transactional smile, nothing personal. She is a small slim woman with a cap of soft brown hair, freckles, and a scrubbed, youthful look. She wears pleated skirts, fresh neat blouses buttoned to the throat, pale sweaters, sometimes a black ribbon tie. She moves gracefully and makes very little noise. Robert once told her he had never met anyone so self-contained as she was. (His women have usually been talkative, stylishly effective, though careless about some of the details, tense, lively, "interesting.")

Peg said she didn't know what he meant.

He started to explain what a self-contained person was like. At that time, he had a very faulty comprehension of Gilmore vocabulary—he could still make mistakes about it—and he took too seriously the limits that were usually observed in daily exchanges.

"I know what the words mean," Peg said, smiling. "I just don't understand how you mean it about me."

Of course she knew what the words meant. Peg took courses, a different course each winter, choosing from what was offered at the local high school. She took a course on the History of Art, one on Great Civilizations of the East, one on Discoveries and Explorations Through the Ages. She went to class one night a week, even if she was very tired or had a cold. She wrote tests and prepared papers. Sometimes Robert would find a page covered with her small neat handwriting on top of the refrigerator or the dresser in their room.

Therefore we see that the importance of Prince Henry the Navigator was in the inspiration and encouragement of other explorers for Portugal, even though he did not go on voyages himself.

He was moved by her earnest statements, her painfully careful small handwriting, and angry that she never got more than a B-plus for these papers she worked so hard at.

"I don't do it for the marks," Peg said. Her cheekbones reddened under the freckles, as if she was making some kind of personal confession. "I do it for the enjoyment."

Robert was up before dawn on Monday morning, standing at the kitchen counter drinking his coffee, looking out at the fields covered with snow. The sky was clear, and the temperatures had dropped. It was going to be one of the bright, cold, hard January days that come after weeks of west wind, of blowing and falling snow. Creeks, rivers, ponds frozen over. Lake Huron frozen over as far as you could see. Perhaps all the way this year. That had happened, though rarely.

He had to drive to Keneally, to the Kuiper store there. Ice on the roof was causing water underneath to back up and leak through the ceiling. He would have to chop up the ice and get the roof clear. It would take him at least half the day.

All the repair work and upkeep on the store and on this house is done by Robert himself. He has learned to do plumbing and wiring. He enjoys the feeling that he can manage it. He enjoys the difficulty, and the difficulty of winter, here. Not much more than a hundred miles from Toronto, it is a different country. The snowbelt. Coming up here to live was not unlike heading into the wilderness, after all. Blizzards still isolate the towns and villages. Winter comes down hard on the country, settles down just the way the two-mile-high ice did thousands of years ago. People live within the winter in a way outsiders do not understand. They are watchful, provident, fatigued, exhilarated.

A thing he likes about this house is the back view, over the open country. That makes up for the straggling dead-end street without trees or sidewalks. The street was opened up after the war, when it was taken for granted that everybody would be using cars, not walking anywhere. And so they did. The houses are fairly close to the street and to each other, and when everybody who lives in the houses is home, cars take up nearly all the space where sidewalks, boulevards, shade trees might have been.

Robert, of course, was willing to buy another house. He assumed they would do that. There were—there are—fine old houses for sale in Gilmore, at prices that are a joke, by city standards. Peg said she couldn't see herself living in those places. He offered to build her a new house in the subdivision on the other side of town. She didn't want that either. She wanted to stay in this house, which was the first house she and the boys had lived in on their own. So Robert bought it—she was only renting—and built on the master bedroom and another bathroom, and made a television room in the basement. He got some help from Kevin, less from Clayton. The house still looked, from the street, like the house he had parked in front of the first time he drove Peg home from work. One and a half stories high, with a steep roof and a living-room window divided into square panes like the window on a Christmas card. White aluminum siding, narrow black shutters, black trim. Back in Toronto, he had thought of Peg living in this house. He had thought of her patterned, limited, serious, and desirable life.

He noticed the Weebles' eggs sitting on the counter. He thought of taking them over. But it was too early. The door would be locked. He didn't want to wake them. Peg could take the eggs when she left to open up the store. He took the Magic Marker that was sitting on the ledge under her reminder pad, and wrote on a paper towel, *Don't forget eggs to W's. Love, Robert*. These eggs were no cheaper than the ones you bought at the supermarket. It was just that Robert liked getting them from a farm. And they were brown. Peg said city people all had a thing about brown eggs—they thought brown eggs were more natural somehow, like brown sugar.

When he backed his car out, he saw that the Weebles' car was in their carport. So they were home from wherever they had been last night. Then he saw that the snow thrown up across the front of their driveway by the town snowplow had not been cleared. The plow must have gone by during the night. But he himself hadn't had to shovel any snow; there hadn't been any fresh snow overnight and the plow hadn't been out. The snow was from yesterday. They couldn't have been out last night. Unless they were walking. The sidewalks were not cleared, except along the main street and the school streets, and it was difficult to walk along the narrowed streets with their banks of snow, but, being new to town, they might have set out not realizing that.

He didn't look closely enough to see if there were footprints.

He pictured what happened. First from the constable's report, then from Peg's.

Peg came out of the house at about twenty after eight. Clayton had already gone off to school, and Kevin, getting over an ear infection, was down in the basement room playing a Billy Idol tape and watching a game show on television. Peg had not forgotten the eggs. She got into her car and turned on the engine to warm it up, then walked out to the street, stepped over the Weebles' uncleared snow, and went up their driveway to the side door. She was wearing her white knitted scarf and tam and her lilac-colored, down-filled coat. Those coats made most of the women in Gilmore look like barrels, but Peg looked all right, being so slender.

The houses on the street were originally of only three designs. But by now most of them had been so altered, with new windows, porches, wings, and decks, that it was hard to find true mates anymore. The Weebles' house had been built as a mirror image of the Kuipers', but the front window had been changed, its Christmas-card panes taken out, and the roof had been lifted, so that there was a large upstairs window overlooking the street. The siding was pale green and the trim white, and there were no shutters.

The side door opened into a utility room, just as Peg's door did at home. She knocked lightly at first, thinking that they would be in the kitchen, which was only a few steps up from the utility room. She had noticed the car, of course, and wondered if they had got home late and were sleeping in. (She hadn't thought yet about the snow's not having been shovelled, and the fact that the plow hadn't been past in the night. That was something that occurred to her later on when she got into her own car and backed it out.) She knocked louder and louder. Her face was stinging already in the bright cold. She tried the door and found that it wasn't locked. She opened it and stepped into shelter and called.

The little room was dark. There was no light to speak of coming down from the kitchen, and there was a bamboo curtain over the side door. She set the eggs on the clothes dryer, and was going to leave them there. Then she thought she had better take them up into the kitchen, in case the Weebles wanted eggs for breakfast and had run out. They wouldn't think of looking in the utility room.

(This, in fact, was Robert's explanation to himself. She didn't say all that, but he forgot she didn't. She just said, "I thought I might as well take them up to the kitchen.")

The kitchen had those same bamboo curtains over the sink window and over the breakfast-nook windows, which meant that though the room faced east, like the Kuipers' kitchen, and though the sun was fully up by this time, not much light could get in. The day hadn't begun here.

But the house was warm. Perhaps they'd got up a while ago and turned up the thermostat, then gone back to bed. Perhaps they left it up all night—though they had seemed to Peg to be thriftier than that. She set the eggs on the counter by the sink. The layout of the kitchen was almost exactly the same as her own. She noticed a few dishes stacked, rinsed, but not washed, as if they'd had something to eat before they went to bed.

She called again from the living-room doorway.

The living room was perfectly tidy. It looked to Peg somehow too perfectly tidy, but that—as she said to Robert—was probably the way the living room of a retired couple was bound to look to a woman used to having children around. Peg had never in her life had quite as much tidiness around her as she might have liked, having gone from a family home where there were six children to her in-laws' crowded farmhouse, which she crowded further with her own babies. She had told Robert a story about once asking for a beautiful bar of soap for Christmas, pink soap with a raised design of roses on it. She got it, and she used to hide it after every use so that it wouldn't get cracked and moldy in the cracks, the way soap always did in that house. She was grown up at that time, or thought she was.

She had stamped the snow off her boots in the utility room. Nevertheless she hesitated to walk across the clean, pale-beige living-room carpet. She called again. She used the Weebles' first names, which she barely knew. Walter and Nora. They had moved in last April, and since then they had been away on two trips, so she didn't feel she knew them at all well, but it seemed silly to be calling, "Mr. and Mrs. Weeble. Are you up yet, Mr. and Mrs. Weeble?"

No answer.

They had an open staircase going up from the living room, just as Peg and Robert did. Peg walked now across the clean, pale carpet to the foot of the stairs, which were carpeted in the same material. She started to climb. She did not call again.

She must have known then or she would have called. It would be the normal thing to do, to keep calling the closer you got to where people might be sleeping. To warn them. They might be deeply asleep. Drunk. That wasn't the custom of the Weebles, so far as anybody knew, but nobody knew them that well. Retired people. Early retirement. He had been an accountant; she had been a teacher. They had lived in Hamilton. They had chosen Gilmore because Walter Weeble used to have an aunt and uncle here, whom he visited as a child. Both dead now, the aunt and uncle, but the place must have held pleasant memories for him. And it was cheap; this was surely a cheaper house than they could have afforded. They meant to spend their money travelling. No children.

She didn't call; she didn't halt again. She climbed the stairs and didn't look around as she came up; she faced straight ahead. Ahead was the bathroom, with the door open. It was clean and empty.

She turned at the top of the stairs toward the Weebles' bedroom. She had never been upstairs in this house before, but she knew where that would be. It would be the extended room at the front, with the wide window overlooking the street.

The door of that room was open.

Peg came downstairs and left the house by the kitchen, the utility room, the side door. Her footprints showed on the carpet and on the linoleum tiles, and outside on the snow. She closed the door after herself. Her car had been running all this time and was sitting in its own little cloud of steam. She got in and backed out and drove to the police station in the Town Hall.

"It's a bitter cold morning, Peg," the constable said.

"Yes, it is."

"So what can I do for you?"

. . .

Robert got more, from Karen.

Karen Adams was the clerk in the Gilmore Arcade. She was a young married woman, solidly built, usually good-humored, alert without particularly seeming to be so, efficient without a lot of bustle. She got along well with the customers; she got along with Peg and Robert. She had known Peg longer, of course. She defended her against those people who said Peg had got her nose in the air since she married rich. Karen said Peg hadn't changed from what she always was. But after today she said, "I always believed Peg and me to be friends, but now I'm not so sure."

Karen started work at ten. She arrived a little before that and asked if there had been many customers in yet, and Peg said no, nobody.

"I don't wonder," Karen said. "It's too cold. If there was any wind, it'd be murder."

Peg had made coffee. They had a new coffee maker, Robert's Christmas present to the store. They used to have to get take-outs from the bakery up the street.

"Isn't this thing marvellous?" Karen said as she got her coffee.

Peg said yes. She was wiping up some marks on the floor.

"Oh-oh," said Karen. "Was that me or you?"

"I think it was me," Peg said.

"So I didn't think anything of it," Karen said later. "I thought she must've tracked in some mud. I didn't stop to think, Where would you get down to mud with all this snow on the ground?"

After a while, a customer came in, and it was Celia Simms, and she had heard. Karen was at the cash, and Peg was at the back, checking some invoices. Celia told Karen. She didn't know much; she didn't know how it had been done or that Peg was involved.

Karen shouted to the back of the store. "Peg! Peg! Something terrible has happened, and it's your next-door neighbors!"

Peg called back, "I know."

Celia lifted her eyebrows at Karen—she was one of those who didn't like Peg's attitude—and Karen loyally turned aside and waited till Celia went out of the store. Then she hurried to the back, making the hangers jingle on the racks.

"Both the Weebles are shot dead, Peg. Did you know that?"

Peg said, "Yes. I found them."

"You did! When did you?"

"This morning, just before I came in to work."

"They were murdered!"

"It was a murder-suicide," Peg said. "He shot her and then he shot himself. That's what happened."

"When she told me that," Karen said, "I started to shake. I shook all over and I couldn't stop myself." Telling Robert this, she shook again, to demonstrate, and pushed her hands up inside the sleeves of her blue plush jogging suit.

"So I said, 'What did you do when you found them,' and she said, 'I went and told the police.' I said, 'Did you scream, or what?' I said didn't her legs buckle, because I know mine would've. I can't imagine how I would've got myself out of there. She said she didn't remember much about getting out, but she did remember closing the door, the outside door, and thinking, Make sure that's closed in case some dog could get in. Isn't that awful? She was right, but it's awful to think of. Do you think she's in shock?"

"No," Robert said. "I think she's all right."

This conversation was taking place at the back of the store in the afternoon, when Peg had gone out to get a sandwich.

"She had not said one word to me. Nothing. I said, 'How come you never said a word about this, Peg,' and she said, 'I knew you'd find out pretty soon.' I said yes, but she could've told me. 'I'm sorry,' she says. 'I'm sorry.' Just like she's apologizing for some little thing like using my coffee mug. Only, Peg would never do that."

Robert had finished what he was doing at the Keneally store around noon, and decided to drive back to Gilmore before getting anything to eat. There was a highway diner just outside of town, on the way in from Keneally, and he thought that he would stop there. A few truckers and travellers were usually eating in the diner, but most of the trade was local—farmers on the way home, business and working men who had driven out from town. Robert liked this place, and he had entered it today with a feeling of buoyant expectation. He was hungry from his work in the cold air, and aware of the brilliance of the day, with the snow on the fields looking sculpted, dazzling, as permanent as marble. He had the sense he had fairly often in Gilmore, the sense of walking onto an informal stage, where a rambling, agreeable play was in progress. And he knew his lines—or knew, at least, that his improvisations would not fail. His whole life in Gilmore sometimes seemed to have this quality, but if he ever tried to describe it that way, it would sound as if it was an artificial life, something contrived, not entirely serious. And the very opposite was true. So when he met somebody from his old life, as he sometimes did when he went to Toronto, and was asked how he liked living in Gilmore, he would say, "I can't tell you how much I like it!" which was exactly the truth.

"Why didn't you get in touch with me?"

"You were up on the roof."

"You could have called the store and told Ellie. She would have told me."

"What good would that have done?"

"I could at least have come home."

He had come straight from the diner to the store, without eating what he had ordered. He did not think he would find Peg in any state of collapse—he knew her well enough for that—but he did think she would want to go home, let him fix her a drink, spend some time telling him about it.

She didn't want that. She wanted to go up the street to the bakery to get her usual lunch—a roll with ham and cheese.

"I let Karen go out to eat, but I haven't had time. Should I bring one back for you? If you didn't eat at the diner, I might as well."

When she brought him the sandwich, he sat and ate it at the desk where she had been doing invoices. She put fresh coffee and water into the coffee maker.

"I can't imagine how we got along without this thing."

He looked at Peg's lilac-colored coat hanging beside Karen's red coat on the washroom door. On the lilac coat there was a long crusty smear of reddish-brown paint, down to the hemline.

Of course that wasn't paint. But on her coat? How did she get blood on her coat? She must have brushed up against them in that room. She must have got close.

Then he remembered the talk in the diner, and realized she wouldn't have needed to get that close. She could have got blood from the door frame. The constable had been in the diner, and he said there was blood everywhere, and not just blood.

"He shouldn't ever have used a shotgun for that kind of business," one of the men at the diner said.

Somebody else said, "Maybe a shotgun was all he had."

It was busy in the store most of the afternoon. People on the street, in the bakery and the café and the bank and the post office, talking. People wanted to talk face to face. They had to get out and do it, in spite of the cold. Talking on the phone was not enough.

What had gone on at first, Robert gathered, was that people had got on the phone, just phoned anybody they could think of who might not have heard. Karen had phoned her friend Shirley, who was at home in bed with the flu, and her mother, who was in the hospital with a broken hip. It turned out her mother knew already—the whole hospital knew. And Shirley said, "My sister beat you to it."

It was true that people valued and looked forward to the moment of breaking the news—Karen was annoyed at Shirley's sister, who didn't work and could get to the phone whenever she wanted to—but there was real kindness and consideration behind this impulse, as well. Robert thought so. "I knew she wouldn't want not to know," Karen said, and that was true. Nobody would want not to know. To go out into the street, not knowing. To go around doing all the usual daily things, not knowing. He himself felt troubled, even slightly humiliated, to think that he hadn't known; Peg hadn't let him know.

Talk ran backward from the events of the morning. Where were the Weebles seen, and in what harmlessness and innocence, and how close to the moment when everything was changed?

She had stood in line at the Bank of Montreal on Friday afternoon.

He had got a haircut on Saturday morning.

They were together, buying groceries, in the I.G.A. on Friday evening at about eight o'clock.

What did they buy? A good supply? Specials, advertised bargains, more than enough to last for a couple of days?

More than enough. A bag of potatoes, for one thing.

Then reasons. The talk turned to reasons. Naturally. There had been no theories put forward in the diner. Nobody knew the reason, nobody could imagine. But by the end of the afternoon there were too many explanations to choose from.

Financial problems. He had been mixed up in some bad investment scheme in Hamilton. Some wild money-making deal that had fallen through. All their money was gone and they would have to live out the rest of their lives on the old-age pension.

They had owed money on their income taxes. Being an accountant, he thought he know how to fix things, but he had been found out. He would be exposed, perhaps charged, shamed publicly, left poor. Even if it was only cheating the government, it would still be a disgrace when that kind of thing came out.

Was it a lot of money?

Certainly. A lot.

It was not money at all. They were ill. One of them or both of them. Cancer. Crippling arthritis. Alzheimer's disease. Recurrent mental problems. It was health, not money. It was suffering and helplessness they feared, not poverty.

A division of opinion became evident between men and women. It was nearly always the men who believed and insisted that the trouble had been money, and it was the women who talked of illness. Who would kill themselves just because they were poor, said some women scornfully. Or even because they might go to jail? It was always a woman, too, who suggested unhappiness in the marriage, who hinted at the drama of a discovered infidelity or the memory of an old one.

Robert listened to all these explanations but did not believe any of them. Loss of money, cancer, Alzheimer's disease. Equally plausible, these seemed to him, equally hollow and useless. What happened was that he believed each of them for about five minutes, no longer. If he could have believed one of them, hung on to it, it would have been as if something had taken its claws out of his chest and permitted him to breathe.

("They weren't Gilmore people, not really," a woman said to him in the bank. Then she looked embarrassed. "I don't mean like you.")

Peg kept busy getting some children's sweaters, mitts, snowsuits ready for the January sale. People came up to her when she was marking the tags, and she said, "Can I help you," so that they were placed right away in the position of being customers, and had to say that there was something they were looking for. The Arcade carried ladies' and children's clothes, sheets, towels, knitting wool, kitchenware, bulk candy, magazines, mugs, artificial flowers, and plenty of other things besides, so it was not hard to think of something.

What was it they were really looking for? Surely not much in the way of details, description. Very few people actually want that, or will admit they do, in a greedy and straightforward way. They want it, they don't want it. They start asking, they stop themselves. They listen and they back away. Perhaps they wanted from Peg just some kind of acknowledgment, some word or look that would send them away, saying, "Peg Kuiper is absolutely shattered." "I saw Peg Kuiper. She didn't say much but you could tell she was absolutely shattered."

Some people tried to talk to her, anyway.

"Wasn't that terrible what happened down by you?"

"Yes, it was."

"You must have known them a little bit, living next door."

"Not really. We hardly knew them at all."

"You never noticed anything that would've led you to think this could've happened?"

"We never noticed anything at all."

Robert pictured the Weebles getting into and out of their car in the driveway. That was where he had most often seen them. He recalled their Boxing Day visit. Her gray legs made him think of a nun. Her mention of virginity had embarrassed Peg and the boys. She reminded Robert a little of the kind of women he used to know. Her husband was less talkative, though not shy. They talked about Mexican food, which it seemed the husband had not liked. He did not like eating in restaurants.

Peg had said, "Oh, men never do!"

That surprised Robert, who asked her afterward did that mean she wanted to eat out more often?

"I just said that to take her side. I thought he was glaring at her a bit."

Was he glaring? Robert had not noticed. The man seemed too self-controlled to glare at his wife in public. Too well disposed, on the whole, perhaps in some way too indolent, to glare at anybody anywhere.

But it wasn't like Peg to exaggerate.

Bits of information kept arriving. The maiden name of Nora Weeble. Driscoll. Nora Driscoll. Someone knew a woman who had taught at the same school with her in Hamilton. Well-liked as a teacher, a fashionable dresser, she had some trouble keeping order. She had taken a French Conversation course, and a course in French cooking.

Some women here had asked her if she'd be interested in starting a book club, and she had said yes.

He had been more of a joiner in Hamilton than he was here. The Rotary Club. The Lions Club. Perhaps it had been for business reasons.

They were not churchgoers, as far as anybody knew, not in either place.

(Robert was right about the reasons. In Gilmore everything becomes known, sooner or later. Secrecy and confidentiality are seen to be against the public interest. There is a network of people who are married to or related to the people who work in the offices where all the records are kept.

There was no investment scheme, in Hamilton or anywhere else. No income-tax investigation. No problem about money. No cancer, tricky heart, high blood pressure. She had consulted the doctor about headaches, but the doctor did not think they were migraines, or anything serious.

At the funeral on Thursday, the United church minister, who usually took up the slack in the cases of no known affiliation, spoke about the pressures and tensions of modern life but gave no more specific clues. Some people were disappointed, as if they expected him to do that—or thought that he might at least mention the dangers of falling away from faith and church membership, the sin of despair. Other people thought that saying anything more than he did say would have been in bad taste.)

Another person who thought Peg should have let him know was Kevin. He was waiting for them when they got home. He was still wearing his pajamas.

Why hadn't she come back to the house instead of driving to the police station? Why hadn't she called to him? She could have come back and phoned. Kevin could have phoned. At the very least, she could have called him from the store.

He had been down in the basement all morning, watching television. He hadn't heard the police come; he hadn't seen them go in or out. He had not known anything about what was going on until his girlfriend, Shanna, phoned him from school at lunch hour.

"She said they took the bodies out in garbage bags."

"How would she know?" said Clayton. "I thought she was at school."

"Somebody told her."

"She got that from television."

"She *said* they took them out in garbage bags."

"Shanna is a cretin. She is only good for one thing."

"Some people aren't good for anything."

Clayton was sixteen, Kevin fourteen. Two years apart in age but three years apart at school, because Clayton was accelerated and Kevin was not.

"Cut it out," Peg said. She had brought up some spaghetti

sauce from the freezer and was thawing it in the double boiler. "Clayton. Kevin. Get busy and make me some salad."

Kevin said, "I'm sick. I might contaminate it."

He picked up the tablecloth and wrapped it around his shoulders like a shawl.

"Do we have to eat off that?" Clayton said. "Now he's got his crud on it?"

Peg said to Robert, "Are we having wine?"

Saturday and Sunday nights they usually had wine, but tonight Robert had not thought about it. He went down to the basement to get it. When he came back, Peg was sliding spaghetti into the cooker and Kevin had discarded the tablecloth. Clayton was making the salad. Clayton was small-boned, like his mother, and fiercely driven. A star runner, a demon examination writer.

Kevin was prowling around the kitchen, getting in the way, talking to Peg. Kevin was taller already than Clayton or Peg, perhaps taller than Robert. He had large shoulders and skinny legs and black hair that he wore in the nearest thing he dared to a Mohawk cut—Shanna cut it for him. His pale skin often broke out in pimples. Girls didn't seem to mind.

"So was there?" Kevin said. "Was there blood and guck all over?"

"Ghoul," said Clayton.

"Those were human beings, Kevin," Robert said.

"Were," said Kevin. "I know they *were* human beings. I mixed their drinks on Boxing Day. She drank gin and he drank rye. They were human beings then, but all they are now is chemicals. Mom? What did you see first? Shanna said there was blood and guck even out in the hallway."

"He's brutalized from all the TV he watches," Clayton said. "He thinks it was some video. He can't tell real blood from video blood."

"Mom? Was it splashed?"

Robert has a rule about letting Peg deal with her sons unless she asks for his help. But this time he said, "Kevin, you know it's about time you shut up."

"He can't help it," Clayton said. "Being ghoulish."

"You, too, Clayton. You, too."

But after a moment Clayton said, "Mom? Did you scream?"

"No," said Peg thoughtfully. "I didn't. I guess because there wasn't anybody to hear me. So I didn't."

"I might have heard you," said Kevin, cautiously trying a comeback.

"You had the television on."

"I didn't have the sound on. I had my tape on. I might have heard you through the tape if you screamed loud enough."

Peg lifted a strand of the spaghetti to try it. Robert was watching her, from time to time. He would have said he was watching to see if she was in any kind of trouble, if she seemed numb, or strange, or showed a quiver, if she dropped things or made the pots clatter. But in fact he was watching her just because there was no sign of such difficulty and because he knew there wouldn't be. She was preparing an ordinary meal, listening to the boys in her usual mildly censorious but unruffled way. The only thing more apparent than usual to Robert was her gracefulness, lightness, quickness, and ease around the kitchen.

Her tone to her sons, under its severity, seemed shockingly serene.

"Kevin, go and get some clothes on, if you want to eat at the table."

"I can eat in my pajamas."

"No."

"I can eat in bed."

"Not spaghetti, you can't."

While they were washing up the pots and pans together—Clayton had gone for his run and Kevin was talking to Shanna on the phone—Peg told Robert her part of the story. He didn't ask her to, in so many words. He started off with "So when you went over, the door wasn't locked?" and she began to tell him.

"You don't mind talking about it?" Robert said.

"I knew you'd want to know."

She told him she knew what was wrong—at least, she knew that something was terribly wrong—before she started up the stairs.

"Were you frightened?"

"No. I didn't think about it like that—being frightened."

"There could have been somebody up there with a gun."

"No. I knew there wasn't. I knew there wasn't anybody but me alive in the house. Then I saw his leg, I saw his leg stretched out into the hall, and I knew then, but I had to go on in and make sure."

Robert said, "I understand that."

"It wasn't the foot he had taken the shoe off that was out there. He took the shoe off his other foot, so he could use that foot to pull the trigger when he shot himself. That was how he did it."

Robert knew all about that already, from the talk in the diner.

"So," said Peg. "That's really about all."

She shook dishwater from her hands, dried them, and, with a critical look, began rubbing in lotion.

Clayton came in at the side door. He stamped the snow from his shoes and ran up the steps.

"You should see the cars," he said. "Stupid cars all crawling along this street. Then they have to turn around at the end and crawl back. I wish they'd get stuck. I stood out there and gave them dirty looks, but I started to freeze so I had to come in."

"It's natural," Robert said. "It seems stupid but it's natural. They can't believe it, so they want to see where it happened."

"I don't see their problem," Clayton said. "I don't see why they can't believe it. Mom could believe it all right. Mom wasn't surprised."

"Well, of course I was," Peg said, and this was the first time Robert had noticed any sort of edge to her voice. "Of course I was surprised, Clayton. Just because I didn't break out screaming."

"You weren't surprised they could do it."

"I hardly knew them. We hardly knew the Weebles."

"I guess they had a fight," said Clayton.

"We don't know that," Peg said, stubbornly working the lotion into her skin. "We don't know if they had a fight, or what."

"When you and Dad used to have those fights?" Clayton said. "Remember, after we first moved to town? When he would be home? Over by the car wash? When you used to have those fights, you know what I used to think? I used to think one of you was going to come and kill me with a knife."

"That's not true," said Peg.

"It is true. I did."

Peg sat down at the table and covered her mouth with her hands. Clayton's mouth twitched. He couldn't seem to stop it, so he turned it into a little, taunting, twitching smile.

"That's what I used to lie in bed and think."

"Clayton. We would never either one of us ever have hurt you."

Robert believed it was time that he said something.

"What this is like," he said, "it's like an earthquake or a volcano. It's that kind of happening. It's a kind of fit. People can take a fit like the earth takes a fit. But it only happens once in a long while. It's a freak occurrence."

"Earthquakes and volcanoes aren't freaks," said Clayton, with a certain dry pleasure. "If you want to call that a fit, you'd have to call it a periodic fit. Such as people have, married people have."

"We don't," said Robert. He looked at Peg as if waiting for her to agree with him.

But Peg was looking at Clayton. She who always seemed pale and silky and assenting, but hard to follow as a watermark in fine paper, looked dried out, chalky, her outlines fixed in steady, helpless, unapologetic pain.

"No," said Clayton. "No, not you."

Robert told them that he was going for a walk. When he got outside, he saw that Clayton was right. There were cars nosing along the street, turning at the end, nosing their way back again. Getting a look. Inside those cars were just the same people, probably the very same people, he had been talking to during the afternoon. But now they seemed joined to their cars, making some new kind of monster that came poking around in a brutally curious way.

To avoid them, he went down a short dead-end street that branched off theirs. No houses had ever been built on this street, so it was not plowed. But the snow was hard, and easy to walk on. He didn't notice how easy it was to walk on until he realized that he had gone beyond the end of the street and up a slope, which was not a slope of the land at all, but a drift of snow. The drift neatly covered the fence that usually separated the street from the field. He had walked over the fence without knowing what he was doing. The snow was that hard.

He walked here and there, testing. The crust took his weight without a whisper or a crack. It was the same everywhere. You could walk over the snowy fields as if you were walking on cement. (This morning, looking at the snow, hadn't he thought of marble?) But this paving was not flat. It rose and dipped in a way that had not much to do with the contours of the ground underneath. The snow created its own landscape, which was sweeping, in a grand and arbitrary style.

Instead of walking around on the plowed streets of town, he could walk over the fields. He could cut across to the diner on the highway, which stayed open until midnight. He would have a cup of coffee there, turn around, and walk home.

One night, about six months before Robert married Peg, he and Lee were sitting drinking in his apartment. They were having an argument about whether it was permissible, or sickening, to have your family initial on your silverware. All of a sudden, the argument split open—Robert couldn't remember how, but it split open, and they found themselves saying the cruellest things to each other that they could imagine. Their voices changed from the raised pitch and speed of argument, and they spoke quietly with a subtle loathing.

"You always make me think of a dog," Lee said. "You always make me think of one of those dogs that push up on people and paw them, with their big disgusting tongues hanging out. You're so eager. All your friendliness and eagerness—that's really aggression. I'm not the only one who thinks this about you. A lot of people avoid you. They can't stand you. You'd be surprised. You push and paw in that eager pathetic way, but you have a calculating look. That's why I don't care if I hurt you."

"Maybe I should tell you one of the things I don't like, then," said Robert reasonably. "It's the way you laugh. On the phone particularly. You laugh at the end of practically every sentence. I used to think it was a nervous tic, but it always really annoyed me. And I've figured out why. You're always telling somebody about what a raw deal you're getting somewhere or some unkind thing a person said to you—that's about two-thirds of your horrendously boring self-centered conversation. And then you laugh. Ha-ha, you can take it, you don't expect anything better. That laugh is sick."

After some more of this, they started to laugh themselves, Robert and Lee, but it was not the laughter of a breakthrough into reconciliation; they did not fall upon each other in relief, crying, "What rot, I didn't mean it, did you mean it?" ("No, of course not, of course I didn't mean it.") They laughed in recognition of their extremity, just as they might have laughed at another time, in the middle of quite different, astoundingly tender declarations. They trembled with murderous pleasure, with the excitement of saying what could never be retracted; they exulted in wounds inflicted but also in wounds received, and one or the other said at some point, "This is the first time we've spoken the truth since we've known each other!" For even things that came to them more or less on the spur of the moment seemed the most urgent truths that had been hardening for a long time and pushing to get out.

It wasn't so far from laughing to making love, which they did, all with no retraction. Robert made barking noises, as a dog should, and nuzzled Lee in a bruising way, snapping with real appetite at her flesh. Afterward they were enormously and finally sick of each other but no longer disposed to blame.

"There are things I just absolutely and eternally want to forget about," Robert had told Peg. He talked to her about cutting his losses, abandoning old bad habits, old deceptions and self-deceptions, mistaken notions about life, and about himself. He said that he had been an emotional spendthrift, had thrown himself into hopeless and painful entanglements as a way of avoiding anything that had normal possibilities. That was all experiment and posturing, rejection of the ordinary, decent contracts of life. So he said to her. Errors of avoidance, when he had thought he was running risks and getting intense experiences.

"Errors of avoidance that I mistook for errors of passion," he said, then thought that he sounded pretentious when he was actually sweating with sincerity, with the effort and the relief.

In return, Peg gave him facts.

We lived with Dave's parents. There was never enough hot water for the baby's wash. Finally we got out and came to town and we lived beside the car wash. Dave was only with us weekends then. It was very noisy, especially at night. Then Dave got another job, he went up North, and I rented this place.

Errors of avoidance, errors of passion. She didn't say.

Dave had a kidney problem when he was little and he was out of school a whole winter. He read a book about the Arctic. It was probably the only book he ever read that he didn't have to. Anyway, he always dreamed about it; he wanted to go there. So finally he did.

A man doesn't just drive farther and farther away in his trucks until he disappears from his wife's view. Not even if he has always dreamed of the Arctic. Things happen before he goes. Marriage knots aren't going to slip apart painlessly, with the pull of distance. There's got to be some wrenching and slashing. But she didn't say, and he didn't ask, or even think much about that, till now.

He walked very quickly over the snow crust, and when he reached the diner he found that he didn't want to go in yet. He would cross the highway and walk a little farther, then go into the diner to get warmed up on his way home.

By the time he was on his way home, the police car that was parked at the diner ought to be gone. The night constable was in there now, taking his break. This was not the same man Robert had seen and listened to when he dropped in on his way home from Keneally. This man would not have seen anything at first hand. He hadn't talked to Peg. Nevertheless he would be talking about it; everybody in the diner would be talking about it, going over the same scene and the same questions, the possibilities. No blame to them.

When they saw Robert, they would want to know how Peg was.

There was one thing he was going to ask her, just before Clayton came in. At least, he was turning the question over in his mind, wondering if it would be all right to ask her. A discrepancy, a detail, in the midst of so many abominable details.

And now he knew it wouldn't be all right; it would never be all right. It had nothing to do with him. One discrepancy, one detail—one lie—that would never have anything to do with him.

Walking on this magic surface, he did not grow tired. He grew lighter, if anything. He was taking himself farther and farther away from town, although for a while he didn't realize this. In the clear air, the lights of Gilmore were so bright they seemed only half a field away, instead of half a mile, then a mile and a half, then two miles. Very fine flakes of snow, fine as dust, and glittering, lay on the crust that held him. There was a glitter, too, around the branches of the trees and bushes that he was getting closer to. It wasn't like the casing around twigs and delicate branches that an ice storm leaves. It was as if the wood itself had altered and begun to sparkle.

This is the very weather in which noses and fingers are frozen. But nothing felt cold.

He was getting quite close to a large woodlot. He was crossing a long slanting shelf of snow, with the trees ahead and to one side of him. Over there, to the side, something caught his eye. There was a new kind of glitter under the trees. A congestion of shapes, with black holes in them, and unmatched arms or petals reaching up to the lower branches of the trees. He headed toward these shapes, but whatever they were did not become clear. They did not look like anything he knew. They did not look like anything, except perhaps a bit like armed giants half collapsed, frozen in combat, or like the jumbled towers of a crazy small-scale city—a space-age, small-scale city. He kept waiting for an explanation, and not getting one, until he got very close. He was so close he could almost have touched one of these monstrosities before he saw that they were just old cars. Old cars and trucks and even a school bus that had been pushed in under the trees and left. Some were completely overturned, and some were tipped over one another at odd angles. They were partly filled, partly covered, with snow. The black holes were their gutted insides. Twisted bits of chrome, fragments of headlights, were glittering.

He thought of himself telling Peg about this—how close he had to get before he saw that what amazed him and bewildered him so was nothing but old wrecks, and how he then felt disappointed, but also like laughing. They needed some new thing to talk about. Now he felt more like going home.

At noon, when the constable in the diner was giving his account, he had described how the force of the shot threw Walter Weeble backward. "It blasted him partways out of the room. His head was laying out in the hall. What was left of it was laying out in the hall."

Not a leg. Not the indicative leg, whole and decent in its trousers, the shod foot. That was not what anybody turning at the top of the stairs would see and would have to step over, step through, in order to go into the bedroom and look at the rest of what was there.

The Moon in the Orange Street Skating Rink

Sam got a surprise, walking into Callie's variety and confectionery store. He had expected a clutter of groceries, cheap bits and pieces, a stale smell, maybe faded tinsel ropes, old overlooked Christmas decorations. Instead, he found a place mostly taken up with video games. Hand-lettered signs in red and blue crayon warned against alcohol, fighting, loitering, and swearing. The store was full of jittery electronic noise and flashing light and menacing, modern-day, oddly shaved and painted children. But behind the counter sat Callie, quite painted up herself, under a pinkish-blond wig. She was reading a paperback.

Sam asked for cigarettes, to test her. She laid down the book, and he looked at the title. *My Love Where the High Winds Blow*, by Veronica Gray. She gave him his change and settled her sweater around her shoulders and picked up her book, all without looking at him. Her sweater was covered with little jiggly balls of pink and white wool, like popcorn. She waited till the last minute to speak to him.

"You taken up smoking in your old age, Sam?"

"I thought you didn't know me."

"I'd know your hide in a tannery," said Callie, pleased with herself. "I knew you the minute you walked in that door."

Sam is sixty-nine years old, a widower. He is staying at the Three Little Pigs Motel, out on the highway, for a few days while on his way to visit his married daughter in Pennsylvania. For all he used to tell his wife about Gallagher, he would never bring her back to see it. Instead, they went to Hawaii, to Europe, even to Japan.

Now he goes for walks in Gallagher. Often he is the only person walking. The traffic is heavy, and not as varied as it used to be. Manufacturing has given way to service industries. Things look to Sam a bit scruffy. But that could be because he lives now in Victoria—in Oak Bay, an expensive and pretty neighborhood full of well-off retired people like himself.

Kernaghan's boarding house used to be the last house—last building—on the edge of town. It's still there, still close to the sidewalk. But the town has spread a little at all its edges. A Petro-Car gas station. A Canadian Tire Store with a big parking lot. Some new, low houses. Kernaghan's has been painted a pale, wintry blue, but otherwise looks neglected. Instead of the front veranda, where the boarders each had a chair, Sam sees a glassed-in porch entirely filled up with batts of insulating material, an upended mattress, screens, and heavy old storm windows. The house used to be light tan, and the trim was brown. Everything was terribly clean. Dust was a problem, the road being so close and not paved at that time. There were always horses going by, and people on foot, as well as cars and farm trucks. "You simply have to keep after it," said Miss Kernaghan, in an ominous way, referring to the dust. As a matter of fact, it was Callie who kept after it. Callie Kernaghan was nineteen when Sam and Edgar Grazier first saw her, and she could have passed for twelve. A demon worker. Some people called her a drudge, Miss Kernaghan's little drudge, or they called her slavey—Slavey Kernaghan. The mistake they made was in thinking that she minded.

Sometimes a woman coming in from the country, lugging her butter and eggs, would take a rest on the front steps. Or a girl would sit there to take off her rubber boots and put on her town shoes—hiding the boots in the ditch until she put them on again on her way home. Then Miss Kernaghan would call out, from the darkness behind the dining-room window, "This is not a park bench!" Miss Kernaghan was a big, square-shouldered, awkward woman, flat in front and back, with hennaed hair and a looming white-powdered face and a thickly painted, sullenly drooping mouth.

Stories of lasciviousness hung around her, dimmer, harder to substantiate than the stories of her amazing avarice and stinginess. Callie, supposedly a foundling, was said by some to be Miss Kernaghan's own daughter. But her boarders had to toe the line. No drinking, no smoking, no bad language or bad morals, she told the Grazier boys on their first day. No eating in the bedrooms, she told them later, after Thanksgiving, when they brought a large, greasy box of sweet buns from home. "It attracts mice," she said.

Miss Kernaghan said fairly often that she had never had boys before. She sounded as if she was doing them a favor. She had four other boarders. A widow lady, Mrs. Cruze, very old but able to look after herself; a business lady, Miss Verne, who was a bookkeeper in the glove factory; a bachelor, Adam Delahunt, who worked in the bank and taught Sunday school; and a stylish, contemptuous young woman, Alice Peel, who was engaged to a policeman and worked as a telephone operator. These four took up the upstairs bedrooms. Miss Kernaghan herself slept on the couch in the dining room, and Callie slept on the couch in the kitchen. Sam and Edgar got the attic. Two narrow metal-frame beds had been set up on either side of a chest of drawers and a rag rug.

After they had taken a look around, Sam pushed Edgar into going down and asking if there was any place they could hang their clothes. "I didn't think boys like you would have a lot of clothes," Miss Kernaghan said. "I never had boys before. Why can't you do like Mr. Delahunt? He puts his trousers under the mattress every night, and that keeps the crease in them grand."

Edgar thought that was the end of it, but in a little while Callie came with a broom handle and some wire. She stood on the bureau and contrived a clothespole with loops of wire around a beam.

"We could easy do that," Sam said. They looked with curiosity but little pleasure at her floppy gray undergarments. She didn't answer. She had even brought some clothes hangers. Somehow they knew already that this was all her own doing.

"Thank you, Callie," said Edgar, a slender boy with a crown of fair curls, turning on her the diffident, sweet-natured smile that had had no success downstairs.

Callie spoke in the rough voice that she used in the grocery store when demanding good potatoes. "Will that be all right for yez?"

Sam and Edgar were cousins—not brothers, as most people thought. They were the same age—seventeen—and had been sent to board in Gallagher while they went to business college. They had grown up about ten miles from here, and had gone to the same country school and village continuation school. After a year at business college, they could get jobs in banks or offices or be apprenticed to accountants. They were not going back to the farm.

What they really wanted to do, and had wanted since they were about ten years old, was to become acrobats. They had practiced for years and put on displays when the continuation school gave its concerts. That school had no gym, but there were some parallel bars and a balancing rail and mats in the basement. At home, they practiced in the barn, and on the grass in fine weather. How do acrobats earn a living? Sam was the one who had begun to ask that question. He could not picture Edgar and himself in a circus. They were not dark enough, for one thing. (He had an idea that the people who worked in circuses were all Gypsies.) He thought there must be acrobats going around on their own, doing stunts at fairs and in church halls. He remembered seeing some when he was younger. Where were they from? How did they get paid? How did you find out about joining them? Such questions troubled Sam more and more and never seemed to bother Edgar at all.

In the early fall, after supper, while there was still some light in the evenings, they practiced in the vacant lot across the street from Kernaghan's, where the ground was fairly level. They wore their undershirts and woollen pants. They limbered up by doing cartwheels and handstands and headstands, somersaults and double somersaults, and then welded themselves together. They shaped their bodies into signs—into hieroglyphs—eliminating to an astonishing degree their separateness and making the bumps of heads and shoulders incidental. Sometimes, of course, these creations toppled, everything came apart, arms and legs flew free, and grappling bodies reappeared—just two boys' bodies, one tall and slight, the other shorter and sturdier. They began again, building jerkily. The balancing bodies swayed. They might topple, they might hold. All depended on whether they could subdue themselves into that pure line, invisibly join themselves, attain the magic balance. Yes. No. Yes. Again.

They had an audience of boarders sitting on the porch. Alice Peel took no notice. If she was not out with her fiancé, she was in her room attending to the upkeep of her clothes and person—painting her nails, doing up her hair or taking it out, plucking her eyebrows, washing her sweaters and silk stockings, cleaning her shoes. Adam Delahunt was a busy person, too—he had meetings of the Temperance Society and the Gideons to go to, social activities of his Sunday-school class to superintend. But he sat for a while and watched with Mrs. Cruze and Miss Verne and Miss Kernaghan. Mrs. Cruze still had good eyesight and she loved the show. She stamped her cane on the porch floor and yelled, "Get him, boy! Get him!" as if the stunts were some sort of wrestling match.

Mr. Delahunt told Sam and Edgar about his Sunday-school class, called the Triple-Vs. The Vs stood for Virtue, Vigor, and Victory. He said that if they joined they could get to use the United church gymnasium. But the boys were Coldwater Baptists at home, so they could not accept.

If Callie watched, it was from behind windows. She always had her work.

Miss Kernaghan said that so much exercise would give those boys terrible appetites.

When Sam thought of himself and Edgar practicing in that vacant lot—it was now part of the Canadian Tire parking space—he always seemed to be sitting on the porch, too, looking at the two boys striving and falling and pulling themselves up on the grass—one figure soaring briefly above the other, triumphantly handbalanced—and then the cheerful separate tumbling. These memories have a certain damp brown shading. Perhaps from the wallpaper in the Kernaghan house. The trees that lined the road at that time were elms, and their leaf color in fall was a brown-spotted gold.

The leaves were shaped like a candle flame. These leaves fell in his mind on a windless evening with the sky clear but the sunset veiled and the countryside misty. The town, under leaves and the smoke of burning leaves, was mysterious and difficult, a world on its own, with its church spires and factory whistles, rich houses and row houses, networks, catchwords, vested interests. He had been warned; he had been told town people were snotty. That was not the half of it.

The exercise did increase the Grazier boys' appetites, but those would have been terrible anyway. They were used to farm meals and had never imagined people could exist on such portions as were served here. They saw with amazement that Miss Verne left half of what little she got on her plate, and that Alice Peel rejected potatoes, bread, bacon, cocoa as a threat to her figure; turnips, cabbage, beans as a threat to her digestion; and anything with raisins in it simply because she couldn't stand them. They could not figure out any way to get what Alice Peel turned down or what Miss Verne left on her plate, though it would surely have been fair.

At ten-thirty in the evening, Miss Kernaghan produced what she called "the evening lunch." This was a plate of sliced bread, some butter and jam, and cups of cocoa or tea. Coffee was not served in that house. Miss Kernaghan said it was American and corroded your gullet. The butter was cut up beforehand into meager pats, and the dish of jam was set in the middle of the table, where nobody could reach it easily. Miss Kernaghan remarked that sweet things spoiled the taste of bread and butter. The other boarders deferred to her out of long habit, but between them Sam and Edgar cleaned out the dish. Soon the amount of jam dwindled to two separate spoonfuls. The cocoa was made with water, with a little skim milk added to make a skin and to support Miss Kernaghan's claim that it was made with milk entirely.

Nobody challenged her. Miss Kernaghan told lies not to fool people but to stump them. If a boarder said, "It was a bit chilly upstairs last night," Miss Kernaghan would say at once, "I can't understand that. I had a roaring fire going. The pipes were too hot to lay your hand on them." The fact of the matter would be that she had let the fire die down or go out altogether. The boarder would know or strongly suspect this, but what was a boarder's suspicion against Miss Kernaghan's firm, flashy lie? Mrs. Cruze would actually apologize, Miss Verne would mutter about her chilblains, Mr. Delahunt and Alice Peel would look sulky but would not argue.

Sam and Edgar had to spend their whole allowance of pocket money, which wasn't much, on food. At first they got hot dogs at the Cozy Grill. Then Sam figured out that they would be farther ahead buying a package of jam tarts or Fig Newtons at the grocery store. They had to eat the whole package on the way home, because of the rule about no food in the bedrooms, They liked the hot dogs, but they had never felt really comfortable at the Cozy Grill, which was full of noisy high-school students, younger and a lot brassier than they were. Sam felt some possibility of insult, though none ever developed. On the way back to Kernaghan's from the grocery store, they had to pass the Cozy Grill and then Dixon's, a drugstore with an ice-cream parlor in the back. That was where their fellow-students from the business college went for cherry Cokes and banana splits after school and in the evenings. Passing Dixon's windows, they stopped chewing, looked stolidly straight ahead. They would never go inside.

They were the only farm boys at business college, and their clothes set them apart. They had no light-blue or light-brown V-neck sweaters, no grownup-looking gray trousers, only these stiff woollen breeches, thick home-knit sweaters, old suit jackets worn as sports coats. They wore shirts and ties because it was required, but they had only one tie each and a couple of shirts. Miss Kernaghan allowed only one shirt a week in the washing, so Sam and Edgar often had dirty collars and cuffs, and even stains—probably from jam tarts—that they had unsuccessfully tried to sponge away.

And there was another problem, related partly to clothes and partly to the bodies inside. There was never much hot water at the boarding house, and Alice Peel used up more than her share. In the sleepy mornings, the boys splashed their hands and faces as they had done at home. They carried around and were used to the settled smell of their bodies and daily-worn clothes, a record of their efforts and exertions. Perhaps this was a lucky thing. Otherwise, girls might have paid more attention to Edgar, whose looks they liked, and not to Sam, with his floppy sandy hair and freckles and his habit of keeping his head down, as if he were thinking of rooting for something. There would have been a wedge between them. Or, to put it another way, the wedge would have been there sooner.

Winter came and put an end to the acrobatic stunts in the vacant lot. Now Sam and Edgar longed to go skating. The rink was only a couple of blocks away, on Orange Street, and on skating nights, which were Mondays and Thursdays, they could hear the music. They had brought their skates with them to Gallagher. They had skated almost as long as they could remember, on the swamp pond or the outdoor rink in the village. Here skating cost fifteen cents, and the only way for them to afford that was to give up the extra food. But the cold weather was making their appetites fiercer than ever.

They walked over to the rink on a Sunday night when there was nobody around and again on a Monday night when the evening's skating was over and there was nobody to keep them from going inside. They went in and mingled with the people leaving the ice and taking off their skates. They had a good look around before the lights were turned off. On their way home, and in their room, they talked quietly. Sam enjoyed figuring out a way that they could get in for nothing, but he did not picture them actually doing it. Edgar took for granted that they would go from plan to action.

"We can't," said Sam. "Neither of us are small enough."

Edgar didn't answer, and Sam thought that was the end of it. He should have known better.

The Orange Street Skating Rink, in Sam's memory, is a long, dark ramshackle shed. A dim, moving light shows through the cracks between the boards. The music comes from gramophone records that are hoarse and scratchy—to listen to them is like reaching for the music through a wavering wall of thorns. "Tales from the Vienna Woods," "The Merry Widow," "The Gold and Silver

Waltz," "The Sleeping Beauty." The moving light seen through the cracks comes from a fixture called "the moon." The moon, which shines from the roof of the rink, is a yellow bulb inside a large tin can, a syrup tin, from which one end has been cut away. The other lights are turned off when the moon is turned on. A system of wires and ropes makes it possible to pull the tin can this way and that, creating an impression of shifting light—the source, the strong yellow bulb, being deeply hidden.

The rinkie-dinks controlled the moon. Rinkie-dinks were boys from ten or eleven to fifteen or sixteen years old. They cleaned the ice and shovelled the snow out the snow door, which was a snugly fitted flap low in the wall, hooked on the inside. Besides the ropes that controlled the moon, they worked the shutters that covered the openings in the roof—opened for air, closed against driving snow. The rinkie-dinks collected the money and would sometimes shortchange girls who were afraid of them, but they didn't cheat Blinker. He had somehow fooled them into thinking he had every skater counted. Blinker was the rink manager, a sallow, skinny, and unfriendly man. He and his friends sat in his room, beyond the men's toilet and changing room. In there was a wood stove, with a tall, blackened conical coffeepot sitting on top, and some straight-backed chairs with rungs missing, and a few old, filthy armchairs. The plank floor, like all the floors and benches and wallboards in the rink, was cut and scarred by fresh and old skate marks and darkened with smoke and dirt. The room where the men sat was hot and smoky and it was assumed they drank liquor in there, though perhaps it was only coffee out of the stained enamel mugs. Of course, there was a story that boys had once got in before the men arrived, and had peed in the coffeepot. Another story was that one of his friends had done that when Blinker went to scoop up the admission money.

The rinkie-dinks could be busy or idle around parts of the rink, climbing the wall ladders, walking along the benches, even running along the platform, which had no guardrail, under the roof openings. Sometimes they would wiggle through these openings onto the roof, and get back in the same way. Some of the time, of course, they skated. They got in for nothing.

So did Sam and Edgar and Callie, soon enough. They came along when the skating was well under way and the rink full and noisy. Close to one corner of the building were some cherry trees, and a very light person could climb one of these trees and drop onto the roof. Then this very light, bold, and agile person could scramble along the roof and crawl through one of the openings and jump to the platform underneath, risking a fall to the ice below and broken bones or even death. But boys risked that all the time. From the platform you could climb down a wall ladder, then work your way around the benches and slip over the wall of the passage made for shovelling out snow. Then it was a matter of crouching in the shadow, watching for the right moment, unhooking the snow door, and letting in the two who were waiting outside: Sam and Edgar, who lost no time putting on their skates and taking to the ice.

Why did others not manage the same trick, Sam might be asked on those occasions, years and years later, when he chose to tell the story, and he always said maybe they did, he wouldn't know about it. The rinkie-dinks of course could have opened the door to any number of friends, but they were not disposed to do so, being quite jealous of their own privileges. And few of the night skaters were small enough and light and quick and brave enough to get in through the roof. Children might have tried it, but they skated on Saturday afternoons and didn't have the advantage of darkness. And why was Callie not noticed? Well, she was very quick, and she was never careless; she waited her time. She wore a ragged, ill-fitting set of clothes—breeches, windbreaker, cloth cap. There were always boys around who were dressed in cast-off raggedy clothes. And the town was just big enough that not every face could be placed instantly. There were two public schools, and a boy from one, noticing her, would just think she went to the other.

Sam's wife once asked, "How did you persuade her?" Callie—what was in it for Callie, who never owned a pair of skates?

"Callie's life was work," Sam said. "So anything that wasn't work—that was a thrill for her." But he wondered—how *did* they persuade her? It must have been a dare. Making friends with Callie at first had been something like making friends with a testy and suspicious little dog, and later on it had been like making friends with the twelve-year-old she looked to be. At first she wouldn't stop work to look at them. They admired the needlework picture she was making, of green hills and a round blue pond and a large sailboat, and she pulled it to her chest as if they were making fun of her. "Do you make the pictures up yourself?" said Sam, meaning it as a compliment, but she was incensed.

"You send away for them," she said. "You send to Cincinnati."

They persisted. Why? Because she was a little slavey, forever out of things, queer-looking, undersized, and compared to her they were in the mainstream, they were fortunate. They could be mean or kind to her as they pleased, and it pleased them to be kind. Also, it was a challenge. Jokes and dares were what finally disarmed her. They brought her tiny lumps of coal wrapped in chocolate papers. She put dried thistles under their sheets. She told them she had never refused a dare. That was the secret of Callie—she would never say that anything was too much for her. Far from being oppressed by all the work she had to do, she gloried in it. One night, when Sam was doing his accounting at the dining-room table, she thrust a school notebook under his nose.

"What's this, Callie?"

"I don't know!"

It was her scrapbook, and pasted in it were newspaper items about herself. The newspaper had invited people to enter into competitions. Who could do the most bound buttonholes in eight hours? Who could can the most raspberries in a single day? Who had crocheted the most amazing number of bedspreads, tablecloths, runners, and doilies? Callie, Callie, Callie, Callie Kernaghan, again and again. In her own estimation, she was no slavey but a prodigy pitying the slothful lives of others.

It was only on Monday nights that they could go skating, because that was the night Miss Kernaghan played bingo at the Legion Hall. Callie kept her boy's clothes in the woodshed. They came from a ragbag of things belonging to Mrs. Cruze, who had brought it with her from her old home, intending to make quilts, but never got around to it. All except the cap. That had belonged to Adam Delahunt, who put it in a bundle of things he gave to

Callie to save for the Missionary Society, but Miss Kernaghan told Callie just to put those things down in the cellar, in case.

Callie could have slipped off from the skating rink as soon as her job was done—she could have walked out by the main entrance and nobody would have bothered her. But she never did. She climbed over the top of the benches, walked along testing the boards for springiness, climbed partway up one of the ladders, and swung out on one hand, one foot, hanging over the partition and watching the skaters. Edgar and Sam never stopped skating till the moon was turned off and the music stopped and the other lights came on. Sometimes they raced each other, darting in and out among the sedate couples and rows of unsteady girls. Sometimes they showed off, gliding down the ice with their arms spread. (Edgar was the more gifted skater, though not so ruthless a racer—he could have done fancy skating, if boys did it then.) They never skated with girls, but that wasn't so much because they were scared to ask as that they didn't want to be kept to anybody else's measure. Callie waited for them outside when the skating was over, and they walked home together, three boys. Callie didn't do any ostentatious whistling or snowballing to show she was a boy. She had a scuffling boy's walk, thoughtful but independent, alert for possibilities—a fight or an adventure. Her heavy, rough black hair was stuffed up under the cloth cap, and kept it from being too big for her head. Without the hair around it, her face looked less pale and scrunched up—that spitting, mocking, fierce look she sometimes had was gone and she looked sober and self-respecting. They called her Cal.

They came into the house the back way. The boys went upstairs and Callie changed her clothes in the icy woodshed. She had ten minutes or so to get the evening lunch on the table.

When Sam and Edgar lay in bed in the dark on Monday nights after skating, they talked more than was usual. Edgar was apt to bring up the name of Chrissie Young, his girlfriend last year, at home. Edgar claimed to be sexually experienced. He said he had done it to Chrissie last winter, when they went tobogganing after dark and ran into a snowdrift. Sam didn't think this was possible, given the cold, their clothing, the brief time before other tobogganers caught up with them. But he wasn't sure, and, listening, he grew restless and perhaps jealous. He mentioned other girls, girls who had been at the skating rink wearing short flared skirts and little fur-trimmed jackets. Sam and Edgar compared what they had seen when these girls twirled around or when one of them fell on the ice. What would you do to Shirley, or Doris, Sam asked Edgar, and quickly passed on, in a spirit of strangely mixed ridicule and excitement, to ask him what he would do to other girls and women, more and more unlikely, caught where they couldn't defend themselves. Teachers at the business college—mannish-looking Miss Lewisohn, who taught accounting, and brittle Miss Parkinson, who taught typing. The fat woman in the post office, the anemic blonde in Eaton's Order Office. Housewives who showed off their behinds in the back yard, bending over clothes baskets. The grotesque nature of certain choices excited them more than the grace and prettiness of girls who were officially admired. Alice Peel was dismissed almost perfunctorily—they tied her to her bed and ravished her on their way down to supper. Miss Verne was spread quite publicly on the stairs, having been caught exciting herself with her legs around the newel post. They spared old Mrs. Cruze—they had some limits, after all. What about Miss Kernaghan, with her rheumatism, her layers of rusty clothes, her queer painted mouth? They had heard stories, everybody had. Callie was supposed to be the child of a Bible salesman, a boarder. They imagined the Bible salesman doing it in place of themselves, plugging old Miss Kernaghan. Over and over, the Bible salesman rams her, tears her ancient bloomers, smears her hungry mouth, drives her to croaks and groans of the most extreme need and gratification.

"Callie, too," said Edgar.

What about Callie? The joys of the game stopped for Sam when she was mentioned. The fact that she, too, was female came to him as an embarrassment. You would think he had discovered something disgusting and pitiable about himself.

Edgar didn't mean that they should just imagine what could be done to Callie.

"We could get her to. I bet we could."

Sam said, "She's too small."

"No, she's not."

That persuading Sam does remember, and it was accomplished by dares, which makes him think the skating-rink adventure must have been managed the same way. A Saturday morning when the winter was nearly over, when the farmers' sleighs, driven over the packed snow, grated on patches of bare ground as they passed Kernaghan's house. Callie coming up the attic stairs with the wet mop, scrub pail, dust rags. She kicked the rag rug down the stairs so that she could shake it out the door. She stripped the beds of the flannelette sheets, with their intimate, cozy smell. No fresh air enters the Kernaghan house. Outside the windows are the storm windows. This is the time and place for Callie's seduction.

That is not a suitable word for it. Callie cross and impatient at first, keeping at her work, then sullen, then oddly tractable. Taunting her with being scared was surely the effective tactic. They must have known, by then, her real age, but they still treated her as if she were an imp to be cajoled—didn't think of stroking or flattering her as if she were a girl.

Even with her cooperation, it was nothing like as easy as they had imagined. Sam became convinced that the story about Chrissie was a lie, even though Edgar was invoking Chrissie's name at the moment.

"Come on," Edgar said. "I'll show you what I do to my girlfriend. Here's what I do to Chrissie."

"I bet," said Callie sourly, but she let herself be pulled down on the narrow mattress. The elastic of her winter bloomers had left red rings around her legs and waist. A flannel vest, buttoned over an undershirt, her brown ribbed stockings, held up by long, lumpy suspenders. Nothing but the bloomers was taken off. Edgar said the suspenders were hurting him and went to undo them, but Callie cried out, "Leave those alone!" as if they were what she had to protect.

Something very important is missing from Sam's memory of that morning—blood. He has no doubt of Callie's virginity, remembering Edgar's struggles, then his own, such jabbing and prodding and bafflement. Callie lay beneath them each in turn, half-grudging, half-obliging, putting up with them and not complaining that anything hurt. She would never do that. But she would not do anything, specifically, to help.

"Open your legs," said Edgar urgently.

"They're open already."

The reason he doesn't remember blood is probably that there wasn't any. They did not get far enough. Callie was so thin her hipbones stood up, yet she seemed quite extensive to Sam, and unwieldy and complicated. Cold and sticky where Edgar had wet her, dry otherwise, with unexpected bumps and flaps and blind alleys—a leathery feel to her. When he thought of this afterward, he still wasn't sure that he had found out what girls were like. It was as if they had used a doll or a compliant puppy. When he got off her, he saw that she had goose bumps where her skin was bare, all around that tuft of dead-looking hair. Also, that their wet had soaked one stocking. Callie wiped herself with the dust rag—granted, it looked to be a clean one—and said it reminded her of when somebody blew their nose.

"You're not mad?" said Sam, meaning partly that, and partly, you won't tell? "Did we hurt you?"

Callie said, "It would take a lot more than that stupid business to hurt me."

There was no more skating after that. The weather got too mild.

Miss Kernaghan's rheumatism was worse. There was more work than ever for Callie. Edgar got tonsillitis and stayed home from classes. Sam, on his own at the business college, realized how much he had come to enjoy it. He liked the noise of the typewriters—the warning of the bells, the carriages banging back. He liked ruling the account-book pages with a straight pen, making the prescribed heavy and fine lines. He especially liked figuring out percentages and quickly adding up columns of numbers, and dealing with the problems of Mr. X and Mr. B, who owned a lumberyard and a chain of hardware stores, respectively.

Edgar was out of school nearly three weeks. When he came back, he had fallen behind in everything. His typing was slower and sloppier than it had been at Christmastime, he smeared ink on the ruler, and he could not understand interest tables. He seemed listless, he grew discouraged, he stared out the window. The lady teachers were somewhat softened by his looks—he was lighter and paler since his illness; even his hair seemed fairer—and he got away with this indolence and ineptitude for a while. He made some efforts, occasionally tried to do homework with Sam, or went to the typing room at noon to practice. But no improvement lasted, or was enough. He took days off.

While he was sick, Edgar had received a get-well card. It showed a green dragon in striped pajamas propped up in bed. On the front of the card were the words "Sorry to Hear your Tail is Draggon," and inside "Hope that Soon, You'll have it Waggon." Down at the bottom, in pencil, was written the name Chrissie.

But Chrissie was in Stratford, training to be a nurse. How would she know Edgar was sick? The envelope, with Edgar's name on it, had come through the mail but had a local postmark.

"You sent it," Edgar said. "I know it's not her."

"I did not," said Sam truthfully.

"You sent it." Edgar was hoarse and feverish and racked with disappointment. "You didn't even write in ink."

"How much money have we got in the bank?" Edgar wanted to know. This was early May. They had enough to pay their board until the end of the term.

Edgar had not been to the college for several days. He had been to the railway station, and he had asked the price of a one-way ticket to Toronto. He said he meant to go alone if Sam wouldn't go with him. He was wild to get away. It didn't take long for Sam to find out why.

"Callie might have a baby."

"She isn't old enough," said Sam. Then he remembered that she was. But he explained to Edgar that he was sure they hadn't been sufficiently thorough.

"I'm not talking about that time," said Edgar, in a sulky voice.

That was the first Sam knew about what had been going on when Edgar stayed away from school. But Sam misunderstood again. He thought Callie had told Edgar that she was in trouble. She hadn't. She hadn't given him any such information or asked for anything or made any threats. But Edgar was frightened. His panic seemed to be making him half sick. They bought a package of cake doughnuts at the grocery store and sat on the stone wall in front of the Anglican church to eat them. Edgar took one bite and held the doughnut in his hand.

Sam said that they had only five more weeks at college.

"I'm not going back there anyway. I'm too far behind," said Edgar.

Sam did not say that he had pictured himself lately working in a bank, a business-college graduate. He saw himself in a three-piece suit in the tellers' cage. He would have grown a mustache. Some tellers became bank managers. It had just recently occurred to him that bank managers did not come into the world ready-made. They were something else first.

He asked Edgar what kind of jobs they could get in Toronto.

"We could do stunts," Edgar said. "We could do stunts on the sidewalk."

Now Sam saw what he was up against. Edgar was not joking. He sat there with one bite out of his doughnut and proposed this way of making a living in Toronto. Stunts on the sidewalk.

What about their parents? This only started crazier plans.

"You could tell them I was kidnapped."

"What about the police?" said Sam. "The police go looking for anybody that's kidnapped. They'd find you."

"Then don't tell them I'm kidnapped," Edgar said. "Tell them I saw a murder and I have to go into hiding. Tell them I saw a body in a sack pushed off the Cedar Bush Bridge and I saw the men that did it and later I met them on the street and they recognized me. Tell them that. Tell them not to go to the police or say anything about it, because my life is at stake."

"How did you know there was a body in the sack?" said Sam idiotically. "Don't talk anymore about it. I have to think."

But all the way back to Kernaghan's Edgar did nothing but talk, elaborating on this story or on another, which involved his having been recruited by the government to be a spy, having to dye his hair black and change his name.

They got to the boarding house just as Alice Peel and her fiancé, the policeman, were coming out the front door.

"Go round the back," said Edgar.

The kitchen door was wide open. Callie had been cleaning the stovepipes. Now she had them all in place again, and was cleaning the stove. She was polishing the black part of it with waxed bread papers and the trim with a clean rag. The stove was a wonderful sight, like black marble set with silver, but Callie herself was smudged from head to foot. Even her eyelids were black. She was singing "My Darling Nellie Grey," and she made it go very fast, to help with the polishing.

"Oh, my darling Nellie Grey,
They have taken you away,
And I'll never see my darling
anymore."

Miss Kernaghan sat at the table, drinking a cup of hot water. Besides her rheumatism, she was troubled with indigestion. Creaks came from her joints, and powerful rumbles, groans, and even whistles, from her deep insides. Her face took no notice.

"You boys," she said. "What have you been doing?"

"Walking," said Edgar.

"You aren't doing your stunts anymore."

Sam said, "The ground's too wet."

"Sit down," said Miss Kernaghan.

Sam could hear Edgar's shaky breathing. His own stomach felt very heavy, as if all work on the mass of doughnuts—he had eaten all but one of them—had ceased. Could Callie have told? She didn't look up at them.

"I never told you boys how Callie was born," Miss Kernaghan said. And she started right in to tell them.

"It was in the Queen's Hotel in Stratford. I was staying there with my friend Louie Green. Louie Green and I ran a millinery shop. We were on our way to Toronto to get our spring trim. But it was winter. In fact, it was a blizzard blowing. We were the only ones for supper. We were coming out of the dining room afterwards and the hotel door blew open and in came three people. It was the driver that worked for the hotel, that met the trains, and a woman and a man. The man and the driver were hanging on to the woman and hauling her between them. She was howling and yelling and she was puffed up to a terrible size. They got her on the settee, but she slid off it onto the floor. She was only a girl, eighteen or nineteen years old. The baby popped right out of her on the floor. The man just sat down on the settee and put his head between his legs. I was the one had to run and call for the hotelkeeper and his wife. They came running and their dog running ahead of them, barking. Louie was hanging on to the banisters afraid she might faint. Everything happening at once.

"The driver was French-Canadian, so he had probably seen a baby born before. He bit the cord with his teeth and tied it up with some dirty string out of his pocket. He grabbed a rug and stuffed it up between her legs. Blood was coming out of her as dark as fly poison—it was spreading across the floor. He yelled for somebody to get snow, and the husband, or whatever he was, he never even lifted his head. It was Louie ran out and got her hands full, and when the driver saw what a piddling little bit she brought he just swore at her and threw it down. Then he kicked the dog, because it was getting too interested. He kicked it so hard it landed across the room and the hotel woman was screaming it was killed. I picked the baby up and wrapped it in my jacket. That was Callie. What a sickly-looking thing. The dog wasn't killed at all. The rugs were soaked with blood and the Frenchman swearing a blue streak. She was dead but she was still bleeding.

"Louie was the one wanted us to take her. The husband said he would get in touch but he never did. We had to get a bottle and boil up milk and corn syrup and make her a bed in a drawer. Louie let on to be very fond of her, but within a year Louie got married and went to live in Regina and has never been back. So much for fond."

Sam thought that this was all most probably a lie. Nevertheless it had a terrible effect on him. Why tell them this now? Truth or lies didn't matter, or whether someone had kicked a dog or bled to death. What mattered was Miss Kernaghan's cold emphasis as she told this, her veiled and surely unfriendly purpose, her random ferocity.

Callie hadn't stopped work for one word of the story. She had subdued but not entirely given up her singing. The kitchen was full of light in the spring evening, and smelled of Callie's harsh soaps and powders. Sam had sometimes before had a sense of being in trouble, but he had always known exactly what the trouble was and what the punishment would be, and he could think his way past it. Now he got the feeling that there was a kind of trouble whose extent you couldn't know and punishments you couldn't fathom. It wasn't even Miss Kernaghan's ill will they had to fear. What was it? Did Edgar know? Edgar could feel something being prepared—a paralyzing swipe. He thought it had to do with Callie and a baby and what they had done. Sam had a sense of larger implications. But he had to see that Edgar's instincts were right.

On Saturday morning, they walked through the back streets to the station. They had left the house when Callie went to do the weekend shopping, pulling a child's wagon behind her for the groceries. They had taken their money out of the bank. They had wedged a note in their door that would drop out when the door was opened: "We have gone. Sam. Edgar."

The words "We have gone" had been typed the day before at the college by Sam, but their names were signed by hand. Sam had thought of adding "Board paid till Monday" or "Will write to parents." But surely Miss Kernaghan would know that their board was paid till Monday and saying they would write to their parents would be a tip-off that they hadn't just gone home. "We have gone" seemed foolish, but he was afraid that if they didn't leave something there would be an alarm and a search.

They left behind the heavy, shabby books they intended to sell at the end of term—*Accounting Practice, Business Arithmetic*—and put what clothes they could into two brown-paper bags.

The morning was fine and a lot of people were out-of-doors. Children had taken over the sidewalks for ball-bouncing, hopscotch, skipping. They had to have their say about the stuffed paper bags.

"What've you got in them bags?"

"Dead cats," said Edgar. He swung his bag at a girl's head.

But she was bold. "What are you going to do with them?"

"Sell them to the Chinaman for chop-cat-suey," said Edgar in a threatening voice.

So they got past and heard the girl chanting behind them, "Chop-cat-suey! Chop-cat-suey! Eat-it-pooey!" Nearer the station, these groups of children thinned out, vanished. Now it was boys twelve or thirteen—some of the same boys who had hung around the skating rink—who were loitering near the platform, picking up cigarette butts, trying to light them. They aped manly insolence and would not have been caught dead asking questions.

"You boys given yourself plenty of time," said the station agent. The train did not go till half past twelve, but they had timed their getaway according to Callie's shopping. "You know where you're going in the city? Anybody going to meet you?"

Sam was not prepared for this, but Edgar said, "My sister."

He did not have one.

"She live there? You going to stay at her place?"

"Her and her husband's," said Edgar. "She's married."

Sam could see what was coming next.

"What part of Toronto they live in?"

But Edgar was equal. "North part," he said. "Doesn't every city have a north part?" The station agent seemed about satisfied. "Hang on to your money," he told them.

They sat on the bench facing the board fence across the tracks, holding their tickets and their brown bags. Sam was counting up in his head how much money they had to hang on to. He had been to Toronto once with his father when he was ten years old. He remembered some confusion about a streetcar. They tried to get on at the wrong door, or get off at the wrong door. People shouted at them. His father muttered that they were all damn fools. Sam felt that he had to hold himself ready for a great assault, try to anticipate the complexities ahead so they wouldn't take him by surprise. Then something came into his head that was like a present. He didn't know where it came from. The Y.M.C.A. They could go to the Y.M.C.A. and stay there that night. It would be late in the afternoon when they got in. They would first get something to eat, then ask somebody the way to the Y.M.C.A. Probably they could walk.

He told Edgar what they would do. "Then tomorrow we'll walk around and get to know the streets and find out where is the cheapest place to eat."

He knew that Edgar would accept any plan at the moment. Edgar had no notion yet of Toronto, in spite of that unexpected invention of a sister and a brother-in-law. Edgar was sitting here on the bench at the station, full of the idea of the train coming in and of their getting on. The blast of the whistle, the departure—the escape. Escape like an explosion, setting them free. He never saw them getting off the train, with their paper bags, in a banging, jarring, crowded, utterly bewildering new place. But Sam felt better now that he had a starting plan. If one good idea could occur to him out of the blue, why not another?

After a while, other people began to gather, waiting for the same train. Two ladies dressed up to go shopping in Stratford. Their varnished straw hats showed that it was getting close to summer. An old man in a shiny black suit carrying a cardboard box secured with twine. The boys who hung around and didn't go anywhere were nevertheless getting ready for the train's arrival—sitting all together at the end of the platform, dangling their legs. A couple of dogs were patrolling the platform in a semi-official way, sniffing at a trunk and some waiting parcels, sizing up the baggage cart, even looking down the tracks as if they knew as well as anybody else which direction the train was coming from.

As soon as they heard the whistle blowing for the crossroads west of town, Sam and Edgar got up and stood at the edge of the platform. When the train arrived, it seemed a very good sign that they had chosen to stand in the exact spot at which the conductor stepped down, carrying the little step. After he had spent an interminable time assisting a woman with a baby, a suitcase, and two small children, they were able to get on. They went ahead of the ladies in summer hats, the man with the box, and whoever else had lined up. They didn't once look behind. They walked to the end of the almost empty car and chose to sit where they could face each other, on the side of the train that looked out on the board fence, not on the platform. The same board fence they had been staring at for over three-quarters of an hour. They had to sit there for two or three minutes while there was the usual commotion outside, important-sounding shouts, and the conductor's voice crying, *"Board!"* in a way that transformed the word from a human sound to a train sound. Then the train began to move. They were moving. They each had one arm still around a brown bag and a ticket held in the other hand. They were moving. They watched the boards of the fence to prove it. They left the fence behind altogether and were passing through the diminished outskirts of the town—the back yards, back sheds, back porches, apple trees in bloom. Lilacs straggling by the tracks, gone wild.

While they were looking out the window, and before the town was entirely gone, a boy sat down in the seat across the aisle from them. Sam's impression was that one of those boys loitering on the platform had slipped onto the train, or somehow connived to get a free ride, perhaps out to the junction. Without really looking, he got an idea of the way the boy was dressed—too shabbily and carelessly to be going on any real trip. Then he did look, and he saw that the boy was holding a ticket, just as they were.

On the winter nights when they walked to the skating rink, they had not often looked at each other. Under the streetlights, they had watched their turning shadows on the snow. Inside the rink, the artificial moon altered colors and left some areas in near darkness. So the clothes this boy was wearing did not send any immediate message across the aisle. Except that they were not the kind of clothes usually worn on a trip. Rubber boots, heavy breeches with stains of oil or paint on them, a windbreaker torn under one arm and too warm for the day, a large, unsuitable cap.

How had Callie got past the station agent in that outfit? The same station agent who looked Sam and Edgar over so inquisitively, who wanted to know where they were planning to stay and who was meeting them, had let this absurd and dirty and ragged pretend-boy buy a ticket (to Toronto—Callie was guessing, and she guessed right) and walk out onto the platform without one word, one question. This contributed to the boys' feeling, when they recognized her, that she was exercising powers that didn't fall far short of being miraculous. (Maybe Edgar, in particular, felt this.) How had she known? How had she got the money? How was she here?

None of it was impossible. She had come back with the groceries and gone up to the attic. (Why? She didn't say.) She had found the note and guessed at once they hadn't gone home to the farm and weren't hitchhiking on the highway. She knew when the train left. She knew two places it went to—Stratford and Toronto. She stole the money for her ticket from the metal box under the hymn books in the piano bench. (Miss Kernaghan, of course, did not trust banks.) By the time she got to the station and was buying her ticket, the train was coming in and the station agent had a lot of things to think about, no time to ask questions. There was a great deal of luck involved—lucky timing and lucky guessing every step of the way—but that was all. It was not magic, not quite.

Sam and Edgar had not recognized the clothes, and there was no particular movement or gesture that alerted them. The boy Callie sat looking out the window, head partly turned away from them. Sam would never know exactly when he first knew it was Callie, or how the knowledge came to him, and whether he looked at Edgar or simply knew that Edgar knew the same thing he did and at the same time. This was knowledge that seemed to have simply leaked out into the air and to be waiting there to be absorbed. They passed through a long cut, with grassy banks fresh on either side, and crossed the Cedar Bush Bridge—the same bridge where boys from town dared each other to climb down and cling to the supports under the ties while the train passed over their heads. (Would Callie have done that if they had dared her?) By the time they were across this bridge, they both knew that it was Callie sitting across from them. And each of them knew the other knew.

Edgar spoke first. "Do you want to move over with us?"

Callie got up and moved across the aisle, sitting down beside Edgar. She had her boy's look on—a look not so sly or quarrelsome as her usual look. She was a good-humored boy, more or less, with reasonable expectations.

It was Sam she spoke to. "Don't you mind riding backwards?"

Sam said no.

Next, she asked them what they had in the bags, and they both spoke at once.

Edgar said, "Dead cats."

Sam said, "Lunch."

They didn't feel as if they were caught. Right away they had understood that Callie hadn't come to bring them back. She was joining them. In her boy's clothes, she reminded them of the cold nights of luck and cunning, the plan that went without a hitch, the free skating, speed and delight, deception and pleasure. When nothing went wrong, nothing could go wrong, triumph was certain, all their moves timely. Callie, who had got herself on this train with stolen money and in boy's clothes, seemed to lift threats rather than pose them. Even Sam stopped thinking about what they would do in Toronto, whether their money would last. If he had been functioning in his usual way, he would have seen that Callie's presence was bound to bring them all sorts of trouble once they descended into the real world, but he was not functioning that way and he did not see anything like trouble. At the moment, he saw power—Callie's power, when she wouldn't be left behind—generously distributed to all of them. The moment was flooded—with power, it seemed, and with possibility. But this was just happiness. It was really just happiness.

That was how Sam's story—which had left some details and reasons out along the way—always ended. If he was asked how things went from there, he might say, "Well, it was a little more complicated than we expected, but we all survived." Meaning, specifically, that the Y.M.C.A. clerk, who was eating an egg-and-onion sandwich, did not take two minutes to figure out that there was something wrong about Callie. Questions. Lies, sneers, threats, phone calls. Abducting a minor. Trying to sneak a girl into the Y.M.C.A. for immoral purposes. Where are her parents? Who knows she's here? Who gave her permission? Who takes responsibility? A policeman on the scene. Two policemen. A full confession and a phone call, and the station agent remembers everything. He remembers lies. Miss Kernaghan has already missed the money and promises no forgiveness. Never wants to lay eyes on. A foundling born in a hotel lobby, parents probably not married, taken in and sheltered, ingratitude, bad blood. Let that be a lesson. Disgrace in plenty, even if Callie isn't a minor.

Meaning, further, that they all went on living, and many things happened. He himself, even in those first confused and humiliating days in Toronto, got the idea that a place like this, a city, with midday shadows in its deep, narrow downtown streets, its seriously ornamented offices, its constant movement and jangling streetcars, could be the place for him. A place to work and make money. So he stayed on, stayed at the Y.M.C.A., where his crisis—his and Edgar's and Callie's—was soon forgotten and something else happened next week. He got a job, and after a few years saw that this wasn't really the place to make money; the West was the place to make money. So he moved on.

Edgar and Callie went home to the farm with Edgar's parents. But they did not stay there long. Miss Kernaghan found she could not manage without them.

Callie's store is in a building she and Edgar own. The variety store and a hairdressing place downstairs, their living quarters upstairs.

(The hairdressing place is where the grocery used to be—the same grocery where Sam and Edgar used to buy jam tarts. "But who wants to hear about that?," Callie says. "Who wants to hear about the way things used to be?")

Sam's idea of good taste has been formed by his wife's grays and whites and blues and straight lines and single vases. Callie's place upstairs is stunning. Gold brocade draped to suggest a large window where no window is. Gold plushy carpet, rough white plaster ceiling sparkling with stars. One wall is a dull-gold mirror in which Sam sees himself crisscrossed by veins of black and silver. Lights hang from chains, in globes of amber glass.

In the midst of this sits Edgar, like a polished ornament, seldom moving, Of the three of them, he has kept his looks the best. He had the most to keep. He is tall, frail, beautifully groomed and dressed. Callie shaves him. She washes his hair every day, and it is white and glistening like the angel hair on Christmas trees. He can dress himself, but she puts everything out for him—trousers, socks, and matched tie and pocket handkerchief, soft shirts of deep blue or burgundy, which set off his pink cheeks and his hair.

"He had a little turn," says Callie. "Four years ago in May. He didn't lose his speech or anything, but I took him to the doctor and he said yes, he's had a little turn. But he's healthy. He's good."

Callie has given Sam permission to take Edgar for a walk. She spends her days in the store. Edgar is waiting upstairs in front of the television set. He knows Sam, seems glad to see him. He nods readily when Sam says, "Just get your overcoat on. Then we're off." Sam brings a new, light-gray overcoat and a gray cap from the closet, then, on second thought, a pair of rubbers to protect Edgar's shining shoes.

"Okay?" says Sam, but Edgar makes a gesture, meaning, "Just a moment." He is watching a handsome young woman interviewing an older woman. The older woman makes dolls. The dolls are made of dough. Though they are of different sizes, they all have the same expression, which is, in Sam's opinion, idiotic. Edgar seems to be quite taken with them. Or perhaps it is the interviewer, with her shaggy gold hair.

Sam stands until that's over. Then the weather comes on, and Edgar motions for him to sit down. That makes sense—to see what the weather is going to be before they start walking. Sam means to head up Orange Street—where a senior citizens' complex has replaced the skating rink and the cherry trees—and go around to the old Kernaghan house and the Canadian Tire lot. After the weather, Sam stays for the news, because there is something about a new tax regulation that interests him. Commercials keep interrupting, of course, but finally the news is over. Some figure skaters come on. After an hour or so has passed, Sam realizes there is no hope of budging Edgar.

Whenever Sam says anything, Edgar raises his hand, as if to say he'll have time to listen in a minute. He is never annoyed. He gives everything the same pleased attention. He smiles as he watches the skaters in their twinkly outfits. He seems guileless, but Sam detects satisfaction.

On the false mantel over the electric fireplace is a photograph of Callie and Edgar in wedding clothes. Callie's veil, in the style of a long-ago time, is attached to a cap trimmed with pearls and pulled down over her forehead. She sits in an armchair with her arms full of roses, and Edgar stands behind, staunch and slender.

Sam knows this picture was not taken on their wedding day. Many people in those days put on their wedding clothes and went to the photographer's studio on a later occasion. But these are not even their wedding clothes. Sam remembers that some woman connected with the Y.M.C.A. got Callie a dress, and it was a shapeless dull-pink affair. Edgar had no new clothes at all, and they were hastily married in Toronto by a minister neither of them knew. This photograph is meant to give quite a different impression. Perhaps it was taken years later. Callie looks a good deal older than on her real wedding day, her face broader, heavier, more authoritative. In fact, she slightly resembles Miss Kernaghan.

That is the thing that can never be understood—why Edgar spoke up the first night in Toronto and said that he and Callie were going to be married. There was no necessity—none that Sam could see. Callie was not pregnant and, in fact, as far as Sam knows she never became pregnant. Perhaps she really was too small, or not developed in the usual way. Edgar went ahead and did what nobody was making him do, took what he had run away from. Did he feel compunction; did he feel there are things from which there is no escape? He said that he and Callie were going to be married. But that was not what they were going to do—that was not what they were planning, surely? When Sam looked across at them on the train, and all three of them laughed with relief, it couldn't have been because they foresaw an outcome like this. They were just laughing. They were happy. They were free.

Fifty years too late to ask, Sam thinks. And even at the time he was too amazed. Edgar became a person he didn't know. Callie drew back, into her sorry female state. The moment of happiness he shared with them remained in his mind, but he never knew what to make of it. Do such moments really mean, as they seem to, that we have a life of happiness with which we only occasionally, knowingly, intersect? Do they shed such light before and after that all that has happened to us in our lives—or that we've made happen—can be dismissed?

When Callie comes upstairs, he doesn't mention the wedding picture. "I've got the electrician downstairs," Callie says. "So I've got to go down again and keep an eye on him. I don't want him sitting smoking a cigarette and charging me."

He is learning the things not to mention. Miss Kernaghan, the boarding house, the skating rink. Old times. This harping on old times by one who has been away to one who has stayed put is irritating—it is a subtle form of insult. And Callie is learning not to ask him how much his house cost, how much his condominium in Hawaii cost, how much he spent on various vacations and on his daughter's wedding—in short, she's learning that she will never find out how much money he has.

He can see another thing she's wondering about. He sees the

question wrinkling further the deep, blue-painted nests around her eyes, eyes that show now a lifetime of fairly successful efforts and calculations.

What does Sam want? That's what Callie wonders.

He thinks of telling her he might stay until he finds out. He might become a boarder.

"Edgar didn't seem to want to go out," Sam says. "He didn't seem to want to go out after all."

"No," says Callie. "No. He's happy."

Jesse and Meribeth

In high school, I had a tender, loyal, boring friendship with a girl named MaryBeth Crocker. I gave myself up to it, as I did to the warm, shallow, rather murky waters of the Maitland River in summer, when I lay on my back, and just fluttered my hands and feet, and was carried downstream.

This began one day in Music period, when there were not enough songbooks to go around and we were told to double up—boys with boys, of course, and girls with girls. I was looking around for some other girl who didn't have a special friend to sit with, and MaryBeth slipped into the seat beside me. She was new to the school then; she had come to live with her sister Beatrice, who was a nurse and worked at the local hospital. Their mother was dead; their father had remarried.

MaryBeth was a short girl, rather chubby but graceful, with large eyes that shaded from hazel-green to dark brown, an almond-colored skin free entirely of spots or freckles, and a pretty mouth that often had a slightly perplexed and pouting expression, as if she recalled a secret hurt. I could smell the flowery soap she washed with. Its sweetness penetrated the layers of dust and disinfectant and sweat, the old school smells—the dreamy boredom, the stale anxiety. I felt astonished, almost dismayed, at being chosen. For weeks afterward, I would wake up in the morning knowing I was happy and not knowing why. Then I would remember this moment.

MaryBeth and I often spoke of it. She said that her heart had been pounding as she skittered over to my seat, but she told herself it's now or never.

In the books I had read all through my childhood, girls were bound two by two in fast friendship, in exquisite devotion. They promised never to tell each other's secrets or keep anything hidden from each other, or form a deep and lasting friendship with any other girl. Marriage made no difference. They grew up and fell in love and got married, but they remained first in each other's heart. They named their daughters after each other and were ready to nurse each other through contagious illnesses or perjure themselves in court on each other's behalf. This was the solemn rigmarole of loyalty, the formal sentimentality that I now wanted, or thought appropriate, and imposed on MaryBeth. We swore and promised and confided. She went along with it all; she had a tender nature. She liked to snuggle up when she thought of something sad or frightening, and to hold hands.

That first fall we walked out of town along the railway tracks and told each other all the illnesses or accidents we had had in our lives, what things we were afraid of and what were our favorite colors, jewels, flowers, movie stars, desserts, soft drinks, and ice-cream flavors. We decided how many children we would have and which sex, and what their names would be. Also the color of our husbands' hair and eyes and what we would like them to do for a living. MaryBeth was afraid of the cows in the fields, and possible snakes along the track. We filled our hands with the silk from burst milkweed pods, the softest-feeling thing there is on earth, then let it all loose to hang on other dry weeds, like bits of snow or flowers.

"That's what they made parachutes out of in the war," I told MaryBeth. That wasn't true, but I believed it.

Sometimes we went to the house where MaryBeth shared a room with Beatrice. We sat on the porch sewing or went up to their room. The house was large, plain, painted yellow, and had an uncared-for look about it. It was just off the main street. The owners were a blind man and his wife, who had a couple of rooms at the back. The blind man sat and peeled potatoes for his wife, or crocheted the doilies and dresser runners that she took around to stores in town and tried to sell.

The girls in the house might dare each other to run down and chat with him when his wife was out. They dared each other to go down in their bras and panties or with nothing on at all. He seemed to guess what kind of game was going on. "Come over here," he would say. "Come closer, I can't hear you." Or, "Come and let me touch your dress. Let me see if I can guess what color it is."

MaryBeth would never play that game; she hated even to hear about it. She thought some girls were disgusting.

The girls she lived with were always in a ferment. They had feuds and alliances and fits of not speaking. Once, a girl pulled out a clump of another girl's hair because of an argument over some nail polish.

Brisk and ominous notes were taped to the medicine cabinet in the bathroom:

> *Sweaters should be dried in a person's own room because of the stink it makes with wool drying. Attention, A.M. and S.D.*
>
> *To Whom It May Concern, I have smelled my Evening in Paris on you and I don't appreciate it. You can buy your own. Sincerely, B.P.*

Things were always being washed: stockings and brassières and garter belts and sweaters—and, of course, hair. You couldn't turn around in the bathroom without having something flap in your face.

Cooking was done on hot plates. Girls who were saving money to buy things for their hope chests, or to move to the city, cooked Kraft Dinners. Others brought in greasy, delicious-smelling brown bags from the diner around the corner. French fries, hamburgers, jumbo hot dogs, doughnuts. Girls who were dieting cursed and slammed their doors as these smells went up the stairs.

From time to time, MaryBeth's sister Beatrice was dieting. She drank vinegar to take away her appetite. She drank glycerine to strengthen her fingernails.

"She wants to get a boyfriend—it makes me sick," MaryBeth said.

When MaryBeth and Beatrice were friends, they borrowed each other's clothes without asking, cuddled in bed, and told each other how their hair looked from behind. When they weren't, they stopped speaking. Then MaryBeth would cook up a rich bubbly mess of brown sugar, butter, and coconut on the hot plate, and wave the fragrant saucepan under Beatrice's nose before she and I commenced eating it with spoons. Or she would go to the store and buy a bag of marshmallows, which she claimed were Beatrice's favorite thing. The idea was to eat them in front of her. I didn't like to eat marshmallows raw—their puffy blandness slightly disgusted me—but MaryBeth would pop one into her mouth and hold it there like a cork, sticking her face in front of Beatrice's. Not quite knowing how to behave at such times, I would go through the closet.

MaryBeth's father didn't want her living with him, but he gave her plenty of money for clothes. She had a dark-blue winter coat with a squirrel collar that I thought luxurious. She had many drawstring blouses, a fashion of the time—pink, yellow, mauve, sky blue, lime green. And a coveted armload of silver bangles. Two all-round pleated skirts I remember—navy-blue and white, turquoise and cerise. I looked at all these things with more homage than envy. I dangled the heavy bangles on my fingers, inspected the dainty powder puffs and the eyebrow tweezers. I myself was not allowed to pluck my eyebrows, and had to put on my makeup in the washroom of the Town Hall on the way to school. During the school year, I lived in town with my Aunt Ena, who was strict. All I had for a powder puff was a gritty scrap of flannel, decidedly sordid-looking. Beside MaryBeth, I felt that I was a crude piece of work altogether, with my strong legs and hefty bosom—robust and sweaty and ill-clad, undeserving, grateful. And at the same time, deeply, naturally, unspeakably, unthinkably—I could not speak or think about it—superior.

After the summer holidays, which she spent with her father and stepmother in Toronto, MaryBeth said that we should not walk out on the railway tracks anymore, it might get us a bad reputation.

She said that it was the new style to wear a scarf over your hair, even on a sunny day, and she brought back several gauzy squares for this purpose. She told me to choose one, and I chose the pink shading into rose, and she cried admiringly, "Oh, that's the very prettiest!" So I tried to give it back. We had a pretend-argument, and I ended up keeping it.

She told me about the things there were to buy in Eaton's and Simpson's, and how she nearly got her heel stuck in an escalator, and some unkind things her stepmother had said, and the plots of movies she had seen. She had gone on rides at the Exhibition that made her sick, and she had been accosted by a man on a streetcar. He wore a gray suit and a gray fedora and offered to take her to the Riverdale Zoo.

Sometimes now I felt myself slipping away while MaryBeth talked. I felt my thoughts slipping off as they did at school during the explanation of a mathematical problem, or at the beginning of the big prayer before the sermon at church. Not that I wished to be elsewhere, or even to be alone. I understood that this was what friendship was like.

We had decided to change the spelling of our names. Mine was to become Jesse instead of Jessie and hers was to be Meribeth, not MaryBeth. We signed these names to the test papers we turned in at school.

The teacher waved my paper in the air. "I can't give a mark to this person, because I don't know who this person is," she said. "Who is this Jesse?" She spelled the name out loud. "That is a boy's name. Does anybody here know a boy named Jesse?"

Not a word was said about the name Meribeth. That was typical. MaryBeth was a favorite with everybody, on account of her looks and her clothes and her exotic situation, as well as her soft, flattering voice and polite ways. Rough girls and caustic teachers alike were taken with her. Boys were, too, of course, but she said her sister wouldn't let her go out with them. I never knew if this was true or not. MaryBeth was adept at small fibs, gentle refusals.

She gave up spelling her name the new way, since I wasn't to be allowed to change mine. We continued to use the special spelling when we signed our notes to each other or wrote letters in the summer.

When I was halfway through my third year at high school, my Aunt Ena got me a job. I was to work for the Crydermans, two days a week, after school. Aunt Ena knew the Crydermans because she was their cleaning lady. I was to do some ironing and tidying up, and I was to get the vegetables ready for supper.

"That's dinner, in their books," Aunt Ena said, in such a flat voice you couldn't tell whether she censured the Crydermans for affectation, or conceded them a superior position that gave them a right to it, or simply wished to state that whatever they said or did was completely outside of her range of understanding and ought to be outside of mine.

Aunt Ena was my father's aunt, she was that old. She was the cleaning lady in town rather as a doctor might be the Doctor, or a music teacher the Music Teacher. She was respected. She didn't accept leftover food, no matter how delicious, or take home cast-off clothing, no matter how excellent its condition. Many of the women she worked for felt bound to do some sort of hurry-up cleaning before she arrived, and took their own empty liquor bottles out to the garbage. Aunt Ena was not fooled.

She and her daughter, Floris, and her son, George, lived in a narrow, tidy house on a steep street where the houses were close together and so near to the street that you could almost touch the porch railings from the sidewalk. My room was behind the kitchen—a former pantry, with pale-green tongue-in-groove walls. I tried to count the boards as I lay in bed, but always had to give up. In the wintertime, I took all my clothes into bed in the morning and got dressed under the covers. There was no provision for heating a pantry.

Aunt Ena came home worn out from exercising her authority all over town. But she roused herself; she exercised it over us as well. She made us understand—Floris and George and me—that we were all superior people in spite of, or perhaps because of, relative poverty. She made us understand that we had to confirm this every day of our lives by having our shoes cleaned and our buttons sewn on, by not using coarse language, by not smoking (in the case of women), by getting high marks (me), and by never touching alcohol (everybody). Nobody has a good word to say nowadays for such narrowness and proud caution and threadbare decency. I don't myself, but I didn't think at the time that I was suffering much from it. I learned how to circumvent some rules and I went along with others, and in general I accepted that even a superiority based on such hard notions was better than no superiority at all. And I didn't plan to live on there, like George and Floris.

Floris had been married once for a short time, but she did not seem to have derived any sense of importance from it. She worked in the shoe store and went to choir practice and was addicted to jigsaw puzzles, of the kind that take up a whole card table. Though I pestered her for it, she would not give me any satisfactory account of her romance or her marriage or her young husband's death from blood poisoning—a story I would have liked to use, to counterbalance MaryBeth's true tragic story of the death of her mother. Floris had large gray-blue eyes set so far apart that they almost seemed to be looking in different directions. There was an estranged, helpless expression in them.

George had not gone past Grade 4 at school. He worked at the piano factory, where he answered to the name of Dumbo without apparent resentment or embarrassment. He was so shy and quiet that he could make Floris with her tired petulance seem spirited. He cut pictures out of magazines and pinned them up around his room—not pictures of half-clothed pretty girls but just of things he liked the look of: an airplane, a chocolate cake, Elsie the Borden cow. He could play Chinese checkers, and sometimes invited me to have a game. Usually I told him I was too busy.

When I brought MaryBeth home to supper, Aunt Ena criticized the noise the bangles made at the table and wondered that a girl of that age was allowed to pluck her eyebrows. She also said—in George's hearing—that my friend did not seem to be blessed with a lot of brains. I was not surprised. Neither MaryBeth nor I expected anything but the most artificial, painful, formal contact with the world of adults.

The Cryderman house was still called the Steuer house. Until not so long ago, Mrs. Cryderman had been Evangeline Steuer. The house had been built by Dr. Steuer, her father. It was set back from the street on a smooth, built-up terrace, and was unlike any other house in town. In fact, it was unlike any other house I had ever seen, reminding me of a bank or some important public building. It was one story high, and flat-roofed, with low French windows, classical pillars, a balustrade around the roof with an urn at each corner. Urns also flanked the front steps. The urns and the balustrade and the pillars had all been painted a creamy white, and the house itself was covered with pale-pink stucco. By this time, both the paint and the stucco were beginning to flake and look dingy.

I started going there in February. The urns were piled high with snow like dishes full of ice cream, and the various bushes in the yard looked as if polar-bear rugs had been thrown over them. There was just a little meandering path to the front door, instead of the broad neat walkway other people shovelled.

"Mr. Cryderman doesn't shovel the snow because he doesn't believe it's permanent," Mrs. Cryderman said. "He thinks he'll wake up some morning and it'll be all gone. Like fog. He wasn't prepared for this!"

Mrs. Cryderman talked emphatically, as if everything she said was drastically important, and at the same time she made everything sound like a joke. This way of talking was entirely new to me.

Once inside that house, you never got a view of outside, except through the kitchen window over the sink. The living room was where Mrs. Cryderman spent her days, lying on the sofa, with ashtrays and cups and glasses and magazines and cushions all around her. She wore a Chinese dressing gown, or a long dark-green robe of brushed wool, or a jacket of quilted black satin—quickly ash-sprinkled—and a pair of maternity pants. The jacket would flap open and give me a glimpse of her stomach, already queerly swollen. She had the lamps turned on and the wine-colored curtains drawn across the windows, and sometimes she burned a little cone of incense in a brass dish. I loved those cones, a dusty-pink color, lying snug as bullets in their pretty box, retaining their shape magically as they turned to ash. The room was full of marvels—Chinese furniture of carved black wood, vases of peacock feathers and pampas grass, fans spread against the faded red walls, heaps of velvet cushions, satin cushions with gold tassels.

The first thing I had to do was tidy up. I picked up the city newspapers strewn on the floor, put the cushions back on the chairs and sofas, gathered up the cups with cold tea or coffee in them and the plates with their hardened scraps of food and the glasses in which there might be slices of soggy fruit, dregs of wine—sweet, weakened, but still faintly alcoholic mixtures. In the kitchen, I drank anything that was left and sucked the fruit to get the strange taste of liquor.

Mrs. Cryderman's baby was expected in late June or early July. The uncertainty of the date was due to the irregularity of her menstrual cycle. (This was the first time I had ever heard anybody say "menstrual." We said "monthlies" or "the curse" or used more roundabout expressions.) She herself was certain that she got pregnant on the night of Mr. Cryderman's birthday when she was full of champagne. The twenty-ninth of September. The birthday was Mr. Cryderman's thirty-third. Mrs. Cryderman was forty. She said she might as well own up to it, she was a cradle robber. And she was paying the price. Forty was too old to have a baby. It was too old to have a first baby. It was a mistake.

She pointed out the damage. First, the pale-brown blotches on her face and neck, which she said were all over her. They made me think of the flesh of pears beginning to go rotten—that soft discoloration, the discouraging faint deep bruises. Next, she showed her varicose veins, which kept her lying on the sofa. Cranberry-colored spiders, greenish lumps all over her legs. They turned black when she stood up. Before she put her feet to the floor, she had to wrap her legs in long, tight, rubbery bandages.

"Take my advice and have your babies while you're young," she said. "Go out and get pregnant immediately, if possible. I thought I was above all this. Ha-ha!" She did have a little sense, because she said, "Don't ever tell your aunt the way I talk to you!"

When Mrs. Cryderman was Evangeline Steuer, she didn't live in this house, only visited it from time to time, often with friends. Her appearances in town were brief and noteworthy. I had seen her driving her car with the top down, an orange scarf over her dark page-boy hair. I had seen her in the drugstore, wearing shorts and a halter, her legs and midriff sleek and tanned as if bound in brown silk. She was laughing that time, and loudly admitting to a hang-over. I had seen her in church wearing a gauzy black hat with pink silk roses, a party hat. She didn't belong here; she belonged in the world we saw in magazines and movies—a world of glossy triviality, of hard-faced wisecracking comedians, music in public ballrooms, pink neon cocktail glasses tipped over bar doors. She was our link with that world, our proof that it existed, and we existed with it, that its frittering vice and cruel luxury were not entirely unconnected with us. As long as she stayed there, making her whirlwind visits home, she was forgiven, perhaps distantly admired. Even my Aunt Ena, who had to deal with the broken glass in the fireplace, the fried chicken trodden into the rug, the shoe polish on the rim of the bathtub, was able to grant Evangeline Steuer some unholy privilege—though perhaps it was only the privilege of being an example of how money made you shameless, leisure made you useless, self-indulgence marked you out for some showy disaster.

But now what had Evangeline Steuer done? She had become a Mrs., like anybody else. She had bought the local newspaper for her husband to run. She was expecting a baby. She had lost her function, mixed things up. It was one thing to be a smoking, drinking, profane, and glamorous bachelor girl, and quite another thing to be a smoking, drinking, profane, and no longer glamorous expectant mother.

"Don't pay any attention to me, Jessie. I never had to lie around like this before. I was always in the action before. All that brute of a doctor does is tell me I'll be worse before I'm better. 'Whatever goes in has to come out. Five minutes' pleasure, nine months' misery.' I said to him, 'What do you mean, *five* minutes?' "

I did pay attention. I had never got such an earful or eyeful before. I told MaryBeth everything. I described the living room, Mrs. Cryderman's outfits, the bottles in the buffet with their gold and green and ruby-colored contents, the tins of unfamiliar eatables in the kitchen cupboards—smoked oysters, anchovies, puréed chestnuts, artichokes, as well as the big tinned hams and fruit puddings. I told about the veins, the bandages and blotches—making these things sound even worse than they were—and about Mrs. Cryderman's long-distance conversations with her friends. Her friends' names were Bunt, Pookie, Pug, and Spitty, so you could not tell if they were men or women. Her own name, among them, was Jelly. After she finished talking to them on the phone, she told me about money they had lost or accidents they had had or practical jokes they had played, or very complicated and unusual romances they were having.

Aunt Ena noticed that I was not getting much ironing done. I said that it was not my fault—Mrs. Cryderman kept me in the living room, talking. Aunt Ena said there was nothing to stop me setting up the ironing board in the living room if Mrs. Cryderman insisted on conversation.

"Let her talk," Aunt Ena said. "You iron. That's what you're paid for."

"I don't mind you ironing in here, but you'll have to scram out the minute Mr. Cryderman gets home," Mrs. Cryderman said. "He hates that—any kind of domestic stuff going on where he's around."

She told me that Mr. Cryderman had been born and brought up in Brisbane, Australia, in a big house with banana trees all around, and that his mother had colored maids. I thought this sounded a little mixed up, as if *Gone With the Wind* had got into Australia, but I thought it might be true. She said that Mr. Cryderman had left Australia and become a journalist in Singapore, and then he was with the British Army in Burma when they were defeated by the Japanese. Mr. Cryderman had walked from Burma into India.

"With a little bunch of British soldiers and some Americans

and native girls—nurses. No hanky-panky, though. All those girls did was sing hymns. They'd all been Christianized. 'Onward, Christian Soldiers'! Anyway, they were in no condition to carry on. Sick and wounded, walking day after day in the terrible heat. Charged by wild elephants. He's going to write a book about it. Mr. Cryderman is. They had to build their own rafts and float downriver. They had malaria. They walked over the Himalayas. They were heroes and nobody has even heard about it."

I thought that sounded fishy, too. Terrible heat in the Himalayas, which were known to be covered with eternal snow.

"I said to Bunt, 'Eric fought with the British in Burma,' and Bunt said, 'The British didn't fight in Burma—the Japs wiped their ass on the British in Burma.' People don't know a damn thing. Bunt couldn't walk to the top of Yonge Street."

Years later, maybe a quarter of a century later, I read about the walk that General Stilwell led out of Burma into India, through the pass above Tamu and down the Chindwin River. In the party were some British commandos, dirty and half starved. Eric Cryderman might have been one of them.

The meeting of Mr. and Mrs. Cryderman took place when he showed up one day to sublet her apartment in Toronto. He was planning to work as a journalist in Canada. She was planning to drive to Mexico with friends. She never made it. As soon as she saw Mr. Cryderman, that was that. Her friends all told her not to marry him. Seven years younger than she was, divorced—with a wife and child somewhere in Australia—and he had no money. Everybody said he was an adventurer. But she was not daunted. She married him within six weeks and didn't invite any of them to the wedding.

I thought that I should contribute something to the conversation, so I said, "Why were they against him just because he was adventurous?"

"Ha-ha!" said Mrs. Cryderman. "That wasn't what they meant. They meant he was after my money. Which I can't even persuade him to live on while he writes a book about his experiences. He has to be independent. He has to write about what the fool bridesmaids wore and the trousseau tea and all the blather at the town council, and it's driving him crazy. He is the most talented man I ever met, and someday you'll be bragging that you knew him!"

As soon as we heard Mr. Cryderman at the door, I whisked the ironing basket away into the kitchen, as directed. Mrs. Cryderman would call out, in a new, silly-sweet, mocking, anxious voice, "Is that my honey-boy home? Is that Little Lord Fauntleroy? Is it the Mad Dingo?"

Mr. Cryderman, taking off his boots in the hall, would reply that it was Dick Tracy, or Barnacle Bill the Sailor. Then he would come into the living room and go straight to the sofa, where she lay with arms outstretched. They did smacking kisses, while I beat an awkward retreat with the ironing board.

"He married her for her money," I said to MaryBeth.

MaryBeth wanted to know what he looked like.

"Like something dug up out of a bog," I said. But that was Aunt Ena's description after she first laid eyes on Mr. Cryderman. I repeated it because I liked the sound of it. I didn't really find it apt. It was true that Mr. Cryderman was thin, tall and thin, and that he had a sallow complexion. But he didn't have a moldy or sickly look. In fact, he had a kind of light-boned, sharp-featured, crisp good looks, a kind of looks very popular at the time. A pencil-line mustache, cool squinting eyes, a sarcastic half-smile.

"Like a snake in the grass," I amended. "But she is out of her mind in love with him." I acted out their daily reunion, smacking my lips and flinging my arms about.

Mrs. Cryderman told Mr. Cryderman that I read like a demon and was a genius at history. This was because I had straightened out some confusion of hers in connection with a historical novel she was trying to read. I had explained how Peter the Great was connected to Catherine the Great.

"Is that so?" said Mr. Cryderman. His accent made him sound both softer and meaner than a Canadian. "Who is your favorite writer?"

"Dostoyevsky," I said, or thought I said.

"Dostoy-vetsky," said Mr. Cryderman thoughtfully. "What is your favorite book by him?"

I was too flustered to notice the imitation.

"The Brothers Karamazov," I said. That was the only book by Dostoyevsky that I had read. I had read it through the night in the cold of the back bedroom, in my haste and greed skipping a lot of the Grand Inquisitor and other parts where I had got bogged down.

"Which is your favorite brother?" said Mr. Cryderman, smiling as if he had got me into a corner.

"Mitya," I said. By this time, I wasn't so nervous and would have liked to go on, explaining why this was so—that Alyosha was too angelic and Ivan too intellectual, and so on. On the way home, I imagined that I had done this, and that while I spoke, the expression on Mr. Cryderman's face had changed to one of respect and delicate chagrin. Then I realized the mistake I had made, in pronunciation.

I didn't get a chance to go on, because Mrs. Cryderman cried out from the sofa, "Favorites, favorites! Who is everybody's favorite big old bloated old pregnant lady? That's what I want to know!"

However much I mocked the Crydermans to MaryBeth, I wanted something from them. Attention. Recognition. I liked Mrs. Cryderman's saying I was a genius at history, even though I knew it was a silly thing to say. I would have valued what he said more. I thought that he looked down on this town and everybody in it. He didn't care what they thought of him for not shovelling his walk. I wanted to snip one little hole in his contempt.

Just the same, he had to be called honey-boy, and submit to those kisses.

MaryBeth had new things to tell me, too. Beatrice had a boyfriend, and hoped to be engaged. MaryBeth said they were going at it hot and heavy.

Beatrice's boyfriend was an apprentice barber. He visited her in the afternoons, when she got home from her shift at the hospital and there was a lull in barbershop business. The other girls who lived in the house were at work then, and MaryBeth and I would not have been there, either, if we had been tactful enough to loiter around the school, or go for Cokes, or spend time looking in store windows. But MaryBeth insisted on making a beeline for the rooming house.

We would find Beatrice making up the bed. She took all the covers off and tucked in the sheet with a professional briskness. Then she laid an absorbent cotton pad across the sheet at a strategic place. I was reminded of the days when I used to sleep shamefully over rubber, being an occasional bed wetter.

Now she replaced the top covers, smoothed and tidied them, hiding the secret. She plumped up the pillows, turned a corner of the top sheet down over the quilt. A queasy feeling of childhood lust came back to me, a recollection of bedclothes intimacies. Rough blankets, comforting flannelette sheets, secrets.

Down the hall to the bathroom went Beatrice, having to fix up the appropriate part of herself as she had fixed the bed. She had a serious, dutiful look on her face, a look of housewifely preoccupation. She still had not spoken one word to us.

"I wouldn't be surprised if she went ahead and did it right in front of us," said MaryBeth loudly as we passed the bathroom door on our way downstairs. The water was running. What exactly did Beatrice do? I thought it involved sponges.

We sat on the veranda steps. The swing had been taken down for the winter and not been put back yet.

"She has no shame," MaryBeth said. "And I have to sleep in the same bed. She thinks if she puts the pad over the sheet it's all right. She stole that pad from the hospital. You could never trust her, even when she was little. Once, we had a fight and she said, 'Let's make up, shake hands,' and when I took her hand to shake, she had a baby toad in it and the toad had gone to the bathroom on her."

The snow was not quite gone; a nippy wind was blowing the smell of swamps and creeks and floodwaters into town. But the barber's apprentice hadn't bothered to put on a coat. He came hurrying along the alley in his white smock, head down, purposefully. He wasn't prepared to see us.

"Hi there!" he said with false assurance, nervous jocularity.

MaryBeth wouldn't answer him, and I couldn't, either, out of loyalty. We didn't get up, but shifted apart, giving him just enough room to go up the steps. I listened for, but couldn't hear, the opening and closing of the bedroom door.

"They might as well be two dogs," MaryBeth said. "Two dogs doing it."

I thought about what was going on at that very moment. The greeting, the look exchanged, the removal of clothing. In what order? Accompanied by what words and caresses? Would they be frenzied or methodical? Would they roll on the bed half-undressed, or proceed as at the doctor's? I thought the latter way would be more like them.

Take that off. Yes. Now lie down. Open your legs. Calm orders, dumb obedience. Beatrice glazed, submissive. The barber's apprentice, that scrawny, blotchy-necked fellow, grown imperious, ready to wield his perverse power. Now. Yes. Now.

"One time, a boy asked me to do it," MaryBeth said. "I nearly got him expelled." She told me how, in Grade 7, a boy had passed her a note that said, "Do you want to F.?" and she had shown the note to the teacher.

"Somebody wants me to do it," I said. I was very surprised at myself. I kept my eyes down and did not look at MaryBeth. Who? she said, and what did he say exactly, and where did he say it? When? Was it anybody in our class? Why hadn't I told her?

She bumped down to the step below me, so that she could look into my face. She put her hands on my knees. "We promised we'd tell each other everything," she said.

I shook my head.

"It hurts my feelings a lot you haven't told me."

I rubbed my lips together as if to hold the secret in. "Actually, he's in love with me," I said.

"Jessie! Tell me!"

She promised me the use of her Eversharp pencil until the end of the school year. I did not respond. She said I could use her fountain pen as well. Her Eversharp pencil and her fountain pen, the set.

I had been planning to tease her for a little longer, then to tell her that it was all a joke. I did not even have anybody's name in my head, in the beginning. I did now, but it was too outrageous. I couldn't believe that I would ever say it.

"Jessie, I'll give you a bangle. Not lend. I said *give.* I'll give you whichever bangle you want and you can keep it."

"If I was going to tell his name, I wouldn't do it for a bangle," I said.

"I'll swear to God I won't tell. Cross my heart and hope to die."

"Just swear to God."

"I will. I swear to God, Jessie. I've sworn to God."

"Mr. Cryderman," I said softly. I felt wonderfully lightened, not burdened, by my lie. "It's him."

MaryBeth took her hands off my knees and sat up straight. "He's old," she said. "You said he was ugly! He's married!"

"I never said ugly," I said. "He's only thirty-three."

"You don't even like him!"

"Sometimes when you fall in love, it starts out that way."

Once, I knew an old woman who said to me, when talking about her life, that she had spent three years having an affair with Robert Browning. She was not in the least senile; she was a very competent and straightforward old woman. She didn't say she loved Browning's writing, or spent all her time reading about him. She didn't say she had fantasies. "Oh, yes," she said, "and then there was the three years' affair I had with Robert Browning." I waited for her to laugh or add some little explanatory word, but she did not do so. I have to think, then, that the affair she conducted in her imagination was so serious and strenuous that she forbade herself to describe it as imaginary.

The affair I conducted that spring with Mr. Cryderman—in my head, and in front of MaryBeth—may not have been that important in my life, but it kept me busy. There was no more sense of drift and boredom, when MaryBeth and I were together. I had to keep arranging and rearranging things, then fit them into place by means of the bits of information I chose to give out. I consummated the affair but did not tell her, and was glad afterward because

I decided to unconsummate it. I couldn't adequately imagine the sequence of moves or what would be said afterward. I didn't at all mind the lying. Once I had taken the plunge into falsehood—by saying Mr. Cryderman's name—falsehood felt wonderfully comfortable.

It wasn't just by what I told, but by how I looked, that I dramatized what was going on. I did some contrary things. I didn't pull my belts tight and make up my face and display myself as a youthful temptress. Instead, I took to wearing my hair in braids wrapped around my head, and I left off rouge and lipstick, though I still powdered heavily to make myself look pale. I went to school in a baggy crêpe blouse of Aunt Ena's. I told MaryBeth that Mr. Cryderman had asked me to dress like this and braid my hair. He could not bear the thought of anyone else looking at my hair or seeing the outline of my breasts. He suffered from his burden of love. I, too, suffered. I bowed my shoulders; I had a chastened air. The passions are no light matter, was my message to MaryBeth. Guilt and misgiving and a glowering desire must be seen as my daily companions.

Mr. Cryderman's, as well. In my imagination, he grew bold. He fondled and whispered, then rebuked himself, groaned, became devout, and kissed my eyelids.

What about the real Mr. Cryderman? Did all this make me tremble when I heard him at the door, lie in wait for him, hope for a sign? Not in the least. When he began to play his role in my imagination, he faded in reality. I no longer hoped for an interesting conversation, or even a nod in the direction of my existence. In my mind, I had improved his looks somewhat—given him a healthier color, rolled back his customary slight sneer to expose a gloomy tenderness. I avoided looking at him in the flesh, so that I would not have to change him all over again.

MaryBeth probed for details but took no pleasure in any of this. She urged me never to surrender. "Couldn't you tell Mrs. Cryderman on him?" she said.

"It would kill her. She might die anyway when she has the baby."

"Would you get married if she did?"

"I'm underage."

"He could wait. If he loves you like he says. He'd need somebody to look after the baby. Would he get all her money?"

Mention of the baby made me think of something real, and unpleasant and embarrassing, that had happened recently at the Crydermans'. Mrs. Cryderman had called me to come and see the baby kicking her. She was lying on the sofa with her robe pulled up, a cushion covering the most private part of her. "There, see!" she cried, and I saw it, not a flutter on the surface but an underground shifting and rolling of the whole blotchy mound. Her navel stuck out like a cork ready to pop. My arms and forehead broke out in a sweat. I felt a hard ball of disgust pushing up in my throat. She laughed and the cushion fell off. I ran to the kitchen.

"Jessie, what are you scared of? I don't think one of them ever came out that way yet!"

Two more scenes at the Crydermans'.

Mr. Cryderman is home early. He and Mrs. Cryderman are together in the living room when I arrive after school. Mrs. Cryderman still keeps the curtains closed all day, though it's spring outside, hot May weather. She says this is so nobody can look in and see the shape she's in.

I come in out of the hot, bright afternoon and find the incense burning in the stuffy, curtained room and the two pale Crydermans giggling and having drinks. He is sitting on the sofa with her feet in his lap.

"Time to join the celebration!" says Mr. Cryderman. "It's our farewell party! Our fare-thee-well party, Jessie. Farewell, begone, goodbye!"

"Control yourself!" says Mrs. Cryderman, beating her bare heels against his legs. "We aren't gone yet. We have to wait till the monstrous infant is born."

Drunk, I think. I had often seen them drinking, but up until now had not been able to spot any interesting alterations in behavior.

"Eric is going to write his book," says Mrs. Cryderman.

"Eric is going to write his book," says Mr. Cryderman, in a silly high-pitched voice.

"You are!" says Mrs. Cryderman, drumming her heels some more. "And we are getting out of here the instant the monster is born."

"Is it really a monster?" says Mr. Cryderman. "Has it got two heads? Can we put it in the freak show and make a lot of money?"

"We don't need money."

"I do."

"I wish you'd cut that out. I don't know if it's got two heads, but it feels as if it's got fifty feet. It frightened Jessie the other day."

She tells him how I ran.

"You have to get used to these things, Jessie," says Mr. Cryderman. "Girls in some parts of the world have a baby or two already by the time they're your age. You can't cheat Nature. Little brown girls, practically babies themselves, they've got babies."

"Oh, I'm sure," says Mrs. Cryderman. "Jessie, be a lamb. You know what gin is, don't you? Put a little gin in this glass and fill it up with orange juice, so I can get my vitamin C."

I take her glass. Mr. Cryderman tries to get up, but she holds him down until he says, "Cigarettes. I think they're in the bedroom."

When he comes back from the bedroom, he enters the kitchen, not the living room. I'm at the sink, filling up the ice-cube tray.

"Did you find any?" calls Mrs. Cryderman.

"Just checking out here."

He has a package of cigarettes in his hand, but rummages noisily in the cupboard beside the sink. He presses against me, side to side. He puts his hand on my shoulder, squeezes. He moves that hand across my back, touches my bare neck. I stand with the ice tray in my hands, looking out the window at an old bus parked in the back lane, behind the gospel hall. The words "Calvary Tabernacle" are painted on its side.

Just the tips of Mr. Cryderman's fingers move on my throat. Their touch is light at first as drops of water. Then heavier. Heavier and heavier, finally stroking my skin as if they would leave furrows.

"Found some."

When I take Mrs. Cryderman her drink, Mr. Cryderman is sitting in the armchair by the stand-up ashtray.

"Come sit where you were," she says, in her silly-sweet voice.

"I'm smoking."

My throat tingles as if it had taken a blow.

The second scene a few days later, on the next regular day of my employment.

Mr. Cryderman is working in the garden. He is in his shirt sleeves, still wearing his tie, hacking away with a hoe at the vines that cover a little tumbledown summerhouse in a corner of the yard. He calls to me warningly, and waits for me to come over to him through the uncut grass. He says that Mrs. Cryderman is not well. The doctor has given her something to put her to sleep, to keep her still and quiet so that the baby won't be born too soon. He says that I'd better not go inside today.

I am standing a couple of yards away from him. Now he says, "Come over here. Here. There's something I want to ask you."

I go closer, with shaking legs, but all he does is point to a vigorous, leafy, red-stalked plant at his feet.

"What is this thing, do you know? Should I dig it up? I can't tell what's a weed around here and what isn't."

It is a rhubarb plant, familiar to me as grass or dandelions.

"I don't know," I say, and at the moment I don't.

"You don't know? What good are you to me, Jessie? Isn't this a queer little hole of a place?" He waves at the summerhouse. "I don't know what it was built for. Midgets?"

He grabs some vines, tears them loose, and says, "Step in."

I do. Inside, it is a wonderfully secret place, shady and neglected, with drifts of leafy debris on the bumpy earth floor. It is true that the roof is very low. Both of us have to bend over.

"Are you hot?" asks Mr. Cryderman.

"No." In fact, chilly waves are passing over me—waves of weakness, physical dismay.

"Yes, you are. You're all sweaty under that mop of hair."

He touches my neck in a matter-of-fact way, like a doctor checking the evidence, then moves his hand to my cheek and hairline.

"Even your forehead is sweaty."

I can smell cigarettes on his fingers, and the inky machinery smell of the newspaper office. All I want is to be equal to this. Ever since Mr. Cryderman touched my throat at the kitchen sink, I have felt that I am seeing the power of my own lies, my own fantasy. I am a person capable of wizardry but helpless. There is nothing to do but submit, submit to the consequences. I am wondering whether the passionate attack will take place here, without further preparation—here in the shelter of the summerhouse, on the earth floor, among the dead leaves and scratchy twigs that perhaps conceal the dead bodies of mice or birds. I do know one thing, and that is that the lovelorn declarations, the delicate pleas and moonings often voiced by Mr. Cryderman in my imagination, are going to have no place on the agenda.

"You think I'm going to kiss you, Jessie?" says Mr. Cryderman. "I have no doubt you're a handy kisser. No," he says, as if I've specifically asked him. "No, Jessie. Let's sit down."

There are boards attached to the summerhouse walls that serve as benches. Some are broken. I sit on one that isn't, and he sits on another. We lean forward to escape the tough branches that have broken through the latticework walls.

He lays his hand on my knee, on my cotton skirt.

"What about Mrs. Cryderman, Jessie? Do you think she'd be very happy if she could see us now?"

I take this to be a rhetorical question, but he repeats it, and I have to say, "No."

"Because I did to her what you might like me to do to you, she's going to have a baby, and she isn't going to have an easy time of it."

He strokes my leg through the thin cotton. "You're an impulsive girl, Jessie. You shouldn't go inside places like this with men just because they ask you. You shouldn't be so ready to let them kiss you. I think you're hot-blooded. Aren't you? You're hot-blooded. You've got some lessons to learn."

And this is how things continue—the stroking and the lecturing, coming at me together. He is telling me I'm to blame, while his fingers start up these flutters under my skin, rousing a tender, distant ache. His dry voice reproaches me. His hand rouses and his words shame me, and something in his voice mocks, mocks endlessly, at both these responses. I don't understand that this isn't fair. At least, I don't think of protesting that it isn't fair. I feel shame all right, and confusion, and longing. But I am not ashamed of what he's telling me I should be ashamed of. I'm ashamed of being caught out, made foolish, of being so enticed and scolded. And I can't stop it.

"One thing you will have to learn, Jessie. To consider other people. The reality of other people. It sounds simple but it can be difficult. For you it will be difficult."

He may be referring to his wife, whom I am not considering. But I understand this differently. Isn't it true that all the people I know in the world so far are hardly more than puppets for me, serving the glossy contrivings of my imagination? It's true. He has hit the nail on the head, as Aunt Ena is fond of saying. But hitting the nail on the head in a matter like this, in a matter of intimate failure, isn't apt to make people abashed and grateful and eager to change their ways. Pride hardens, instead, over the nakedly perceived fault. So mine does now. Pride hardens, pride deals with all those craven licks of sweetness, douses the hope of pleasure, the deep-seated glow of invitation. What do I want with anybody who can know so much about me? In fact, if I could wipe him off the face of the earth now, I would.

He feels the change. He takes his hand away and gets up. He tells me to go out ahead of him, to go home. He may have said a couple of cautionary words, in addition, but I was not listening anymore.

On top of this, MaryBeth announced that she did not believe me. "I did at first. I did. But then I started to wonder."

"We broke off," I said. "It's all over."

"I don't believe you," said MaryBeth, in a trembling voice, grieving and shaking her head. "I don't believe there was anything going on between you and him at all. I had to tell you. Don't be mad. I had to."

I didn't answer her. I walked along quickly. We were on the way to school. We had met as usual at the Dominion Bank corner and she had waited three blocks before blurting out what she had to say. She had to trot to keep up with me. Just before we caught up with some other girls—just before I called out their names with a great show of friendliness and good humor—I gave her a bitter look. I gave her the look deserved by a traitor. And I thought she did deserve it. She was wrong—plenty had gone on between me and Mr. Cryderman. She was right, too, of course. But I suppressed all thought of that with ferocious ease. You can feel the same rush of justified anger, whether you are rightfully or wrongfully accused.

Without quite planning to, I took up a policy of not speaking to MaryBeth. When she came up to me in the cloakroom and said softly, "Are we walking home together, Jessie," I didn't answer. When she walked along beside me, I pretended she wasn't there. Examinations had begun, our schedules were disrupted; it was easy to avoid her.

A letter appeared, folded into my French book. I didn't read it all the way through. She said that I was hurting her, that she couldn't eat, she cried in bed at night, she got such blinding headaches from crying that she couldn't see the questions on the examinations and would fail. She apologized, she wished that she had kept her mouth shut; how could she tell me she was sorry when I wouldn't even speak to her? She knew one thing—she would never have the heart to treat me as I was treating her.

I looked ahead to the end of the letter and saw two intertwined hearts made up of little x's, with our two names inside. Jesse and Meribeth. I didn't read any more.

I wanted to get rid of her. I was tired of her complaints and confidences, her pretty face and gentle nature. I had got beyond her, beyond needing anything she had to offer. But there was more to it than that. Her puffy eyes, her stricken looks satisfied something in me. I felt the better for wounding her. No doubt about it. I got back a little of whatever I had lost in the Crydermans' summerhouse.

A few years after this—not a long time to me now, but a long time then—I was walking down the main street of that town where I had gone to high school. I was a graduate student by then. I had won scholarships and no longer mispronounced Dostoyevsky. Aunt Ena was dead. She sat down and died, just after waxing a floor. Floris was married. It seemed that she had been courted for years, in secret, by the druggist who had the shop next door to the shoe store, but Aunt Ena objected to him: he drank (that is, he drank a little), and was a Catholic. Floris had two baby boys, one right after the other, and she put an auburn rinse on her hair and drank beer with her husband in the evenings. George lived with them. He drank beer, too, and helped look after the babies. Floris was not shy or irritable anymore. She wanted to be friends now; she gave me flowered scarves and costume jewellery which I could not wear, and lotions and lipstick from the drugstore that I was glad of. She asked me to come and visit whenever I liked. Sometimes I did, and the hectic domesticity, the baby-centered chores and pleasures, soon drove me out to walk.

I was walking down the main street and I heard a rap on a window. It was the window of the insurance agent's office, and the person rapping was MaryBeth, who worked there. During her last year in high school, she had taken the typing and bookkeeping course. She lived with Beatrice and Beatrice's husband, who soon had a barbershop of his own. She didn't try to be friends with me during that year. We would cross the street or look into a store window when we saw each other coming—though that was from awkwardness more than real enmity. Then she got the job in the insurance agent's office.

The Crydermans were gone before that. They shut up the house and went away to Toronto before the baby was born. It was a boy—quite normal, as far as anybody knew. Aunt Ena was disgusted with them for not closing the house down properly. She said there would be rats in it. But they sold it. They sold the newspaper. They were completely gone.

MaryBeth motioned for me to come inside.

"It's been ages since I saw you," she said, as if we had parted most amicably. She plugged the electric kettle in, to make us instant coffee. The insurance agent was out.

She was fatter than she used to be, but still pretty, with her look of a bruised nestling. Dressed as nicely as ever, a flattering soft blue sweater, brushed wool over the tender breasts. She kept chocolates in a desk drawer and jam tarts in a tin. She offered me marzipan fruit wrapped in foil. She asked me if I was still going to school and what courses I was taking. I told her a little bit about my studies and ambitions.

"That's wonderful," she said, without malice. "I always knew you were smart." Then she said she had been sorry to hear about my Aunt Ena and she thought it was nice about Floris. She had heard that Floris's little fellows were really cute.

Beatrice had girls. They were cute, too, but rather spoiled.

We both said how lucky it was that she had spotted me, and we vowed to get together sometime for a real visit—something I knew she did not intend any more than I did. She admired my angora scarf and tam, asked if I had got them in the city.

I said yes, and the only problem was they shed terribly.

"Keep them in the fridge overnight," she said. "I don't know why, but it works."

I opened the door, and the wind blew in from the street.

"Remember how crazy we used to be?" said MaryBeth, in a voice full of plaintive surprise. She had to turn this way and that, grabbing papers.

I thought of Mr. Cryderman and all my lies, and my abysmal confusion in the summerhouse.

"Those days will never come again," said MaryBeth, flinging herself across the desk to hold things down.

I laughed and said just as well, and quickly shut the door. I waved from outside.

I felt such changes then—from fifteen to seventeen, from seventeen to nineteen—that it didn't occur to me how much I had been myself, all along. I saw MaryBeth shut in, with her treats and her typewriter, growing sweeter and fatter, and the Crydermans fixed, far away, in their everlasting negotiations, but myself shedding dreams and lies and vows and errors, unaccountable. I didn't see that I was the same one, embracing, repudiating. I thought I could turn myself inside out, over and over again, and tumble through the world scot free.

ESKIMO

Mary Jo can hear what Dr. Streeter would have to say.

"Regular little United Nations back here."

Mary Jo, knowing how to handle him, would remark that there was always first class.

He would say that he didn't propose paying an arm and a leg for the privilege of swilling free champagne.

"Anyway, you know what's up in first class? Japs. Japanese businessmen on their way home from buying up some more of the country."

Mary Jo might say then that Japanese hardly seemed foreign to her anymore. She would say this thoughtfully, as if she was wondering about it, almost talking to herself.

"I mean, they hardly seem like a foreign race."

"Well, you seem foreign to them, and you better not forget it."

When he had got these remarks off his chest, Dr. Streeter would not be displeased. He would settle down beside her, glad they had these front seats where there was room for his legs. A tall, bulky man, florid and white-haired, he would stand out here—a slightly clumsy but noble-headed giant—among the darker skins, the more compact and fine-boned races, in their flashy or picturesque clothes. He would settle down as if he had a right to be here, as if he had a right to be on this earth—which only other men of his age and race, dressed and thinking like him, could really match.

But he isn't stretching his legs out beside her, grumbling and content. She is off to Tahiti by herself. His Christmas present to her, this holiday. She has an aisle seat, and the window seat is empty.

"He has the mind of a dinosaur, that's all," said Dr. Streeter's daughter, Rhea, not long ago, talking to Mary Jo about what seems to be her favorite subject—her father. She has a list of favorite subjects, favorite serious subjects—nuclear proliferation, acid rain, unemployment, as well as racial bigotry and the situation of women—but the road into them always appears to be through her father. Her father is not far from being the cause of all this, in Rhea's mind. He is behind bombs and pollution and poverty and discrimination. And Mary Jo has to admit that there are things he says that would lead you to this conclusion.

"That's just his opinions," Mary Jo said. She pictured a certain kind of dinosaur, the one with the frill of bony plates along its spine—a showy armor, almost like decoration. "Men have to have their opinions."

What a stupid thing to say, especially to Rhea. Rhea is twenty-five years old, unemployed, a fat, breezy, pretty girl who rides around on a motorcycle. When Mary Jo said that, Rhea just stared at her for a minute, smiling her fat leisurely smile. Then she said softly, "Why, Mary Jo? Why do men have to have their opinions? So women can sit around clicking their tongues while men wreck the world?"

She had taken off her motorcycle helmet and set it down, wet from the rain, on Mary Jo's desk. She was shaking out her long, dark, tangled hair.

"No man is wrecking my world," said Mary Jo spiritedly, picking up the helmet and setting it on the floor. She didn't feel as equal to this conversation as she sounded. What was it Rhea wanted, really, when she came into her father's office and started up on these rambling complaints? She surely didn't expect Mary Jo to agree with her. No. She wanted and expected Mary Jo to defend her father, so that she could be amused and scornful (Oh, sure, Mary Jo, you think he's God!), and at the same time reassured. Mary Jo was supposed to do the work this girl's mother should have done—making her understand her father, and forgive and admire him. But Dr. Streeter's wife is not one for forgiving or admiring anybody, least of all her husband. She is a drinker, and thinks herself a wit. Sometimes she will phone the office and ask if she may speak to the Great Healer. A big, loud, untidy woman, with wild white hair, who likes to spend her time with actors—she is on the board of the local theater—and so-called poet—English professors from the university, where she has been working on her Ph.D. for the last several years.

"A man like your father, who saves lives every day," said Mary Jo to Rhea—making a point she had often made before—"can hardly be said to be wrecking the world." Mary Jo did not defend Dr. Streeter just because he was a man, and a father, not at all; it was not for those reasons she thought his wife should have instilled some respect for him in his children. It was because he was the best cardiologist in that part of the country, because he gave himself over every day to the gray-faced people in his waiting room, the heart cases, people living in fear, in pain. His life was given over.

In spite of the helmet, some of Rhea's hair had got wet, and she was shaking raindrops over Mary Jo's desk.

"Rhea, watch it, please."

"What is your world, Mary Jo?"

"I haven't got time to tell you."

"You're so busy helping my dad."

Mary Jo has been working for Dr. Streeter for twelve years, living in the apartment upstairs for ten. When Rhea was younger—a boisterous, overweight, strenuous, but likable teenager—she used to like to visit Mary Jo in the apartment, and Mary Jo would have to be sure that all signs of Dr. Streeter's regular, though not lengthy, times there were out of the way. Now Rhea must know all about that, but does not make direct investigations. She often seems to be probing, skirting the subject. Mary Jo remains bland and unforthcoming, but sometimes the effort tire her.

"It's nice you're going to Tahiti, though," said Rhea, still smiling in her dangerous way, her hair and eyes sparkling. "Have you always wanted to go there?"

"Of course," said Mary Jo. "Who wouldn't?"

"Not that he doesn't owe it to you. It's about time he paid you back some of your devotion, I think."

Mary Jo, without answering, went on writing up her records. After a while, Rhea calmed down and began to discuss the possibility of getting some money out of her father for repairs to her motorcycle—which was what she had come into the office for in the first place.

Why is it that Rhea always knows the tricky question to ask, in spite of her predictable mockery, lectures, and propaganda? "Have you always wanted to go there?" Tahiti is, in fact, a place where Mary Jo has never thought of going. Tahiti to her means palm trees, red flowers, curling turquoise waves, and the sort of tropical luxuriance and indolence that has never interested her. The gift has something unimaginative but touching about it, like the chocolates on St. Valentine's Day.

A winter holiday in Tahiti! I bet you're excited about it!

Well, I certainly am!

She has told patients, and her friends, and her sisters—whom she suspects of thinking she doesn't have much of a life—how excited she is. And she couldn't sleep last night, if that counts for anything. Before six o'clock this morning—it seems a long time ago—she stood at the window of her apartment, wearing new clothes from the skin out, waiting for the taxi to take her to the airport. A short, bumpy flight to Toronto, a longer flight from Toronto to Vancouver, and here she is, launched over the Pacific Ocean. A stop at Honolulu, then Tahiti. She can't go back on it.

Greece would have been better. Or Scandinavia. Well, perhaps not Scandinavia at this time of year. Ireland. Last summer, Dr. Streeter and his wife went to Ireland. His wife is "working on" some Irish poet. Mary Jo does not for a minute suppose that they had a good time. Who could have a good time with such an unkempt, capricious, disruptive woman? She believes they drank quite a bit. He went salmon-fishing. They stayed in a castle. Their holidays—and his holidays alone, usually fishing trips—are always expensive, and seem to Mary Jo ritualized and burdensome. His house, too, his social life and family life—it's all like that, she thinks, all prescribed, bleak, and costly.

When Mary Jo started working for Dr. Streeter, she had had her nursing degree for three years, but she had never had any extra money, because she was paying back money borrowed for her education and helping her sisters with theirs. She came from a small town in Huron County. Her father worked on the town maintenance crew. Her mother had died of what was called "heart disease"—something Mary Jo later knew was a heart problem that Dr. Streeter could have detected and recommended surgery for.

As soon as she had enough money, Mary Jo started getting some work done on her teeth. She was self-conscious about them; she never wore lipstick and was careful of how she smiled. She had her eyeteeth pulled and the front teeth filed. She still didn't like the way they looked, so she got braces. She planned to lighten her hair—which was plain brown—and buy some new clothes, perhaps even move away and get a different sort of job once the braces came off. By the time they did, her life was changed without these stratagems.

Some of the other changes came, in the course of time. From a serious-looking thick-waisted girl with an attentive manner, a gentle voice, a heavy bosom, she has become a slender well-dressed woman with short blond-streaked hair—prettier now than other women of her age who were so much prettier than she when they were all young—and an agreeable but decisive way of talking. It's hard to tell how much difference any of this makes to Dr. Streeter. He used to tell her not to get too glamorous or somebody would spot her and grab her away from him. She was uneasy with this talk, finding a discouraging message in it. He stopped saying such things, and she was glad. Just recently he has started up again, with reference to her trip to Tahiti. But she thinks she knows better now how to deal with him, and she teases him, saying, You never know, and, Stranger things have happened.

He liked her when the braces were still on. They were on the first time he made love to her. She turned her head aside, conscious that a mouthful of metal might not be pleasing. He shut his eyes, and she wondered if it might be for that reason. Later she learned that he always closed his eyes. He doesn't want to be reminded of himself at such times, and probably not of her, either. His is a fierce but solitary relish.

Across the aisle from Mary Jo are two empty seats and then a young family, mother and father and baby and a little girl about two years old. Italian or Greek or Spanish, Mary Jo thinks, and she soon finds out from their conversation with the stewardess that they are Greek, but living now in Perth, Australia. Their row of seats under the movie screen is the only place on the plane that could have provided room for their equipment and family operations. Insulated bags, plastic food dishes, baby-sized pillows, the folding cot that makes into a seat, milk bottles, juice bottles, and an enormous panda bear for the consolation of the little girl. Both parents busy themselves continually with the children—changing them into pastel pajamas, feeding them, joggling them, singing to them. Yes, they tell the admiring stewardess, very close, only fourteen months between them. The baby is a boy. He has a slight teething problem. She has occasional fits of jealousy. Both are very fond of bananas. Hers whole, his mashed. Get his bib, dear, out of the blue bag. The washcloth, too, he's drooling a bit. No, the washcloth isn't there, it's in the plastic. Hurry. There it is. Hurry. Good.

Mary Jo is surprised at how ill-disposed she feels toward this harmless family. Why are you shovelling food into him? she feels like saying (for they have mixed up some cereal in a blue bowl). Solid food is a total waste at his age; it just gives you more to mop up at both ends. What a fuss, what accumulation and display and satisfaction, just because they have managed to reproduce. Also, they are delaying the stewardess when she might be serving the drinks.

In the row behind them is another sort of young family, Indian. The mother wears a gold-embroidered red sari, the father a tight cream-colored suit. Slim, silent, gold-laden mother; well-fed, indolent-looking father, listening to the rock channel on his headphones. You can tell it's the rock channel by the movement of his fingers on the cream cloth stretched over his full thighs. Between these two parents sit two little girls, all in red, with gold bracelets and earrings and patent-leather shoes, and a younger brother, maybe as old as the little Greek girl in front, dressed up in a suit that is a miniature copy of his father's—vest, fly, pockets, and all. The stewardess offers crayons and coloring books, but the little girls, glistening with gold, just giggle and hide their faces. She brings them glasses of ginger ale. The little brother shakes his head at the ginger ale. He climbs on his mother's lap, and she fetches out of her sari a shadowy, serviceable breast. He settles there, lolls and sucks, with his eyes open, looking blissful and commanding.

This way of going on doesn't suit Mary Jo any better. She is not used to feeling such aversion; she knows it is not reasonable. She is never like this in the office. No matter what difficulties develop there, or how tired she is, she deals easily with any sort of strange or rude behavior, with unpleasant habits, sour smells, impossible questions. Something is wrong with her. She didn't sleep. Her throat feels slightly raw and her head heavy. There is a hum in her head. She may be getting a fever. But it's more likely that her body is protesting its removal too quickly, by ever-increasing distance, from its place of habitual attachment and rest. This morning, she could see from her window a corner of Victoria Park, the snow under the streetlights and the bare trees. The apartment and the office are in a handsome old brick house owned by Dr. Streeter, in a row of similar houses given over to such uses. Mary Jo looked at the slushy streets, the dirty February snow, the gray walls of these houses, a tall office block, with its night lights on, that she could see beyond the park. She wanted nothing so much as to stay. She wanted to cancel the taxi, change her new suède suit for her uniform, go downstairs and put on coffee and water the plants, prepare for another long day of problems and routine, fear and reassurance, dread to be held in check—some of the time—by talk about the dismal weather. She loves the office, the waiting room, the lights on in the darkening icy afternoons; she loves the challenge and the monotony. At the end of the day, Dr. Streeter sometimes comes upstairs with her; she makes supper, and he stays for part of the evening. His wife is out at meetings, classes, poetry readings; she is out drinking or has come home and gone straight to bed.

When the stewardess gets around to asking her, Mary Jo orders a vodka martini. She always chooses vodka, hoping it's true that you can't smell it. For obvious reasons, Dr. Streeter dislikes the smell of liquor on a woman.

Here come two new people down the aisle, changing their seats, evidently, creating problems with the drinks cart. Another stewardess comes fussing behind them. She and the woman of the pair are carrying shopping bags, a travelling bag, an umbrella. The man walks ahead and doesn't carry anything. They take the seats directly across from Mary Jo, beside the Greek family. They try to stow their paraphernalia under the seat, but it won't go.

The stewardess says that there is lots of room in the overhead bins.

No. Low growls of protest from the man, muttered apologies from the woman. The stewardess is given to understand that they intend to keep an eye on all their belongings. Now that the drinks cart has moved on, they can see a place where things might go—in front of Mary Jo, and behind the little jump seat used by a stewardess at takeoff and landing.

The stewardess says she hopes that won't be too much in the lady's way. Her bright voice suggests a certain amount of difficulty already undergone with these passengers. Mary Jo says no, it will be quite all right. The couple settle down then, the man in the aisle seat. He gives another growl, peremptory but not ill-humored, and the stewardess brings two whiskeys. He raises his glass slightly, in Mary Jo's direction. A lordly gesture that might be a thank-you. It is certainly not an apology.

He is a corpulent man, probably older than Dr. Streeter, but more buoyant. An incautious, unpredictable-looking man, with rather long gray hair and new, expensive clothes. Sandals over brown socks, rust-colored trousers, bright yellow shirt, a handsome gold suède jacket with many little tabs and pleats and pockets. His skin is brown and his eyes are slightly slanted. Not Japanese or Chinese—what is he? Mary Jo has a feeling that she has seen him before. Not as a patient, not in the office. Where?

The woman peers around his shoulder, smiling with her lips closed, pleasantly creasing her broad face. Her eyes have a more definite slant than his, and her skin is paler. Her black hair is parted in the middle and held with an elastic band in a childish ponytail. Her clothes are cheap and decent and maybe fairly new—brown slacks, flowered blouse—but not in keeping with his. When she came along the aisle with the shopping bags, she looked middle-aged—thick-waisted and round-shouldered. But now, smiling at Mary Jo around the man's bulky shoulder, she looks quite young. There is something odd about the smile itself. What that is becomes apparent when she opens her mouth and says something to the man. Her front teeth are missing, all across the top. That is what gives the smile such a secretive yet innocent look—a look of sly, durable merriment such as an old woman's smile might have, or a baby's.

Now Mary Jo thinks she has an idea about where she might have seen the man across the aisle before. A few weeks ago, she watched a television program about a tribe that lived in one of the high valleys of Afghanistan, near the Tibetan border. The film had been shot a few years ago, before the Russians came in. The people of the tribe lived in skin houses, and their wealth was in herds of sheep and goats and in fine horses. One man seemed to have cornered most of this wealth, and had become the ruler of the tribe, not through hereditary right but through force of personality and financial power. He was called "the Khan." He had beautiful rugs in his skin house, and a radio, and several wives or concubines.

That's who this man reminds her of—the Khan. And isn't it possible, isn't it really possible, that that's who he might be? He might have left his country, got out before the Russians came, with his rugs and women and perhaps a horde of gold, though not likely his goats and sheep and horses. If you travel the world in great airliners, aren't you bound to see, sooner or later, somebody you have seen on television? And it could easily be an exotic ruler, just as easily as an entertainer or a politician or a faith healer. In these days of upheaval, it could be somebody who had been photographed as a curiosity, a relic even, in a shut-off country, and is now turned loose like everybody else.

The woman must be one of his wives. The youngest, maybe the favorite, to be taken on a trip like this. He has taken her to Canada or the United States, where he has put his sons in school. He has taken her to a dentist to get her fitted with false teeth. Perhaps she has the teeth in her handbag, is just getting used to them, doesn't wear them yet all the time.

Mary Jo feels cheered up by her own invention, and perhaps also by the vodka. In her head, she starts to compose a letter describing these two, and mentioning the television program. Of course the letter is to Dr. Streeter, who was sitting on the couch beside her—but had fallen asleep—while she watched it. She mentions the woman's teeth and the possibility that they might have been removed on purpose, to comply with some strange notion of improving a female's appearance.

"If he asks me to join his harem, I promise I won't agree to any such weird procedures!"

The movie screen is being lowered. Mary Jo obediently turns out her light. She thinks of ordering another drink but decides against it. Alcohol is more potent at this altitude. She tries to watch the movie, but the images are much elongated from this angle. They seem doleful and absurd. There is murder in the first two minutes—some girl with marvellous silvery hair is being stalked through empty corridors and apparently shot, right behind the credits. Mary Jo almost immediately loses interest, and after a while takes off her headphones. When she does so, she becomes aware of some sort of argument going on across the aisle.

The woman, or girl, seems to be trying to get up. The man pushes her down. He grumbles at her. She replies in a voice that wanders from complaint to reassurance and back to complaint. He appears to lose interest, tilts his head back to watch the figures on the screen. The girl eases her way out of the seat and stumbles over him. He growls in earnest now, and grabs her leg. To Mary Jo's surprise, the girl speaks to him in English.

"I am not," she says stubbornly. "I am not. Drunk." She says this in the passionate, hopeless tone that drunk people will often use when arguing that they are not.

The man releases her with a sound of disgust.

"You can't boss me," she says, and there are tears now in her voice and eyes. "You're not my father." Instead of going down the aisle to the washroom—if that was what she had in mind—she remains standing within his reach, looking mournfully down at him. He makes a feint to grab at her again, a swift, brutal movement, as if this time, next time, he intends really to hurt her. She stumbles aside. He turns his attention back to the screen.

Still the girl doesn't move off down the aisle. She leans over Mary Jo.

"Excuse me," she says. She smiles with her eyes full of tears. Her baffled, offended face is creased with this wide, closed-mouthed smile, of apology or conspiracy. "Excuse me."

"That's all right," says Mary Jo, thinking the girl is apologizing for the quarrel. Then she sees that "Excuse me" means "May I get past?" The girl wants to step over Mary Jo's legs, which are stretched out for comfort, crossed at the ankles. She wants to sit down in the window seat.

Mary Jo makes way. The girl sits down, wipes her eyes with a straight-across movement of her forefinger, and gives a loud snuffle that sounds businesslike and conclusive. What now?

"Don't tell nobody," the girl says. "Don't tell nobody."

She lays her broad hand on Mary Jo's knee, then takes it away.

"No," says Mary Jo. But who would she tell and why would she tell about such a formless bit of a quarrel?

"Don't tell nobody. I am Eskimo."

Of course Mary Jo has known ever since the girl got into the aisle and opened her mouth that it was all nonsense about the Khan and the favorite wife. She nods, but the word "Eskimo" bothers her more than the fact. That isn't the word to use anymore, is it? "Inuit." That's the word they use now.

"He is Métis. I am Eskimo."

All right, then. Métis and Eskimo. Fellow-Canadians. A joke on me, thinks Mary Jo. In her head, she'll have to start a different sort of letter.

"Don't tell nobody."

The girl behaves as if she is confessing something—a shameful secret, a damaging mistake. She is frightened but trying to be dignified. She says again, "Don't tell nobody," and she puts her fingers for a few seconds across Mary Jo's mouth. Mary Jo can feel the heat of her skin and the tremor that runs through the girl's fingers and her whole body. She is like an animal in an entirely uncommunicable panic.

"No. No, I won't," says Mary Jo again. The best thing to do, she thinks, is to pretend to understand everything contained in this request.

"Are you going to Tahiti?" she says conversationally. She knows how an ordinary question at a moment like this can provide a bridge over somebody's terror.

The girl's smile breaks open as if she appreciates the purpose of the question, its kindness, though in her case it can hardly be enough. "He's going to Hawaii," the girl says. "Me, too."

Mary Jo glances across the aisle. The man's head is lolling. He may have dozed off. Even when she has turned away, she can feel the girl's heat and quivering.

"How old are you?" says Mary Jo. She doesn't really know why she asks this.

The girl shakes her head, as if her age is indeed an absurd and deplorable fact. "I am Eskimo."

What has that to do with it? She says it as if it might be a code word, which Mary Jo would eventually understand.

"Yes. But how old are you?" says Mary Jo more confidently. "Are you twenty? Are you over twenty? Eighteen?"

More headshaking and embarrassment, more smiling. "Don't tell nobody."

"How old?"

"I am Eskimo. I am sixteen."

Mary Jo looks across the aisle again to make sure the man isn't listening. He seems to be asleep.

"Sixteen?"

The girl wags her head heavily, almost laughing. And doesn't stop trembling.

"Are you? No? Yes? Yes."

Again those thick fingers passed like feathers over Mary Jo's mouth.

"Do you want to go to Hawaii with him? Is it all right?"

"He is going to Hawaii. Me, too."

"Listen," says Mary Jo, speaking softly and carefully. "I am going to get up and walk to the back of the plane. I am going to where the washrooms are. The toilets. I'll wait for you back there. After a moment, you get up and come back. You come to the back of the plane where the toilets are and we'll talk there. It's better to talk there. All right? Do you understand me? All right."

She gets up unhurriedly, retrieves her jacket, which has slipped down on the seat, rearranges it. The man rolls his head on the cushion, gives her a glazed, gloomy look, the look of a dog half-asleep. His eyes slide under the lids and his head turns away.

"All right?" Mary Jo mouths the words at the girl without a sound.

The girl presses her fingers over her own mouth, her smile.

Mary Jo walks to the back of the plane. Earlier, she removed her boots and put on slippers. Now she pads along comfortably, but misses the feeling of competence and resolution that boots can give.

She has to get in the lineup for the toilets, because there is nowhere else to stand. The line extends into the little space by the window where she intended to wait. She keeps looking around, waiting for the girl to come up behind her. Not yet. Other, taller people join the line and she has to keep peering around them, wanting to make sure the girl can see where she is. She has to move forward with the line, and when it's her turn she has no choice but to go in. It's time she went, anyway.

She gets out as quickly as possible. The girl is still not there.

Not in the lineup. Not hanging around the galley or sitting in any of the back seats. The line is shorter now and there is room for Mary Jo to stand by the window. She waits there, shivering, wishing she had brought her jacket.

In the washroom, she didn't take time to put on fresh lipstick. She does so now, looking at her reflection in the dark window. Suppose she decided to speak to somebody about the girl—what would they think of her? She could speak to somebody now—that older, rather grim-looking stewardess with the coppery eye makeup, who seems to be in charge, or the steward, who looks distracted but more approachable. She could tell them what the girl had said, and about her trembling. She could voice her suspicions. But what do those amount to? The girl has not really said anything that suspicions can be firmly based on. She is Eskimo, she is sixteen, she is going to Hawaii with a much older man who is not her father. Is sixteen underage? Is taking a girl to Hawaii a crime? She may be more than sixteen after all; she certainly looks it. She may be drunk and lying. She may be his wife, though she doesn't wear a ring. He may certainly be some sort of relative. If Mary Jo says anything now, she will be seen as a meddling woman, who has had one drink and may have had more. She may be seen as someone trying to get hold of the girl for her own purposes.

The girl herself will have to say more if anything is to be done.

You can't be helped if you don't ask for it.

You will have to say what you want.

You will have to say.

Mary Jo walks slowly back to her seat, checking on the way to see if the girl has moved, if she is sitting somewhere else. She looks for the large docile head with its black ponytail.

Nowhere.

But when she is nearly back to her seat she sees that the girl has moved. She has moved back to where she was sitting before beside the man. They have been provided with two more whiskeys.

Perhaps he grabbed her when she got up, and forced her to sit down with him. Mary Jo should have seen that the girl went first. But could she have persuaded her, made her understand? Did the girl really understand that help was being offered?

Mary Jo stands in the aisle putting on her jacket. She looks down at the couple, but they don't look at her. She sits down and snaps on her reading light, then turns it off. Nobody is watching the movie anymore. The Greek baby is crying, and the father is walking it up and down the aisle. The little Indian girls have toppled over on each other, and their brother is asleep in his mother's narrow lap.

Dr. Streeter would soon put Mary Jo straight about this. Some kinds of concern—he has made her admit this—are little more than frivolity and self-indulgence. With their self-indulgent good intentions, people are apt to do more harm than good. And that is what she might do in this case.

Yes. But he could always turn to what was inside people, inside their chests. If this girl had a faulty heart, even if she was twenty years older, forty years older, than she is, even if her life was totally muddled and useless and her brain half-rotted with drink—even then he would put himself completely at her service. He withheld nothing, he used himself up in such rescues or attempted rescues. If it was a problem of the real heart, the bloody, pumping, burdened heart inside a person's chest.

Dr. Streeter's voice has an underlying sadness. It's not only his voice. His breathing is sad. An incurable, calm, and decent sadness is what he breathes out over the phone before you even hear his voice. He would be displeased if you told him that. Not that he particularly wishes to be thought jolly. But he would think it unnecessary, impertinent, for anybody to assume that he is sad.

This sadness seems to come from obedience. Mary Jo can just recognize that, never understand it. She thinks there is an obedience about men that women can't understand. (What would Rhea say to that?) It's not the things he knows about—Mary Jo could manage that—but the things he accepts that make a difference. He baffles her, and compels her. She loves this man with a baffled, cautious, permanent love.

When she pictures him, she always sees him wearing his brown three-piece suit, an old-fashioned suit that makes him look like a doctor from his classically poor and rural childhood. He has good-looking casual clothes and she has seen him in them, but she thinks he isn't at ease in them. He isn't at ease with being rich, she thinks, though he feels an obligation to be so and a hatred for any government that would prevent him. All obedience, acceptance, sadness.

He wouldn't believe her if she told him that. Nobody would.

She is shivering, even with her jacket on. She seems to have caught something of the girl's persistent and peculiar agitation. Perhaps she really is sick, has a fever. She twists around, trying to compose herself. She closes her eyes but cannot keep them closed. She cannot stop herself from watching what is going on across the aisle.

What is going on is something she should have the sense and decency to turn away from. But she hasn't, and she doesn't.

The whiskey glasses are empty. The girl has leaned forward and is kissing the man's face. His head is resting against the cushion and he does not stir. She leans over him, her eyes closed, or almost closed, her face broad and pale and impassive, a true moon face. She kisses his lips, his cheeks, his eyelids, his forehead. He offers himself to her; he permits her. She kisses him and licks him. She licks his nose, the faint stubble of his cheeks and neck and chin. She licks him all over his face, then takes a breath and resumes her kissing.

This is unhurried, not greedy. It is not mechanical, either. There is no trace of compulsion. The girl is in earnest; she is in a trance of devotion. True devotion. Nothing so presumptuous as forgiveness or consolation. A ritual that takes every bit of her concentration and her self but in which her self is lost. It could go on forever.

Even when the girl's eyes open and she looks straight out across the aisle, with an expression that is not dazed and unaware 'but direct and shocking—even then, Mary Jo has to keep looking. Only with a jolting effort, and after an immeasurable amount of time, is she able to pull her own eyes away.

If anybody was to ask her what she was feeling while she watched this, Mary Jo would have said that she felt sick. And she would have meant it. Not just sick with the beginnings of a fever or whatever it is that's making her dull and shivery, but sick with revulsion, as if she could feel the slow journeys of the warm, thick tongue over her face. Then, when she takes her eyes away, something else is released, and that is desire—sudden and punishing as a rush of loose earth down a mountainside.

At the same time, she is listening to Dr. Streeter's voice, and it says clearly, "You know, that girl's teeth were probably knocked out. In some brawl."

This is Dr. Streeter's familiar, reasonable voice, asking that some facts, some conditions, should be recognized. But she has put something new into it—a sly and natural satisfaction. He is not just sad, not just accepting; he is satisfied that some things should be so. The satisfaction far back in his voice matches the loosening feeling in her body. She feels a physical shame and aversion, a heat that seems to spread from her stomach. This passes, the wave of it passes, but the aversion remains. Aversion, disgust, dislike spreading out from you can be worse than pain. It would be a worse condition to live in. Once she has thought this, and put some sort of name to what she is feeling, she is a little steadier. It must be the strangeness of being on the flight, and the drink, and the confusion offered by that girl, and perhaps a virus, that she is struggling with. Dr. Streeter's voice is next thing to a real delusion, but it isn't a delusion; she knows she manufactured it herself. Manufactured what she could then turn away from, so purely hating him. If such a feeling became real, if a delusion like that got the better of her, she would be in a state too dreary to think about.

She sets about deliberately to calm herself down. She breathes deeply and pretends that she is going to sleep. She starts telling herself a story in which things work out better. Suppose the girl had followed her to the back of the plane a while ago; suppose they had been able to talk? The story slips ahead, somehow, to the waiting room in Honolulu. Mary Jo sees herself sitting there in a room with stunted, potted palm trees, on a padded bench. The man and the girl walk past her. The girl is walking ahead, carrying the shopping bags. The man has the travelling bag slung over his shoulder and he is carrying the umbrella. With the end of the furled umbrella, he gives the girl a poke. Nothing to hurt her or even surprise her.

A joke. The girl scurries and giggles and looks around her with an expression of endless apology, embarrassment, helplessness, good humor. Then Mary Jo catches her eye, without the man's noticing. Mary Jo gets up and walks across the waiting room and reaches the bright, tiled refuge of the ladies' washroom.

And this time the girl does follow her.

Mary Jo runs the cold water. She splashes it over her own face, in a gesture of encouragement.

She urges the girl to do the same.

She speaks to her calmly and irresistibly.

"That's right. Cool your face off. Get your head clear. You have to think clearly. You have to think very clearly. Now. What is it? What is it you want? What are you afraid of? Don't be afraid. He can't come in here. We've got time. You can tell me what you want and I can help you. I can get in touch with the authorities."

But the story halts at this point. Mary Jo has hit a dry spot, and her dream—for she is dreaming by now—translates this in its unsubtle way into an irregular, surprising patch of rust where the enamel has worn away at the bottom of the sink.

What a badly maintained ladies' room.

"Is it always like this in the tropics?" says Mary Jo to the woman standing beside her at the next sink, and this woman covers her sink with her hands as if she doesn't want Mary Jo to look at or use it. (Not that Mary Jo was intending to.) She is a large, white-haired woman in a red sari, and she seems to have some authority in the ladies' room. Mary Jo looks around for the Eskimo girl and is bewildered to see her lying on the floor. She has shrunk, and has a rubbery look, a crude face like a doll's. But the real shock is that her head has come loose from her body, though it is still attached by an internal elastic band.

"You'll get a chance to choose your own," says the white-haired woman, and Mary Jo thinks this means your own punishment. She knows she is in no danger of that—she is not responsible, she didn't hit the girl or push her to the floor. The woman is crazy.

"I'm sorry," she says, "but I have to get back to the plane."

But this is later, and they are no longer in the ladies' room.

They are back in Dr. Streeter's office and Mary Jo has a sense of a dim scramble of events she can't keep track of, of lapses in time she hasn't noted. She still thinks about getting back on the plane, but how is she to find the waiting room, let alone get to Honolulu?

A large figure entirely wrapped up in bandages is carried past, and Mary Jo means to find out who it is, what has happened, why they are bringing a victim of burns in here.

The woman in the red sari is there, too. She says to Mary Jo, in quite a friendly way, "The court is in the garden?"

This may mean that Mary Jo is still to be accused of something, and that there is a court being conducted in the garden. On the other hand, the word "court" may refer to Dr. Streeter. The woman may mean "count," being mixed up in her spelling. If that's so, she intends to mock him. Calling him the count is a joke, and "in the garden" means something else, too, which Mary Jo will have to concentrate hard on to figure out.

But the woman opens her hand and shows Mary Jo some small blue flowers—like snowdrops, but blue—and explains that these are "court" and that "court" means flowers.

A ruse, and Mary Jo knows it, but she can't concentrate because she's waking up. In a jumbo jet over the Pacific Ocean, with the movie screen furled and the lights mostly out and even the baby asleep. She can't get back through the various curtains of the dream to the clear part, in the ladies' room, when the cold water was streaming down their faces and she—Mary Jo—was telling the girl how she could save herself. She can't get back there. People all around her are sleeping under blankets, with their heads on small orange pillows. Somehow a pillow and a blanket have been provided for her as well. The man and the girl across the aisle are asleep with their mouths open, and Mary Jo is lifted to the surface by their duet of eloquent, innocent snores.

This is the beginning of her holiday.

A Queer Streak

I *Anonymous Letters*

Violet's mother—Aunt Ivie—had three little boys, three baby boys, and she lost them. Then she had the three girls. Perhaps to console herself for the bad luck she had already suffered, in a back corner of South Sherbrooke Township—or perhaps to make up, ahead of time, for a lack of motherly feelings—she gave the girls the fanciest names she could think of: Opal Violet, Dawn Rose, and Bonnie Hope. She may not have thought of those names as anything but temporary decorations. Violet wondered—did her mother ever picture her daughers having to drag such names around sixty or seventy years later, when they were heavy, faded women? She may have thought her girls were going to die, too.

"Lost" meant that somebody died. "She lost them" meant they died. Violet knew that. Nevertheless she imagined. Aunt Ivie—her mother—wandering into a swampy field, which was the waste ground on the far side of the barn, a twilight place full of coarse grass and alder bushes. There Aunt Ivie, in the mournful light, mislaid her baby children. Violet would slip down the edge of the barnyard to the waste ground, then cautiously enter it. She would stand hidden by the red-stemmed alder and nameless thornbushes (it always seemed to be some damp, desolate time of year when she did this—late fall or early spring), and she would let the cold water cover the toes of her rubber boots. She would contemplate getting lost. Lost babies. The water welled up through the tough grass.

Farther in, there were ponds and sinkholes. She had been warned. She shuffled on, watching the water creep up on her boots. She never told them. They never knew where she went. Lost.

The parlor was the other place that she could sneak to by herself. The window blinds were down to the sills; the air had a weight and thickness, as if it were cut into a block that exactly filled the room. In certain fixed places could be found the flushed, spiky shell with the roar of the sea caught inside it; the figure of the little kilted Scotsman holding a glass of amber liquid that would tilt but never spill; a fan made entirely out of glossy black feathers; a plate that was a souvenir of Niagara Falls and showed the same picture as the Shredded Wheat box. And a framed picture on the wall that affected Violet so intensely that she couldn't look at it when she first came into the room. She had to work her way around to it, keeping it always in a corner of her vision. It showed a king with his crown on, and three tall, queenly-looking ladies in dark dresses. The king was asleep, or dead. They were all on the shore of the sea, with a boat waiting, and there was something coming out of this picture into the room—a smooth, dark wave of unbearable sweetness and sorrow. That seemed a promise to Violet; it was connected with her future, her own life, in a way she couldn't explain or think about. She couldn't even look at the picture if there was anybody else in the room. But in that room there seldom was anybody else.

Violet's father was called King Billy, King Billy Thoms, though William was not in his name. There was also a horse called King Billy, a dapple-gray horse that was their driver, hitched to the cutter in wintertime and the buggy in summer. (There was not to be a car on that place until Violet was grown up and bought one in the nineteen-thirties.)

The name King Billy was usually connected with the parade, the Orange Walk, on the twelfth of July. A man chosen to be King Billy, wearing a cardboard crown and a raggedy purple cloak, would ride at the head of the parade. He was supposed to ride a white horse, but sometimes a dapple-gray was the best that could be found.

Violet never knew if the horse or her father, or both, had figured in this parade, either separately or together. Confusion abounded, in the world as she knew it, and adults as often as not resented being asked to set it straight.

But she did know that her father, at one time in his life, had worked on a train up North that ran through the wild bush where bears were. Loggers would ride this train on the weekends, coming out of the bush to get drunk, and if they got too rambunctious on the way back, King Billy would stop the train and kick them off. No matter where the train was at the time. In the middle of the wilderness—no matter. He kicked them off. He was a fighter. He had got that job because he was a fighter.

Another story, from further back in his life. He had gone to a dance, when he was a young man, up on the Snow Road, where he came from. Some other young fellows who were there had insulted him, and he had to take their insults because he did not know a thing about fighting. But after that he got some lessons from an old prizefighter, a real one, who was living in Sharbot Lake. Another night, another dance—the same thing as before. The same kind of insults. Except that this time King Billy lit into them and cleaned up on them, one by one.

Lit into them and cleaned up on them, one by one.

No more insults of that kind anywhere up in that country.

No more.

(The insults had to do with being a bastard. He didn't say so, but Violet figured it out from her mother's muttering. "Your daddy didn't have *no people*," Aunt Ivie said, in her dark, puzzled, grudging way. "He never did. He just didn't have *no people* at all.")

Violet was five years older than her sister Dawn Rose, and six years older than Bonnie Hope. Those two were thick as thieves, but mainly docile. They were redheads, like King Billy. Dawn Rose was chubby and ruddy and broad-faced. Bonnie Hope was small-boned and big-headed, with hair that grew at first in wisps and patches, so that she looked like a wobbly young bird. Violet was dark-haired, and tall for her age, and strong like her mother. She had a long, handsome face and dark blue eyes that looked at first to be black. Later on, when Trevor Auston was in love with her, he had some nice things to say about the color of her eyes matching up with her name.

Violet's mother, as well as her father, had an odd name, being called Aunt Ivie most of the time even by her own children. That was because she was the youngest of a large family. She had plenty of people, though they didn't often come to see her. All the old or precious things in the house—those things in the parlor, and a certain humpbacked trunk, and some tarnished spoons—came from Aunt Ivie's family, who had a farm on the shores of White Lake. Aunt Ivie had stayed there so long, unmarried, that her nieces' and nephews' name for her became everybody's name, and her daughters, too, chose it over Mama.

Nobody ever thought she would marry. She said so herself. And when she did marry the little bold redheaded man who looked so odd beside her, people said she didn't seem to stand the change too well. She lost those first boy babies, and she didn't take too happily to the responsibility of running a house. She liked to work outside, hoeing in the garden or splitting wood, as she had always done at home. She milked the cows and cleaned out the stable and took care of the hens. It was Violet, getting older, who took over the housework.

By the time she was ten years old, Violet had become quite house-proud and dictatorial, in a sporadic way. She would spend all Saturday scouring and waxing, then yell and throw herself on the couch and grind her teeth in a rage when people tracked in mud and manure.

"That girl will grow up, and she won't have nothing but stumps in her mouth, and serve her right for her temper," Aunt Ivie said, as if she was talking about some neighbor child. Aunt Ivie was usually the one who had tracked in the mud and ruined the floor.

Another Saturday there would be baking, and making up recipes. One whole summer, Violet was trying to invent a drink like Coca-Cola, which would be famous and delicious and make them a fortune. She tried out on herself and her sisters all sorts of combinations of berry juice, vanilla, bottled fruit essences, and spices. Sometimes they were all off in the long grass in the orchard, throwing up. The younger girls usually did what Violet told them to, and believed what she said. One day, the butcher's man arrived to buy the young calves, and Violet told Dawn Rose and Bonnie Hope that sometimes the butcher's man was not satisfied with the meat on the calves and went after juicy little children to make them into steaks and chops and sausages. She told this out of the blue and for her own amusement, as far as she could recall later on when she made things into stories. The little girls tried to hide themselves in the haymow and King Billy heard their commotion and chased them out. They told what Violet had said and King Billy said they should be smacked for swallowing such nonsense. He said he was a man with a mule for a wife and a hooligan daughter running his house. Dawn Rose and Bonnie Hope ran to confront Violet.

"Liar! Butchers don't chop up children! You told a lie, liar!"

Violet, who was cleaning out the stove at the time, said nothing. She picked up a pan of ashes—warm but, fortunately, not hot—and dumped it on their heads. They knew enough not to tell a second time. They ran outside and rolled in the grass and shook themselves like dogs, trying to get the ashes out of their hair and ears and eyes and underwear. Down in a corner of the orchard, they started their own playhouse, with pulled grass heaped up for seats and bits of broken china for dishes. They vowed not to tell Violet.

But they couldn't keep away from her. She put their hair up in rags to curl it; she dressed them in costumes made from old curtains; she painted their faces, using concoctions of berry juice and flour and stove polish. She found out about the playhouse and had ideas for furnishing it that were superior to theirs. Even on the days when she had no time for them at all, they had to watch what she was doing.

She was painting a design of red roses on the black and worn-out kitchen linoleum.

She was cutting a scalloped edge on all the old green window blinds for elegance.

It did seem as if ordinary family life had been turned upside down at their place. At other farms, it would usually be the children you would see first as you came up the lane—children playing, or doing some chore. The mother would be hidden in the house. Here it was Aunt Ivie you would see, hilling up the potatoes or just prowling around the yard or the chicken run, wearing rubber boots and a man's felt hat and a dingy assortment of sweaters, skirt, droopy slip and apron, and wrinkled, spattered stockings. It was Violet who ruled in the house, Violet who decided when and if to pass out the pieces of bread and butter and corn syrup. It was as if King Billy and Aunt Ivie had not quite understood how to go about making an ordinary life, even if they had meant to.

But the family got along. They milked the cows and sold the milk to the cheese factory and raised the calves for the butcher and cut the hay. They were members of the Anglican church, though they didn't often attend, owing to the problems of getting Aunt Ivie cleaned up. They did go sometimes to the card parties in the schoolhouse. Aunt Ivie could play cards, and she would remove her apron and felt hat to do so, though she wouldn't change her boots. King Billy had some reputation as a singer, and after the card-playing, people would try to get him to entertain. He liked to sing songs he had learned from the loggers that were never written down. He sang with his fists clenched and his eyes closed, resolutely:

"On the Opeongo Line I drove a span of bays,
One summer once upon a time for Hooligan and Hayes,
Now that them bays is dead and gone and grim old age is mine,
I'm dreamin' that I'm teamin', on the Opeongo Line."

Who was Hooligan? Who was Hayes?

"Some outfit," said King Billy, expansive from the singing.

Violet went to high school in town, and after that to normal school in Ottawa. People wondered where King Billy got the money. If he still had some put by from his railway pay, that meant he had got some money from Aunt Ivie's family when he took her off their hands and bought the farm. King Billy said he didn't grudge Violet an education—he thought being a teacher would suit her. But he didn't have anything extra for her. Before she started at high school, she went across the fields to the next farm, carrying a piece of Roman-striped crêpe she had found in the trunk. She wanted to learn to use the sewing machine, so that she could make herself a dress. And so she did, though the neighbor woman said it was the oddest-looking outfit for a schoolgirl that she ever hoped to see.

Violet came home every weekend when she was at high school, and told her sisters about Latin and basketball, and looked after the house as before. But when she went away to Ottawa, she stayed until Christmas. Dawn Rose and Bonnie Hope were big enough by then to take care of the house, but whether they did or not was another matter. Dawn Rose was actually big enough to be starting high school, but she had failed her last year at the local school and was repeating it. She and Bonnie Hope were in the same class.

When Violet came home for the Christmas holidays, she had changed a great deal. But she thought it was everything and everybody else that had changed.

She wanted to know if they had always talked this way. What way? With an accent. Weren't they doing it on purpose, to sound funny? Weren't they saying "youse" on purpose, to sound funny?

She had forgotten where some things were kept, and was astonished to find the frying pan under the stove. She took a dislike to the dog, Tigger, who was allowed to stay in the house now that he was getting old. She said he smelled, and that the couch blanket was full of dog hairs.

She said the parlor smelled moldy and the walls needed papering.

But it was her sisters themselves who got the full force of her surprise and displeasure. They had grown since the summer. Dawn Rose was a big stout girl now, with loose breasts jiggling inside her dress, and a broad red face whose childish expression of secretiveness had changed to a look that seemed stupid and stubborn. She had developed womanly smells, and she did not wash. Bonnie Hope was still childish in body, but her frizzy red hair was never combed out properly and she was covered with fleabites that she got from playing with the barn cats.

Violet hardly knew how to go about cleaning these two up. The worst was that they had become rebellious, looked at each other and snickered when she talked to them, avoided her, were mulish and silent. They acted as if they had some idiotic secret.

And so they did, they had a secret, but it did not come out until quite a while later, not until after the events of the next summer, and then indirectly, with Bonnie Hope telling some girls who told another who told another, and others getting to hear about it, then a neighbor woman, who finally told Violet.

In late fall of that year—the year Violet went away to normal school—Dawn Rose had begun to menstruate. She was so affronted by this development that she went down to the creek and sat in the cold water, resolved to get the bleeding stopped. She took off her shoes and stockings and underpants and sat there, in the shallow, icy water. She washed the blood out of her underpants and wrung them out and put them on wet. She didn't catch cold, she didn't get sick, and she didn't menstruate again all year. The neighbor woman said that such a procedure could have affected her brain.

"Driving all that bad blood back into her system, it could have."

Violet's only pleasure that Christmas was in talking about her boyfriend, whose name was Trevor Auston. She showed her sisters his picture. It was cut from a newspaper. He wore his clerical collar.

"He looks like a minister," said Dawn Rose, snickering.

"He is. That picture's from when he was ordained. Don't you think he's handsome?"

Trevor Auston was handsome. He was a dark-haired young man with narrowed eyes and a perfect nose, a chin flung up in the air, and a thin-lipped, confident, even gracious smile.

Bonnie Hope said, "He must be old, to be a minister."

"He just got to be a minister," said Violet. "He's twenty-six. He isn't an Anglican minister, he's a United Church minister," she said, as if that made a difference. And to her it did. Violet had changed churches in Ottawa. She said that at the United church there was a lot more going on. There was a badminton club—both she and Trevor played—and a drama club, as well as skating parties, tobogganing parties, hayrides, socials. It was at a Halloween social in the church basement, bobbing for apples, that Violet and Trevor first met. Or first talked, because Violet of course had noticed him before in church, where he was the assistant minister. He said that he had noticed her, too. And she thought that maybe he had. A group of girls from the normal school all went to that church together, partly on Trevor's account, and they played a game, trying to catch his eye. When everybody was standing up singing the hymns, they stared at him, and if he looked back they dropped their eyes at once. Waves of giggles would spread along the row. But Violet sang right back at him as if her eyes had just lit on him by accident:

"Rise up, oh men of God
And gird your armour on—"

Locked eyes during the hymn-singing. The virile hymns of the old Methodists and the scourging psalms of the Presbyterians had come together in this new United Church. The ministry then, in that church, attracted vigorous young men intent on power, not too unlike the young men who went into politics. A fine voice and a good profile did no harm.

Locked eyes. Kisses at the door of Violet's boarding house. The cool, nicely shaved, but still slightly bristling and foreign male cheek, the decent but promising smell of talc and shaving lotion. Soon enough they were slipping into the shadows beside the doorway, pressing together through their winter clothing. They had to have serious talks about self-control, and these talks were in themselves inflammatory. They became more and more convinced that if they were married, they would be having the kind of pleasures that nearly make you faint when you think about them.

Soon after Violet got back from her Christmas holidays, they became engaged. Then they had other things to think about and look forward to besides sex. A responsible and important sort of life lay ahead of them. They were asked to dinner as an engaged couple, by older ministers and rich and powerful members of the congregation. Violet had made herself one good dress, a cranberry wool serge with box pleats—a great improvement over the Roman-striped crêpe creation.

At those dinners, they had tomato juice to start with. Pitchers of iced water sat on the tables. No one in that church could touch alcoholic beverages. Even their Communion wine was grape juice. But there were great roasts of beef or pork, or turkeys, on silver platters, roasted potatoes and onions and slatherings of gravy, then rich cakes and pies and divinely molded puddings with whipped cream. Eating was not a sin. Cardplaying was a sin, except for a specially created Methodist card game called Lost Heir; dancing was a sin for some, and moviegoing was a sin for some, and going to any kind of entertainment except a concert of sacred music for which one did not pay was a sin for all on Sundays.

This was a change for Violet after the easygoing Anglicanism of her childhood, and the rules—if there were any rules—at home. She wondered what Trevor would say if he could see King Billy downing his tot of whiskey every morning before he started out to do the chores. Trevor had spoken of going home with her to meet her family, but she had been able to put him off. They could not go on Sunday because of his church services, and they could not go during the week because of her classes. She tried to push the idea of home out of her mind for now.

The strictness of the United Church might have been something to get used to, but the feelings of purpose and importance about it, the briskness and energy, were very agreeable to Violet. It was as if the ministers and top parishioners all had jobs in some thriving and important company. The role of a minister's wife she could see as hard and challenging, but that did not discourage her. She could see herself teaching Sunday school, raising money for missions, leading in prayer, sitting nicely dressed in the front pew listening to Trevor, tirelessly pouring tea out of a silver pot.

She didn't plan to spend the summer at home. She would visit for a week, once her exams were over, then work for the summer in the church office in Ottawa. She had applied for a teaching job in Bell's Corners, close by. She meant to teach for one year, then get married.

The week before exams were due to start, she got a letter from home. It was not from King Billy or Aunt Ivie—they didn't write letters—but from the woman on the next farm, the owner of the sewing machine. Her name was Annabelle Wrioley and she took some interest in Violet. She had no daughter of her own. She used to think that Violet was a terror, but now she thought she was a go-getter.

Annabelle said she was sorry to bother Violet at this time, but thought she should be told. There was trouble at home. What the trouble was she didn't like to say in a letter. If Violet could see her way to coming home on the train, she could go to town and meet her. She and her husband had a car now.

So Violet came home on the train.

"I have to tell you straight out," said Annabelle. "It's your father. He's in danger."

Violet thought she meant that King Billy was sick. But it wasn't that. He had been getting strange letters. Terrible letters. They were threats on his life.

What was in those letters, Annabelle said, was disgusting beyond belief.

Out at home, it looked as if all daily life had been suspended. The whole family was frightened. They were afraid to go to the back pasture to get the cows, afraid to go to the far end of the cellar, or to the well or toilet after dark. King Billy was a man willing even now to get into a fight, but he was unnerved by the idea of an unknown enemy waiting to pounce. He could not walk from the house to the barn without whirling around to see if there was anybody behind him. When he milked the cows, he turned them around in their stalls so that he could be in a corner where nobody could sneak up on him. Aunt Ivie did the same.

Aunt Ivie went around the house with a stick, beating on cupboard doors and the tops of chests and trunks and saying, "If you're in there, you better stay in there until you suffocate to death! You murderer!"

The murderer would have to be a midget, Violet said, to be hiding in any of those places.

Dawn Rose and Bonnie Hope were staying home from school, although it was the time of year when they should have been preparing to write the entrance examinations. They were afraid to get undressed at night, and their clothes were all wrinkled and sour-smelling.

Meals were not being cooked. But the neighbors brought food. There seemed to be always some visitor sitting at the kitchen table, a neighbor, or even someone not well known to the family who had heard about their trouble and come from a distance. The dishes were being washed in cold water if they were washed at all, and the dog was the only one interested in cleaning up the floor.

King Billy had been sitting up all night to keep watch. Aunt Ivie barricaded herself behind the bedroom door.

Violet asked about the letters. They were brought out, spread for her inspection on the oilcloth of the table, as they had been spread before all the neighbors and visitors.

Here was the letter that had come first, in the regular mail. Then the one that came second, also through the mail. After that the notes were found in different places around the farm.

On top of a cream can in the stable.

Tacked to the barn door.

Wrapped around the handle of the milk pail that King Billy used every day.

Some argument started up about just which note was found in which place.

"What about the postmark?" Violet cut in. "Where are the envelopes of the ones that came in the mail?"

They didn't know. They didn't know where the envelopes had got to.

"I want to see where they were posted from," said Violet.

"Don't make no difference where it was posted from seeing he knows right where to find us," Aunt Ivie said. "Anyway, he don't post them now. He sneaks up here after dark and leaves them. Sneaks right around here after dark and leaves them—he knows where to find us."

"What about Tigger?" said Violet. "Didn't he bark?"

No. But Tigger was getting too old now to be much of a watchdog. And with all the visitors coming and going he had practically given up barking altogether.

"He likely wouldn't bark if he seen all the hosts of hell coming in at the gate," King Billy said.

The first note told King Billy that he might as well sell off all his cows. He was a marked man. He would never live to cut the hay. He was as good as dead.

That had sent King Billy to the doctor. He took it that there might be something wrong with him that could be read in his face. But the doctor thumped him and listened to his heart and shone a light in his eyes and charged him two dollars and told him he was sound.

What a fool ignoramus you were to go to the doctor, the next letter said. *You could have saved your two-dollar bill to wipe your dirty old arse. I never told you that you were going to die of any disease. You are going to be killed. That is what is going to happen to you. You aren't safe no matter how good your health is. I can come in your house at night and slit your throat. I can shoot you from behind a tree. I can sneak up from behind and throw a rope around you and strangle you and you will never even see my face, so what do you think of that?*

So it wasn't a fortune-teller or somebody who could read the future. It was an enemy, who planned to do the job himself.

> *I wouldn't mind killing your ugly wife and your stupid kids while I'm at it.*
>
> *You ought to be thrown down the toilet hole head first. You bowlegged stupid rotten pig. You ought to have your things cut off with a razor blade. You are a liar, too. All those fights you said you won are a lie.*
>
> *I could stick a knife in you and catch your blood in a bowl and make a blood pudding. I would feed it to the pigs.*
>
> *How would you like a red-hot poker in your eye?*

When she finished reading, Violet said, "The thing to do is to show these to the police."

She had forgotten that the police did not exist out here in that abstract, official way. There was a policeman, but he was in town, and furthermore King Billy had had a run-in with him last winter. According to King Billy's story, a car driven by Lawyer Boot Lomax had skidded into King Billy's cutter at an intersection, and Lomax had summoned the policeman.

"Arrest that man for failing to stop at an intersection!" shouted Boot Lomax (drunk), waving his hand in its big fur-lined glove.

King Billy jumped up on the hard, heaped-up snow and readied his fists. "Ain't no brass buttons going to put the cuffs on me!"

It was all talked out in the end, but just the same it would be bad policy to go to that policeman.

"He's going to have it in for me, no matter. Could be even him is writing them."

But Aunt Ivie said it was that tramp. She remembered a bad-looking tramp who had come to the door years ago, and when she gave him a piece of bread he didn't say thank you. He said, "Haven't you got any bologna?"

King Billy thought more likely it could be a man he had hired once to help with the hay. The man quit after a day and a half because he couldn't stand working in the mow. He said he had nearly choked to death up there on the dust and the hayseeds, and he wanted fifty cents extra for the damage to his lungs.

"I'll give you fifty cents!" King Billy yelled at him. He jabbed at the air with a pitchfork. "Come over here and you'll get your fifty cents!"

Or could it be somebody settling an old score, one of those fellows he had kicked off the train long ago? One of those fellows from further back than that, that he had cleaned up on at the dance?

Aunt Ivie recalled a boy who had thought the world of her when she was young. He had gone out West but might have come back, and just heard that she was married.

"After all this time to come ragin' after you?" King Billy said. "That's not what I'd call likely!"

"He thought the world of me, just the same."

Violet was studying the notes. They were printed in pencil, on cheap lined paper. The pencil strokes were dark, as if the writer kept bearing down hard. There was no rubbing out or problem with the spelling—for instance, of a word like "ignoramus." There was an understanding of sentences and capital letters. But how much could that tell you?

The door was bolted at night. The blinds were drawn down to the sills. King Billy laid the shotgun on the table and set a glass of whiskey beside it.

Violet dashed the whiskey into the slop pail. "You don't need that," she said.

King Billy raised his hand to her—though he was not a man to strike his wife or his children.

Violet backed off but went on talking. "You don't need to stay awake. I'll stay awake. I'm fresh and you're tired. Go on, Papa. You need to sleep, not drink."

After some arguing, this was agreed on. King Billy made Violet show him that she knew how to use the shotgun. Then he went off to sleep in the parlor, on the hard couch there. Aunt Ivie had already pushed the dresser against the bedroom door and it would take too much yelling and explaining to get her to push it away.

Violet turned up the lamp and got the ink bottle from the shelf and started writing to Trevor to tell him what the trouble was. Without boasting, just telling what was happening, she let him see how she was taking over and calming people down, how she was prepared to defend her family. She even told about throwing out the whiskey, explaining that it was due to the strain on his nerves that her father had thought of resorting to whiskey in the first place. She did not say that she was afraid. She described the stillness, darkness, and loneliness of the early-summer night. And to someone who had been living in a town or city, it was very dark and lonely—but not so still, after all. Not if you were listening for something. It was full of faint noises, distant and nearby, of trees lifting and stirring and animals shifting and feeding. Lying outside the door, Tigger made the noise once or twice that meant he was dreaming about barking.

Violet signed her letter *Your loving and longing future wife,* then added, *with all my heart*. She turned the lamp down and raised a window blind and sat there keeping watch. In her letter, she had said that the countryside looked lovely now with the buttercups blooming along the roads, but as she sat watching to see if any moving shape detached itself from the bulging shadows in the yard, and listening for soft footsteps, she thought that she really hated the country. Parks were nicer for grass and flowers, and the trees along the streets in Ottawa were as fine as you could ask for. Order prevailed there, and some sort of intelligence. Out here was emptiness, rumor, and absurdity. What would the people who had asked her to dinner think if they could see her sitting here with a shotgun in front of her?

Suppose the intruder, the murderer, did come up the steps? She would have to shoot at him. Any wound from a shotgun would be terrible, that close. There would be a court case and her picture would be in the papers. HILLBILLY SQUABBLE.

If she didn't hit him, it would be worse.

When she heard a thump, she was on her feet, with her heart pounding. Instead of picking up the gun, she had pushed it away. She had thought the sound was on the porch, but when she heard it again she knew it was upstairs. She knew, too, that she had been asleep.

It was only her sisters. Bonnie Hope had to go outside to the toilet.

Violet lit the lantern for them. "You didn't need to both get up," she said. "I could have gone with you."

Bonnie Hope shook her head and pulled on Dawn Rose's hand. "I want her," she said.

This fright seemed to be making them into near imbeciles. They would not look at Violet. Could they even remember the days when they had, and she had instructed and spoiled them, and tried to make them pretty?

"Why can't you wear your nightgowns?" Violet said sadly,

and closed the door. She sat by the gun until they came back and went to bed. Then she lit the stove and made coffee, because she was afraid of falling asleep again.

When she saw the sky getting light, she opened the door. The dog stood up, shivered all over, and went to drink from the plugged dishpan by the pump. The yard was surrounded by white mist. Between the house and the barn was a rocky hump of land, and the rocks were dark with the dampness of night. What was their farm but a few acres of shallow soil scattered in among rubbly hills and swamp? What folly to think you could settle in there and live a life and raise a family.

On the top step was an out-of-place object—a neat, glistening horse bun. Violet looked for a stick to push it off with, then saw the piece of paper underneath.

Don't think your stuck-up slut of a daughter can help you. I see you all the time and I hate her and you. How would you like to get this rammed down your throat?

He must have put it here during the last hour of the night, while she was drinking her coffee at the kitchen table. He could have looked in through the window and seen her. She ran to wake her sisters to ask if they had seen anything when they went out, and they said no, nothing. They had gone down those steps and back up with the lantern, and there was nothing. He had put it there since.

One thing this told Violet that she was glad of. Aunt Ivie could have had nothing to do with it. Aunt Ivie had been shut up in her room all night. Not that Violet really thought that her mother was spiteful enough or crazy enough to do such a thing. But she knew what people said. She knew there would be people now saying they were not too surprised about what was going on here. They would just be saying that certain people attract peculiar troubles, that in the vicinity of certain people things are more likely to happen.

Violet worked all day at cleaning up. Her letter to Trevor lay on the dresser. She never got down to the mailbox with it. People dropped in, and it was the same as yesterday—the same talk, the same suspicions and speculations. The only difference was that there was the new note to show.

Annabelle brought them fresh bread. She read the note and said, "It just makes me sick to my stomach. So close, too. You could've almost heard him breathing, Violet. Your nerves must be about shot."

"There's not nobody can realize it," said Aunt Ivie proudly. "What us up here are going through."

"Anybody even steps on this place after dark," King Billy said, "from now on he's likely to get shot. And that's all I've got to say."

After they had eaten supper, and milked, and turned out the cows, Violet took her letter down to the mailbox for the mailman to pick up in the morning. She set the pennies on top of it for the stamp. She climbed up on the bank behind the mailbox and sat down.

Nobody went by on the road. The days were at their longest now; the sun was just going down. A killdeer went cheeping by with a wing dragging, trying to get her to follow. Its eggs must be somewhere close by. Killdeers laid their eggs practically on the road, right on the gravel, then had to spend their time trying to lure people away.

She was getting as bad as King Billy, thinking she sensed somebody behind her. She tried not to look around, but couldn't stop herself. She jumped up and turned, all at once, and saw a streak of red hair caught by the low sun, behind a juniper bush.

It was Dawn Rose and Bonnie Hope.

"What are you doing there, trying to scare me?" Violet said bitterly. "Aren't all of us scared enough already? I can see you! What do you think you're doing?"

They came out, and showed her what they had been doing—picking the wild strawberries.

Between the time she first saw the streak of red hair and the time she saw the red strawberries in their hands, Violet knew. But she would never get it out of them unless she coaxed and pleaded, and seemed to admire and sympathize. Maybe not even then.

"Can't I have a berry?" she said. "Are you mad at me? I know your secret.

"I know," she said. "I know who wrote those letters. I know it was you. You played a good trick on them, didn't you?"

Bonnie Hope's face started twitching. She clamped her teeth down on her bottom lip. Dawn Rose's face didn't change at all. But Violet saw her fist close on the berries she had picked. Red juice oozed out between Dawn Rose's fingers. Then she seemed to decide that Violet was on her side—or that she didn't care—and she smiled. This smile, or grin, was one that Violet thought she would never forget. It was innocent and evil, like the smile of some trusted person turned or revealed to be an enemy in a dream. It was the smile of chubby little Dawn Rose, her sister, and the grin of a cold, sly, full-grown, slatternly, bad-hearted stranger.

It was all Dawn Rose's doing. That came out. It all came out now. Dawn Rose had written all the letters and figured out where to put them, and Bonnie Hope had not done anything but stand by and keep her mouth shut. The first two letters were posted from town. The first time was when Dawn Rose had been taken to town to see the doctor for her earache. The second was when they had gone along with Annabelle for the ride. (Annabelle found a reason to go to town almost every day, now that she had the car.) Both times it had been easy to get to the post office. Then Dawn Rose had started putting the notes in other places.

Bonnie Hope was giggling faintly. Then she started to hiccup, and next to sob.

"Be quiet!" said Violet. "It wasn't you!"

Dawn Rose did not show any such signs of fright or remorse. She cupped her hands to her face to eat the squashed berries. She didn't even ask if Violet was going to tell. And Violet didn't ask her why she had done it. Violet thought that if she did ask, point-blank, Dawn Rose would probably say that she had done it for a joke. That would be bad enough. But what if she didn't say anything?

After her sisters had gone upstairs that night, Violet told King Billy that he wouldn't have to sit up anymore.

"Why's that?"

"Get Mother out here and I'll tell you." She was conscious of saying "Mother" instead of "Aunt Ivie" or even "Mama."

King Billy banged on the bedroom door. "Move that stuff away and get out here! Violet wants you!"

Violet let up the window shades and unbolted and opened the door. She stood the shotgun in the corner.

Her news took a long time to sink in. Both parents sat with their shoulders slumped and their hands on their knees and looks of deprivation and bewilderment on their faces. King Billy seemed to comprehend first.

"What's she got against me?" he said.

That was all he kept saying, and all he ever could say when he thought about it.

"What do you think she could've had against me?"

Aunt Ivie got up and put on her hat. She felt the night air coming in through the screen door.

"People get their laugh on us now," she said.

"Don't tell them," said Violet. (As if that would be possible.) "Don't tell them anything. Let it die down."

Aunt Ivie rocked herself on the couch, in her felt hat and dismal nightgown and rubber boots. "They'll say we got a queer streak in this family now, for sure."

Violet told her parents to go to bed, and they went, as if they were the children. Though she hadn't been to bed last night, and her eyes felt as they had been rubbed with sandpaper, she was sure she could never sleep herself. She got down all the letters that Dawn Rose had written from their place behind the clock, and folded them without looking at them and put them in an envelope. She wrote a note and put it in with them, and addressed the envelope to Trevor.

We have found out who wrote these, her note said. *It was my sister. She is fourteen years old. I don't know if she is crazy, or what. I don't know what I should do. I want you to come and get me and take me away. I hate it here. You can see what her mind is like. I can't sleep here. Please if you love me come and get me and take me away.*

She took this envelope down to the mailbox in the dark, and put in the pennies for the stamp. She had actually forgotten the other letter and the pennies already there. It seemed as if that letter had gone off days before.

She lay down on the hard parlor couch. In the dark, she couldn't see the picture that she used to think so powerful, so magical. She tired to remember the feeling it had given her. She fell asleep very soon.

Why did Violet do this? Why did she send those ugly letters to Trevor, and put such a note in with them? Did she really want to be rescued, told what to do? Did she want his help with the problem of Dawn Rose—his prayers, even? (Since this whole thing began, Violet hadn't given a thought to praying, or involving God in any way.)

She would never know why she had done it. She was sleepless and strung-up and her better judgment had deserted her. That was all.

The day after those letters were collected, Violet herself was standing by the mailbox in the morning. She wanted to get a ride into town with the mailman, so that she could catch the one-o'clock train to Ottawa.

"You folks got some bad business going on?" the mailman said. "Some bad business with your daddy?"

"That's all right," said Violet. "That's all over."

She knew that mail posted here was delivered in Ottawa the next day. There were two deliveries, one in the morning and one in the afternoon. If Trevor was out all day—and he usually was—his letters would be left waiting for him on the hall table of the house where he boarded, the house of a minister's widow. The front door was usually left unlocked. Violet could get to the letters before he did.

Trevor was at home. He had a bad summer cold. He was sitting in his study with a white scarf wrapped like a bandage around his throat.

"Don't come near me, I'm full of germs," he said as Violet crossed the room toward him. From his tone of voice, you would have thought she was.

"You forgot to leave the door open," he said. The door of the study had to be left open when Violet was in there, so that the minister's widow would not be scandalized.

Spread out on his desk, among his books and sermon notes, were all the smudged, creased, disgraceful letters that Dawn Rose had written.

"Sit down," said Trevor, in a tired, croaking voice. "Sit down, Violet."

So she had to sit in front of his desk, like some unhappy parishioner, some poor young woman who had got into trouble.

He said that he was not surprised to see her. He had thought she might show up. Those were his words. "*Show up*."

"You were going to tear them up if you got here first," he said.

Yes. Exactly.

"So I would never have known," he said.

"I would have told you someday."

"I doubt it," said Trevor, in his miserable croaking voice. Then he cleared his throat and said, "I'm sorry, but I doubt it," in an attempt to be kinder, more patient, more ministerial.

They talked from midafternoon until dark. Trevor talked. He rubbed the outside of his throat to keep his voice going. He talked until his throat was quite raw, stopped for a rest, and talked again. He didn't say a single thing that Violet couldn't have predicted, from the moment when he first raised his eyes to her. From the moment when he said, "Don't come near me."

And in the letter that she received from him, a few days later—in which he said the final things he couldn't quite bring himself to say to her face—there was also not one word she didn't know ahead of time. She could have written it for him. (All the letters written by Dawn Rose were enclosed.)

A minister, unfortunately, is never quite free to love and choose for himself. A minister's wife must be someone who doesn't bring with her any problem that might distract her husband and deflect him from serving God and his congregation. A minister's wife also must not have anything in her background or connections that would ever give rise to gossip or cause a scandal. Her life is often difficult, and it is necessary that she should have the very best of physical and mental health, with no hereditary taint or weakness, in order to undertake it.

All this came out with a great deal of repetition and enlargement and sidetracking, and in the middle of it they had some sort of wrangle about bringing Dawn Rose to see some doctors here, getting her put away somewhere. Trevor said that Dawn Rose was obviously a very deranged sort of person.

But instead of feeling that she wanted the problem of Dawn Rose solved for her by Trevor, Violet now seemed to feel that she had to protect Dawn Rose against him.

"Couldn't we ask God to cure her?" she said.

She knew by his look that he thought she was being insolent. It was up to him to mention God, not her. But he said calmly that it was through doctors and treatment that God cured people. Through doctors and treatment and laws and institutions. That was how God worked.

"There is a kind of female insanity that strikes at that age," he said. "You know what I mean. She hates men. She blames them. That's obvious. She has an insane hatred of men."

Later, Violet wondered if he had been trying to keep a door open for her then. If she had agreed to Dawn Rose's banishment, would he have broken off their engagement? Perhaps not. Though he tried to sound so superior and sensible, he, too, was probably feeling desperate.

Several times he had to say the same thing to her. "I won't talk to you, I can't talk to you, unless you stop crying."

The minister's widow came in and asked if they wanted supper. They said no, and she went away, disapproving. Trevor said he couldn't swallow. When it was getting dark, they went out. They walked down the street to a drugstore, and ordered two milkshakes, and a chicken sandwich for Violet. The chicken felt like bits of wood in her mouth. They walked on to the Y.W.C.A., where she could get a room for the night. (The room at her boarding house was being held for her, but she couldn't face going there.) She said she would catch the early-morning train.

"You don't have to do that," said Trevor. "We could have breakfast. My voice is gone now."

It was. He was whispering.

"I'll pick you up," he whispered. "I'll pick you up at eight-thirty."

But never touched, again, his mouth or his cool cheek to hers.

The early train left at ten to eight, and Violet was on it. She planned to write to the woman at the boarding house and to the church office where she had meant to work. She would not write her examinations. She could not stay in Ottawa another day. Her head ached horribly in the morning sunlight. This time, she really had not closed her eyes all night. When the train began to move, it was as if Trevor was being pulled away from her. More than Trevor. Her whole life was being pulled away from her—her future, her love, her luck, and her hopes. All that was being pulled off like skin, and hurt as much, and left her raw and stinging.

Did she despise him, then? If she did, she didn't know it. That wasn't something she could know about. If he had come after her, she would have gone back to him—gladly, gladly. Until the last minute, she hoped that he would come running onto the station platform. He knew when the early train left. He might wake up, and know what she was doing, and come after her. If he had done that, she would have given in about Dawn Rose; she would have done anything he wanted.

But he hadn't come after her, he hadn't come. No face was his; she couldn't bear to look at anybody.

At moments like this, thought Violet, it must be at moments like this that people do the things you hear about, and read about in the newspapers. The things you try to imagine, or try not to imagine. She could imagine it, she could feel what it would be like. The quick sunny flight, then the smack of the gravelly bank. Drowning yourself would be pleasanter, but would require a firmer purpose. You'd have to keep wanting it, still wanting it, hugging the water, gulping it down.

Unless you jumped from a bridge.

Could this be Violet? Could she be the person thinking these thoughts, reduced to such possibilities, her life turned upside down? She felt as if she was watching a play, and yet she was inside it, inside the play; she was in crazy danger. She closed her eyes and prayed rapidly—that, too, part of the play, but real: the first time in her life, she thought, that she had really prayed.

Deliver me. Deliver me. Restore me to my rightful mind. Please. Please hurry. Please.

And what she afterward believed that she learned on this train trip, which took less than two hours altogether, was that prayers are answered. Desperate prayers are answered. She would believe that she had never had an inkling before of what prayers could be, or the answers could be. Now something settled on her in the train, and bound her. Words settled on her, and were like cool, cool cloths, binding her.

It was not your purpose to marry him.

It was not the purpose of your life.

Not to marry Trevor. Not the purpose of your life.

Your life has a purpose, and you know what it is.

To look after them. All of them, all of your family, and Dawn Rose in particular. To look after all of them, and Dawn Rose in particular.

She was looking out the window, understanding this. The sun shone on the feathery June grass and the buttercups and toadflax and the old smooth rocks, on all the ragged countryside that she would never care for, and the word that came into her mind was "golden."

A golden opportunity.

What for?

You know what for. To give in. To give up. Care for them. Live for others.

That was the way Violet saw to leave her pain behind. A weight gone off her. If she would bow down and leave her old self behind as well, and all her ideas of what her life should be, the weight, the pain, the humiliation would all go magically. And she could still be chosen. She could be like the June grass that the morning light passed through, and lit up like pink feathers or streaks of sunrise cloud. If she prayed enough and tried enough, that would be possible.

People said that King Billy was never the same after his scare. Never really. They said that he got old, withered visibly. But he had been old, fairly old, when it all happened. He was a man who hadn't married till he was over forty. He went on milking the cows, getting back and forth to the barn through a few more hard winters, then died of pneumonia.

Dawn Rose and Bonnie Hope had gone to live in town by that time. They didn't go to high school. They got jobs in the shoe factory. Bonnie Hope became reasonably pretty and sociable, and she caught the eye of a salesman named Collard. They were married, and moved to Edmonton. Bonnie Hope had three daughters. She wrote proper letters home.

Dawn Rose's looks and manners improved, too. She was known in the shoe factory as a hard worker, a person not to be crossed, and one who could tell some good jokes if she was in the mood for it. She married, too—a farmer named Kemp, from the southern part of the county. No strange behavior or queerness or craziness ever surfaced in her again. She was said to have a blunt way with her—that was all. She had a son.

Violet went on living with Aunt Ivie on the farm. She had a job in the municipal telephone office. She bought a car, so that she could drive back and forth to work. Couldn't she have managed to write her teacher's examinations another year? Perhaps so. Perhaps not. When she gave up, she gave up. She didn't believe in trying to get back. She was good at her job.

Aunt Ivie still prowled the yard and the orchard, looking for where some hens might have hidden their eggs. She wore her hat and her boots. She tried to remember to scrape her boots off at the door, so that Violet wouldn't throw a tantrum.

But Violet never did that anymore.

. . .

One afternoon when she was off work, Violet drove over to see Dawn Rose. They were friendly—Dawn Rose's husband liked Violet—there was no reason not to arrive unexpectedly.

She found the doors of the house open. It was a warm summer day. Dawn Rose, who was very stout now, came out on the porch and said that it wasn't a good day for visiting, she was varnishing the floors. And indeed this was so—Violet could smell the varnish. Dawn Rose didn't offer lemonade or ask Violet to sit down on the porch. Just that day she was too busy.

Her little timid-looking fat son, who had the odd name of Dane, came up and clung to her legs. He usually liked Violet, but today he made strange.

Violet drove away. She didn't know, of course, that in a year Dawn Rose would be dead of a blood clot resulting from chronic phlebitis. It wasn't Dawn Rose she was thinking of, but herself, as she drove along a low stretch of road with trees and thick brush on either side and heard a voice say, "Her life is tragic."

"Her life is tragic," the voice said clearly and without any special emotion, and Violet, as if blinded, ran the car right off the road. There wasn't much of a ditch at all, but the ground there was boggy and she couldn't get the car out of it. She walked around and looked at where her wheels were, then stood by the car waiting for somebody to come along and give her a shove.

But when she did hear a car coming, she knew she didn't want to be found. She couldn't bear to be. She ran from the road into the woods, into the brush, and she was caught. She was caught then by berry bushes, little hawthorns. Held fast. Hiding because she didn't want to be seen, if her life was tragic.

II. *Possession*

Dane believes that he has one memory of Violet—his mother's sister—from a time before his mother died. He remembers very little from that far back. He hardly remembers his mother. He has one picture of his mother standing in front of the mirror at the kitchen sink, tucking her red hair under a navy-blue straw hat. He remembers a bright red ribbon on the hat. She must have been getting ready to go to church. And he can see a swollen leg, of a dull-brown color, that he associates with her last sickness. But he doubts if he ever saw that. Why would her leg be such a color? He must have heard people talking about it. He heard them say that her leg was as big as a barrel.

He thinks he remembers Violet coming for supper, as she sometimes did, bringing with her a pudding, which she set outside in the snow to keep cool. (None of the farmhouses had a refrigerator in those days.) Then it snowed, and the snow covered the pudding dish, which sank from sight. Dane remembers Violet tramping around in the snowy yard after dark, calling, "Pudding, pudding, here pudding!" as if it was a dog. Himself laughing immoderately, and his mother and father laughing in the doorway, and Violet elaborating the performance, stopping to whistle.

Not long after his mother died, his grandmother died—the one who lived with Violet, and wore a black hat, and called the hens in what sounded exactly like their own language, a tireless crooning and clucking. Then Violet sold the farm and moved to town, where she got a job with Bell Telephone. That was during the Second World War, when there was a shortage of men, and Violet soon became manager. There was some feeling that she should have stepped down when the war was over, given the job back to some man who had a family to support. Dane recalls hearing somebody say that—a woman, maybe one of his father's sisters, saying that it would have been the gracious thing to do. But his father said no, Violet did right. He said Violet had spunk.

Instead of the dull, draped, beaded dresses that married women—mothers—wore, Violet wore skirts and blouses. She wore pleated skirts of lively plaid, navy-blue or gray gabardine, with wonderful blouses of ivory satin, ruffled white georgette, pink or yellow or silvery rayon crêpe. The color of her good coat was royal purple, and it had a silver-fox collar. Her hair was not finger-waved, or permanented, but done up in a thick, dark, regal-looking roll. Her complexion was powdered, delicately pink, like the large seashell she owned and would let Dane listen to. Dane knows now that she dressed, and looked, like a certain kind of businesswoman, professional woman, of those days. Stylish but ladylike, shapely though not exactly slender, neither matronly nor girlish. What he took to be so remarkable and unique was not really so. This was the truth he discovered about most things as he got older. Just the same, his memory protects Violet from any sense of repetition, or classification, there's no way that long-ago Violet can be diminished.

In town, Violet lived in an apartment over the Royal Bank. You had to go up a long, closed-in flight of stairs. The long windows in the living room were called French doors. They opened out onto two tiny balconies with waist-high railings of wrought iron. The walls were painted, not papered. They were a pale green. Violet bought a new sofa and chair upholstered in a rich moss-green fabric, and a coffee table with a glass tray that fitted over the wooden top. The curtains were called drapes, and had pull cords. As they closed over the windows, a pattern of shiny cream-colored leaves rippled out across the dull cream background. There was no ceiling light—just floor lamps. In the kitchen there were knotty-pine cupboards and a knotty-pine breakfast nook. Another flight of steps—these were open and steep—led down to a little hedged-in back yard, which only Violet had the use of. It was as tidily enclosed, as susceptible to arrangement and decoration, as any living room.

During the first two years he went to high school in town, Dane visited Violet fairly often. He stayed overnight in the apartment when the weather was stormy. Violet made him up a bed on the moss-green sofa. He was a skinny, ravenous, redheaded boy in those days—nobody can credit the skinniness now—and Violet fed him well. She made him hot chocolate with whipped cream to drink at bedtime. She served him creamed chicken in tart shells, and layer cakes, and something called gravel pie, which was made with maple syrup. She ate one piece, and he ate the rest. This was a great change from the rough-and-ready meals at home with his father and the hired man. Violet told him stories about her own childhood on the farm, with his mother and the other sister, who lived out in Edmonton now, and their mother and father, whom she called "characters." Everybody was a character in those stories; everything was shaped to be funny.

She had bought a record player, and she played records for him, asking him to choose his favorite. His favorite was the record she got as a bonus when she joined a record club that would introduce her to classical music. It was *The Birds*, by Respighi. Her favorite was *Kenneth McKellar Singing Sacred and Secular Songs*.

She didn't come out to the farm anymore. Dane's father, when he stopped to pick Dane up, never had time for a cup of coffee. Perhaps he was afraid to sit down in such an elegant apartment in his farm clothes. Perhaps he still held a little grudge against Violet for what she had done at church.

Violet had made a choice there, right at the beginning of her town life. The church had two doors. One door was used by country people—the reason for this originally being that it was nearer to the drive shed—and the other by town people. Inside, the pattern was maintained: town people on one side of the church, country people on the other. There was no definable feeling of superiority or inferiority involved; that was just the way it was. Even country people who had retired and moved to town made a point of not using the town door, though that might mean going out of their way, walking right past it, to the country door.

Violet's move, and her job, certainly made her a town person. But when she first came to that church, Dane and his father were the only people in it that she knew. Choosing the country side would have shown loyalty, and a certain kind of pride, a forgoing of privilege. (For it was true that most of the elders and ushers and Sunday-school teachers were chosen from the town side, just as most of the fancy hats and fashionable ladies' outfits appeared over there.) Choosing the town side, which was what Violet did, showed an acceptance of status, perhaps even a wish for more.

Dane's father teased her on the sidewalk afterward. "You like the company over there?"

"It just seemed handier," Violet said, pretending not to know what he was talking about. "I don't know about the company. I think some fellow had a dead cigar in his pocket."

Dane wished so much that Violet hadn't done that. It wasn't

that he wanted anything serious to happen between Violet and his father—for instance, marriage. He couldn't imagine that. He just wanted them to be on the same side, so that could be his side.

On an afternoon in June, when he had finished writing one of his exams, Dane went around to Violet's apartment to get a book he had left there. He was allowed to use the apartment to study in while she was at work. He would open the French doors and let in the smell of the countryside just freed of snow, with its full creeks and leaky swamps and yellowing willow trees and steaming furrows. Dust came in, too, but he always thought he could wipe that up before she got home. He walked around and around in the pale bright living room, tamping down chunks of information, feeling lordly. Everything in the room got bits of whatever he was learning attached to it. There was a dark picture of a dead king and some stately ladies that he would always look at when he was memorizing poetry. The ladies reminded him in a strange way of Violet.

He hadn't known whether Violet would be home, because her afternoon off varied from week to week. But he heard her voice as he came up the stairs.

"It's me," he called, and waited for her to come out of the kitchen and ask about his exam.

Instead she called back to him, "Dane! Dane, I wasn't expecting you! Come and have coffee with us!"

She introduced him to the two people in the kitchen, a man and wife. The Tebbutts. The man was standing by the counter and the woman was sitting in the breakfast nook. Dane knew the man by sight. Wyck Tebbutt, who sold insurance. He was supposed to have been a professional baseball player, but that would have been a long time ago. He was a trim, small, courteous man, always rather nattily dressed, with a deft athlete's modest confidence.

Violet didn't ask Dane anything about his exam, but went on fussing about getting the coffee ready. First she got out breakfast cups, then rejected them and got down her good china. She spread a cloth on the breakfast-nook table. There was a faint scorch mark on it from the iron.

"Well, I'm mortified!" said Violet laughing.

Wyck Tebbutt laughed, too. "So you should be, so you should be!" he said.

Violet's nervous laugh, and her ignoring him, displeased Dane considerably. She had been in town for several years now, and she had made several changes in herself, which he seemed to be just now noticing all together. Her hair was not done up in a roll anymore; it was short and curled. And its dark-brown color was not the same as it used to be. Now it had a rich, dull look, like chocolate fudge. Her lipstick was too heavy, too bright a red, and the grain of her skin had coarsened. Also, she had put on a lot of weight, especially around the hips. The harmony of her figure was spoiled—it almost looked as if she was wearing some kind of cage or contraption under her skirt.

As soon as his coffee was poured, Wyck Tebbutt said that he would just take his cup down into the yard, because he wanted to see how those new rosebushes were getting on.

"Oh, I think they've got some kind of a bug!" said Violet, as if the fact delighted her. "I'm afraid they have, Wyck!"

All this time, the wife was talking, and she went right on, hardly noticing that her husband had left. She talked to Violet and even to Dane, but she was really just talking into the air. She talked about her appointments with the doctor, and the chiropractor. She said that she had a headache that was like red-hot irons being clamped on her temples. And she had another kind of shooting pain down the side of her neck that was like hundreds of needles being driven into her flesh. She wouldn't allow a break; she was like a helpless little talking machine set up in a corner of the breakfast nook, her large sad eyes going blank as soon as they fixed on you.

This was the sort of person, this was the sort of talk, that Violet was so good at imitating.

And now she was deferring. She was listening, or pretending to listen, to this woman with an interest the woman didn't even notice or need. Was it because the husband had walked out? Was Violet feeling a concern about his rudeness to his wife? She did keep glancing down into the back yard.

"I just have to see what Wyck thinks about that bug," she

said, and she was off, down the back steps, at what seemed like a heavy and undignified trot.

"All they are interested in is their money," the wife said.

Dane got up to get himself more coffee. He stood at the stove and lifted the coffeepot inquiringly while she talked.

"I shouldn't have drunk the amount I already have," she said. "Ninety percent of my stomach is scar tissue."

Dane looked down at her husband and Violet, who were leaning together over the young rosebushes. No doubt they were talking about the roses, and bugs, and bug killer and blight. Nothing so crude as a touch would occur. Wyck, holding his coffee cup, delicately lifted one leaf, then another, with his foot. Violet's look travelled down obediently to the leaf held against his polished shoe.

It would be wrong to say that Dane understood anything right then. But he forgot the woman who was talking and the coffeepot he was holding. He felt a secret, a breath of others' intimacy. Something he didn't want to know about, but would have to.

Not so long afterward, he was with his father on the street, and he saw Wyck coming toward them. His father said, "Hello, Wyck," in a certain calm, respectful voice men use to greet other men they don't know—or perhaps don't want to know—too well. Dane had veered off to look into the hardware store window.

"Don't you know Wyck Tebbutt?" his father said. "I thought you might've run into him at Violet's."

Then Dane felt it again—the breath he hated. He hated it more now, because it was all around him. It was all around him if even his father knew.

He didn't want to understand the extent of Violet's treachery. He already knew that he would never forgive her.

Now Dane is a broad-shouldered ruddy man with the worn outlines of a teddy bear and a beard that is almost entirely gray. He has grown to look more and more like his mother. He is an architect. He went away from home to college, and for a long time he lived and worked in other places, but he came back several years ago, and is kept busy now restoring the churches and town halls and business blocks and houses that were considered eyesores at the time he left. He lives in the house he grew up in, the house his father was born and died in, a hundred-and-fifty-year-old stone house that he and Theo have gradually brought back to something like its original style.

He lives with Theo, who is a social worker.

When Dane first told Wyck and Violet (he has forgiven her—them—long ago) that somebody named Theo was moving in with him, Wyck said, "I take that to mean you finally turned up a serious girlfriend."

Violet didn't say anything.

"A man friend," Dane said gently. "It isn't easy to tell, from the name."

"Well. That's him's and your business," Wyck said affably. The only sign he gave that he might be shaken was in saying "him's" and not noticing.

"Theo. Yes," said Violet. "That is hard to tell."

This was in the little two-bedroom house on the edge of town that Violet moved to after she retired from the phone company. Wyck had moved in with her after his wife died and they were able to marry. The house was one of a row of very similar houses strung out along a country road in front of a cornfield. Wyck's things were moved in on top of Violet's, and the low-ceilinged rooms seemed crowded, the arrangement temporary and haphazard. The moss-green sofa looked bulky and old-fashioned under an afghan made by Wyck's wife. A large black velvet painting, belonging to Wyck, took up most of one living-room wall. It depicted a bull and a bullfighter. Wyck's old sporting trophies and the silver tray presented to him by the insurance company sat on the mantel beside Violet's old shell and tippling Scotsman.

All those old dust catchers, Violet calls them.

But she kept Wyck's things there even after Wyck himself was gone. He died during the Grey Cap game, at the end of November. Violet phoned Dane, who listened to her at first with his eyes on the television screen.

"I went down to the church," Violet said. "I took some things down for the rummage sale, and then I went and got us a bottle of whiskey, and when I got back, as soon as I opened the door, I said, 'Wyck,' and he didn't answer. I saw the back of his head in a funny position. It was bent towards the arm of his chair. I went around in front of him and turned off the television."

"What do you mean?" said Dane. "Aunt Violet? What's the matter?"

"Oh, he's dead," said Violet, as if Dane had been questioning it. "He would have to be dead to let me turn off the football game." She spoke in a loud, emphatic voice with an unnatural joviality—as if she was covering up some embarrassment.

When he drove into town, he found her sitting on the front step.

"I'm a fool," she said. "I can't go inside. What an idiot I am, Dane." Her voice was still jarring, loud and bright.

Theo said later that many old people were like that when someone close to them died. "They get past grief," he said. "Or it's a different kind."

All winter, Violet seemed to be all right, driving her car when the weather permitted, going to church, going to the senior citizens' club to play cards. Then, just when the hot months were starting and you'd think she would most enjoy getting out, she announced to Dane that she didn't intend to drive anymore.

He thought the trouble might be with her eyesight. He suggested an appointment to see if she needed stronger glasses.

"I see well enough," she said. "My trouble is not being sure of what I see."

What did she mean by that?

"I see things I know aren't there."

How did she know they were not there?

"Because I still have enough sense that I can tell. My brain gets the message through and tells me that's ridiculous. But what if it doesn't get through all the time? How am I going to know? I can get my groceries delivered. Most old people get their groceries delivered. I am an old person. They are not going to miss me that much at the A.&P."

But Dane knew how much she enjoyed going to the A.&P., and he thought that he or Theo would have to try to get her there once a week. That was where she got the special strong coffee that Wyck had drunk, and she usually liked to look at the smoked meats and back bacon—both favorite things of Wyck's—though she seldom bought any.

"For instance," said Violet. "The other morning, I saw King Billy."

"You saw my granddaddy?" Dane said, laughing. "Well. How was he?"

"I saw King Billy the horse," said Violet shortly. "I came out of my room and there he was poking his head in at the dining-room window."

She said she had known him right away. His familiar, foolish, dapple-gray head. She told him to go on, get out of there, and he lifted his head over the sill and moved off in a leisurely kind of way. Violet went on into the kitchen to start her breakfast, and then several things occurred to her.

King Billy the horse had been dead for about sixty-five years.

That couldn't have been the milkman's horse, either, because milkmen hadn't driven horses since around 1950. They drove trucks.

No. They didn't drive anything, because milk was not delivered anymore. It didn't even come in bottles. You picked it up at the store in cartons or in plastic bags.

There was glass in the dining-room window that had not been broken.

"I was never especially fond of that horse, either," said Violet. "I was never *un*-fond of it, but if I had my choice of anything or anyone I wanted to see that's gone, it wouldn't be that horse."

"What would it be?" said Dane, trying to keep the conversation on a light level, though he wasn't at all happy about what he heard. "What would be your choice?"

But Violet made an unpleasant sound—a balky sort of grunt, *annhh*—as if his question angered and exasperated her. A look of deliberate, even ill-natured stupidity—the visual equivalent of that grunt—passed over her face.

It happened that a few nights later Dane was watching a television program about people in South America—mostly women—who believe themselves to be invaded and possessed, from time to time and in special circumstances, by spirits. The look on their faces reminded him of that look on Violet's. The difference was that they courted this possession, and he was sure Violet didn't. Nothing in her wanted to be overtaken by a helpless and distracted, dull and stubborn old woman, with a memory or imagination out of control, bulging at random through the present scene. Trying to keep that old woman in check was bound to make her short-tempered. In fact, he had seen her—now he remembered, he had seen her tilt her head to the side and give it a quick slap, as people do to get rid of a buzzing, unwelcome presence.

A week or so further into the summer, she phoned him. "Dane. Did I tell you about this pair I see, going by my house?"

"Pair of what, Aunt Violet?"

"Girls. I think so. Boys don't have long hair anymore, do they? They're dressed in army clothes, it looks like, but I don't know whether that means anything. One is short and one is tall. I see them go by this house and look at it. They walk out the road and back."

"Maybe they're collecting bottles. People do."

"They don't have anything to put bottles in. It's this house. They have some interest in it."

"Aunt Violet? Are you sure?"

"Yes, I know, I ask myself, too. But they're not anybody I've ever known. They're not anybody I know that's dead. That's something."

He thought he should get around to see her, find out what was going on. But before he got there, she phoned again.

"Dane. I just wanted to tell you. About those girls I noticed walking by the house. They are girls. They're just dressed up in army outfits. They came and knocked on my door. They said they were looking for a Violet Thoms. I said there was no such person living here, and they looked very downcast. Then I said there was a Violet Tebbutt, and would she do?"

She seemed in high spirits. Dane was busy; he had a meeting

with some town councillors in half an hour. He also had a toothache. But he said, "You were right, then. So who are they?"

"That's the surprise," said Violet. "They are not just any girls. One of them is your cousin. I mean, the daughter of your cousin. Donna Collard's daughter. Do you know who I'm talking about? Your cousin Donna Collard? Her married name is McNie."

"No," said Dane.

"Your Aunt Bonnie Hope, out in Edmonton, she was married to a man named Collard, Roy Collard, and she had three daughters. Elinor and Ruth and Donna. Now do you know who I mean?"

"I never met them," he said.

"No. Well, Donna Collard married a McNie, I forget his first name, and they live in Prince George, British Columbia, and this is their daughter. Heather. This is their daughter Heather that has been walking past my house. The other girl is her friend. Gillian."

Dane didn't say anything for a minute, and Violet said, "Dane? I hope you don't think that I'm confused about this?"

He laughed. He said, "I'll have to come around and see them."

"They are very polite and good-hearted," said Violet, "in spite of how they might look."

He was fairly sure that these girls were real, but everything was slightly out of focus to him at the time. (He had a low-grade fever, though he didn't know it yet, and eventually would have to have a root-canal job done on his tooth.) He actually thought that he should ask around town to find out if anybody else had seen them. When he did get around to doing this, sometime later, he found out that a couple of girls of that description had been staying at the hotel, that they owned a beat-up blue Datsun but walked a lot, in town and out, and were generally thought to be woman's libbers. People didn't think much of their outfits, but they didn't cause any trouble, except for getting into some sort of argument with the exotic dancer at the hotel.

In the meantime, he had heard a lot from Violet. She phoned him at home, when his mouth was so sore he could hardly talk, and said it was too bad he wasn't feeling well—otherwise he could have got to meet Heather and Gillian.

"Heather is the tall one," Violet said. "She has long, fair hair and a narrow build. If she resembles Bonnie Hope at all, it is in her teeth. But Heather's teeth suit her face better and they are beautifully white. Gillian is a nice-looking sort of girl, with curly hair and a tan. Heather has that fair skin that burns. They wear the same sort of clothes—you know, the army pants and work shirts and boys' boots—but Gillian always has a belt on and her collar turned up, and on her it looks like more of a style. Gillian is more confident, but I think Heather is more intelligent. She is the one more genuinely interested."

"What in?" said Dane. "What are they, anyway—students?"

"They've been to university," Violet said. "I don't know what they were studying. They've been to France and Mexico. In Mexico, they stayed on an island that was called the Isle of Women. It was a women-ruled society. They belong to a theater and they make up plays. They make up their own plays. They don't take some writer's plays or do plays that have been done before. It's all women, in this theater. They made me a lovely supper. Dane, I wish you could have been here. They made a salad with artichoke hearts in it."

"Violet sounds as if she's on drugs," said Dane to Theo. "She sounds as if they've got her spinning."

When he could talk again, he called her. "What are those girls interested in, Aunt Violet? Are they interested in old china and jewellery and things?"

"They are not," said Violet crossly. "They are interested in family history. They are interested in our family and what I can remember about what it was like. I had to tell them what the reservoir was on a stove."

"What would they want to know that for?"

"Oh. They have some idea. They have some idea about doing a play."

"What do they know about plays?"

"Didn't I tell you they've acted in plays? They've made up their own plays and acted in them, in this women's theater."

"What sort of play are they going to make up?"

"I don't know. I don't know if they'll do it. They're just interested in what it was like in the old days."

"That's all the style now," Dane said. "To be interested in that."

"They're not just letting on to be, Dane. They really are."

But he thought that she didn't sound so buoyant this time.

"You know they change all the names," she said. "When they do make up a play, they change all the names and places. But I think they just like finding out about things, and talking. They're not all that young, but they seem young, they're so curious. And lighthearted."

"Your face looks different," said Dane to Violet when he finally got to visit her again. "Have you lost weight?"

Violet said, "I wouldn't think so."

Dane had lost twelve pounds himself but she did not notice. She seemed cheerful but agitated. She kept getting up and sitting down, looking out the window, moving things around on the kitchen counter for no reason.

The girls had gone.

"They're not coming back?" said Dane.

Yes, they were. Violet thought they were coming back. She didn't know just when.

"They're off to find their island, I guess," said Dane. "Their island ruled by women."

"I don't know," said Violet. "I think they've gone to Montreal."

Dane didn't like to think that he could be made to feel so irritable and suspicious by two girls he hadn't even met. He was almost ready to blame it on the medication he still had to take for his tooth. There was a sense he had of something concealed from him—all around him, but concealed—a tiresome, silly, malicious sort of secret.

"You've cut your hair," he said. That was why her face looked different.

"They cut it. They said it was a Joan of Arc style." Violet

smiled ironically, much as she used to, and touched her hair. "I told them I hoped I wouldn't end up burned at the stake."

She held her head in her hands, and rocked back and forth.

"They've tired you," Dane said. "They've tired you, Aunt Violet."

"It's going through all that," said Violet. She jerked her head toward the back bedroom. "It's what I have to get to work on in there."

In Violet's back bedroom there were boxes of papers, and an old humpbacked trunk that had belonged to her mother. Dane thought that it was full of papers, too. Old high-school notes, normal-school notes, report cards, records and correspondence from her years with the phone company, minutes of meetings, letters, postcards. Anything that had writing on it, she had probably kept.

She said that all these papers had to be sorted out. It had to be done before the girls got back. There were things she had promised them.

"What things?"

"Just things."

Were they coming back soon?

Violet said yes. She expected so, yes. As she thought of this, her hands were patting and rubbing at the tabletop. She took a bite of a cookie, and crumbled what was left of it. Dane saw her sweep the crumbs into her hand and put them in her coffee.

"That's what they sent," she said, and pushed in front of him a card he had noticed that was propped against her sugar bowl. It was a homemade card with childishly crayoned violets on it, and red hearts. She seemed to intend that he should read it, so he did.

Thank you a million, million times for your help and openness. You have given us a wonderful story. It is a classic story of anti-patriarchal rage. Your gift to us, can we give it to others? What is called Female Craziness is nothing but centuries of Frustration and Oppression. The part about the creek is wonderful just by itself and how many women can identify!

Across the bottom, in capitals, had been written: LONGING TO SEE DOCUMENTS. PLEASE NEXT TIME. LOVE AND GRATITUDE.

"What is all this about?" said Dane. "Why do you have to sort things out for them? Why can't they just go through the whole mess and find what they want for themselves?"

"Because I am so ashamed!" said Violet vehemently. "I don't want anybody to see."

He told her there was nothing, nothing, to be ashamed of.

"I shouldn't have used the word 'mess.' It's just that you've accumulated a lot, over the years. Some of it is probably very interesting."

"There is more to it than anybody knows! And I am the one has to deal with it!"

"Anti-patriarchal rage," said Dane, taking up the card again. "What do they mean by that?" He wondered why they used capitals for Female Craziness and Frustration and Oppression.

"I'll tell you," said Violet. "I'll just tell you. You don't know what I've got to contend with. There's things that are not so nice. I went in there and opened up that old trunk to have a look at what was inside, and what do you think I found, Dane? It was full of filth. Horse manure. Set out in rows. On purpose. Inside my trunk in my own house, that's what I find." She began to sniffle, in an uncharacteristic, unattractive, self-pitying way.

When Dane told Theo this, Theo smiled, then said, "I'm sorry. What did she say then?"

"I told her I'd go and look at it, and she said she'd cleaned it all out."

"Yes. Well. It looks as if something snapped, doesn't it? I thought I could see it coming."

Dane remembered what else she'd said, but he didn't mention it. It didn't matter.

"That's a disgusting trick, isn't it?" she'd said, whimpering. "That's the trick of a stunted mind!"

Violet's front door was standing open at noon the next day when Dane drove down her road, heading out of town. He didn't usually take this route. That he did today was not surprising, considering how much Violet had been on his mind in the last several hours.

He must have come in the door just as the flames started up in the kitchen. He saw their light ahead of him on the kitchen wall. He ran back there, and caught Violet heaping papers on top of the gas stove. She had turned on the burners.

Dane grabbed a scatter rug from the hall to shield himself so that he could turn off the gas. Burning papers flew into the air. There were heaps of paper all over the floor, some papers still in boxes. Violet was evidently intending to burn them all.

"Oh, Jesus, Aunt Violet!" Dane was yelling. "Jesus, Jesus, what are you doing! Get out of here! Get out!"

Violet was standing in the middle of the room, rooted there like a big dark stump, with scraps of fiery paper flying all around her.

"Get out!" Dane yelled, and turned her around and pushed her toward the back door. Then, all of a sudden, her speed was as extraordinary as her stillness had been. She ran or lurched to the door, opened it, and crossed the back porch. Instead of going down the steps, she went off the edge, falling headfirst into some rosebushes that Wyck had planted.

Dane didn't know right away that she had fallen. He was too busy in the kitchen.

Luckily, paper in heaps or bundles doesn't catch fire as readily as most people think it does. Dane was more afraid of the curtains catching, or the dry paint behind the stove. Violet wasn't anything like the careful housekeeper she used to be, and the walls were greasy. He brought the scatter rug down on the flames that were shooting up from the stove, then remembered the fire extinguisher that he himself had bought for Violet and insisted she keep on the kitchen counter. He went stumbling around the room with the fire extinguisher, chasing flaming birds that fell down as bits of charred paper. He was impeded by the piles of paper on the floor. But the curtains didn't catch. The wall behind the stove had broken out in paint blisters, but it didn't catch either. He kept at the chase, and in five minutes, maybe less, he had the fire out. Just the bits of burned paper, dirty moth wings, were lying over everything—a mess.

When he saw Violet on the ground between the rosebushes, he thought the worst. He was afraid she had had a stroke, or a heart attack, or at the very least broken her hip in the fall. But she was conscious, struggling to push herself up, groaning. He got hold of her, and lifted her. With many grunts and exclamations of dismay coming from them both, he helped her to the back steps and set her down.

"What's this blood on you?" he said. Her arms were smeared with dirt and blood.

"It's from the roses," Violet said. He knew then, by her voice, that there was nothing broken in her.

"The roses scratched me something fierce," she said. "Dane, you're a terrible sight. You're a terrible sight, you're all black!"

Tears and sweat ran together down his face. He put his hand up to his cheek, and it came away black. "Smoke," he said.

She was so calm that he thought perhaps she had had a tiny stroke, a loss of memory, just enough to let her mind skip over the fire. But she hadn't.

"I didn't even use any coal oil," she said. "Dane, I didn't use coal oil or anything. What would make it flare up like that?"

"It wasn't a wood stove, Aunt Violet. It was on top of the gas burners."

"Oh, Lord."

"You must have thought you were burning papers in the wood stove."

"I must have. What a thing to do. And you came and put it out."

He was trying to pick the black bits of paper out of her hair, but they disintegrated under his fingers. They fell to smaller bits, and were lost.

"I have you to thank," said Violet.

"What we ought to do now," he said, "is take you over to the hospital, just to make sure you're all right. You could have a rest for a few days while we see about cleaning up the kitchen. Would that be all right?"

She made some groaning but peaceable sound that meant yes.

"Then maybe you'd like to come out and stay with us for a while."

He would talk to Theo that night; they would have to manage something.

"You'd have to watch me that I didn't burn the place down."

"That's all right."

"Oh, Dane. It's no joke."

Violet died in the hospital, the third night, without any warning. A delayed reaction, perhaps. Shock. Dane burned all the papers in the back-yard incinerator. She never told him to; she never mentioned what she had been doing. She never mentioned the girls again, or anything that had happened that summer. He just felt that he should finish what she had started. He planned, as he burned, what he would say to those girls, but by the time he finished, he thought he was being too hard on them—they had brought her happiness, as much as trouble.

While they were still sitting on the back steps, in the hot, thinly clouded early afternoon, with the green wall of corn in front of them, Violet had touched her scratches and said, "These remind me."

"I should put some Dettol on them," said Dane.

"Sit still. Do you think there is any kind of infection that hasn't run its course through my veins by now?"

He sat still, and she said, "You know, Wyck and I were friends, Dane, a long, long time before we were able to get married?"

"Yes."

"Well, these scratches remind me of the way we met, to be friends the way we were, because of course we knew each other by sight. I was driving my first car, the V-8 that you wouldn't remember, and I ran it off the road. I ran it into a bit of a ditch and I couldn't get out. So I heard a car coming, and I waited, and then I couldn't face it."

"You were embarrassed you'd run off the road?"

"I was feeling badly. That was why I'd run off the road. I was feeling badly for no reason, or just a little reason. I couldn't face anybody, and I ran off into the bushes and right away I got stuck. I turned and twisted and couldn't get loose, and the more I turned the more I got scratched. I was in a light summer dress. But the car stopped anyway. It was Wyck. I never told you this, Dane?"

No.

"It was Wyck driving someplace by himself. He said, stay still there, and he came over and started pulling the berry canes and branches off me. I felt like a buffalo in a trap. But he didn't laugh at me—he didn't seem the least surprised to find a person in that predicament. I was the one who started laughing. Seeing him going round so dutiful in his light-blue summer suit."

She ran her hands up and down her arms, tracing the scratches with her fingertips, patting them.

"What was I just talking about?"

"When you were caught in the bushes, and Wyck was working you out."

She patted her arms rapidly and shook her head and made that noise in her throat, of impatience or disgust. *Annhh.*

She sat up straight and said, in a clear, but confiding voice, "There is a wild pig running through the corn."

"And you were laughing," Dane said, as if he hadn't heard that.

"Yes," said Violet, nodding several times and struggling to be patient. "Yes. We were."

Circle of Prayer

Trudy threw a jug across the room. It didn't reach the opposite wall; it didn't hurt anybody, it didn't even break.

This was the jug without a handle—cement-colored with brown streaks on it, rough as sandpaper to the touch—that Dan made the winter he took pottery classes. He made six little handleless cups to go with it. The jug and the cups were supposed to be for sake, but the local liquor store doesn't carry sake. Once, they brought some home from a trip, but they didn't really like it. So the jug Dan made sits on the highest open shelf in the kitchen, and a few odd items of value are kept in it. Trudy's wedding ring and her engagement ring, the medal Robin won for all-round excellence in Grade 8, a long, two-strand necklace of jet beads that belonged to Dan's mother and was willed to Robin. Trudy won't let her wear it yet.

Trudy came home from work a little after midnight; she entered the house in the dark. Just the little stove light was on—she and Robin always left that on for each other. Trudy didn't need any other light. She climbed up on a chair without even letting go of her bag, got down the jug, and fished around inside it.

It was gone. Of course. She had known it would be gone.

She went through the dark house to Robin's room, still with her bag over her arm, the jug in her hand. She turned on the overhead light. Robin groaned and turned over, pulled the pillow over her head. Shamming.

"Your grandmother's necklace," Trudy said. "Why did you do that? Are you insane?"

Robin shammed a sleepy groan. All the clothes she owned, it seemed, old and new and clean and dirty, were scattered on the floor, on the chair, the desk, the dresser, even on the bed itself. On the wall was a huge poster showing a hippopotamus, with the words underneath "Why Was I Born So Beautiful?" And another poster showing Terry Fox running along a rainy highway, with a whole cavalcade of cars behind him. Dirty glasses, empty yogurt containers, school notes, a Tampax still in its wrapper, the stuffed snake and tiger Robin had had since before she went to school, a collage of pictures of her cat Sausage, who had been run over two years ago. Red and blue ribbons that she had won for jumping, or running, or throwing basketballs.

"You answer me!" said Trudy. "You tell me why you did it!"

She threw the jug. But it was heavier than she'd thought, or else at the very moment of throwing it she lost conviction, because it didn't hit the wall; it fell on the rug beside the dresser and rolled on the floor, undamaged.

You threw a jug at me that time. You could have killed me.

Not at you. I didn't throw it at you.

You could have killed me.

Proof that Robin was shamming: She started up in a fright, but it wasn't the blank fright of somebody who'd been asleep. She looked scared, but underneath that childish, scared look was another look—stubborn, calculating, disdainful.

"It was so beautiful. And it was valuable. It belonged to your grandmother."

"I thought it belonged to me," said Robin.

"That girl wasn't even your friend. Christ, you didn't have a good word to say for her this morning."

"You don't know who is my friend!" Robin's face flushed a

bright pink and her eyes filled with tears, but her scornful, stubborn expression didn't change. "I knew her. I talked to her. So get out!"

Trudy works at the Home for Mentally Handicapped Adults. Few people call it that. Older people in town still say "the Misses Weir's house," and a number of others, including Robin—and, presumably, most of those her age—call it the Half-Wit House.

The house has a ramp now for wheelchairs, because some of the mentally handicapped may be physically handicapped as well, and it has a swimming pool in the back yard, which caused a certain amount of discussion when it was installed at taxpayers' expense. Otherwise the house looks pretty much the way it always did—the white wooden walls, the dark-green curlicues on the gables, the steep roof and dark screened side porch, and the deep lawn in front shaded by soft maple trees.

This month, Trudy works the four-to-midnight shift. Yesterday afternoon, she parked her car in front and walked up the drive thinking how nice the house looked, peaceful as in the days of the Misses Weir, who must have served iced tea and read library books, or played croquet, whatever people did then.

Always some piece of news, some wrangle or excitement, once you get inside. The men came to fix the pool but they didn't fix it. They went away again. It isn't fixed yet.

"We don't get no use of it, soon summer be over," Josephine said.

"It's not even the middle of June, you're saying summer'll be over," Kelvin said. "You think before you talk. Did you hear about the young girl that was killed out in the country?" he said to Trudy.

Trudy had started to mix two batches of frozen lemonade, one pink and one plain. When he said that, she smashed the spoon down on the frozen chunk so hard that some of the liquid spilled over.

"How, Kelvin?"

She was afraid she would hear that a girl was dragged off a country road, raped in the woods, strangled, beaten, left there. Robin goes running along the country roads in her white shorts and T-shirt, a headband on her flying hair. Robin's hair is golden; her legs and arms are golden. Her cheeks and limbs are downy, not shiny—you wouldn't be surprised to see a cloud of pollen delicately floating and settling behind her when she runs. Cars hoot at her and she isn't bothered. Foul threats are yelled at her, and she yells foul threats back.

"Driving a truck," Kelvin said.

Trudy's heart eased. Robin doesn't know how to drive yet.

"Fourteen years old, she didn't know how to drive," Kelvin said. "She got in the truck, and the first thing you know, she ran it into a tree. Where was her parents? That's what I'd like to know. They weren't watching out for her. She got in the truck when she didn't know how to drive and ran it into a tree. Fourteen. That's too young."

Kelvin goes uptown by himself; he hears all the news. He is fifty-two years old, still slim and boyish-looking, well-shaved, with soft, short, clean dark hair. He goes to the barbershop every day, because he can't quite manage to shave himself. Epilepsy, then surgery, an infected bone-flap, many more operations, a permanent mild difficulty with feet and fingers, a gentle head fog. The fog doesn't obscure facts, just motives. Perhaps he shouldn't be in the Home at all, but where else? Anyway, he likes it. He says he likes it. He tells the others they shouldn't complain; they should be more careful, they should behave themselves. He picks up the soft-drink cans and beer bottles that people have thrown into the front yard—though of course it isn't his job to do that.

When Janet came in just before midnight to relieve Trudy, she had the same story to tell.

"I guess you heard about that fifteen-year-old girl?"

When Janet starts telling you something like this, she always starts off with "I guess you heard." *I guess you heard Wilma and Ted are breaking up*, she says. *I guess you heard Alvin Stead had a heart attack*.

"Kelvin told me," Trudy said. "Only he said she was fourteen."

"Fifteen," Janet said. "She must've been in Robin's class at school. She didn't know how to drive. She didn't even get out of the lane."

"Was she drunk?" said Trudy. Robin won't go near alcohol,

or dope, or cigarettes, or even coffee, she's so fanatical about what she puts into her body.

"I don't think so. Stoned, maybe. It was early in the evening. She was home with her sister. Their parents were out. Her sister's boyfriend came over—it was his truck, and he either gave her the keys to the truck or she took them. You hear different versions. You hear that they sent her out for something, they wanted to get rid of her, and you hear she just took the keys and went. Anyway, she ran it right into a tree in the lane."

"Jesus," said Trudy.

"I know. It's so idiotic. It's getting so you hate to think about your kids growing up. Did everybody take their medication okay? What's Kelvin watching?"

Kelvin was still up, sitting in the living room watching TV.

"It's somebody being interviewed. He wrote a book about schizophrenics," Trudy told Janet.

Anything he comes across about mental problems, Kelvin has to watch, or try to read.

"I think it depresses him, the more he watches that kind of thing," Janet said. "Do you know I found out today I have to make five hundred roses out of pink Kleenex for my niece Laurel's wedding? For the car. She said I promised I'd make the roses for the car. Well, I didn't. I don't remember promising a thing. Are you going to come over and help me?"

"Sure," said Trudy.

"I guess the real reason I want him to get off the schizophrenics is I want to watch the old *Dallas*," said Janet. She and Trudy disagree about this. Trudy can't stand to watch those old reruns of *Dallas*, to see the characters, with their younger, plumper faces, going through tribulations and bound up in romantic complications they and the audience have now forgotten all about. That's what's so hilarious, Janet says; it's so unbelievable it's wonderful. All that happens and they just forget about it and go on. But to Trudy it doesn't seem so unbelievable that the characters would go from one thing to the next thing—forgetful, hopeful, photogenic, forever changing their clothes. That it's not so unbelievable is the thing she really can't stand.

Robin, the next morning, said, "Oh, probably. All those people she hung around with drink. They party all the time. They're self-destructive. It's her own fault. Even if her sister told her to go, she didn't have to go. She didn't have to be so stupid."

"What was her name?" Trudy said.

"Tracy Lee," said Robin with distaste. She stepped on the pedal of the garbage tin, lifted rather than lowered the container of yogurt she had just emptied, and dropped it in. She was wearing bikini underpants and a T-shirt that said "If I Want to Listen to an Asshole, I'll Fart."

"That shirt still bothers me," Trudy said. "Some things are disgusting but funny, and some things are more disgusting than funny."

"What's the problem?" said Robin. " I sleep alone."

Trudy sat outside, in her wrapper, drinking coffee while the day got hot. There is a little brick-paved space by the side door that she and Dan always called the patio. She sat there. This is a solar-heated house, with big panels of glass in the south-sloping roof—the oddest-looking house in town. It's odd inside, too, with the open shelves in the kitchen instead of cupboards, and the living room up some stairs, looking out over the fields at the back. She and Dan, for a joke, gave parts of it the most conventional, suburban-sounding names—the patio, the powder room, the master bedroom. Dan always had to joke about the way he was living. He built the house himself—Trudy did a lot of the painting and staining—and it was a success. Rain didn't leak in around the panels, and part of the house's heat really did come from the sun. Most people who have the ideas, or ideals, that Dan has aren't very practical. They can't fix things or make things; they don't understand wiring or carpentry, or whatever it is they need to understand. Dan is good at everything—at gardening, cutting wood, building a house. He is especially good at repairing motors. He used to travel around getting jobs as an auto mechanic, a small-engines repairman. That's how he ended up here. He came here to visit Marlene, got a job as a mechanic, became a working partner in an auto-repair business, and before he knew it—married to Trudy, not Marlene—he was a small-town businessman, a member of the Kinsmen. All without shaving off his nineteen-sixties beard or trimming his hair any more than he wanted to. The town was too small and Dan was too smart for that to be necessary.

Now Dan lives in a townhouse in Richmond Hill with a girl named Genevieve. She is studying law. She was married when she was very young, and has three little children. Dan met her three years ago when her camper broke down a few miles outside of town. He told Trudy about her that night. The rented camper, the three little children hardly more than babies, the lively little divorced mother with her hair in pigtails. Her bravery, her poverty, her plans to enter law school. If the camper hadn't been easily fixed, he was going to invite her and her children to spend the night. She was on her way to her parents' summer place at Pointe au Baril.

"Then she can't be all that poor," Trudy said.

"You can be poor and have rich parents," Dan said.

"No, you can't."

Last summer, Robin went to Richmond Hill for a month's visit. She came home early. She said it was a madhouse. The oldest child has to go to a special reading clinic, the middle one wets the bed. Genevieve spends all her time in the law library, studying. No wonder. Dan shops for bargains, cooks, looks after the children, grows vegetables, drives a taxi on Saturdays and Sundays. He wants to set up a motorcycle-repair business in the garage, but he can't get a permit; the neighbors are against it.

He told Robin he was happy. Never happier, he said. Robin came home firmly grownup—severe, sarcastic, determined. She had some slight, steady grudge she hadn't had before. Trudy couldn't worm it out of her, couldn't tease it out of her; the time when she could do that was over.

Robin came home at noon and changed her clothes. She put on a light, flowered cotton blouse and ironed a pale-blue cotton skirt.

She said that some of the girls from the class might be going around to the funeral home after school.

"I forgot you had that skirt," said Trudy. If she thought that was going to start a conversation, she was mistaken.

The first time Trudy met Dan, she was drunk. She was nineteen years old, tall and skinny (she still is), with a wild head of curly black hair (it is cropped short now and showing the gray as black hair does). She was very tanned, wearing jeans and a tie-dyed T-shirt. No brassière and no need. This was in Muskoka in August, at a hotel bar where they had a band. She was camping with girlfriends. He was there with his fiancée, Marlene. He had taken Marlene home to meet his mother, who lived in Muskoka on an island in an empty hotel. When Trudy was nineteen, he was twenty-eight. She danced around by herself, giddy and drunk, in front of the table where he sat with Marlene, a meek-looking blonde with a big pink shelf of bosom all embroidered in little fake pearls. Trudy just danced in front of him until he got up and joined her. At the end of the dance, he asked her name, and took her back and introduced her to Marlene.

"This is Judy," he said. Trudy collapsed, laughing, into the chair beside Marlene's. Dan took Marlene up to dance. Trudy finished off Marlene's beer and went looking for her friends.

"How do you do?" she said to them. "I'm Judy!"

He caught up with her at the door of the bar. He had ditched Marlene when he saw Trudy leaving. A man who could change course quickly, see the possibilities, flare up with new enthusiasm. He told people later that he was in love with Trudy before he even knew her real name. But he told Trudy that he cried when he and Marlene were parting.

"I have feelings," he said. "I'm not ashamed to show them."

Trudy had no feelings for Marlene at all. Marlene was over thirty—what could she expect? Marlene still lives in town, works at the Hydro office, is not married. When Trudy and Dan were having one of their conversations about Genevieve, Trudy said, "Marlene must be thinking I got what's coming to me."

Dan said he had heard that Marlene had joined the Fellowship of Bible Christians. The women weren't allowed makeup and had to wear a kind of bonnet to church on Sundays.

"She won't be able to have a thought in her head but forgiving," Dan said.

Trudy said, "I bet."

This is what happened at the funeral home, as Trudy got the story from both Kelvin and Janet.

The girls from Tracy Lee's class all showed up together after school. This was during what was called the visitation, when the family waited beside Tracy Lee's open casket to receive friends. Her parents were there, her married brother and his wife, her sister, and even her sister's boyfriend who owned the truck. They stood in a row and people lined up to say a few words to them. A lot of people came. They always do, in a case like this. Tracy Lee's grandmother was at the end of the row in a brocade-covered chair. She wasn't able to stand up for very long.

All the chairs at the funeral home are upholstered in this white-and-gold brocade. The curtains are the same, the wallpaper almost matches. There are little wall-bracket lights behind heavy pink glass. Trudy has been there several times and knows what it's like. But Robin and most of these girls had never been inside the place before. They didn't know what to expect. Some of them began to cry as soon as they got inside the door.

The curtains were closed. Soft music was playing—not exactly church music but it sounded like it. Tracy Lee's coffin was white with gold trim, matching all the brocade and the wallpaper. It had a lining of pleated pink satin. A pink satin pillow. Tracy Lee had not a mark on her face. She was not made up quite as usual, because the undertaker had done it. But she was wearing her favorite earrings, turquoise-colored triangles and yellow crescents, two to each ear. (Some people thought that was in bad taste.) On the part of the coffin that covered her from the waist down, there was a big heart-shaped pillow of pink roses.

The girls lined up to speak to the family. They shook hands, they said sorry-for-your-loss, just the way everybody else did. When they got through that, when all of them had let the grandmother squash their cool hands between her warm, swollen, freckled ones, they lined up again, in a straggling sort of way, and began to go past the coffin. Many were crying now, shivering. What could you expect? Young girls.

But they began to sing as they went past. With difficulty at first, shyly, but with growing confidence in their sad, sweet voices, they sang:

> *"Now, while the blossom still clings to the vine,*
> *I'll taste your strawberries, I'll drink your sweet wine—"*

They had planned the whole thing, of course, beforehand; they had got that song off a record. They believed that it was an old hymn.

So they filed past, singing, looking down at Tracy Lee, and it was noticed that they were dropping things into the coffin. They were slipping the rings off their fingers and the bracelets from their arms, and taking the earrings out of their ears. They were undoing necklaces, and bowing to pull chains and long strands of beads over their heads. Everybody gave something. All this jewellery went flashing and sparkling down on the dead girl, to lie beside her in her coffin. One girl pulled the bright combs out of her hair, let those go.

And nobody made a move to stop it. How could anyone interrupt? It was like a religious ceremony. The girls behaved as if they'd been told what to do, as if this was what was always done on such occasions. They sang, they wept, they dropped their jewellery. The sense of ritual made every one of them graceful.

The family wouldn't stop it. They thought it was beautiful.

"It was like church," Tracy Lee's mother said, and her grandmother said, "All those lovely young girls loved Tracy Lee. If they wanted to give their jewellery to show how they loved her, that's their business. It's not anybody else's business. I thought it was beautiful."

Tracy Lee's sister broke down and cried. It was the first time she had done so.

Dan said, "This is a test of love."

Of Trudy's love, he meant. Trudy started singing, "Please release me, let me go—"

She clapped a hand to her chest, danced in swoops around the room, singing. Dan was near laughing, near crying. He couldn't help it; he came and hugged her and they danced together, staggering. They were fairly drunk. All that June (it was two years ago), they were drinking gin, in between and during their scenes. They were drinking, weeping, arguing, explaining, and Trudy had to keep running to the liquor store. Yet she can't remember ever feeling really drunk or having a hangover. Except that she felt so tired all the time, as if she had logs chained to her ankles.

She kept joking. She called Genevieve "Jenny the Feeb."

"This is just like wanting to give up the business and become a potter," she said. "Maybe you should have done that. I wasn't really against it. You gave up on it. And when you wanted to go to Peru. We could still do that."

"All those things were just straws in the wind," Dan said.

"I should have known when you started watching the Ombudsman on TV," Trudy said. "It was the legal angle, wasn't it? You were never so interested in that kind of thing before."

"This will open life up for you, too," Dan said. "You can be more than just my wife."

"Sure. I think I'll be a brain surgeon."

"You're very smart. You're a wonderful woman. You're brave."

"Sure you're not talking about Jenny the Feeb?"

"No, you. You, Trudy. I still love you. You can't understand that I still love you."

Not for years had he had so much to say about how he loved her. He loved her skinny bones, her curly hair, her roughening skin, her way of coming into a room with a stride that shook the windows, her jokes, her clowning, her tough talk. He loved her mind and her soul. He always would. But the part of his life that had been bound up with hers was over.

"That is just talk. That is talking like an idiot!" Trudy said. "Robin, go back to bed!" For Robin in her skimpy nightgown was standing at the top of the steps.

"I can hear you yelling and screaming," Robin said.

"We weren't yelling and screaming," Trudy said. "We're trying to talk about something private."

"What?"

"I told you, it's something private."

When Robin sulked off to bed, Dan said, "I think we should tell her. It's better for kids to know. Genevieve doesn't have any secrets from her kids. Josie's only five, and she came into the bedroom one afternoon—"

Then Trudy did start yelling and screaming. She clawed through a cushion cover. "You stop telling me about your sweet fucking Genevieve and her sweet fucking bedroom and her asshole kids—you shut up, don't tell me anymore! You're just a big dribbling mouth without any brains. I don't care what you do, just shut up!"

Dan left. He packed a suitcase; he went off to Richmond Hill. He was back in five days. Just outside of town, he had stopped the car to pick Trudy a bouquet of wildflowers. He told her he was back for good, it was over.

"You don't say?" said Trudy.

But she put the flowers in water. Dusty pink milkweed flowers that smelled like face powder, black-eyed Susans, wild sweet peas, and orange lilies that must have got loose from old disappeared gardens.

"So you couldn't stand the pace?" she said.

"I knew you wouldn't fall all over me," Dan said. "You wouldn't be you if you did. And what I came back to is you."

She went to the liquor store, and this time bought champagne. For a month—it was still summer—they were back together being happy. She never really found out what had happened at Genevieve's house. Dan said he'd been having a middle-aged fit, that was all. He'd come to his senses. His life was here, with her and Robin.

"You're talking like a marriage-advice column," Trudy said.

"Okay. Forget the whole thing."

"We better," she said. She could imagine the kids, the confusion, the friends—old boyfriends, maybe—that he hadn't been prepared for. Jokes and opinions that he couldn't understand. That was possible. The music he liked, the way he talked—even his hair and his beard—might be out of style.

They went on family drives, picnics. They lay out in the grass behind the house at night, looking at the stars. The stars were a new interest of Dan's; he got a map. They hugged and kissed each other frequently and tried out some new things—or things they hadn't done for a long time—when they made love.

At this time, the road in front of the house was being paved. They'd built their house on a hillside at the edge of town, past the other houses, but trucks were using this street quite a bit now, avoiding the main streets, so the town was paving it. Trudy got so used to the noise and constant vibration she said she could feel herself jiggling all night, even when everything was quiet. Work started at seven in the morning. They woke up at the bottom of a river of noise. Dan dragged himself out of bed then, losing the hour of sleep that he loved best. There was a smell of diesel fuel in the air.

She woke up one night to find him not in bed. She listened to hear noises in the kitchen or the bathroom, but she couldn't. She got up and walked through the house. There were no lights on. She found him sitting outside, just outside the door, not having a drink or a glass of milk or a coffee, sitting with his back to the street.

Trudy looked out at the torn-up earth and the huge stalled machinery. "Isn't the quiet lovely?" she said.

He didn't say anything.

Oh. Oh.

She realized what she'd been thinking when she found his side of the bed empty and couldn't hear him anywhere in the house. Not that he'd left her, but that he'd done worse. Done away with himself. With all their happiness and hugging and kissing and stars and picnics, she could think that.

"You can't forget her," she said. "You love her."

"I don't know what to do."

She was glad just to hear him speak. She said, "You'll have to go and try again."

"There's no guarantee I can stay," he said. "I can't ask you to stand by."

"No," said Trudy. "If you go, that's it."

"If I go, that's it."

He seemed paralyzed. She felt that he might just sit there, repeating what she said, never be able to move or speak for himself again.

"If you feel like this, that's all there is to it," she said. "You don't have to choose. You're already gone."

That worked. He stood up stiffly, came over, and put his arms around her. He stroked her back.

"Come back to bed," he said. "We can rest for a little while yet."

"No. You've got to be gone when Robin wakes up. If we go back to bed, it'll just start all over again."

She made him a thermos of coffee. He packed the bag he had taken with him before. All Trudy's movements seemed skillful and perfect, as they never were, usually. She felt serene. She felt as if they were an old couple, moving in harmony, in wordless love, past injury, past forgiving. Their goodbye was hardly a ripple. She went outside with him. It was between four-thirty and five o'clock; the sky was beginning to lighten and the birds to wake, everything was drenched in dew. There stood the big harmless machinery, stranded in the ruts of the road.

"Good thing it isn't last night—you couldn't have got out," she said. She meant that the road hadn't been navigable. It was just yesterday that they had graded a narrow track for local traffic.

"Good thing," he said.

Goodbye.

"All I want is to know why you did it. Did you just do it for show? Like your father—for show? It's not the necklace so much. But it was a beautiful thing—I love jet beads. It was the only thing we had of your grandmother's. It was your right, but you have no right to take me by surprise like that. I deserve an explanation. I always loved jet beads. Why?"

"I blame the family," Janet says. "It was up to them to stop it. Some of the stuff was just plastic—those junk earrings and bracelets—but what Robin threw in, that was a crime. And she wasn't the only one. There were birthstone rings and gold chains. Somebody said a diamond cluster ring, but I don't know if I believe that. They said the girl inherited it, like Robin. You didn't ever have it evaluated, did you?"

"I don't know if jet is worth anything," Trudy says.

They are sitting in Janet's front room, making roses out of pink Kleenex.

"It's just stupid," Trudy says.

"Well. There is one thing you could do," says Janet. "I don't hardly know how to mention it."

"What?"

"Pray."

Trudy'd had the feeling, from Janet's tone, that she was going to tell her something serious and unpleasant, something about herself—Trudy—that was affecting her life and that everybody knew except her. Now she wants to laugh, after bracing herself. She doesn't know what to say.

"You don't pray, do you?" Janet says.

"I haven't got anything against it," Trudy says. "I wasn't brought up to be religious."

"It's not strictly speaking religious," Janet says. "I mean, it's not connected with any church. This is just some of us that pray. I can't tell you the names of anybody in it, but most of them you know. It's supposed to be secret. It's called the Circle of Prayer."

"Like at high school," Trudy says. "At high school there were secret societies, and you weren't supposed to tell who was in them. Only I wasn't."

"I was in everything going." Janet sighs. "This is actually more on the serious side. Though some people in it don't take it seriously enough, I don't think. Some people, they'll pray that they'll find a parking spot, or they'll pray they get good weather for their holidays. That isn't what it's for. But that's just individual praying. What the Circle is really about is, you phone up somebody that is in it and tell them what it is you're worried about, or upset about, and ask them to pray for you. And they do. And they phone one other person that's in the Circle, and they phone another and it goes all around, and we pray for one person, all together."

Trudy throws a rose away. "That's botched. Is it all women?"

"There isn't any rule it has to be. But it is, yes. Men would be too embarrassed. I was embarrassed at first. Only the first person you phone knows your name, who it is that's being prayed for, but in a town like this nearly everybody can guess. But if we started gossiping and ratting on each other it wouldn't work, and everybody knows that. So we don't. And it does work."

"Like how?" Trudy says.

"Well, one girl banged up her car. She did eight hundred dollars' damage, and it was kind of a tricky situation, where she wasn't sure her insurance would cover it, and neither was her husband—he was raging mad—but we all prayed, and the insurance came through without a hitch. That's only one example."

"There wouldn't be much point in praying to get the necklace back when it's in the coffin and the funeral's this morning," Trudy says.

"It's not up to you to say that. You don't say what's possible or impossible. You just ask for what you want. Because it says in the Bible, 'Ask and it shall be given.' How can you be helped if you won't ask? You can't, that's for sure. What about when Dan left—what if you'd prayed then? I wasn't in the Circle then, or I would have said something to you. Even if I knew you'd resist it, I would have said something. A lot of people resist. Now, even—it doesn't sound too great with that girl, but how do you know, maybe even now it might work? It might not be too late."

"All right," says Trudy, in a hard, cheerful voice. "All right." She pushes all the floppy flowers off her lap. "I'll just get down on my knees right now and pray that I get Dan back. I'll pray that I get the necklace back and I get Dan back, and why do I have to stop there? I can pray that Tracy Lee never died. I can pray that she comes back to life. Why didn't her mother ever think of that?"

Good news. The swimming pool is fixed. They'll be able to fill it tomorrow. But Kelvin is depressed. Early this afternoon—partly to keep them from bothering the men who were working on the pool—he took Marie and Josephine uptown. He let them get ice-cream cones. He told them to pay attention and eat the ice cream up quickly, because the sun was hot and it would melt. They licked at their cones now and then, as if they had all day. Ice cream was soon dribbling down their chins and down their arms. Kelvin had grabbed a handful of paper napkins, but he couldn't wipe it up fast enough. They were a mess. A spectacle. They didn't care. Kelvin told them they weren't so pretty that they could afford to look like that.

"Some people don't like the look of us anyway," he said. "Some people don't even think we should be allowed uptown. People just get used to seeing us and not staring at us like freaks and you make a mess and spoil it."

They laughed at him. He could have cowed Marie if he had her alone, but not when she was with Josephine. Josephine was one who needed some old-fashioned discipline, in Kelvin's opinion. Kelvin had been in places where people didn't get away with anything like they got away with here. He didn't agree with hitting. He had seen plenty of it done, but he didn't agree with it, even on the hand. But a person like Josephine could be shut up in her room. She could be made to sit in a corner, she could be put on bread and water, and it would do a lot of good. All Marie needed was a talking-to—she had a weak personality. But Josephine was a devil.

"I'll talk to both of them," Trudy says. "I'll tell them to say they're sorry."

"I want for them to *be* sorry," Kelvin says. "I don't care if they say they are. I'm not taking them ever again."

Later, when all the others are in bed, Trudy gets him to sit down to play cards with her on the screened veranda. They play

Crazy Eights. Kelvin says that's all he can manage tonight; his head is sore.

Uptown, a man said to him, "Hey, which one of them two is your girlfriend?"

"Stupid," Trudy says. "He was a stupid jerk."

The man talking to the first man said, "Which one you going to marry?"

"They don't know you, Kelvin. They're just stupid."

But they did know him. One was Reg Hooper, one was Bud DeLisle. Bud DeLisle that sold real estate. They knew him. They had talked to him in the barbershop; they called him Kelvin. "Hey, Kelvin, which one you going to marry?"

"Nerds," says Trudy. "That's what Robin would say."

"You think they're your friend, but they're not," says Kelvin. "How many times I see that happen."

Trudy goes to the kitchen to put on coffee. She wants to have fresh coffee to offer Janet when she comes in. She apologized this morning, and Janet said all right, I know you're upset. It really is all right. Sometimes you think they're your friend, and they are.

She looks at all the mugs hanging on their hooks. She and Janet shopped all over to find them. A mug with each one's name. Marie, Josephine, Arthur, Kelvin, Shirley, George, Dorinda. You'd think Dorinda would be the hardest name to find, but actually the hardest was Shirley. Even the people who can't read have learned to recognize their own mugs, by color and pattern.

One day, two new mugs appeared, bought by Kelvin. One said Trudy, the other Janet.

"I'm not going to be too overjoyed seeing my name in that lineup," Janet said. "But I wouldn't hurt his feelings for a million dollars."

For a honeymoon, Dan took Trudy to the island on the lake where his mother's hotel was. The hotel was closed down, but his mother still lived there. Dan's father was dead, and she lived there alone. She took a boat with an outboard motor across the water to get her groceries. She sometimes made a mistake and called Trudy Marlene.

The hotel wasn't much. It was a white wooden box in a clearing by the shore. Some little boxes of cabins were stuck behind it. Dan and Trudy stayed in one of the cabins. Every cabin had a wood stove. Dan built a fire at night to take off the chill. But the blankets were damp and heavy when he and Trudy woke up in the morning.

Dan caught fish and cooked them. He and Trudy climbed the big rock behind the cabins and picked blueberries. He asked her if she knew how to make a piecrust, and she didn't. So he showed her, rolling out the dough with a whiskey bottle.

In the morning there was a mist over the lake, just as you see in the movies or in a painting.

One afternoon, Dan stayed out longer than usual, fishing. Trudy kept busy for a while in the kitchen, rubbing the dust off things, washing some jars. It was the oldest, darkest kitchen she had ever seen, with wooden racks for the dinner plates to dry in. She went outside and climbed the rock by herself, thinking she would pick some blueberries. But it was already dark under the trees; the evergreens made it dark, and she didn't like the idea of wild animals. She sat on the rock looking down on the roof of the hotel, the old dead leaves and broken shingles. She heard a piano being played. She scrambled down the rock and followed the music around to the front of the building. She walked along the front veranda and stopped at a window, looking into the room that used to be the lounge. The room with the blackened stone fireplace, the lumpy leather chairs, the horrible mounted fish.

Dan's mother was there, playing the piano. A tall, straight-backed old woman, with her gray-black hair twisted into such a tiny knot. She sat and played the piano, without any lights on, in the half-dark, half-bare room.

Dan had said that his mother came from a rich family. She had taken piano lessons, dancing lessons; she had gone around the world when she was a young girl. There was a picture of her on a camel. But she wasn't playing a classical piece, the sort of thing you'd expect her to have learned. She was playing "It's Three O'Clock in the Morning." When she got to the end, she started in again. Maybe it was a special favorite of hers, something she had danced to in the old days. Or maybe she wasn't satisfied yet that she had got it right.

Why does Trudy now remember this moment? She sees her young self looking in the window at the old woman playing the piano. The dim room, with its oversize beams and fireplace and the lonely leather chairs. The clattering, faltering, persistent piano music. Trudy remembers that so clearly and it seems she stood outside her own body, which ached then from the punishing pleasures of love. She stood outside her own happiness in a tide of sadness. And the opposite thing happened the morning Dan left. Then she stood outside her own unhappiness in a tide of what seemed unreasonably like love. But it was the same thing, really, when you got outside. What are those times that stand out, clear patches in your life— what do they have to do with it? They aren't exactly promises. Breathing spaces. Is that all?

She goes into the front hall and listens for any noise from upstairs.

All quiet there, all medicated.

The phone rings right beside her head.

"Are you still there?" Robin says. "You're not gone?"

"I'm still here."

"Can I run over and ride back with you? I didn't do my run earlier because it was so hot."

You threw the jug. You could have killed me.

Yes.

Kelvin, waiting at the card table, under the light, looks bleached and old. There's a pool of light whitening his brown hair. His face sags, waiting. He looks old, sunk into himself, wrapped in a thick bewilderment, nearly lost to her.

"Kelvin, do you pray?" says Trudy. She didn't know she was going to ask him that. "I mean, it's none of my business. But, like for anything specific?"

He's got an answer for her, which is rather surprising. He

pulls his face up, as if he might have felt the tug he needed to bring him to the surface.

"If I was smart enough to know what to pray for," he says, "then I wouldn't have to."

He smiles at her, with some oblique notion of conspiracy, offering his halfway joke. It's not meant as comfort, particularly. Yet it radiates—what he said, the way he said it, just the fact that he's there again, radiates, expands the way some silliness can, when you're very tired. In this way, when she was young, and high, a person or a moment could become a lily floating on the cloudy river water, perfect and familiar.

WHITE DUMP

I

"I don't know what color," says Denise, answering a question of Magda's. "I don't really remember any color in this house at all."

"Of course you don't," says Magda sympathetically. "There was no light in the house, so there was no color. There was no attempt. So dreary, I couldn't believe."

As well as having the old, deep, light-denying veranda on the Log House torn down, Magda—to whom Denise's father, Laurence, is now married—has put in skylights and painted some walls white, others yellow. She has hung up fabrics from Mexico and Morocco, and rugs from Quebec. Pine dressers and tables have replaced badly painted junk. There is a hot tub surrounded by windows and greenery, and a splendid kitchen. All this must have cost a lot of money. No doubt Laurence is rich enough now to manage it. He owns a small factory, near Ottawa, that manufactures plastics, specializing in window panels and lampshades that look like stained glass. The designs are pretty, the colors not too garish, and Magda has stuck a few of them around the Log House in inconspicuous places.

Magda is an Englishwoman, not a Hungarian as her name might suggest. She used to be a dancer, then a dancing teacher. She is a short, thick-waisted woman, still graceful, with a smooth, pale neck and a lovely, floating crown of silver-gold hair. She is wearing a plain gray dress and a shawl of muted, flowery colors that is sometimes draped over the settee in her bedroom.

"Magda is style through and through," Denise said once, to her brother, Peter.

"What's wrong with that?" said Peter. He is a computer engineer in California and comes home perhaps once a year. He can't understand why Denise is still so bound up with these people.

"Nothing," said Denise. "But you go to the Log House, and there is not even a jumble of scarves lying on an old chest. There is a *calculated* jumble. There is not a whisk or bowl hanging up in the kitchen that is not the most elegant whisk or bowl you could buy."

Peter looked at her and didn't say anything. Denise said, "Okay."

Denise has driven up from Toronto, as she does once or twice every summer, to visit her father and her stepmother. Laurence and Magda spend the whole season here, and are talking of selling the house in Ottawa, of living here year-round. The three of them are sitting out on the brick patio that has replaced part of the veranda, one Sunday afternoon in late August. Magda's ginger pots are full of late-blooming flowers—geraniums the only ones that Denise can name. They are drinking wine-and-soda—the real drinks will come out when the dinner guests arrive. So far, there have been no preposterous arguments. Driving up here, Denise determined there wouldn't be. In the car, she played Mozart tapes to steady and encourage herself. She made resolves. So far, so good.

Denise runs a Women's Centre in Toronto. She gets beaten women into shelters, finds doctors and lawyers for them, goes after private and public money, makes speeches, holds meetings, deals with varied and sometimes dangerous mix-ups of life. She makes less money than a clerk in a government liquor store.

Laurence has said that this is a typical pattern for a girl of affluent background.

He has said that the Women's Centre is a good idea for those who really need it. But he sometimes wonders.

What does he sometimes wonder?

Frankly, he sometimes wonders if some of those women—some of them—aren't enjoying all the attention they are getting, claiming to be battered and raped, and so on.

Laurence customarily lays the bait, Denise snaps it up. (Magda floats on top of these conversations, smiling at her flowers.)

Taxpayers' money. Helping those who won't help themselves. Get rid of acid rain, we lose jobs; your unions would squawk.

"They're not *my* unions."

"If you vote New Democrat, they're your unions. Who runs the New Democrats?"

Denise can't tell if he really believes what he says, or half believes it, or just feels compelled to say these things to her. She has gone out in tears more than once, got into her car, driven back to Toronto. Her lover, a cheerful Marxist from a Caribbean island, whom she doesn't bring home, says that old men, successful old men, in a capitalist industrial society are almost purely evil; there is nothing left in them but raging defenses and greed. Denise argues with him, too. Her father is not an old man, in the first place. Her father is a good person, underneath.

"I'm sick of your male definitions and airtight male arguments," she says. Then she says thoughtfully, "Also, I'm sick of hearing myself say 'male' like that." She knows better than to bring up the fact that if she lasts through the argument, her father will give her a check for the Centre.

Today her resolve has held. She has caught the twinkle of the bait but has been able to slip past, a clever innocent-seeming fish, talking mostly to Magda, admiring various details of house renovation. Laurence, an ironic-looking, handsome man with a full gray mustache and soft, thinning gray-brown hair, a tall man with a little sag now to his shoulders and his stomach, has got up several times and walked to the lake and back, to the road and back, has sighed deeply, showing his dissatisfaction with this female talk.

Finally he speaks abruptly to Denise, breaking through what Magda is saying.

"How is your mother?"

"Fine," says Denise. "As far as I know, fine."

Isabel lives far away, in the Comox Valley, in British Columbia.

"So—how is the goat farming?"

The man Isabel lives with is a commercial fisherman who used to be a TV cameraman. They live on a small farm and rent the land, or part of it, to a man who raises goats. At some point, Denise revealed this fact to Laurence (she has taken care not to reveal the fact that the man is several years younger than Isabel and that the relationship is periodically "unstable"), and Laurence has ever since insisted that Isabel and her paramour (his word) are engaged in goat farming. His questions bring to mind a world of rural hardship: muddy toil with refractory animals, poverty, some sort of ghastly outdated idealism.

"Fine," says Denise, smiling.

Usually she argues, points out the error in fact, accuses him of distortion, ill will, mischief.

"Enough counterculture left out there to buy goat milk?"

"I would think so."

Laurence's lips twitch under his mustache impatiently. She keeps on looking at him, maintaining an expression of innocent, impudent cheerfulness. Then he gives an abrupt laugh.

"Goat milk!" he says.

"Is this the new in-joke?" says Magda. "What am I missing? Goat milk?"

Laurence says, "Magda, did you know that on my fortieth birthday Denise took me up in a plane?"

"I didn't actually fly it," says Denise.

"My fortieth birthday, 1969. The year of the moon shot. The moon shot was actually just a couple of days after. She'd heard me say I often wished I could get a look at this country from a thousand feet up. I'd go over it flying from Ottawa to Toronto, but I'd never see anything."

"I only paid enough for him to go up, but as it happened we all went up, in a five-seater," Denise says. "For the same price."

"We all went except Isabel," says Laurence. "Somebody had to bow out, so she did."

"I made him drive—Dad drive—blindfolded to the airport," says Denise to Magda. "That is, not drive blindfolded"—they were all laughing—"*ride* blindfolded, so he wouldn't know where we were going and it would be a complete surprise."

"Mother drove," says Laurence. "I imagine I could have driven blindfolded better. Why did she drive and not Isabel?"

"We had to go in Grandma's car. The Peugeot wouldn't take us all, and I had to have us all go to watch you because it was my big deal. My present. I was an awful stage manager."

"We flew all down the Rideau Lake system," Laurence says. "Mother loved it. Remember she'd had a bad experience that morning, with the hippies? So it was good for her. The pilot was very generous. Of course he had his wife working. She made cakes, didn't she?"

Denise says, "She was a caterer."

"She made my birthday cake," says Laurence. "That same birthday. I found that out later."

"Didn't Isabel?" says Magda. "Didn't Isabel make the cake?"

"The oven wasn't working," says Denise, her voice gone cautionary and slightly regretful.

"Ah," says Magda. "What was the bad experience?"

When Denise and Peter and their parents arrived at the Log House every summer from Ottawa, the children's grandmother Sophie would be there already, having driven up from Toronto, and the house would be opened, aired, and cleaned as much as it was ever going to be. Denise would run through all the dim cavelike rooms and hug the lumpy cushions, making a drama out of her delight at being there. But it was a true delight. The house smelled of trodden bits of cedar, never-conquered dampness, and winter mice. Everything was always the same. Here was the boring card game that taught you the names of Canadian wildflowers; here was the Scrabble set with the Y and one of the U's missing; here were the dreadful irresistible books from Sophie's childhood, the World War I cartoon book, the unmatched plates, the cracked saucers Sophie used for ashtrays, the knives and forks with their faint, strange taste and smell that was either of metal or of dishwater.

Only Sophie would use the oven. She turned out hard roast potatoes, cakes raw in the middle, chicken bloody at the bone. She never thought of replacing the stove. A rich man's daughter, now poor—she was an assistant professor of Scandinavian languages, and through most of her career university teachers were poor—she had odd spending habits. She always packed sandwiches to eat on a train trip, and she had never visited a hairdresser, but she wouldn't have dreamed of sending Laurence to an ordinary school. She spent money on the Log House grudgingly, not because she didn't love it (she did) but because her instinct told her to put pots under leaks, to tape around warped window frames, to get used to the slant in the floor that indicated one of the foundation posts was crumbling. And however much she needed money, she wouldn't have thought of selling off any of her property around the house—as her brothers long ago had sold the property on either side, most profitably, to cottagers.

Denise's mother and father had a name for Sophie that was a joke between them, and a secret. Old Norse. It seemed that shortly after they had met, Laurence, describing Sophie to Isabel, had said, "My mother isn't quite your average mom. She can read Old Norse. In fact, she *is* sort of an Old Norse."

In the car on the way to the Log House, feeling Sophie's presence ahead of them, they had played this game.

"Is an Old Norse's car window ever mended with black tape?"

"No. If an Old Norse window is broken, it stays broken."

"What is an Old Norse's favorite radio program?"

"Let's see. Let's see. The Metropolitan Opera? Kirsten Flagstad singing Wagner?"

"No. Too obvious. Too élitist."

"Folk Songs of Many Lands?"

"What is an Old Norse breakfast?" said Denise from the back seat. "Porridge!" Porridge was her own most hated thing.

"Porridge with codfish," said Laurence. "Never tell Grandma about this game, Denise. Where does an Old Norse spend a summer vacation?"

"An Old Norse never takes a summer vacation," said Isabel severely. "An Old Norse takes a winter vacation. And goes North."

"Spitzbergen," said Laurence. "The James Bay Lowlands."

"A cruise," said Isabel. "From Tromso to Archangel."

"Isn't there a lot of ice?"

"Well, it's on an icebreaker. And it's very dark, because those cruises only run in December and January."

"Wouldn't Grandma think it was funny, too?" said Denise. She pictured her grandmother coming out of the house and crossing the veranda to meet them—that broad, strong, speckled old woman, with a crown of yellowish-white braids, whose old jackets and sweaters and skirts had some of the smell of the house, whose greeting was calmly affectionate though slightly puzzled. Was she surprised that they had got here so soon, that the children had grown, that Laurence was suddenly so boisterous, that Isabel looked so slim and youthful? Did she know how they'd been joking about her in the car?

"Maybe," said Laurence discouragingly.

"In those old poems she reads," said Isabel, "you know those old Icelandic poems, there is the most terrible gore and hacking people up—women particularly, one slitting her own kids' throats and mixing the blood in her husband's wine. I read that. And then Sophie is such a pacifist and Socialist, isn't it strange?"

Isabel drove into Aubreyville in the morning to get the birthday cake. Denise went with her to hold the cake on the way home. The plane ride was arranged for five in the afternoon. Only Isabel knew about it, having driven Denise to the airport last week. It was all Denise's idea. She was worrying now about the clouds.

"Those streaky ones are okay," said Isabel. "It's the big piled-up white ones that could mean a storm."

"Cumulus," Denise said. "I know. Do you think Daddy is a typical Cancer? Home-loving and food-loving? Hangs on to things?"

"I guess so," said Isabel.

"What did you think when you first met him? I mean, what attracted you? Did you know this was the person you were going to end up married to? I think that's all so weird."

Laurence and Isabel had met in the cafeteria of the university, where Isabel was working as a cashier. She was a first-year student, a poor, bright girl from the factory side of town, wearing a tight pink sweater that Laurence always remembered.

("Woolworth's," said Isabel. "I didn't know any better. I thought the sorority girls were kind of dowdy.")

The first thing she said to Laurence was "That's a mistake." She was pointing to his selection—shepherd's pie.

Laurence was too embarrassed or too stubborn to put it back. "I've had it before and it was okay," he said. He hung about for a moment after he got his change. "It reminds me of what my mother makes."

"Your mother must be an awful cook."

"She is."

He phoned her that night, having asked around to find out her name. "This is shepherd's pie," he said shakily. "Would you go to a movie with me?"

"I'm surprised you're still alive," said Isabel, that brash-talking tight-sweatered girl who was certainly going to be a surprise for Sophie. "Sure."

Denise knew all this by heart. What she was after was something else. "Why did you go out with him? Why did you say, 'Sure'?"

"He was nice-looking," said Isabel. "He seemed interesting."

"Is that all?"

"Well. He didn't act as if he was God's gift to women. He blushed when I spoke to him."

"He often blushes," said Denise. "So do I. It's terrible."

She thought that those two people, Laurence and Isabel, her father and mother, kept something hidden. Something between them. She could feel it welling up fresh and teasing, or lying low and sour, but she could never get to understand what it was, or how it worked. They would not let her.

Aubreyville was a limestone town, built along the river. The old stove foundry, out of which Sophie's father had made his money, was still there on the riverbank. It had been partly converted into a crafts center, where people blew glass and wove shawls and made birdhouses, which they sold on the premises. The name Vogelsang, the German name that had also appeared on the stoves and had contributed to the downfall of the company during the First World War, could still be read, carved in stone, over the door. The handsome house where Sophie had been born had become a nursing home.

The catering woman lived on one of the new streets of town—the streets that Sophie hated. The street was recently paved, broad and black, with smooth curbs. There were no sidewalks. No trees either, no hedges or fences, just some tiny ornamental shrubs with a wire roll to protect them. Split-level and ranch-style houses alternated. Some of the driveways were paved with the glittering white crushed stone called, around Aubreyville, "white marble." On one lawn, three spotted plastic deer were resting; at a doorway, a little black boy held up a lantern for coaches. An arrangement of pink-and-gray-speckled boulders prevented people from crossing a corner lot.

"Plastic rocks," said Isabel. "I wonder if they have weights or are stuck into the ground?"

The catering woman brought the cake out to the car. She was a stout, dark-haired, rather pretty woman in her forties, with heavy green eye shadow and a perfect, gleaming, bouffant hairstyle.

"I've been on the lookout for you," she said. "I have to run some pies over to the Legion. You want to take a look at this and see if it's okay?"

"I'm sure it's lovely," said Isabel, getting out her wallet. Denise took the cake box onto her lap.

"I wish I had a girl this size around to help me," the woman said.

Isabel looked at the two little boys—they were about three and four years old—who were jumping in and out of an inflated wading pool on the lawn. "Are those yours?" she said politely.

"Are you kidding? Those are my daughter's she dumped on me. I've got one married son and one married daughter, and another son—the only time I see him he's in a motorcycle helmet. I was an early starter."

Isabel had begun to back the car out of the drive when Denise gave a cry of surprise. "Mom! That's the pilot!"

A man had come out of the side door and was talking to the catering woman.

"Damn it, Denise, don't scare me like that!" Isabel said. "I thought it was one of the kids running behind the car."

"It's the pilot I was talking to at the airport!"

"He must be her husband. Keep the cake level."

"But isn't that strange? On Daddy's birthday? The woman who made his cake is married to the man who's going to take him up in the plane. *Maybe* he is. He's got a partner. He and his partner give flying lessons and they fly hunters up North in the fall and they fly fishermen to lakes you can only fly to. He told me. Isn't it strange?"

"It's only moderately strange in a place the size of Aubreyville. Denise, you have to *watch* that cake."

Denise subsided, feeling a little insulted. If a grownup had cried out in surprise, Isabel wouldn't have shown such irritation. If a grownup had remarked on this strange coincidence, Isabel would have agreed that it was indeed strange. Denise hated it when Isabel treated her like a child. With her grandmother, or Laurence, she expected a certain denseness and inflexibility. Those two were always the same. But Isabel could be confiding, friendly, infinitely understanding, then remote and irritable. And sometimes the more she gave you, the less you felt satisfied. Denise suspected that her father felt that about Isabel, too.

Today Isabel was wearing a long wraparound skirt of Indian cotton—her hippie skirt, Laurence called it—and a dark-blue halter. She was slim and brown—she tanned well, considering she was a redhead—and until you got close to her she looked only about twenty-five. Even close up, she didn't look more than twenty-nine. So Laurence said. He wouldn't let her cut her dark-red hair, and he supervised her tan, calling out, "Where are you going," in a warning, upset voice, when she tried to move into the shade or go up to the house for a little while.

"If I let her, Isabel would sneak off out of the sun every time my back was turned," Laurence had said to visitors, and Denise had heard Isabel laugh.

"It's true. I've got Laurence to thank. I'd never last long enough on my own to get any kind of a tan. I get the fried-brain feeling."

"Who cares about fried brains if you've got a gorgeous brown body?" said Laurence, in a lordly, farcical way, tap-tapping the smooth stomach bared by Isabel's bikini.

Those little rhythmic slaps made Denise's own stomach go queasy. The only way she could keep from yelling out "Stop it!" was to jump up and rush at the lake with her arms spread wide and silly whoops coming out of her mouth.

When Denise saw the catering woman again, more than a year had gone by. It was nearly the end of August, a close, warm, cloudy day, when they were near the end of their summer's stay at the Log House. Isabel had gone to town on one of that summer's regular trips to the dentist. She was having some complicated work done in Aubreyville, because she liked the dentist there better than the dentist in Ottawa. Sophie had not been at the Log House since the beginning of summer. She was in Wellesley Hospital, in Toronto, having some tests done.

Denise and Peter and their father were in the kitchen making bacon-and-tomato sandwiches for lunch. There were a few things that Laurence believed he could cook better than anybody else, and one of them was bacon. Denise was slicing tomatoes, and Peter was supposed to be buttering the toast, but was reading his book. The radio was on, giving the noon news. Laurence liked to hear the news several times a day.

Denise went to see who was at the front door. She did not immediately recognize the catering woman, who was wearing a more youthful dress this time—a loose dress with swirls of red and blue and purple "psychedelic" colors—and did not look as pretty. Her hair was down over her shoulders.

"Is your mother home?" this woman said.

"I'm sorry, she's not here right now," said Denise, with a

dignified politeness she knew to be slightly offensive. She thought the woman was selling something.

"She is not here," the woman said. "No. She is not here." Her face was puffy and unsmiling, her lipstick clownishly thick, and her eye makeup blotchy. Her voice was heavy with some insinuation Denise could not grasp. She would not talk that way if she was trying to sell something. Could they owe her money? Had Peter run across her property or bothered her dog?

"My father's here," Denise said contritely. "Would you like to talk to him?"

"Your father, yes, I will talk to him," the woman said, and hoisted her large, shiny red handbag up under her arm. "Why don't you go and get him, then?"

Denise realized then that this was the same voice that had said, "I wish I had a girl this size to help me."

"The lady who does catering is at the door," she said to her father.

"The lady who does catering?" he repeated, in a displeased, disbelieving voice, as if she had invented this lady just to interrupt him.

But he wiped his hands and went off down the hall. She heard him say smoothly, "Yes, indeed, what can I do for you?"

And instead of coming back in a few minutes, he took this woman into the dining room; he shut the dining-room door. Why into the dining room? Visitors were taken into the living room. The bacon, lying on a paper towel, was getting cold.

There was a little window high in the door between the kitchen and the dining room. In the days when Sophie was a little girl, there used to be a cook in the kitchen. The cook could watch the progress of the meal through this window to know when to change the dishes.

Denise raised herself on tiptoe.

"Spy," said Peter, without looking up from his book. It was a science-fiction book called *Satan's World*.

"I just want to know when to make the sandwiches," Denise said.

She saw that there had been a reason for going into the dining room. Her father was sitting in his usual place, at the end of the table. The woman was sitting in Peter's usual place, nearest the hall door. She had her purse on the table, and her hands clasped on top of it. Whatever they were talking about demanded a table and straight-backed chairs and an upright, serious position. It was like an interview. Information is being given, questions are being asked, a problem is being considered.

Well, all right, thought Denise. They were talking about a problem. They would finish talking about it, settle it, and it would be over with. Her father would tell the family about it, or not tell them. It would be over.

She turned off the radio. She made the sandwiches. Peter ate his. She waited awhile, then ate hers. They drank Coke, which their father allowed them at lunch. Denise ate and drank too quickly. She sat at the table quietly burping and retasting the bacon, and hearing the terrible sound of a stranger crying in their house.

From the plane on her father's birthday, they had seen some delicate, almost transparent, mounded clouds in the western sky, and Denise had said, "Thunderclouds."

"That's right," said the pilot. "But they're a long ways away."

"It must be pretty dramatic," said Laurence, "flying in a thunderstorm."

"Once, I looked out and I saw blue rings of fire around the propellers," the pilot said. "Round the propellers and the wing tips. Then I saw the same thing round the nose. I put my hand out to touch the glass—this here, the plexiglass—and just as I got within touching distance, flames came shooting out of my fingers. I don't know if I touched the glass or not. I didn't feel anything. Little blue flames. One time in a thunderstorm. That's what they call St. Elmo's fire."

"It's from the electrical discharges in the atmosphere," called Peter from the back seat.

"You're right," the pilot called back.

"Strange," said Laurence.

"It gave me a start."

Denise had a picture in her mind of the pilot with cold blue fire shooting out of his fingertips, and that seemed to her a sign of pain, though he had said he didn't feel anything. She thought of the time she had touched an electric fence. The spurts of sound coming out of the dining room made her remember. Peter went on reading, and they didn't say anything, though she knew he heard the sound, too.

Magda is in the kitchen making the salad. She is humming a tune from an opera. "Home to Our Mountains." Denise is in the dining room setting the table. She hears her father laughing on the patio. The guests have arrived—two pleasant, rich couples, not cottagers. One couple comes from Boston, one from Montreal. They have summer houses in Westfield.

Denise hears her father say, "*Weltschmerz*." He says it as if in quotation marks. He must be quoting some item they all know about, from a magazine they all read.

I should be like Peter, she thinks. I should stop coming here.

But perhaps it's all right, and this is happiness, which she is too stubborn, too childish, too glumly political—too mired in a past that everyone else has abandoned—to accept?

The dining room has been extended to take in the area where part of the veranda was, and the extension is all glass—walls and slanting roof, all glass. In the darkening glass, she sees herself—a tall, careful woman with a long braid, very plainly dressed, setting down on the long pine table, among the prettily overflowing bowls of nasturtiums, little blue glass dishes full of salt. Red-and-orange linen napkins, yellow candles like round pats of butter, thick white country plates with a pattern of grapes around the edges. Layers of forthcoming food and wine, and the talk that cuts off the living air: layers of harmony and satisfaction.

Magda, bearing in the salad, stops humming.

"Your mother—is she happy, out in British Columbia?"

Her fault, Denise thinks. Isabel's.

Unfair, unbidden thoughts can strike her here, reverberating harshly, to no purpose.

"Yes," she says. "Yes. I think so." By which she means that Isabel, at least, has no regrets.

II

Sophie's tread made the floorboards shudder. She was barefoot, naked under the striped terry-cloth bathrobe, in the early morning. She had swum naked in the lake since she was a child and all this shore belonged to her father, down as far as Bryce's farm. If she wanted to swim like that now, she had to get up early in the morning. That was all right. She woke early. Old people did.

After she had her swim, she liked to sit on the rocks and smoke her first cigarette. That was what she was looking for now—not her cigarettes, but her lighter. She looked on the shelf over the sink, in the cutlery drawer—not meaning to make such a clatter—and on the dining-room buffet. Then she remembered that she had been sitting in the living room last night, watching *David Copperfield* on television. And there it was, her lighter, on the grubby arm of the chintz-covered chair.

Laurence had rented a television set so that they could watch the moon shot. She had agreed that that was an occasion the children shouldn't miss—that none of them should miss, said Laurence sternly—but she had supposed it would mean a twenty-four-hour rental, the presence of the television set in the house overnight. Laurence pointed out her mistake. The moon shot would take place Wednesday, the day after tomorrow, and the landing, if all went well, on Sunday. Had she really thought the trip would be only a matter of hours? And Laurence said there would be no hope of renting a decent set if you waited until the last moment. All the cottagers would be after them. So they had got one ten days ahead of time, and Laurence's campaign, ever since it came into the house, had been to get Sophie to watch it. He had been lucky, discovering reruns of last winter's *National Geographic* series: one about the Galápagos Islands, which Sophie watched without protest, and one on America's National Parks, which she said was good but tainted by American boasting. Then there was *David Copperfield,* a British-made series shown every Sunday night in hour-long segments.

"You see what you've been missing?" said Laurence to Sophie. She had refused to have television all these years—not only at the Log House, but in her apartment in Toronto.

"Oh, Laurence. Don't rub it in," said Isabel. Her tone was affectionate but weary. Sophie, saying nothing, was annoyed with Isabel more than with Laurence. How little that girl knew her husband if she expected him to take any triumph discreetly. And how little she knew Sophie if she expected Laurence's pushing to discomfort her. It was his way—their way. He would push and push at Sophie, and no matter what he got out of her it would never be enough. Sophie's capitulation about the television had turned out not to be enough; she didn't really care enough, and that was what Laurence knew.

It was the same about the steps. (Sophie was making her way down the bank now to the lake, scrambling past the wooden forms.) Sophie had not wanted cement steps, preferring logs set into the bank, but had given in, finally, to Laurence's complaints about the logs rotting and the job he had replacing them. Now he called her every day to see the progress he had made.

"I build for the ages," he announced, with a grand gesture. He had made a memorial step for each of them: a palm print, initials, the date—July, 1969.

Sophie slipped from the rocks into the water and swam toward the middle of the lake, into the sunlight. Then she turned onto her back. Though there were cottages all along the shore, most people had been quite decent about not cutting down the trees. She could lie here in the water and look at the high bank of pine and cedar, poplar and soft maple, both white and golden birch. There was no wind, no ripple on the lake except what Sophie had made, yet the birch and poplar leaves turned at their own will, flashed like coins in the sun.

There was movement, not just in the leaves. Sophie saw figures. They were coming down the bank, coming out of the trees close to the rocks where she had left her bathrobe. She lowered her body, so that she wasn't floating but treading water, and watched them.

Two boys and a girl. All three had long hair, waist-length or nearly so, though one of the boys wore his combed back into a ponytail. The ponytailed boy had a beard and wore dark glasses, and a suit jacket with no shirt underneath. The other boy wore only jeans. He had some chains or necklaces, perhaps feathers, dangling down on his thin brown chest. The girl was fat and gypsyish, with a long red skirt and a bandanna tied across her forehead. She had tied her skirt into a floppy knot in front, so that she could more easily get down the bank.

Children—young people—who looked like this were of course no new sight to Sophie. You saw a lot of them around the lake on weekends—the children of cottagers visiting, bringing friends. Sometimes they took over cottages, with no parents present, and held weekend-long parties. The Property Owners' Newsletter had proposed a ban on long hair and "weird forms of dress," to be voluntarily administered by each property holder on his or her own property. People had been invited to write letters supporting or opposing this ban, and Sophie had written opposing it. She stated in her letter that this entire side of the lake had once been Vogelsang property, and that Augustus Vogelsang had left the comparative comfort of Bismarck's Germany to seek the freedom of the New World, in which all individuals might choose how they dressed, spoke, worshipped, and so on.

But she didn't think these three belonged to any of the cottages. They were surely trespassers, nomads. Why did she think so? Something furtive about them—but bold, too, disdainful. She didn't think, however, that any harm would come from them. They were playactors, self-absorbed, not real marauders.

They had seen her bathrobe. They were looking at her, across the water.

Sophie waved. She called out, "Good morning," in a cheerful, hailing tone—to indicate that the greeting was all, that nothing more was expected.

They didn't wave or answer. The girl sat down.

The bare-chested boy picked up Sophie's bathrobe and put it on. He found the cigarettes and the lighter in her pocket, and threw them to the girl, who took a cigarette out and lit it. The other boy sat down and pulled off his boots and splashed his feet in the water.

The boy who had put on the bathrobe did a little shimmy.

His hair was black, beautifully shining, waving over his shoulders. He was imitating a woman, though it surely couldn't be said that he was imitating Sophie. (It did occur to her now that they could have been watching, could have seen her take off her bathrobe and go into the water.)

"Would you please take that off?" called Sophie. "You are welcome to a cigarette, but please put them back in the pocket!"

The boy did another shimmy, this time turning his back to her. The other boy laughed. The girl smoked, and seemed not to pay much attention.

"Take off my bathrobe and put back my cigarettes!"

Sophie started to swim toward the shore, holding her head out of the water. The boy slipped off the bathrobe, picked it up, and tore it in two. The worn material tore easily. He wadded up one half and flung it into the water.

"You young scum!" cried Sophie.

He threw the other half.

The boy with the ponytail was putting on his boots.

The black-haired boy held out his hand to the girl. She shook her head. He dived into the folds of her skirt, she cried out in protest. He threw something else into the water, after the pieces of bathrobe.

Sophie's lighter.

Sophie heard the girl say something—it sounded like "you fucking crud"—and then the three of them began to climb the bank without another look toward the lake. The black-haired boy was leaping gracefully; the other boy followed quickly but more awkwardly; the girl climbed laboriously in her hiked-up skirt. They were all out of sight when Sophie rose out of the water and hoisted herself up onto the rocks.

The girl's cigarette—Sophie's cigarette—was not stubbed out but cast down in a little vein of dirt, dirt and rubbly stones between the rocks.

Sophie sat on the rocks, drawing in deep, ragged breaths. She didn't shiver—she was heated by a somber, useless rage. She needed to compose herself.

She had an image in her mind of the rowboat that used to be

tied up here when she was a child. A safe old tub of a rowboat, rocking on the water by the dock. Every evening, after dinner, Sophie, or Sophie and one of her brothers (they were both dead now), but usually just Sophie, would row down the lake to Bryce's farm to get the milk. A can with a lid, scoured and scalded by the Vogelsangs' cook, was taken along—you wouldn't want to trust any Bryce receptacle. The Bryces didn't have a dock. Their house and barn had their backs turned to the lake; they faced the road. Sophie had to steer the boat into the reeds and throw the rope to the Bryce children who ran down to meet her. They would splash out through the mud and haul on the rope and clamber over the boat while Sophie gave out her usual instructions.

"Don't take the oar out! Don't swamp it! Don't all climb in at one end!"

Barefoot, as they were, she would jump out and run up to the stone dairy house. (It was still there, and served now, Sophie understood, as a cottager's darkroom.) Mr. Bryce or Mrs. Bryce would pour the warm frothy milk into the can.

Some Bryce children were as old as Sophie was and some were older, but all were smaller. How many were there? What were their names? Sophie could recall a Rita, a Sheldon or Selwyn, a George, an Annie. They were always pale children, in spite of the summer sun, and they bore many bites, scratches, scabs, mosquito bites, blackfly bites, fleabites, bloody and festering. That was because they were poor children. It was because they were poor that Rita's—or Annie's—eyes were crossed, and that one of the boys had such queerly uneven shoulders, and that they talked as they did, saying, "We-ez goen to towen," and "bowt," and other things that Sophie could hardly understand. Not one of them knew how to swim. They treated the boat as if it was a strange piece of furniture—something to climb over, get inside. They had no idea of rowing.

Sophie liked to come for the milk by herself, not with one of her brothers, so that she could loiter and talk to the Bryce children, ask them questions and tell them things—something her brothers wouldn't have dreamed of doing. Where did they go to school? What did they get for Christmas? Did they know any songs? When they got used to her, they told her things. They told her about the time the bull got loose and came up to the front door, and the time they saw a ball of lightning dance across the bedroom floor, and about the enormous boil on Selwyn's neck and what ran out of it.

Sophie wanted to invite them to the Log House. She dreamed of giving them baths and clean clothes and putting ointment on their bites, and teaching them to talk properly. Sometimes she had a long, complicated daydream that was all about Christmas for the Bryce family. It included a redecoration and painting of their house, as well as a wholesale cleanup of their yard. Magic glasses appeared, to straighten crossed eyes. There were picture books and electric trains and dolls in taffeta dresses and armies of toy soldiers and heaps of marzipan fruits and animals. (Marzipan was Sophie's favorite treat. A conversation with the Bryces about candy had revealed that they did not know what it was.)

In time, she did get her mother's permission to invite one of them. The one she asked—Rita or Annie—backed out at the last minute, being too shy, and the other came instead. This Annie or Rita wore one of Sophie's bathing suits, which drooped on her ridiculously. And she proved hard to entertain. She would not indicate a preference of any kind. She wouldn't say what sort of sandwiches or cookies or drink she wanted, and wouldn't choose to go on the swing or the teeter-totter, or to play by the water or play with dolls. Her lack of preference seemed to have something superior about it, as if she was adhering to a code of manners Sophie couldn't know anything about. She accepted the treats she was given and allowed Sophie to push her in the swing, all with a steadfast lack of enthusiasm. Finally, Sophie took her down to the water and initiated a program of catching frogs. Sophie wanted to move a whole colony of frogs from the reedy little bay on one side of the dock, around to a pleasant shelf and cave in the rocks on the other side. The frogs made the trip by water. Sophie and the Bryce girl caught them and set them on an inner tube and pushed them around the dock—the water was low, so the Bryce girl could wade—to their new home. By the end of the day, the colony had been moved.

The Bryce girl had died in a house fire, with some young

children, several years later. Or perhaps that was the other one, the one who wouldn't come. Whichever brother inherited the farm sold it to a developer, who was reported to have cheated him. But this brother bought a big car—a Cadillac?—and Sophie used to see him in Aubreyville in the summers. He would give her a squint-eyed look that said he wasn't going to bother speaking unless she did.

Sophie remembered telling the story of the frog-move to Laurence's father—a teacher of German, whose attention she had first attracted by arguing forcefully, in class, for a Westphalian pronunciation. By the time she was a graduate student, she was relentlessly in love with him. Pregnant, she was too proud to ask him to uproot himself, leave his wife, follow her to the Log House, where she waited for Laurence to be born, but she believed that he must do so. He did come here, but only twice, to visit. They sat on the dock and she told him about the frogs and the Bryce girl.

"Of course they were all back in the reeds the next day," she said.

He laughed, and in a comradely way patted her knee. "Ah, Sophie. You see."

And today was Laurence's fortieth birthday. Her son was born on Bastille Day. She sent a postcard: *Male Prisoner let loose July 14, eight pounds nine ounces*. What did his wife think? She was not to know. The Vogelsang family carried the whole thing off with pride, and Sophie went off to another university to qualify for her academic career. She had never lied about being married. But Laurence, at school, had invented a father—his mother's first cousin (therefore having the same name), who was drowned on a canoe trip. Sophie said she understood, but she was disappointed in him.

Late that afternoon, Sophie found herself up in a plane. She had flown twice before—both times in large planes. She had not thought that she would be frightened. She sat in the back seat between her excited grandchildren, Denise and Peter—Laurence was in front, with the pilot—and in fact she could not tell if what she was feeling was fear.

The little plane seemed not to be moving at all, though its

engine had not cut off; it was making a terrible racket. They hovered in the air, a thousand feet or so off the ground. Below were juniper bushes spread like pincushions in the fields, cedars charmingly displayed like toy Christmas trees. There were glittering veins of ripples on the dark water. That toylike, perfect tininess of everything had a peculiar and distressing effect on Sophie. She felt as if it was she, not the things on earth, that had shrunk, was still shrinking—or that they were all shrinking together. This feeling was so strong it caused a tingle in her now tiny, crablike hands and feet—a tingle of exquisite smallness, an awareness of exquisite smallness. Her stomach shrivelled up: her lungs were as much use as empty seed sacs; her heart was the heart of an insect.

"Soon we'll be right over the lake," said Laurence to the children. "See how it's all fields on one side and trees on the other? See, one side is soil over limestone, and the other is the Precambrian shield. One side is rocks and one is reeds. This is what's called a glint lake." (Laurence had studied and enjoyed geology, and at one time she had hoped he might become a geologist instead of a businessman.)

So they were moving, barely. They were moving over the lake. Off to the right Sophie saw Aubreyville spread out, and the white gash of the silica quarry. Her feeling of a mistake, of a very queer and incommunicable problem, did not abate. It wasn't the approach but the aftermath of disaster she felt, in this golden air—as if they were all whisked off and cancelled, curled up into dots, turned to atoms, but they didn't know it.

"Let's see if we can see the roof of the Log House," said Laurence. "My grandfather was a German; he built his house in the trees, like a hunting lodge," he said to the pilot.

"That so?" said the pilot, who probably knew at least that much about the Vogelsangs.

This feeling—Sophie was realizing—wasn't new to her. She'd had it as a child. A genuine shrinking feeling, one of the repertoire of frightening, marvellous feelings, or states, that are available to you when you're very young. Like the sense of hanging upside down, walking on the ceiling, stepping over heightened doorsills. An awful pleasure then, so why not now?

Because it was not her choice, now. She had a sure sense of changes in the offing, that were not her choice.

Laurence pointed out the roof to her, the roof of the Log House. She exclaimed satisfactorily.

Still shrinking, curled up into that sickening dot, but not vanishing, she held herself up there. She held herself up there, using all the powers she had, and said to her grandchildren, Look here, look there, see the shapes on the earth, see the shadows and the light going down in the water.

III.

Sitting by herself is my wife's greatest pleasure.

Isabel sat on the grass near the car, in the shade of some scrawny poplar trees, and thought that this day, a pleasant family day, had been full of hurdles, which she had so far got over. When she woke up this morning, Laurence was wanting to make love to her. She knew that the children would be awake; they would be busy in Denise's room down the hall, preparing the first surprise of the day—a poster with a poem on it, a birthday poem and a collage for their father. If Laurence was interrupted by their trooping in with this—or their pounding on the door, supposing she got up to bolt it—he was going to be in a very bad mood. Denise would be disappointed—in fact, grief-stricken. They would be off to a bad start for the day. But it wouldn't do to put Laurence off, explaining about the children. That would be seen as an instance of her making them more important, considering their feelings ahead of his. The best thing to do seemed to be to hurry him up, and she did that, encouraging him even when he was momentarily distracted by the sound of heavy-footed Sophie, prowling around downstairs, banging open some kitchen drawer.

"What the Christ is the matter with her?" he whispered into Isabel's ear. But she just stroked him as if impatient for further and faster activity. That was effective. Soon everything was all right. He lay on his back holding her hand by the time the children could be heard coming along the hall making a noise like trumpets, a jumbled fanfare. They pushed open the door of their parents' room and entered, holding in front of them the large poster on which the birthday poem was written, in elaborate, crayoned letters of many colors.

"Hail!" they said together, and bowed, lowering the poster. Denise was revealed in a sheet, carrying a tinfoil-covered stick with a silver paper star stuck on one end, and most of Isabel's necklaces, chains, bracelets, and earrings strung around or somehow attached to her person. Peter was just in his pajamas.

They began to recite the poem. Denise's voice was high and intensely dramatic, though self-mocking. Peter's voice trailed a little behind hers, slow and dutiful and uncertainly sardonic.

> *"Hail upon your fortieth year*
> *That marks your fortunate lifetime here!*
> *And I, the Fairy Queen, appear*
> *To wish you health and wealth and love and cheer!"*

Peter, trailing, said, "And *she*, the Fairy Queen, appears," and at the end of the verse Denise said, "Actually, I am the Fairy Godmother but that has too many syllables." She and Peter continued to bow.

Laurence and Isabel laughed and clapped, and asked to see the birthday poster at closer range. All around the poem were pasted figures and scenes and words cut letter by letter out of magazines. This was all in illustration of the past year in the life of the Great L. P. (Long-Playing Laurence Peter) Vogelsang. A business trip to Australia was indicated by a kangaroo jumping over Ayers Rock, and a can of insect repellent.

In Between Exciting Trips, and the caption, *the Great L. P. Found Time for His Special Interests* (a Playboy Bunny displayed her perky tail, and offered a bottle of champagne as large as herself), *and for relaxing with His Lovely Family* (a cross-eyed girl stuck out her tongue, a housewife threateningly waved a mop, and a mud-covered urchin stood on his head). *He Also Considered Taking Up a Second Career* (a cement mixer was shown, with an old codger superimposed). "*Happy Birthday, L. P. the Great*," said a number of farmyard animals wearing party hats and hoisting balloons, "*From Your Many Loyal Fans.*"

"That's remarkable," said Laurence. "I can see you put a lot of work into it. I particularly like the special interests."

"And the loving family," said Denise. "Don't you love them, too?"

"And the loving family," said Laurence.

"Now," said Denise, "the Fairy Godmother is prepared to grant you three wishes."

"You never really need more than one wish," Peter said. "You just wish that all the other wishes you make will come true."

"That wish is not allowed," said Denise. "You get three wishes, but they have to be for three specific things. You can't wish something like you'll always be happy, and you can't wish just that you get all your wishes."

Laurence said, "That's a rather dictatorial Fairy Godmother," and said he wished for a sunny day.

"It already is," said Peter disgustedly.

"Well, I wish for it to stay sunny," said Laurence. Then he wished that he would complete six more steps and that there would be broiled tomatoes and sausages and scrambled eggs for breakfast.

"Lucky you wished for broiled," said Isabel. "The top element is working. I suppose it would be too much to ask the Fairy Godmother to bring Sophie a new stove."

The noise that they all made in the kitchen getting breakfast must have kept them from hearing Sophie's voice raised, down at the lake. They were going to eat on the veranda. Denise had spread a cloth over the picnic table. They came out in procession, Denise carrying the coffee tray, Isabel the platter of hot food, the eggs and sausages and tomatoes, and Peter carrying his own breakfast, which was dry cereal with honey. Laurence was not supposed to have to carry anything, but he had picked up the rack of buttered toast, seeing that otherwise it would be left behind.

Just as they came out on the veranda, Sophie appeared at the top of the bank, naked. She walked directly toward them across the mown grass.

"I have had a very minor catastrophe," she said. "Happy Birthday, Laurence!"

This was the first time Isabel had ever seen an old woman naked. Several things surprised her. The smoothness of the skin compared to the wrinkled condition of Sophie's face, neck, arms, and hands. The smallness of the breasts. (Seeing Sophie clothed, she had always perceived the breasts as being on the same large scale as the rest of her.) They were slung down like little bundles, little hammock bundles, from the broad, freckled chest. The scantiness of the pubic hair, and the color of it, was also unexpected; it had not turned white, but remained a glistening golden brown, and was as light a covering as a very young girl's.

All that white skin, slackly filled, made Isabel think of those French cattle, dingy white cattle, that you sometimes saw now out in the farmers' fields. Charolais.

Sophie of course did not try to shield her breasts with an arm or place a modest hand over her private parts. She didn't hurry past her family. She stood in the sunlight, one foot on the bottom step of the veranda—slightly increasing the intimate view they could all get of her—and said calmly, "Down there, I was dispossessed of my bathrobe. Also my cigarettes and my lighter. My lighter went to the bottom of the lake."

"Christ, Mother!" said Laurence.

He had set the toast rack down in such a hurry that it fell over. He pushed aside the dishes to get hold of the tablecloth.

"Here!" he said, and threw it at her.

Sophie didn't catch it. It fell over her feet.

"Laurence, that's the tablecloth!"

"Never mind," said Laurence. "Just put it on!"

Sophie bent and picked up the tablecloth and looked at it as if examining the pattern. Then she draped it around herself, not very effectively and in no great hurry.

"Thank you, Laurence," she said. She had managed to arrange the tablecloth so that it flapped open at just the worst place. Looking down, she said, "I hope this makes you happier." She started again on her story.

No, thought Isabel, she cannot be that unaware. It has to be on purpose; it has to be a game. Crafty innocence. The stagy old show-off. Showing off her purity, her high-mindedness, her simplicity. Perverse old fraud.

"Denise, run and get another cloth," Isabel said. "Are we going to let this food get cold?"

The idea was—Sophie's idea always was—to make her own son look foolish. To make him look a fool in front of his wife and children. Which he did, standing above Sophie on the veranda, with the shamed blood rising hotly up his neck, staining his ears, his voice artificially lowered to sound a manly reproach, but trembling. That was what Sophie could do, would do, every time she got the chance.

"What arrogant brats," said Isabel, responding to the story. "I thought they were all supposed to be lovely and blissful and looking for enlightenment and so on."

"If only you had worn a bathing suit to go swimming, in the first place," said Laurence.

Then the trip to get the cake, the worry of getting it home intact, the need to nag at Denise so that she would keep it level. A further trip, alone, to the Hi-Way Market to get the ripe field tomatoes Laurence preferred to any that you could buy in the store. Isabel had to plan a top-of-the-stove menu. It had to be something that could be cooked or heated up fairly quickly when they all got home hungry from the trip to the airport. And it should be something that Laurence particularly liked, that Sophie wouldn't find too fancy, and that Peter would eat. She decided on coq au vin, though with that she couldn't be entirely sure of Sophie, or of Peter. After all, it was Laurence's day. She spent the afternoon cooking, watching the time so that they would all be ready to leave for the airport early enough not to throw Denise into a fit of anxiety.

Even with her watching, they were a bit late. Laurence, called to from the top of the steps, answered yes, but did not appear. Isabel had to run down and tell him it was urgent, that there was a surprise connected with his birthday and everything might be ruined if he didn't hurry—it was Denise's particular surprise, furthermore, and she was getting into a state. Even after that, it seemed that Laurence deliberately took his time and was longer than usual washing and changing. He did not approve of so much effort going into preventing one of Denise's states.

But they had got here, and now they were all, except Isabel, up in the plane. That had not been the plan. The plan was that they were all to drive to the airport, watch Laurence get his blindfold removed and be surprised, watch him take off on his birthday ride, and greet him when he came down.

Then the pilot, coming out of the little house that served as an office, and seeing them all there, had said, "How about taking the whole family up? We'll take the five-seater—you get a nicer ride." He smiled at Denise. "I won't charge you any more. It's the end of the day."

"That's very nice of you," said Denise promptly.

"So," said the pilot, looking them over. "All but one."

"That can be me," said Isabel.

"I hope you're not scared," said the pilot, turning his look on her. "No need to be."

He was a man in his forties—maybe he was fifty—with waves of very blond or white hair, probably blond hair going white, combed straight back from his forehead. He was not tall, not as tall as Laurence, but he had heavy shoulders, a thick chest and waist and a little hard swell of belly, not a sag, over his belt. A high, curved forehead, bright blue eyes with a habitual outdoor squint, a look of professional calm and good humor. That same quality in his voice—the good-humored, unhurried, slightly stupid-sounding country voice. She knew what Laurence would say of this man—that he was the salt of the earth. Not noticing something else—something vigilant underneath, and careless or even contemptuous of them, sharply self-possessed.

"You're not scared, are you, ma'am?" said the pilot to Sophie.

"I've never flown in a small plane," said Sophie. "But I don't think I'm scared, no."

"We've none of us ever flown in a small plane. It'll be a great treat," said Laurence. "Thank you."

"I'll just sit here by myself, then." said Isabel, and Laurence laughed.

"Sitting by herself is my wife's greatest pleasure."

If that was so—and it really might be, because she wasn't scared, or only vaguely scared, yet she so much relished the idea of being left behind—it surely wasn't much to her credit. Here she sat and saw her day as hurdles got through. The coq au vin waiting on the back of the stove, the cake got home safely, the wine and tomatoes bought, the birthday brought this far without any real errors or clashes or disappointments. There remained the drive home, the dinner. Then tomorrow Laurence would go to Ottawa for the day, and come back in the evening. He was to be with them Wednesday to watch the moon shot.

Not much to her credit to go through her life thinking, Well, good, now that's over, *that's* over. What was she looking forward to, what bonus was she hoping to get, when this, and this, and this, was over?

Freedom—or not even freedom. Emptiness, a lapse of attention. It seemed all the time that she was having to provide a little more—in the way of attention, enthusiasm, watchfulness—than she was sure she had. She was straining, hoping not to be found out. Found to be as cold at heart as that Old Norse, Sophie.

Sometimes she thought that she had been brought home, in the first place, as a complicated kind of challenge to Sophie. Laurence was in love with her from the beginning, but his love had something to do with the challenge. Quite contradictory things about her were involved: her tarty looks and bad manners (how tarty, and how bad, she had no idea at the time); her high marks and her naïve reliance on them as proof of intelligence; all that evidence she bore of being the brightest pupil from a working-class high school, the sport of an unambitious family.

"Not your typical Business Ad choice, is she, Mother?" said Laurence to Sophie in Isabel's presence. He was enrolled in the one school in the university that Sophie detested—Business Administration.

Sophie said nothing, but smiled directly at Isabel. The smile was not unkind, not scornful of Laurence—it seemed patient—but it said plainly, "Are you ready, are you taking this on?" And Isabel, who was concentrating then on being in love with Laurence's good looks and wit and intelligence and hoped-for experience of life, understood what this meant. It meant that the Laurence she had set herself to love (for in spite of her looks and manner, she was a serious, inexperienced girl who believed in lifelong love and could not imagine connecting herself on any other terms), *that* Laurence had to be propped up, kept going, by constant and clever exertions on her part, by reassurance and good management; he depended on her to make him a man. She did not like Sophie for bringing this to her attention, and she didn't let it touch her decision. This was what love was, or what life was, and she wanted to get started on it. She was lonely, though she thought of herself as solitary. She was the only child of her mother's second marriage; her mother was dead, and her half brothers and half sister were much older, and married. She had a reputation in her family for thinking she was special. She still had it, and since her marriage to Laurence she hardly saw her own relatives.

She read a lot; she dieted and exercised seriously; she had become a good cook. At parties, she flirted with men who did not seriously pursue her. (She had noticed that Laurence was disappointed if she did not create a little stir.) Sometimes she imagined herself overpowered by these men, or others, a partner in most impulsive, ingenious, vigorous couplings. Sometimes she thought of her childhood with a longing that seemed almost as perverse, and had to be kept almost as secret. A sagging awning in front of a corner store might remind her, the smell of heavy dinners cooking at noon, the litter and bare earth around the roots of a big urban shade tree.

When the plane landed, she got up and went to meet them, and she kissed Laurence as if he had returned from a journey. He seemed happy. She thought that she seldom concerned herself about Laurence's being happy. She wanted him to be in a good mood, so that everything would go smoothly, but that was not the same thing.

"It was wonderful," Laurence said. "You could see the changes in the landscape so clearly." He began to tell her about a glint lake.

"It was most enjoyable," said Sophie.

Denise said, "You could see way down into the water. You could see the rocks going down. You could even see sand."

"You could see what kind of boats," said Peter.

"I mean it, Mother. You could see the rocks going down, down, and then sand."

"Could you see any fish?" said Isabel.

The pilot laughed, though he must have heard that often enough before.

"It's really too bad you didn't come up," Laurence said.

"Oh, she will, one day," said the pilot. "She could be out here tomorrow."

They all laughed at his teasing. His bold eyes met Isabel's, and seemed in spite of their boldness to be most innocent, genial, and kind. Respect was not wanting. He was a man who could surely mean no harm, no folly. So it could hardly be true that he was inviting her.

He said goodbye to them then, as a group, and was thanked once more. Isabel thought she knew what it was that had unhinged her. It was Sophie's story. It was the idea of herself, not Sophie, walking naked out of the water toward those capering boys. (In her mind, she had already eliminated the girl.) That made her long for, and imagine, some leaping, radical invitation. She was kindled for it.

When they were walking toward the car, she had to make an effort not to turn around. She imagined that they turned at the same time, they looked at each other, just as in some romantic movie, operatic story, high-school fantasy. They turned at the same time, they looked at each other, they exchanged a promise that was no less real though they might never meet again. And the promise hit her like lightning, split her like lightning, though she moved on smoothly, intact.

Oh, certainly. All of that.

But, it isn't like lightning, it isn't a blow from outside. We only pretend that it is.

"If somebody else wouldn't mind driving," Sophie said. "I'm tired."

. . .

That evening, Isabel was bountifully attentive to Laurence, to her children, to Sophie, who didn't in the least require it. They all felt her happiness. They felt as if an invisible, customary barrier had been removed, as if a transparent curtain had been pulled away. Or perhaps they had only imagined it was there all the time? Laurence forgot to be sharp with Denise, or to treat her as his rival. He did not even bother to struggle with Sophie. Television was not mentioned.

"We saw the silica quarry from the air," he said to Isabel, at dinner. "It was like a snowfield."

"White marble," said Sophie, quoting. "Pretentious stuff. They've put it on all the park paths in Aubreyville, spoiled the park. Glaring."

Isabel said, "You know we used to have the White Dump? At the school I went to—it was behind a biscuit factory, the playground backed on to the factory property. Every now and then, they'd sweep up these quantities of vanilla icing and nuts and hardened marshmallow globs and they'd bring it in barrels and dump it back there and it would shine. It would shine like a pure white mountain. Over at the school, somebody would see it and yell, 'White Dump!' and after school we'd all climb over the fence or run around it. We'd all be over there, scrabbling away at that enormous pile of white candy."

"Did they sweep it off the floor?" said Peter. He sounded rather exhilarated by the idea. "Did you eat it?"

"Of course they did," said Denise. "That was all they had. They were poor children."

"No, no, no," said Isabel. "We were poor but we certainly had candy. We got a nickel now and then to go to the store. It wasn't that. It was something about the White Dump—that there was so much and it was so white and shiny. It was like a kid's dream—the most wonderful promising thing you could ever see."

"Mother and the Socialists would take it all away in the dead of night," said Laurence, "and give you oranges instead."

"If I picture marzipan, I can understand," said Sophie. "Though you'll have to admit it doesn't seem very healthy."

"It must have been terrible," said Isabel. "For our teeth, and everything. But we didn't really get enough to be sick, because there were so many of us and we had to scrabble so hard. It just seemed like the most wonderful thing."

"White Dump!" said Laurence—who, at another time, to such a story might have said something like "Simple pleasures of the poor!" "White Dump," he said, with a mixture of pleasure and irony, a natural appreciation that seemed to be exactly what Isabel wanted.

She shouldn't have been surprised. She knew about Laurence's delicacy and kindness, as well as she knew his bullying and bluffing. She knew the turns of his mind, his changes of heart, the little shifts and noises of his body. They were intimate. They had found out so much about each other that everything had got cancelled out by something else. That was why the sex between them could seem so shamefaced, merely and drearily lustful, like sex between siblings. Love could survive that—had survived it. Look how she loved him at this moment. Isabel felt herself newly, and boundlessly, resourceful.

If his partner was there, if he and his partner were there together, she could say, "I think we left something yesterday. My mother-in-law thinks she dropped her glasses case. Not her glasses. Just the case. It doesn't matter. I thought I'd check."

If he was there alone but came toward her with a blank, pleasant look, inquiring, she might need to have a less trivial reason.

"I just wanted to find out about flying lessons. My husband asked me to find out."

If he was there alone but his look was not so blank—yet it was still necessary that something should be said—she could say, "It was so kind of you to take everybody up yesterday and they did enjoy it. I just dropped by to thank you."

She couldn't believe this; she couldn't believe it would happen. In spite of her reading, her fantasies, the confidences of certain friends, she couldn't believe that people sent and got such messages every day, and acted on them, making their perilous plans, moving into illicit territory (which would turn out to be shockingly like, and unlike, home).

In the years ahead, she would learn to read the signs, both at the beginning and at the end of a love affair. She wouldn't be so astonished at the way the skin of the moment can break open. But astonished enough that she would say one day to her grownup daughter Denise, when they were drinking wine and talking about these things, "I think the best part is always right at the beginning. At the beginning. That's the only pure part." "Perhaps even before the beginning," she said. "Perhaps just when it flashes on you what's possible. That may be the best."

"And the first love affair? I mean the first extra love affair?" (Denise suppressing all censure.) "Is that the best, too?"

"With me, the most passionate. Also the most sordid."

(Referring to the fact that the business was failing, that the pilot asked for, and received, some money from her; also to the grievous scenes of revelation that put an end to the affair and to her marriage, though not to his. Referring, as well, to scenes of such fusing, sundering pleasure that they left both parties flattened, and in a few cases, shedding tears. And to the very first scene, which she could replay in her mind at any time, recalling surprisingly mixed feelings of alarm and tranquillity.

The airport at about nine o'clock in the morning, the silence, sunlight, the dusty distant trees. The small white house that had obviously been hauled here from somewhere else to be the office. No curtains or blinds on its windows. But a piece of picket fence, of all things, a gate. He came out and held the gate open for her. He wore the same clothes that he had worn yesterday, the same light-colored work pants and work shirt with the sleeves rolled up. She wore the same clothes that she had worn. Neither heard what the other said, or could answer in a way that made sense.

Too much ease on his part, or any sign of calculation—worse still, of triumph—would have sent her away. But he didn't make that kind of mistake, probably wasn't tempted to. Men who are successful with women—and he had been successful; she was to find out that he had been successful some times before, in very similar circumstances—men who are gifted in that way are not so light-minded about it as they are thought to be, and not unkind. He was resolute but seemed thoughtful, or even regretful, when he first touched her. A calming, appreciative touch, a slowly increasing declaration, over her bare neck and shoulders, bare arms and back, lightly covered breasts and hips. He spoke to her—some intimate, serious nonsense—while she swayed back and forth in a response that this touch made just bearable.

She felt rescued, lifted, beheld, and safe.)

After dinner, they played charades. Peter was Orion. He did the second syllable by drinking from an imaginary glass, then staggering around and falling down. He was not disqualified, though it was agreed that Orion was a proper name.

"Space is Peter's world, after all," said Denise. Laurence and Isabel laughed. This remark was one that would be quoted from time to time in the household.

Sophie, who never understood the rules of charades—or, at least, could never keep to them—soon gave up the game, and began to read. Her book was *The Poetic Edda*, which she read every summer, but had been neglecting because of the demands of television. When she went to bed, she left it on the arm of her chair.

Isabel, picking it up before she turned out the light, read this verse:

Seinat er at segia;
svá er nu rádit.

(It is too late to talk of this now: it has been decided.)